TUMBLING

Diane McKinney-Whetstone

Scribner Paperback Fiction
Published by Simon & Schuster

SCRIBNER PAPERBACK FICTION
Simon & Schuster Inc.
Rockefeller Center
1230 Avenue of the Americas
New York, NY 10020

First Scribner Paperback Fiction edition 1997
Published by arrangement with
William Morrow & Company, Inc.

SCRIBNER PAPERBACK FICTION and design are
trademarks of Simon & Schuster Inc.

Designed by M. Kristen Bearse
Manufactured in the United States of America

3   5   7   9   10   8   6   4   2

Library of Congress Cataloging-in-Publication Data
McKinney-Whetstone, Diane.
Tumbling / Diane McKinney-Whetstone.
        p.   cm.
        I. Title.
    [PS3563.C3825T86   1997]
    813'.54—dc21   96-51546
                CIP

ISBN 0-684-83724-2

TO MOMMIE AND DADDY

ACKNOWLEDGMENTS

To the Pennsylvania Council on the Arts for funding a time to write; to Pam and Donna at Pam Bernstein and Associates for loving the book when it was still a draft; to Claire Wachtel, my editor at William Morrow, whose pen is sharp and intuitive and ultimately kind, and to her energetic assistant, Tracy Quinn; to those gifted and award-winning writers and patient readers at Rittenhouse Writers' Group, like Sheila Dolan and Bob Michel, who read the whole book early on, and especially James Rahn, the workshop leader, whose honesty creates an atmosphere where writers like me can hobble off a broken porch and make it to Page 1; to dear friends like Mary with whom I've fellowshipped; most of all, to my family, my sisters and brother, Gloria, Paula, Gwen, Elaine, Vernell, and Bobby, through whom the spirit of my parents sustains me; to my teenage twins, Taiwo, my daughter, and Kehinde, my son, who slept late so I could write and whose laughter is still my greatest joy, and to their dad, Greg, my life-mate and truest friend.

Blessings and Love

PART I

ONE

The black predawn air was filled with movement. Its thin coolness rushed through the streets of South Philly, encircling the tight, sturdy row houses. In 1940 the blocks were clean and close. The people who lived here scrubbed their steps every morning until the sand in the concrete sparkled like diamond pins. Then some went to work mopping floors and cooking meals for rich folks, or cleaning fish at the dock, or stitching fine leather shoes or pinch-pleated draperies at the factories on the north side. Some answered phones or crumpled paper for the government. Some tended house and nursed babies. A few were really nurses. One or two taught school. Unless it was the weekend. On the weekend the blocks came to life. They'd cram into Club Royale, where redheaded olives danced in gold-colored liquid. And the music flowed like bubbly. And brown faces laughed for real, not the mannered tee-hees of the workday, but booming laughs. And Sunday they shouted in church and felt the sweet release where grand hats rocked, and high heels stomped or went clickety-clack depending on how the spirit hit.

Right now they slept. Especially if they'd been at Club Royale earlier. They were in a heavy sleep as the moving air wrapped around their chimneys, and stroked their curtained windows, and slid down their banisters. It breezed past the church where the bricks were gray and jutted into the dark air and even shone from the dew that was just beginning to settle. It shimmied over Pop's, the corner store famous for its glass jars filled with sweet pickled pigs' feet. And then dipped past the funeral home owned by the Saunderses, where the Model T hearse was usually

3

parked out front. It blew over the playground where a makeshift swing hanging with tufted, braided clothesline swayed to the rhythm of the dancing air. And then turned on through a short block where Cardplaying-Rose lived; the light from her basement meant that kings and queens and aces were slapping her fold-up table adorned with piles of red and green chips for quarters and dollars and IOUs. And then the night air moved all through Lombard Street and bounced up and down the long block where Noon and Herbie lived. Right now it caressed a brown cardboard box being slipped onto Noon and Herbie's middle step.

Noon was fast asleep this Saturday morning. Still two hours before her faithful church bells would give her the early risers' wake-up call. So she didn't hear quick swishes of leather against concrete rushing straight to her house. Nor did she stir when the rustling sound got louder as sweaty palms shifted the box gently along the steps so that it wouldn't tip. But if Noon or anyone else on the whole of Lombard Street had been only half awake, she surely would have heard the singular whisper tinged with a sadness that was dark as the night. The air heard it, and swallowed it up, and whipped around the corner to push Herbie on home.

Herbie was wide-awake, walking through the streets as the air nudged him on. Heading in after a night of clapping to the beat, then hanging later at Royale because he'd heard Ethel might be coming back, then stepping outside of Royale and running right into Bow, the barber who cut hair at the end of Herbie's block, and having to suffer through a lecture about the wages of sin and ignorance, Herbie appreciated the way the moving air was at his back. He needed a push to get home. The red and white candy cane lamp in front of Bow's barbershop made Herbie mad again as he thought about Bow's finger wagging in his face and his voice all in his ear saying, "Boy, you got a good wife, stop trying to live the fast life, chasing women and hanging in those clubs."

He got some nerve, Herbie thought. He ought to be glad my sweet, pretty mama taught me to respect my elders, or I would have yanked his finger and told him to mind his own business. Herbie kicked at the air as he walked past Bow's. He didn't consider himself a woman chaser anyhow. There was his wife, Noon. And there was Ethel. At least there had been Ethel. He hadn't seen her in several months. But now the thought of her roundness filled his head, the way she moved like fire and made the air crackle when she laughed. The thought warmed him as he pushed up Lombard Street toward home.

The air was moving faster now, impatiently, rushing ahead of Herbie and then doubling back to egg him on. He pulled his jacket closer and picked up his pace. His house was in the middle of a long block. For the past year he and his wife, Noon, lived here with people mostly like him who used to live in the South too. Georgia, South Carolina, Alabama, Mississippi. They brought their dialects, their gospel music and blues, their love for Jesus, children, and candied yams. A few had been here all along, so they said. Like Noon's pastor, Reverend Schell. "My daddy's daddy worked for Harriet Tubman," Reverend Schell was often heard to proclaim. The stories of the perilous journeys on the "Railroad" made for rich metaphor many a Sunday about making it to the promised land. Except that Herbie got it secondhand from Noon. He rarely went to church, didn't particularly care for Reverend Schell's dramatics, and had a few "railroad" stories of his own, as he was a redcap, a porter, at the Thirtieth Street train station.

The air was really dancing now, and whistling, and made Herbie step even faster. Noon would be asleep, he was sure of that. Just as well, he thought, with her problem and all when it came time for them to mix pleasures, just as well. When he thought about Noon, his guilt vibrated in his chest like a tuning fork sitting where his lungs should be. Good churchgoing woman she was. Didn't go to card parties or speakeasies. Content to take care of him and her church business and roast a turkey for somebody's wedding or fry chicken for the gathering after somebody's funeral, or sew organza dresses for somebody's girls for Easter. Nice things. He was almost sorry he was warmed by thoughts of Ethel. But then he pictured Ethel's lips, the thickness and redness, and her drooping eyes that always seemed to be moaning, "baby, baby," and he thought about Noon and her problem, and Bow's finger wagging in his face, and all he could do was say, "Damn," out loud to only the moving air.

The box sat patiently on the steps as Herbie approached his house. He might have tripped over it except that pink yarn fringes hung over the edges. They rippled in the breeze and startled the night as they moved. They startled Herbie too. "What the hell?" he murmured as he stopped sharply and nudged the box with his foot. He pulled back the pink covering. He peered into the box.

5

He stood straight up. He pulled at the end of his long, thin nose and rubbed his hand hard across his head. How many beers had he had at Royale? Only two, not even enough to make him miss a step, certainly not enough to make the night do a strangeness on his mind. He reached in his jacket pocket and snatched out a tin filled with red-topped stick matches. He struck a match and cupped his hands to protect the flame from the air that was circling him in wispy drafts. He leaned into the box guided by the fire. A baby. Damn sure was. Somebody had left a baby right here on his steps.

He sat down on the steps next to the box. He lifted out a dark-haired infant swaddled in a loosely knitted bright pink blanket. His hands felt clumsy and large as he held the baby like a chicken he had just pulled from a crate of ice on Ninth Street. The baby jerked and then cried a loud, agitated cry. "Shit," Herbie said. "You gonna go and do all that crying, someone will think I'm out here trying to hurt you. I'm only trying to figure this out." He brought the baby to his chest. Awkwardly at first. And then he worked up a smooth, gentle rocking motion. The baby hushed. He rested the infant along the length of his thighs. He lit another match and held it high like a torch so he could see the baby's face. He saw the eyes. Dark as coals that shocked him first, then softened him to putty. "What you looking at, huh?" he whispered into the eyes. "You can't see me nohow; don't y'all stay blind till you much older than this?" He felt silly. He had never talked to an infant before. He thought that he should run in the house and wake Noon; she would know what to do. Surely they'd have to turn the baby over to the authorities, but in the meantime Noon would know what to do about feeding it and changing it. He caught himself calling the baby "it" and then wondered if it was really a girl child. "You gotta be a girl, right? I mean, they got you all in pink, I'm just gonna have to trust that you a girl."

The eyes pierced through the predawn air that had gotten quiet around them now and held him as he talked. He knew where he had seen these eyes. Not just their blackness or their roundness, but deep inside, beyond the physical, these eyes had a knowingness about them, a familiarity; these were his mother's eyes. He'd seen eyes like these from time to time after his mother's death: a stray dog that would hang around their Mississippi country house and shock him with his mother's stare, a bird that would allow him to get closer than any normal bird and then look straight through to his soul the way his mother used to do, even the pantry mouse that he couldn't kill because it gripped him with his mother's eyes. His mother came back to him again and again in the eyes. But never before in a human's eyes.

He wondered then where the baby had come from. Dropped out of the sky to stare at him and reinforce Bow's warnings about trying to live the fast life? He dismissed that. His superstitions had their limit. He let the flame go out and drew the child closer into his chest and cradled her head in one hand and, with a deftness that surprised him, rummaged through the box with the other. "Shameful, abandoning you out here under the cover of night like this. No note saying what your name is or nothing. Diapers in here. Bottle in here too. No reason, though; they packed everything in here except the reason why." He stood, still holding the baby's head close to his chest. She smelled of cocoa butter and talc. He rubbed his chin against her hair, which was thick and soft. "I'll take you in to Noon and let her change you and do all that tending-to business." The baby nestled her head in the crook of his neck. He stopped short. He had never had such a sensation as this. As if a blanket of warmth had just peeled away from the chill of the night and covered them both. The air let out a deep contented sigh as Herbie stepped through his front door, holding the baby close as he went.

"Noon," he yelled, once inside the door. "Noon, you gotta come down here and see this. Noon!" He trod tenuously across the buffed-up shine of the hardwood floor. He held the baby's head to his chest as he walked. He stepped onto the thick circle of a throw rug in the center of the room and yanked the cord that turned on the living room chandelier. He eased the baby's head back in his palm so he could see her in the swaying light of the chandelier.

"Herbie, that you? What you got that bright light on in the middle of the night for? Coming in here talking loud this time of night, what's all the commotion?" Noon's voice was generous like her round face, her bow-shaped hips, and her healthy legs. It was what had attracted Herbie to her in the first place, the hips and the legs. He could see the print of the hips even now as she rushed down the stairs in a thick quilted robe.

"Lord have mercy! Where in Jesus name did you get that baby? Where it come from, Herbie?"

"On the steps. I was on my way in from Royale, and this box was on the steps."

"On what steps? Royale's? Ours?" She pulled back Herbie's arm and gently took the baby from him. "And where's the box? Maybe there's a note or something in there."

"Still on the steps, on our steps, I wouldn't go looking through no boxes left on anybody else's steps." He went back out the front door to bring the box in. The space between his chin and his shoulder still held the warmth of the baby's body right where she had nestled her head.

"It is a girl, right?" he asked as he walked back into the living room and put the box at Noon's feet. She was now on the couch smiling exaggerated smiles and otherwise animating her face as she cooed and clucked and amused the contents of the pink covering.

"Oh, yeah, I done already checked her out, she's a girl for real, a newborn baby girl, can't be more than a week by the looks of the cord, and she's gonna need changing she is." She talked more to the baby than to Herbie.

Herbie hovered over Noon as she undid the loosely knitted blanket and inspected the baby's limbs and fingers and toes. "Diapers in the box." He said it with authority. "And be careful with her head."

"Scuse me, Mr. Herbie." Noon turned and looked at him, her small, slanted eyes filled with exclamation. "I been taking care of infants since I was ten; I do know how to hold a baby. I'm just surprised you was able to even get her up the steps and in the house without snapping her spine."

"Well, I did. I even stopped her from crying when we were out front. It just came natural. She was good and content with me holding her too till you came and snatched her right outta my hands."

"I declare 'fore God! You seem to have gotten mighty attached to this baby. I thought a baby was the farthest thing from your mind."

"No, it's just that I can hardly get close enough to you to put you in a family way." He saw Noon flinch, even from where he was standing, looking down on her head that she turned from him. He could see her scalp tighten through the brown twisted papers that she used to curl her

8

hair. He stopped and breathed in hard and said, "I'm sorry, Noon, I shouldn't have said that."

Noon's face was round and soft brown, and the print of her cheekbones was usually lost in the roundness, except that they were showing now as she ground her teeth and swallowed hard, trying to swallow the hurt that always surfaced as a ball in her throat whenever he reminded her of her bedroom problem. It was all Noon could do to just pull her defenses up like a girdle to keep him from seeing the hurt.

Right now the baby helped. "Mercy, mercy," she said, ignoring Herbie, "You 'bout the cutest baby I ever did see, look at those eyes."

"The eyes are something, aren't they?" Herbie said excitedly as he pushed into the space between Noon and the arm of the couch. "What those eyes look like to you?"

"Like black diamonds, that's what they look like." Noon took her voice down to a whisper. The baby's eyes held Noon too. "Wish those eyes could tell me who left you, why they leave you on our steps, who would do such a thing, on a chilly night too, even if they did have you good and bundled. Do they know me, whoever left you, or did they just leave you arbitrarily like?"

The room was completely quiet except for Noon's whispers and the baby's light breathing that sounded like sighs. The chandelier swayed to the hushed rumble of Noon's voice. Herbie pressed himself into the couch and stared in the baby's eyes. He got the same gush of warmth that he had on the steps when she nestled her head along his shoulder.

He fingered the infant's thumb and touched her hair lightly. "Wonder who her parents are, she real light, look to be half white."

"She don't have her true color yet." Now Noon spoke with authority. "Her true color is in the tip of her ears." She pulled the blanket from around the baby's ears. "See, the tips of her ears just a little darker than the rest of her, that's the color she gonna be, good and yellow."

"I done told you 'bout calling people yellow, woman." Herbie said it playfully, mockingly, trying to soften Noon and make up for his sarcasm a minute ago.

"All right, golden then, she gonna be a golden color, like a piece of cornbread." Noon got quiet then as she looked from the newborn to Herbie. The dark hair, the coal black eyes, the light skin, Herbie and the baby had these in common in a striking way. Noon couldn't think it. Suppose this was Herbie's baby. Suppose this whole business of a box on the steps was a made-up tale. Suppose he had just crept from some hellhole with some harlot and had just finished telling her that his wife will take this baby, she can't have any of her own because she can't mix pleasures with a man. She cringed at the thought. Except that she knew Herbie better than that. Terrible liar he was. Lean face showed off every muscle twitch when he was nervous. Thick dark brows couldn't do anything but recess when he was ashamed, even his lips, which were short and full, tightened involuntarily when he was guilty. She watched him as he sat transfixed by the baby's stare. His wide shoulders were rounded, relaxed. He found the box on the steps, she believed that for sure.

When she spoke again, she said, "Guess we gonna have to turn her over to the authorities come daybreak."

"Guess we will," he agreed. "Sure can't keep her. That could get us both locked up." His words felt like lead coming out. He was hoping Noon would say, "We not hardly turning this chile over. No, no, no."

TWO

Daybreak came. The blues went from navy to royal to light with just a speck of pink. Then came the yellow spilling into Noon and Herbie's bedroom. Noon was wide-awake, had been for the past hour. Herbie was snoring, and the baby was be-tween them, fast asleep, looking like butter the way the sunlight was stroking her. The bed was warm. So warm that Noon didn't jump right up when the Saturday morning church bells rang. And when she did get up, it was only because the baby needed feeding. Once that was done, she snuggled back in between the stiff muslin sheets topped with the patchwork quilt that was one-quarter wool. She moved the baby in closer to her body and thought that even though this was the beginning of April, they might need to buy yet one more bin of coal, especially if there was to be a baby in the house. She reminded herself then that they would still have to get in touch with the proper authorities who handled such things like abandoned children. She knew how they would have handled it back home. They would have taken the child to the mouth of the river and dipped her in the name of the Father and the Son and the Holy Ghost and claimed her as their own. No questions about it, none at all. But here in Philadelphia the laws were more complicated. The mother might even come back for the child. City people were so unpredictable; they didn't follow the same rules for living like country folk in the South, where if a thing was done, it was done for good.

The baby squirmed, and Noon leaned on her elbow so she could face her. She pecked the child's forehead and smoothed at her hair and won-dered if she could feel any more motherly about her very own child than she did right now with this abandoned baby next to her and the sunlight splashing in through the stark white curtains. She pictured the mothers she used to help the midwives tend. She'd watch them as their babies suckled their high and firm breasts. How complete they must have felt. How devastated she herself felt when she was examined by Lula, the midwife blessed with the gift of healing. And when Lula had mouthed the words "Shame 'fore God what they to did to you," Noon's heart froze. She felt a chill even now as she remembered how Lula's eyes filled up as she'd covered Noon's lower body with the stiff white sheet as if she were covering the mangled face of a dead child. She'd told Noon then that her womb would never issue forth a birth. Despite the praying over her, the sassafras teas, the salves made from this herb or that leaf, the cornstarch soaks to soothe the pain, the scarring was just too thick, too permanent to dissolve.

She pushed her hand down into her pink flannel nightgown and grabbed at her own breasts. They felt flaccid and heavy. "Young as I am, breasts ain't got no business feeling like this," she muttered. At least they were warm now. At night, when Herbie reached for her, they'd go cold and shrivel up like a prune. At least now they were warm and smooth.

The baby was getting hungry again. Noon could tell because her mouth was pursing and smacking and opening and closing with sucking motions. She listened for Herbie's loud and rhythmic snoring. She pulled her nightgown from her shoulder and lifted her breast and just held it in her hand for a while. Then she closed her eyes tightly and guided her breast straight to the infant's hungry mouth. The baby clamped her mouth around Noon's breast and pulled in hard, instinctively, pulling for milk. Noon felt a pain that started at her nipple and ricocheted through her body to her deepest parts. She almost cried out; were it not for Herbie on the other side of the baby, snoring soundly, she would have cried out. The baby did cry. Pulling on emptiness, she cried, and twisted her head so that Noon's breast fell from her mouth and hung there, wet from the child's spit and exposed.

The commotion jostled Herbie, who sat up with a start. "What's wrong with her, why she acting like that? She all right, Noon? Noon, is she all right?"

"Just hungry, is all," Noon said as she turned quickly so that her back was to Herbie, and then, covering herself up, rolled out of the bed. "I'll warm her bottle, that's all she needs right now; a little milk and she'll go right back to sleep." She pushed her feet into her soft pink slippers and rushed out of the room before Herbie could see her shame.

In the kitchen everything was yellow and orange except for the white sink-tub, next to the off-white gas-powered stove that had set them back $59.95. Noon ran the water hot over her softest dish towel and pressed it to her breast. Guess even that newborn know these breasts can't make no milk, wonder if she know I don't bleed right either, wonder if everybody knows. Wonder if they can look at me and see the best of my feelings were snatched away. She patted herself dry and started mixing milk and water and Karo syrup into the bottle that had been packed in the cardboard box. Still don't mean I can't be a good mother, she thought. Just 'cause my body ain't ripe for it don't mean my heart and my mind ain't. I could sure be a better mother to that child upstairs than her natural mother. Somebody probably know that too. Probably why they left her out there. Somebody know already I'd be as good as Mary was to Jesus. Humph, takes more than dripping titties to make a good mother.

She scuffed out of the kitchen and through the dining room that was as immaculate as the rest of the house. She walked back into the bedroom, where Herbie stood at the window bouncing the infant along his shoulder. His back was bare, and she thought that his shoulders looked wider with the baby's dark hair peeking over the top.

"Aren't you chilly standing next to that drafty window bare-chested?"

"Amazing how much heat this little body sends off," Herbie answered as he turned and smiled as contented a smile as Noon had ever seen.

Noon was struck by the contentment settling in good on Herbie's brow. She knew then that a baby was exactly what Herbie needed to calm him down some, keep him out of those clubs where the women ogled over his honest smile and half-straight hair and eyes as dark as his skin was light. A baby like this might even get him into a church service or two. She felt as sad for him as for herself that they couldn't claim this child as their own.

"You getting mighty attached." Noon took the baby from him. "It's only gonna make it harder when we got to give her up later today."

"I was gonna say the same thing about you getting attached, you know how sensitive you are about things." Herbie rubbed his stomach as he talked.

Noon looked at the baby so that she didn't have to watch his hands make circles over his stomach, which was hairy and flat. "Well, since we on the subject"—she paused and took a deep breath—"I want to get Reverend Schell over here to pray over the chile, later, maybe, after I get her bathed down, and she gets in another nap. I'll feel better knowing she's leaving here under special blessings."

Herbie agreed quickly, even though he wasn't big on prayer in the public sort of way that Reverend Schell went about it. "Okay, you call Schell, and I'll go around the corner and tell Big Carl from the club to stop by. He hears rumors before they're spoken. Maybe he heard of someone having a baby, and now don't have the baby to show."

"I been thinking too," Noon said as she busied herself changing the baby's diaper. "Since today is Saturday and all, and no one's at work down there at City Hall besides maybe the police—well, I was thinking, she might as well stay the weekend. She's sure no trouble, and Pet milk and Karo sure isn't an extra expense. I can pull out a dresser drawer and empty it and line it, and she can sleep right in there."

"Might as well stay the weekend then." Herbie went to Noon and pecked her on the mouth. "If that's what you want, then she can stay the weekend." He looked down on the bed, and the baby's eyes were dancing as Noon pinned the diaper together. He reached in and pinched the baby's cheek and felt the talc- and cocoa-butter-scented warmth he'd felt last night on the steps.

Afternoon came quickly on Saturdays in this part of South Philly. The morning melted from sunrise to afternoon while the neighbors scrubbed the steps outside and poured buckets of bleach and hot water through the back alleys. They shined their windows and did their in-the-house work and then shopped on Ninth Street or South Street or Washington Avenue. One to five was catch-up time: to wonder where the morning went, to sew, to fry hair with a hot comb and a tin of Royal Crown grease, to get in on a card game at Rose's, or a special-call choir rehearsal, to go to Bow's for a cut, Royale for a shot, Pop's for a hoagie, or a car ride to Eden to put flowers on somebody's grave. This Saturday from one until five they crowded into Noon and Herbie's because news of the baby spread as quickly as the morning went.

Reverend Schell came, and Noon's choir member friends, the deacons, people from the block, from around the corner, Big Carl from Royale, and Herbie's buddies from the train station. Somebody brought in a crate of fried chicken, somebody else an army pot filled with potato salad; they brought spirits from the club, coffee from the church. One came with a cradle, another with a large wooden playpen, another with a bag filled up with baby clothes. They piled into the neat Lombard Street row house from the kitchen to the front steps. They sat along the arms of the couch and on the steps and the floor. They clapped and sang, danced worldly dances, prayed holy prayers, and chatted excitedly about the baby in the box.

"Just like that, huh? Box was just sitting on the steps, huh?" Reverend Schell asked, as he sipped at his steaming cup of coffee.

"Just sitting like it was waiting for me to see it," Herbie answered, drinking his chilled wine. "Might have tripped over it in the dark, but they had her all in pink that acted like a light as I was on my way up the steps. Then I picked her up and she started to cry, but I rocked her a little and she got quiet and content like she was just waiting for me to come and rock her."

"You thought about calling the police?" asked Dottie, who lived across the street.

"No need to call the authorities. That child is a gift from God," Reverend Schell boomed. "We got to learn how to handle our own affairs without always getting white folks to intervene."

"Wait a minute," Herbie said slowly. "You saying you think we should keep the chile."

"What else you gonna do with her? Where I come from, which is right here in Philadelphia born and raised, we take care of our own."

"But I thought they were stricter with the laws here in Philadelphia," Herbie said excitedly. Then he called into the dining room, where Noon and a roomful of women were passing the baby from hand to hand.

"Noon," he said, "come on in here. Your reverend is saying we should just keep the baby."

"It's been on my heart to suggest that," Noon spouted as she moved through the throng of people into the living room. "I know down Florida it happened to two families that I know of, somebody left children with them and the people just raised them as their own."

"Well, down in Mississippi," Herbie said, taking the baby from Noon, "everybody raised everybody else's children anyhow. At least it was that way with me since my mama died when I was seven and my daddy was a Pullman porter and away for stretches at a time. My brother and me got all the mothering we needed from any of a number of good-cooking women."

"So y'all in agreement then, right?" Reverend Schell looked from Noon to Herbie. "Y'all gonna keep the baby, right?"

Noon looked at Herbie and smiled, almost shyly. "I was gonna suggest it this morning, but I didn't know how you'd take to such a notion so suddenly, having the finances of a baby's upkeep thrust on you."

"You should have spoken it then," Herbie said. "I was thinking along the same lines, but I thought that was a suggestion that should come from you, you being the woman, and the baby's tending to being your responsibility." He moved in close to Noon and handed the baby back to her and then covered his wife's shoulders with his arms. "I just want you to be happy, Noon."

"Seems like it's settled to me," Reverend Schell said. "God bless the new parents."

"Still seem to me like the court or somebody official needs to be involved," Dottie countered. She rested her hand on Herbie's forearm and squeezed it lightly.

"Now let me say something to you, Sister Dottie," Reverend Schell bellowed, raising his hand high. "What's a bunch of white folks gonna do once they get their hands on this baby? They just gonna turn her over to a foster family, and I'm telling you the Lord has already handpicked the family. Noon and Herbie have just had a blessing laid at their doorsteps. No need to be second-guessing the hand of God. Sometimes the Lord's work and man's work don't always mesh. And when that happens, I'm going with the Lord every time." He loosened his tie and cleared his throat for preaching.

Herbie reached up to Reverend Schell, who towered over him, grabbed Reverend Schell's cup, and put his arm around his shoulder. "Now, Rev, you been a good pastor to my wife this past year that we been here in Philadelphia. And I promise, I do plan to visit you in the House of the Lord one of these Sundays. But Reverend, if you fixing to preach right here and now, we got to trade off cups 'cause I'm sure gonna need some coffee and I do believe you could benefit from some wine."

The rooms from the kitchen to the front door exploded with laughter. These were downtown folks. Holy Ghost–filled to whiskey-inspired, bartender to deacon, jazz singer to choir member, the separations fell away when there was an occasion for a grand coming together such as this.

"I will say this," Cardplaying-Rose offered, "you won't have to worry 'bout that mother coming back for the chile. Whoever left that chile cares for her. They know just what they doing. Ain't coming back. No offense to you, Reverend, but I saw Queen of Hearts in my reading this morning. Means motherly love, they ain't coming back."

"Sister Rose, I agree the mother won't return, but my source is more reliable than a deck of cards. It's the word of God—"

"Rev, Rev, Rev," Herbie cut in. "So what we got to do legally? I mean, what about birth certificates?"

"First thing Monday morning"—Reverend Schell placed his hand on Herbie's shoulder as he spoke—"go down to City Hall, to the department that handles birth certificates. Tell them one of your relatives from down South left the baby for you to raise, and you want to do whatever paperwork you need to do so you don't get any of their undereyed looks when it's time for the chile to get enrolled in school. And you sure don't have to worry about anybody gathered here saying anything different. To intercede in the workings of God that way might bring damnation to us all. Am I right, Sister Dottie?" He looked over at his shoulder and squinted his eyes at Dottie.

"I was only saying that the law—"

"Damnation! Sister Dottie, am I right?" Reverend Schell cut her off.

"You right, Reverend," Dottie mumbled, trying to shake off the collected gaze of the roomful of people.

"Now you give me your Bible," Reverend Schell said, "and I'm gonna make it legal right now in the sight of God. That's what I love about my God, we don't have to wait till Monday morning to do our business with the Lord."

"Ain't it the truth," someone shouted, until sounds of agreement rippled through the whole house.

"Now, what you gonna call her?" Reverend Schell asked as he patted his breast pocket and then handed the Bible to Herbie. "Left my glasses home, but you can do this part. Just turn the gold-trimmed pages of this beautiful white leather Bible to the one marked 'Birth Certificate,' and you take this with you Monday, let them put their official stamp to it."

The memory of the early morning fell over Herbie like a wave as he moved his fingers over the thin, soft pages. He thought about the way the air felt at his back as he pushed up Lombard Street right before he stumbled upon the box. And then the eyes, as the air fanned the flame of the match and made the baby's eyes dance in the flickering light.

"Fannie!" he shouted. "Her name's Fannie. The name just came to me; it fits her too. That name all right by you, Noon?"

"Fannie it is," Noon answered.

"Just put it right there on that top line of that page, then fill in the date and hand it here and let me put my scribble to it." Reverend Schell's voice was filled with jubilation.

They cheered and shouted. Reverend Schell prayed over the infant. Afterward they raised their cups filled with wine, or juice, or milk, or coffee, or vodka, or tea. The merriment even sifted out of the front door, onto the street, where even more people had gathered to hear about the baby in the box.

Noon's round face beamed as she sat propped in the deep green armchair. She ran her hand along the baby's hair and almost seemed to blush. "Fannie," she said again. "Who would've thought it? Noon and Herbie's baby girl named Fannie."

THREE

Herbie didn't have the urge to play cards at Rose's that night, or catch Ella at the Mercantile Hall on Broad Street, or Morris Mosely and the Dukes at O. V. Catto on Sixteenth and Fitzwater. He didn't feel like popping his head into the red- and blue-lit air of any of a half-dozen South Street nightspots, not even his main spot, Club Royale. Big Carl and the guys from the club had told him they'd heard Ethel was back. But he even dismissed, if only for right now, the desire to find her. Noon stayed in too. Tomorrow was Founders' Day at the church, and by right she should have been there to help peel white potatoes, and clean chickens for frying, and snap string beans, and season the shoulders of pork for roasting. But there was a baby in the house. Even the rooms and the furniture seemed to vibrate with a whispered warmth that was like a heartbeat. The kitchen, which looked out past the shed to where the sycamore tree was just pushing out buds, now held a pot half filled with water waiting on the stove to be heated for a bottle. The breakfast room table was adorned with an overturned mixing bowl that covered a plate of peach cobbler or coconut cake depending on Noon's taste for baking; now the table also held a neat row of Pet milk in short cans. The dining room table with the large scalloped legs that looked like a turtle's legs was now covered over with a rubber-backed burlap spread because Noon had used the table's wide sturdiness for washing the baby down. Even in the living room, where the walls were white and smooth and the couch was deep green and soft to sit on, gently folded cotton diapers were now stacked four deep along the couch's arm.

Noon was in the bedroom, where a cedar chest squatted at the foot of the bed and the bedspread was delicate and white like the lacy doilies that adorned the center of the bureau and chest of drawers. The bottom drawer lined with fresh cotton diapers sat along the night table, and the baby snuggled inside.

Noon sat on the cedar chest and stroked her bare foot along the naps in the throw rug and wrote the word "healing" on off-white parchment paper. She pressed it between the gold-edged pages of her take-to-church Bible. She would touch her Bible to the altar tomorrow when Reverend Schell called for special prayer. Between her and God. That's the only way her healing would come. Herbie must never know; her mother had cautioned her over and over. "Man know you tainted, dragged through the woods by those devils, he'll put you down quicker than lightning striking. Plus his anger will get in the way, block the blessings before they even take hold." Noon believed that now more than ever. For the past year she'd been writing the word "baby," then folding the fancy paper into a perfect square, pressing it between her Bible's thin pages, and lightly touching it to the altar Sunday after Sunday. Even though she'd gone through the motions earlier and had her heart prepared for giving the baby up come Monday had Reverend Schell not convinced her otherwise, she'd known. As soon as she'd seen Herbie standing under the chandelier with the baby in his arms, she'd known that that was her "miracle" taking hold. She hoped her healing miracle would take hold as swiftly.

Herbie walked into the bedroom just as Noon placed her Bible on the cedar chest. "Doing a little Scripture reading on a Saturday night, huh?" He asked it softly and then walked straight to the head of the bed and peered into the dresser drawer of a cradle. The baby was sound asleep, and Herbie watched her breathe and wished that the eyes were open so he could see that penetrating stare again.

"She ain't waking no time soon, Herbie; she's exhausted from being passed from hand to hand like she was today."

Herbie was usually irritated when Noon talked as if she knew exactly what he was thinking. But tonight her voice had a whisper to it like the rest of the house that stirred him and made him want Noon's closeness.

"That was sure some get-together, wasn't it?" He moved quickly to the cedar chest and waited for Noon to lift her Bible so he could sit beside her. He sat stiffly at first. Never knew when his closeness would offend her. "I wouldn't have guessed so many colored people could cram into this little house. Reminded me of Mississippi. If something big happened to one of us, everyone showed out just like they did today."

"I love it here, Herbie, I really do." Noon let her head rest upon his shoulder. "Never thought I'd get used to any place after you talked me away from Florida. But this is home now. Whole area is nice. Nice place to raise Fannie up in."

Herbie smiled when Noon talked about raising Fannie. He was glad then that he had plucked Noon from a church congregation instead of from a nightclub. She would do right by this baby that had stared at him and melted his heart. "Yeah, well, I love it here too," he mused. "Always knew I would. My daddy's stories from his years as a Pullman porter got me excited about here. He used to tell us how once the train hissed through Washington, and then Maryland and Delaware, the colored man would start to sit a little straighter, stretch a little wider, jaw muscles would slacken. And then, when the conductor would sing out, 'Phil-a-del-phia' "—Herbie threw his back and crooned the word out in his finest baritone—"the colored man could leave the Jim Crow car and sit anywhere he damned well pleased. Even the hiss of the train would start sounding like joy bells, my daddy used to say. Always knew I'd settle here someday. Even when I was deep in the South touring, I'd be thinking about Philly, those joy bells, and raising a family here someday." He rubbed his chin against Noon's hair. Her hair was thin and soft, and even though it was Saturday night, she hadn't yet set it in rollers of twisted pieces of brown paper bag.

"Raising a family." Noon sighed and leaned in closer to him. "Imagine that. Yesterday this time it was just you and me. Now in the twinkling of an eye we got us a precious little baby. God is good, I tell you. Can't wait to get to church in the morning and praise His name. You might even think of joining me."

Herbie was quiet; then he chuckled and whispered, "My sweet baby with the silky hair, you know your hair is so soft, how you keep it so soft and silky, baby?"

"Don't change the conversation, Herbie." She pushed her head against his shoulder for emphasis. "You went to church long enough to catch my eye, now you act like it's a sin to go. Why you act like that?"

"They say church fulfills your needs." Herbie squeezed Noon's shoulder as he talked. "I went in, saw what I needed was you, and been careful not to wear out my welcome since."

"Well, all I know is it'd be good for that little baby's benefit if both her parents were in church."

"Now, Noon, my daddy rarely went, and he did okay by my brother and me."

"Could have done better."

"And then you know what would have happened." He slapped the cedar chest to punctuate his words. "I would have hurried up and married one of those what you all call worldly women. But seeing as I had a wild streak with that hard-living club life and all, I knew I would need the calming down of a big-legged church girl like you."

Noon blushed when he talked about her legs. And then she got up quickly from the cedar chest and went to the dresser to lay her Bible down.

"Now why you go getting up?" Herbie teased. "I was enjoying that nice soft hair rubbing up against my shoulder."

Noon put her Bible in the center of her dresser just in front of her hand-etched wooden jewelry box. She was used to avoiding his closeness. Early in the morning before the sun even rose, before he had a chance to reach for her the way her mother told her that men did, always pulling on you first thing in the morning, she'd ease out of bed and fix him a big country breakfast instead. At night she'd pretend to be asleep, unmovable. But times like these were the hardest.

"I just wish you would give some more thought to coming to church." She had her back to him now. "Reverend Schell says we're unevenly yoked and it's not good for a marriage."

"The only thing uneven about our 'yoke' "—he made his voice boom like Reverend Schell's as he got up and walked to the dresser and put his arms around her back—"is that I like to do it"—he leaned in and smooched at her neck—"and you don't."

He felt her shoulders stiffen. He had hoped tonight would be different with her so happy over the baby. Maybe she'd relax, let him give her pleasure for once. He started to apologize for bringing it up again. But right now his nature was rising, and he didn't feel like getting dressed and going out and hunting down a woman for his physical release.

He moved his hand across her back in circles; he felt her back stiffen too. "Don't tense up on me, Noon. Not again. Please don't. I need you so bad. It ain't right to deny me of your pleasure like you been doing."

She wanted to open up for him. She wanted to smother him with her body until it made him cry out. But she was afraid of falling into that place where her passions died when she was just twelve. That place that had already claimed her insides. She pressed her hands hard into the dresser.

Herbie's throbbing urged him on. He kissed at the back of her neck. He moved his lips down toward the front around her throat. Her blouse was cotton, and the collar tickled his nose as he tried to get under it with his lips. He wanted her to wrap her arms around him, but he couldn't pull her hands from the dresser.

She could feel him snatching at her elbows, trying to make them bend. I'll fall, she thought. Doesn't he understand if I'm not holding on to something, I'll fall? "Stop it!" she said. "You're gonna make me fall."

"Go ahead and fall, baby, I got you." Herbie was breathing harder and trying to unpry her hands from the dresser. "Hold me," he almost commanded. "Put your arms around me and hold me."

"I can't," she said as she tried to wrestle herself free.

"You got to." His head was buried in the space between her neck and shoulder. His throbbing was rhythmic and painful. "You got to; please, don't do this to me, Noon, not again, don't."

"Get off my hands," she screamed, and then she pushed against him and yanked and pulled and twisted until she felt him relent.

"The hell with this," he shouted. He jabbed the air so hard that Noon backed up until her calves touched the cedar chest. "You supposed to be my damn wife. I ain't supposed to have to fight for this."

"You should have let my hands be." Her arms were now folded tightly across her chest.

"Bullshit. It's always something with you. This shit is crazy. It's crazy, I tell you. And I can't even get a decent explanation out of you about what the hell the problem is."

"You wouldn't understand," she whispered. "And keep your voice down, you gonna wake Fannie."

"Make me understand," he shouted even louder. "We been man and wife for damn near a year. Now the adjustment time is supposed to be over with by now. So you better make me understand or I don't know what's gonna happen here, but something's gotta happen. I got needs, and I gotta feel like I'm giving pleasure to my own damn wife, so you gotta make me understand or something."

"I told you I hurt myself when I was younger, and it left me with female problems, but I'll be all right by and by," she stammered, and then forced the words out. "It's just gonna take me some more time to heal."

"Time? That's all you been saying for the past year. What am I supposed to do while you doing all this damn healing?"

"If you would come to church and hear about the Lord's plan for salvation, that he takes you through trials to test your faith—"

"Bullshit, Noon, the Lord says a man and wife got an obligation to satisfy each other. Don't your reverend preach about that, huh? Why don't you quote him when he say, 'Ladies, y'all know the Lord means for marriage to bring pleasure to you and your mate,' huh, why don't you tell me he says something like that, huh, instead of all that uneven yoke bullshit?"

"Keep your voice down. You want Jeanie next door to hear you?"

"She don't hear our bed rocking against the wall on a regular basis, that's for damn sure, she might as well know that one of us is normal. You hear that, Jeanie?" He pounded at his chest. "I'm normal, this bedroom is mighty quiet night after night, but I'm normal."

Noon sat heavily on the cedar chest and looked at the ceiling, at the three lit bulbs jutting out of the gold-toned sockets until dark spots danced in front of her. She could feel the tears hot behind her eyes, but she wouldn't let them fall this time. She couldn't tell him why she didn't have a nature to her. Couldn't endure the suspicion that would certainly follow her accounting of what those evil people did to her. She heard her mother's voice again: "He'll say you asked for it. Treat you like a street whore, or worse yet, like a devil or a witch, is what he'll do. Block your blessings too, you admit to something like that."

She looked at Herbie standing in front of her, at his fists clenched like his jaw, eyes gone to slits in anger. She could see the hurt through the anger. She at least wished she could make him understand that this was her cross—their cross to bear. Humph! He wouldn't even step foot in the church she had come to love, how could she ever explain that they just had to be patient? Hadn't they just been blessed with a brand-new baby girl? In God's time. She closed her eyes tightly and said that to herself. She got angry then that she couldn't make him understand. Bet if Big Carl from that club told him so, he'd listen, or one of those big butt women that smiled at him from the barstools, bet he'd listen to one of them. She yanked her body from the cedar chest and stomped out of the room, muttering that she had to mix more formula since his old loud mouth was sure to make the baby stir.

Herbie breathed in and out so that it sounded like moans. He sat back down on the cedar chest. He let his back, usually straight and square as the letter H, slump. Then he fell back onto the bed and dragged his hands down his face. "Damn," he said into his palms. "Damn, damn, damn." He really didn't understand what the obstruction was all about. Why Noon would go cold on him, like death. He thought at first that it was a prenuptial thing, that Noon being a good Christian-raised girl was saving herself for marriage. Her body was so soft and quiet that he thought surely it was worth waiting for. But they had been legally bound for a year. In the meantime he had been patient, helped along by taking up with one willing woman or the other so his essence wouldn't back up into his brain and make him go crazy. He thought about Ethel, the one he hadn't seen in several months, the only one outside of Noon he had feelings for. He thought he would go out tonight after all, try to find Ethel. He got up to change.

When Noon came back into the bedroom with Fannie's bottle wrapped in a warm towel, Herbie was already dressed for going out. She didn't look directly at him as she brushed past him to get to the dresser drawer of a cradle. She did cut her eye at him, though, long enough to see that he had on his good navy pants, the ones she took extra time pressing because she'd hoped he'd wear them to church. His white shirt was perfectly starched; it confused her with feelings of pride in her handiwork and rage that the fruits of her talent should be wasted in a devil-filled nightclub. His sleeves were rolled up in neat folds. She had never noticed how hairy his arms were before. He sat on the side of the bed away from Noon and slapped at the black leather of his shoes until the shine came up. The scent of Kiwi polish was thick in the room and almost over-powered the intermittent whiffs of Old Spice aftershave. Noon's eyes started to tear.

She busied herself over the sleeping infant, folding and unfolding the blanket under her chin, smoothing the blanket out, then folding it, then smoothing it again. "That stuff is too strong to be using around the baby," she said through her teeth. "Maybe you should polish your shoes in the cellar from now on till we put her in her own room."

"Maybe I should sleep in the cellar too." Herbie stood as he talked so that his voice got louder.

"Fiery furnace down there, just like hell, you should feel right at home."

"At least the fire moves," he said on his way out of the bedroom. "And it's red hot."

The front door closed with a thump that Noon felt deep in her chest. The door closing woke Fannie. Noon picked her right up, and rocked her, and unwrapped the warm towel from the bottle.

FOUR

Herbie spotted the club immediately as he walked up the Lawnside, New Jersey, hill, mashing the grass hard under his feet. Big Carl had been right earlier when he'd said he'd heard through the grapevine that Ethel was back and singing just across the river. The whole town of Lawnside was celebrating its first hundred years as the oldest Negro town, and the poster board that said "Gert's Tent-Top Nightclub" shouted Ethel's name in exaggerated block letters followed by the slogan "The voice of the century." He wanted to shout too. For six months she had disappeared. No forwarding address, no explanations, just that she had to go down home to take care of some things.

Thick blue-gray smoke billowed from huge barbecue pits that were cooking up ribs and chicken for the hand-clapping, feet-twisting party makers under the tent. The smoke vibrated to the beat of the drums and reminded Herbie of his Mississippi home. The smoke sifting under the tent gave the club a foggy haze, like a foggy dawn. Herbie crowded in and found a seat along a wide bench. He watched big-hipped women in bold-colored dresses of emerald and orange sashaying like bushy-tailed squirrels on an acorn hunt. Tan straw hats and polka-dot ties were nodding and flapping everywhere. Laughter spilled like the gold-colored liquid falling into short glasses. Conversations were loud and light, filled with jive and merriment and to the beat.

This was Herbie's set. He loved to talk to the women, drink gin, and listen to the music. But not tonight. He was on edge about his earlier argument with Noon. Her shutting down when it came time for them to mix pleasures was going to mean the end of their marriage yet. But now they had this new baby, now it was complicated. Plus his stomach was jumpy over seeing Ethel. And there was something about this place: the way the new April grass felt soft and wilted under his feet as he walked up the hill; the southern-style tent sporting red and white balloons; even the smell of fresh-killed pig sizzling over red-hearted chunks of charcoal; this could have been Mississippi instead of New Jersey. Just as he started to drift back there, to the Mississippi cotton, and his mother and baby brother, a lilting voice pulled him back.

"What you drinking, handsome?" It was a high-busted waitress with her red and white ruffled blouse pulled way off the shoulders.

"What you pouring, beautiful?" Herbie turned to look at her but couldn't see her face as she leaned in closer and offered him a tray filled with cheese squares and pimento-stuffed olives pushed onto foil-wrapped toothpicks. He waved his hand and shook his head. "Just bring me whatever y'all dripping from those kegs. And then tell me what time Ethel starts to sing."

"Any minute now," the waitress said as she bent over to talk into his ear so that she could be heard over the foot-stomping good time. "You getting your order in just in time; even the owner stops pouring when Miss Ethel takes to the stage." Her uplifted chest was right in his face, bouncing up and down as she talked. Her breath tickled his ear. Herbie sat up sharply. He didn't want to be stirred right now.

"I guess he do stop pouring," he said as he crossed his ankle over his knee. "I'd stop pouring too if this was my spot."

"Uh-oh," she said, standing straight up now, her face lost in the smoky haze except for her bright red lips, which she was smirking to one side. "Don't tell me you got a thing for Miss Ethel too."

"Why I got to have a thing for her just to recognize her rare talent?" Herbie looked down so he didn't have to look at her lips. "Me and Miss Ethel go way back. I used to play drums in a little quartet, Ethel was on vocals. We're friends. Good, good friends."

"Tell it to your wife, handsome." She placed a red square napkin at his elbow and started to walk away.

"How you know I got a wife?" Herbie grabbed her hand quickly to hold her there, to hear what she had to say.

"It's all in the eyes, sweet daddy," she said as she pulled her hand away.

"What about the eyes?" Herbie's voice had an urgency to it.

"I got to get your drink, handsome; there's more'n you needing service." And calling over her shoulder, she said, "Trust me, sweet thing, it shows."

Herbie didn't want it to show. Whatever it was she was seeing, whether it was his yearnings for Ethel or the long-ago memories this place was jostling in him, Herbie hated that his feelings showed. He used to practice the blank smile of the cool cats that hung out at Club Royale and never let it show. But he thought he looked like someone constipated, straining. He decided that it might be easier just to practice not feeling. Maybe that's what the cool cats had on him.

He fixed his eyes on the small stage. The stage was just a circle, now blackened, raised two feet from the ground. He stared into the circle and traced the outline of the large silver microphone. The cord curled and looped around its base like the tail of an oversized field mouse. A piano and drum set were off to the side. The smoky haze filled with the scent of ribs and chicken sizzling on the grill surrounded the small stage. The smell was still getting to Herbie. He tried to breathe through his mouth. He decided to focus in on the merriment around him. Many of the party people had spilled out of the tent and were dancing in the grass. Their fast feet and shaking hips egged Herbie on to look for a partner and join them on the grass. But then he heard the first strike of a piano key, the slightest rush of a cymbal; he even thought he could hear the yellow light as it spilled down on the small circle of a stage.

A hush moved through the tent like a rushing wave, even drawing the dancers back in. The circle of a stage was fully lit now, ablaze in yellow light. The piano and drums were tapping in sync. Suddenly Ethel stepped out of the shadow into the fiery circle. She was dressed all in red. Even the smoky haze from the barbecue pit retreated like a gentleman bowing. Her roundness filled the stage: her round, droopy eyes with the thick lashes that made her eyes look half asleep; her cheekbones that curved softly, shadowed with bright red rouge; her round lips that were as thick as they were red, and pursed. Even the line that moved down her chest to where her heartbeat rose and fell had a roundness to it. Her gown was tight and cinched in at the waist and made an hourglass of her frame so that when she lowered her head, gracefully acknowledging the rapt attention of the crowd, and then looked up and out, Herbie's insides turned to jelly. "Damn," he said softly, "she would have to look so good."

The crowd clapped and hooted. Somebody yelled, "Come on and sing to me, baby."

Somebody else called, "Just don't take my man."

Ethel laughed and then smiled. And then her rounded face took a serious slant as she pushed the oversized microphone to her healthy lips. The tent was silent again except for the piano and the drums, backdrops to Ethel's voice: loops and waves of passionate moans and tender shrills and trembling so resonant it was smooth.

Herbie was filled with the impulse to just rush the stage. Just grab her from the stage and take her away with him, someplace where he'd be her only audience. He was getting worked up over the thought. But then there was Noon. There was this new baby that had happened quicker than a whirlwind. There were practicalities.

Ethel trilled her first song, "A Good Man Is Hard to Find." And when the club could settle down after clapping and hollering and begging for more, she went into her next song, "Mean to Me." And then, on "It Don't Mean a Thing If It Ain't Got That Swing," she snapped her fingers to the beat and twisted and twirled and put on a show. The club was clapping and thumping as Ethel controlled the rhythm. When she got louder, they got louder too. When she flew her hands in the air, there were hands everywhere. And when she moved her hips from side to side, the top of the tent threatened to blow. Then she laughed, and they were doubled over laughing with her, and she spoke softly and they swooned. Then she rounded out her set and bowed gracefully again and tried to leave the stage. But their applause held her, planted, in the middle of the raised circle of a stage.

She looked out in the audience again. This time she was looking at Herbie, and she said, "I want to sing this one for a special friend." And then she closed her eyes and breathed in deep and started to sing "Summertime."

Herbie closed his eyes too. "Please," he said softly, "don't sing that song." But she was already into it.

30

And Herbie was tumbling through time against his will. He was back there in Mississippi. He was seven years old. The whole black section of town was celebrating the sixtieth anniversary of the end of slavery, with the annual pork roast. It was morning, and already the huge pits were firing up freshly slaughtered pigs. The smell was all through their little country house, and the smell was making Herbie hungry. He and his baby brother were running through the soft grassy dirt chasing balloons of red and white that were floating everywhere. His daddy had just walked down the road humming in the direction of the barbecue smoke, wearing his stark white chef's hat that billowed at the top like a pleated curtain.

And then Ethel sang the part about your daddy's rich and your mama's good-looking. And Herbie was looking in his mama's face, how pretty her face looked when she was asleep. Her skin was light, and her hair was dark and usually pinned back in a bun, but at night she let it fall and the loose, crinkly curls fluffed against the pillow and made her face look even softer. He almost hated to wake her that morning. But as his daddy had left, he'd said, "Your mama must be awful tired this morning. I'm going on and help turn those pigs on the grill; wake her up in a little bit so you can have breakfast and get on into town 'fore the parade starts."

And Herbie was saying, "Wake up, Mommy, please wake up and fix us breakfast." And his mother was still. And he said, "We caught you some runaway balloons, Mommy, wake up and see them, and then you can fix us something to eat. Come on, Mommy, or we'll miss the parade." He shook her again and again, and when she still didn't move, he told his baby brother to bring the big leather strap from the shed.

"What for?" his brother asked.

"Just bring it, now!" Herbie yelled at him. And his brother struggled with the thick strap that almost weighed as much as he did. Herbie took the strap, and drew it high, and smacked it hard against his mother's back.

And his brother covered his eyes and screamed. "Why you whipping Mommy, Herbie? Don't whip Mommy."

And Herbie said, "Mommy, I know you gonna spank me for doing this to you, but I got to wake you, come on, Mommy, please wake up. You never slept like this before, Mommy." And he let the strap strike her back again, and he saw a thickening welt race along her shoulder blade until it opened up, except the blood was brownish instead of bright red.

"Mommy, we're hungry, please wake up and fix us something to eat, please, please, please."

And later that day they had to pry the whip from his hands as he listened to his father sob.

By now Ethel was singing the words that hushed the little baby not to cry. It was too late. His face was in his hands. His shoulders were going up and down. Nobody else noticed, though; they were on their feet calling for more as Ethel exited the stage. Except for the high-busted waitress in the red and white off-the-shoulder blouse; she noticed.

Herbie just stared at the blackened stage, at where Ethel had just been like a red flame. His breath was coming in heaves as he tried to pull himself together.

"What's them married eyes staring at that empty stage for?" It was the waitress again.

"Looking for you, beautiful." Herbie tried to force a smile. She leaned in and placed a fresh beer at his elbow.

"How you know I wanted that?"

"I didn't know. Miss Ethel sent it. Said to tell you to come on back in about fifteen minutes." She exaggerated a smirk as she talked. "And I was gonna take you home with me tonight, Papa. I was gonna work that sadness right outta them eyes."

"What you talking 'bout sadness?" Herbie stood quickly, and smoothed at his pants, and snatched at his collar. "Where's Ethel, doll face? I just want to pay a friendly visit to an old friend and be on my way."

"Whoa, hold it, Mr. Married Man"—she put her palm against his chest—"she said in about fifteen minutes, just calm down, she can't be that good."

Herbie sat back down, embarrassed that he was letting it show again. "I just want to talk to her so I can get on home."

"Yeah, well, you got time, handsome, take your time and finish your beer, she ain't going nowhere. Just relax your fine self," she whispered as she stroked his shoulder and then kneaded his back with the ball of her palm. "She got pretty much the same thing any woman got, even your wife. Miss Ethel just parades hers around a little more, advertises it a little better. But it sure ain't worth no jittery nerves."

"Where she at anyhow?" Herbie asked as he rolled his neck around. "Damn, that feels good what you doing. Where you learn that? What you do, moonlight in a massage parlor?"

"Let your shoulders go limp," she said as she hacked at them with the side of her hands. "You like stone. What weight you carrying in these shoulders? What you do for a living?"

"I carry shit," Herbie answered as he let his shoulders collapse. "I'm a redcap, a porter at the train station, but basically I carry shit."

"White folks' shit, huh?" she asked as she pushed her fingers into his back, working down his spine.

"Who else got heavy shit? I could pack everything I own in a paper bag."

She laughed, and Herbie wished he had paid more attention to her smile earlier. He wanted to turn around and look in her face, but her hands felt so good working his shoulders and his back he couldn't stand to disrupt their rhythm.

"I believe you probably got a lot of stuff," she said to the rhythm of her working hands. "You seem like one of them refined men. I bet your wife keeps a big cedar chest, and your china closet is full with real pieces, and y'all probably got expensive figurines sitting on the coffee table, and I'm sure your wife owns a string of genuine pearls, and she dresses the girls in organza dresses on Sunday mornings with long sashes that tie into big bows."

"How you know I got girls?" Herbie asked, feeling so relaxed now he felt as if he could float off to sleep.

"You do, don't you?"

"Just one, a newborn, name's Fannie."

"A newborn, ain't that nice? No wonder those eyes look so needy; you ain't getting no wifely attention right about now."

"Getting all I can handle."

She laughed out loud and kneaded his shoulders with her palm. "If you say so, sweetness. Where you live?"

"You tell me, you know every damn thing else. All right, I live across the bridge on Lombard Street."

"Oh, yeah, you not far from Royale, and the Budweiser, and Peps, lots of clubs over your way."

"I'm gonna call you Houdini, baby, what don't you know?"

"Your name."

"Herb, what's yours, magic fingers?"

"Houdini," she said, laughing.

"What time you done tonight, Houdini?"

"Right now," she said as she gently moved her hand up and down his back.

"Can I buy you a drink?"

"I don't drink," she said as she moved around to Herbie's side.

"Well, can you at least hang around till I say my hellos to Ethel? It's a for-old-times'-sake meeting." He felt the jelly in his stomach quiver.

"Your neck's getting stiff again, sweetness. You can blow one of my best massages on your desires if you want. But if I was you, I'd just take my fine relaxed behind on home."

"So in other words, you ain't hanging around so we can, you know, so we can talk some more."

"Can't, baby, tomorrow's Sunday, I got to be up and out early."

"Doing what?" Herbie asked, trying to look beyond the red and white ruffled off-the-shoulder blouse to get to her face.

She laughed again, and Herbie wished there were more light under the tent so that he could see her better.

"I usher, baby."

"Usher? At a movie house?" Herbie was thrown off guard.

"At church, tomorrow's Communion Sunday, so it's a long day." She leaned down to kiss Herbie on the cheek. "I really do have to go, Herb, right? I have to go, Herb; like I said, I have an early day. We'll see each other again. I'm right here every weekend."

"Can I reach you otherwise, you got a address?"

"Just look for me here, sweet Herb, since I have a feeling I won't be seeing you in nobody's church."

"For all you know I could be chairman of the Deacon Board."

He watched her disappear into the smoky haze. He listened to her laugh. His back felt like a new back. He could still feel the palm of her hand working it, mashing it, pounding it, until it seemed to open up, expand. It felt wider, as if there were more room on it now to carry all that was heaped on and on it. Day after day. Always some new shit to carry.

He followed the bartender's instructions back to Ethel's dressing room. It was really a trailer on the other side of the tent. The midnight air was misty as he walked across the soft grass. The dirt was almost muddy. Barbecue smoke was still swirling around, making the misty air even grayer. He walked up to the trailer and hesitated and then tapped lightly on the door. No answer. He knocked harder several times. He could see yellow light pouring out of the side window. He waited, then turned the handle and opened the door. "Ethel, you in here?" he called into the trailer. "Ethel, it's me, Herbie. Can I come on in?" He stuck his head in. She was gone.

FIVE

It took the bus ride from Lawnside to Philly for Herbie to let go of his anger at the way Ethel had given him the slip using that fast-talking, back-massaging waitress. Just like Ethel to use something that gives a man pleasure to distract him, he thought. If he hadn't been under a tent filled with people, he reasoned he and the waitress might have mixed pleasures right on that long bench just to give Ethel splitting time. Suddenly the very thought was funny, and his laughter sliced through his anger as the bus reached his stop. Must be that baby that's softening me, he thought as he headed home. He couldn't even hold on to his anger toward Noon when he thought about the baby. "Those eyes," he whispered as he turned onto Lombard Street. "Like that baby got a spell over me." By the time he reached his front steps he had even fixed his mind to apologize to Noon; he had been ready to hurt her for real, call her all kinds of low-down names for the way she'd just shut down on him. But he decided he'd be patient. Find him a little something on the side until Noon came around. She had to come around. Next month they'd be married a year.

He pushed open the door, and the stillness hit him all at once. He walked quickly through the house. The rooms reverberated with silence. Noon wasn't home. It was well past one; where was she on a Saturday night, with the baby no less? He ran straight to the kitchen; still Pet milk in neat rows on the table. He leaned against the chair, relieved. She would be back. He didn't think he had been rough enough to chase her down South.

Shit, a whole year without mixing pleasures with his own wife, some

36

husbands would have wrestled her down and taken it by now. He stopped himself from thinking about it. No need in getting worked up. He went out the front door and looked up and down the long block. He blew into the air that was beginning to spit a light drizzle. Then he saw a figure turn the corner. He jumped off the steps and was halfway to the corner before his eyes focused through the drizzle. Damn, it wasn't Noon, nothing like Noon. It was Bow. Damn, Bow.

"Evening, Bow." He said it with forced politeness.

"Herbie, how are you?" It was more a declaration than it was a question. "I just left your lovely wife and that cherub of an infant over at the church."

"Just going back to get an umbrella," Herbie said, not wanting Bow to know he'd had no idea where his wife was at this hour, "and then over there to the church to escort them on home." Herbie looked down into the street at the trolley tracks that had a greased-down shine from the rain that was falling heavier now.

"No one expected to see Noon over there helping with the preparations tonight. We all thought she'd be too tied up with that new baby that was left on your steps, but she found a way."

"She will find a way, thank you, Bow."

"You might find the way too, young man. One of these days."

"Scuse me?" Herbie put his hands over his head to protect it from the rain.

"To church, boy. Don't play dumb with me. I'm old enough to be your father and feel right justified in telling you that your lifestyle ain't right for a nice Christian lady the likes of Noon."

"Look, Bow, you ain't made it no secret about how you feel about me."

"She is after all a preacher's daughter." Bow talked right over Herbie.

"I take care of my family, okay, Bow."

"Good upbringing, that girl had. Parents was the pinnacle of that community in Florida. I know 'cause I still got kinfolk there."

The rain was falling harder now and landing on Herbie's thick eyelashes and looked like tears. He wiped at his eyes and said, "If you trying to make a point, can you make it so I can go get an umbrella and see my family home, since you obviously ain't interested in what I got to say?"

"Made it, boy." Bow stood unfazed by the rain and smiled. "Guess you better be getting that umbrella."

"You trying to say I ain't good enough for Noon, that's what you trying to say, well, let me tell you, she don't want for nothing, and she sure don't have to hunt down no day job."

"Rain's really falling, Herbie; you best keep your head dry." Bow was still smiling. His teeth were long and straight, and Herbie had the urge to knock them out with his bare fist. Instead he turned and walked swiftly away.

By the time he dashed home to get an umbrella and walked the three and a half blocks to the church, the rain had stopped. He stood across the street, facing the church. Yellow light pulsed out of the church basement. The light was always on and gave a glow to the sidewalk that surrounded the church. The scent of baking sweet potato pies sifted along the damp air and enticed Herbie with a sweet brown nutmeg–tinged aroma. He couldn't force himself across the street, though. He couldn't muster up the desire to walk inside the church.

Inside, they had mostly finished their cooking preparations for tomorrow's Founders' Day celebration. Noon and the ladies, and the deacons, who were there to shuffle the huge pans in and out of the oven. Reverend Schell even lent his hand. Pastor of this church since the Depression from a long line of Schells: His uncle had been pastor, his grandfather before him; his grandfather's oldest brother cofounded the church, oversaw its erection, had the words "A Refuge and a Rock for the Newly Free" etched into the cornerstone of the fine brick structure. Like the Schells before him, this preacher was a working leader, put on his overalls with the rest of them when it was time to paint. Helped with the plumbing, shoveled snow, pitched coal, and on Sunday mornings put on his fancy robe and rocked the congregation, made them shout and clap until it felt like the walls might come tumbling down. Right now he quoted Scriptures to keep the morale of these willing workers lifted high.

The ladies took a break and passed Fannie from hand to hand. They bounced her, fed her, and chattered on about how the Good Lord meant for Noon and Herbie to have that baby and how it wasn't nothing but the hand of the Lord that fixed it so the child would be left in a box on their front steps. And as they spoke, they all were struck by the baby's eyes.

"That stare," Sister Maybell said. "I ain't never seen a baby this young look you in the eye so directly."

"Like she trying to look right through you to your soul," said Pat Saunders.

"That child might likely have a seeing eye," Sister Maybell said softly, almost hauntingly.

"Hope to God she don't," Noon answered. "Too much pressure on a child when they can see into the future. Child down home had one and ended up taking her own life. They think she saw her mother's death a month before it happened, and the knowing of it was more than she could handle."

"Usually the Lord gives them a strong constitution when he gives them that gift of extra sight." Sister Maybell was consoling.

"Noon, Noon." Reverend Schell put his hands on her shoulders. "If God is for us, we need not trouble ourselves over parts of the future that might not even come to pass. He has blessed you with this child, seeing eye or not, and he has given you a concerned pastor and a church family for you to lean on, no matter what the future sends."

"I'll say amen to that," said Sister Maybell. "When my son was killed training for the Negro part of that white man's army, and I was left with the raising of my pretty grandson, Willie, I think I would've surely gone mad with grief if it hadn't been for my Sunday morning release where I could cry out like I could nowhere else. And the whole church, the whole congregation just held me in their arms, rocked me like you rocking that baby right now. You don't know true comfort till you been held and rocked by a whole congregation."

Reverend Schell gushed with pride, and Noon settled down. And Reverend Schell shifted the conversation to the goodness of the Lord, and they sang a little and laughed about such things like the Bible Bandit, who lived not far from there, who'd rob gas stations and always had a Bible in his hand. Then mostly they were done. The meats all cleaned and seasoned and ready for the ovens come daybreak, the macaroni sitting in butter and cheese, the chicken covered over with flour and paprika, the string beans snapped and soaked and swirling around the neck bones, the cakes iced, the biscuits formed; all that was left was to wait for the pies that needed to bake awhile longer. Noon insisted that the rest head on home; she and the baby would stay and wait for the pies. Reverend Schell said that he would wait with Noon too. And when everyone was gone from the church except for Noon and the baby and Reverend Schell, he asked her where the slant to her eyes had gone.

"I declare 'fore God, I don't know what you talking 'bout, Reverend." She played with the dials on the stove and opened the oven and closed it.

"You got small eyes, Noon. They show what they show under them. They get puffy along the bottom and lose that nice slant they got to them."

"Sinuses acting up. Happens most Aprils." She moved to the sink tub and dried it out.

"A good shepherd knows his flock, Noon. You suffering, you need to unburden yourself."

She squeezed water from the dishrag and hung it over the spigot. "Just want to do the Lord's will, Reverend. Gets hard sometimes." Her voice sounded high-pitched and strained.

"It'd help if you and Herbie were evenly yoked, you know that, don't you?"

"It ain't all Herbie, Reverend. He's better than most actually. Worst he does is go into those clubs."

Noon turned then and looked at Reverend Schell. He was leaned against the counter carved out of the wall that separated the kitchen from the auditorium of the church basement. Good preacherly-looking man. Strapping black skin, tall, sturdy frame, expansive shoulders. His rugged features went soft around the eyes that whispered, "Trust me, trust me." His face was expectant. He was used to the unburdening that Noon was about to do. Even though she was generally a keep-to-herself member, she was after all a preacher's daughter. She would trust him when she couldn't trust God. "Trust me, Sister Noon." Not just his eyes now, but his mouth said it too in a voice that was deep and soothing. "Trust your Reverend Schell."

He opened his arms wide as Noon fell into them, saying that it wasn't fair, it wasn't fair. Her insides were scarred. She didn't have a nature to her, and it wasn't fair.

So as Herbie stood on the other side of the street watching the yellow light of the basement against the pavement, Noon and Reverend Schell and the sound-asleep baby were upstairs in the sanctuary. It was dark up there except for two candles hanging over the altar. Reverend Schell had removed the white sheets and communion trays from the altar table that stood at the front and center of the sanctuary. Noon was stretched across the table. Her eyes were clenched like her fists. Reverend Schell had covered her from her shoes to the collar of her dress with the thick white sheets that had just covered the silver trays that held thimble-sized glasses for tomorrow's communion. He stood over her, his hands cupped high in the air. "Touch!" he said into the darkness. The candles flickered as his voice resonated through the sanctuary. "In your holy name, Lord, touch your daughter Noon. Touch, touch, heal, forgive, touch, Lord, touch."

His words gushed forth one after the other, rousing the baby, who was in a basket on the floor next to the altar. She shifted in the basket, and twisted, and worked up a cry. Her whining was lost in the gulf of air that Reverend Schell's voice created.

Noon echoed Reverend Schell's commanding voice with her own shallow whispers. "Please, Lord, heal me, Lord, please, Father, touch me, Lord." Her body moved in a frenzy; she cried out then, begging the Lord for healing.

Reverend Schell moved his hands down; he inched them down through the air as if he were pushing against iron weights. His hands shook as he called on the Lord to touch and heal. He was sweating, as he held his hands two feet above her body. He spoke in whispered babbles. He moved his fingers in ripples across the air. "Have your way, Lord," he whispered. "Have your way."

She couldn't feel anything as Reverend Schell tried to render healing. She did hear the baby crying, though. As Reverend Schell's voice fell to a whisper, the baby had worked up a good strong cry. It pulled Noon to awareness as she writhed along the altar. She was embarrassed, covered over with the communion sheets, convulsing. She had never lost control like that, not even during the most fiery revival. She saw Reverend Schell's shadow cast in the candlelight. How large he appeared as his arms rose and fell, his outline exaggerated by the candle flame's random dance.

She tried to sit up. She needed to get to the baby. Reverend Schell put his hand to her forehead.

"Reverend," she gasped, "Reverend, the baby. Reverend."

He leaned his face in close to hers. "How bad do you want your healing?"

She was confused.

"How bad, Noon? How bad?" His voice was low, tender. His breath was warm as he talked right into her face.

The baby's cry was like a siren, now, getting louder and louder in circles. It pulled Noon toward it. "Reverend!" This time she screamed it crisply like a slap.

He jerked to. He crossed his hands on her face in the center of her forehead. "Sweet Noon," he whispered. "You got to claim your healing, Noon, you got to claim it." He unfolded the communion sheets from around her. He helped her to sit. She felt wobbly as she stepped down from the altar table and smoothed at her dress and leaned quickly to pick up the baby. She rocked her and bounced her and hurried to the kitchen to get her milk.

Herbie couldn't stand it. He leaned up against the lamppost, scraping the silver tip of his closed umbrella against the concrete. The light from the church basement was so constant illuminating the sidewalk. He couldn't stand the waiting. And then he thought he heard a baby, his baby crying. He stomped across the street and pulled open the church door with such force that it banged against the jutting silver gray bricks. "Noon," he called in, "how much cooking you plan on doing here tonight?" He walked down the three steps that led into the church basement. He looked through the carved-out wall and saw Noon holding the baby, feeding her and rocking her as she stood in the middle of the kitchen. She looked so small standing in the center of the large room. She was small, small shoulders and arms, only her hips were broad, and her big, healthy legs. He was just about to scoop her in his arms, tell her how much he loved her, how sorry he was, how he would try to be patient, when Reverend Schell walked up behind him.

"Evening, Herbie. Came to fetch your lovely wife, I see. Well, I wasn't going to hold her much longer. She was tending to the pies, and I was gonna poke some coals around since it's supposed to be chilly come morning, then I was gonna see her home, safely."

"Won't be needing to do that, now, Reverend. In fact, if the pies are near done, maybe you can handle it from here and I can get my family on home."

"Actually they're done," Noon said quickly. She handed the baby to Herbie through the carved-out kitchen window and went to tend to the pies.

"Let me give you a hand there, Sister Noon," Reverend Shell said as he opened the large, heavy oven door. "Careful, don't burn yourself, now, they're hot, real hot."

Noon lifted the copper-colored pies from the oven one at a time as the preacher held the oven door and fanned the heat away so she wouldn't get burned. She could feel warmth now deep in her body in the parts that had been numb since she was twelve. She held each pie carefully as she tried to hold on to the slither of warmth thawing her insides like a thin hot line piercing through a block of ice. She didn't know completely what to make of it, except that maybe her miracle was starting. Maybe the next time Reverend Shell prayed over her the warmth might deepen and spread. "Thank you, Reverend," she said. "That oven door is heavy sure nuff."

"Maybe, for you, but not for me. But that's why I'm your pastor; it's my duty to carry the extra weight." He smiled, and in that instant Noon loved him more than anything.

Herbie cleared his throat as he watched them bustle about the kitchen conversing. Her soft hair was pulled back in a bun, but it looked tousled by Noon's standards; she always kept a brush to it. Her simple dress, a smoky blue color like the air under that Lawnside tent, was belted at the waist, but it had far too many wrinkles for her usual taste. That bothered Herbie, seeing Noon disheveled, especially since she was so particular about things like unbrushed hair and wrinkled clothing. He bounced the baby gently in his arms as Reverend Schell thanked Noon and kissed her cheek lightly.

"I'm ready now," Noon said to Herbie as she walked toward him, glowing.

Reverend Schell extended his oversized hand to Herbie. It caught Herbie off guard, and he had to shift the baby to meet the handshake. He felt suddenly diminished, as if he could never measure up. He was inclined to feel this way from time to time when he was in the company of righteous men.

SIX

Except that Herbie hadn't felt diminished when he'd first seen Noon's preacher daddy. Two years earlier in Florida, where Noon lived the sheltered life of a preacher's daughter. He'd felt inspired that day, uplifted, in love.

He was a drummer then and accustomed to the fast-paced, hepcat-talking, late-night life. He was touring in that part of Florida with a band famous for swing and blues and, to him, the prettiest singer ever to hold a microphone. After he had been on the road for a month, tired and homesick, and after he'd seen that pretty singer, Ethel, leave the club the night before with the headwaiter, he felt like having church.

He ended up at Noon's daddy's church. A prosperous country church made of fine white brick and red and yellow windows stained by hand. It was Noon who ushered him to his seat. Her straight walk in her white usher's uniform stirred him. Her walk was different from the night walk of the club women. Theirs was exaggerated, wide open. Noon had a close walk; there was a stillness to her. He imagined how her thighs must rub together when she walked. He didn't hear much of her daddy's sermon that morning, at least not the words. He went with the rhythm of it though, the buildup, until it crescendoed and people were dancing and shouting, "Yes, yes, Lord, yes!" He imagined himself amidst Noon's closeness, opening her up, calmed by her stillness until the stillness made him shout.

Noon fixed his plate after service. She heaped it with her own macaroni and cheese. The top of it was baked brown. Just below the surface the cheese and butter oozed through the noodle's soft blandness. He watched her as he ate. She moved about the small church kitchen efficiently. Her slight shoulders maneuvered around the bustiness of the older women. Her healthy legs took the weight of her wide, bow-shaped hips. Her legs did all the moving. Her hips stayed remarkably still. He sank into the fluffiness of a yeast roll and imagined that Noon would be like that, soft, buttery-tasting, still.

"That was a mighty fine meal," he said when she came to clear his plate. "Did you have a hand in that?"

"Not only a hand," she said, smiling broadly, "I was up to my elbows in macaroni and cheese."

"Well, some of that softness from those pretty brown arms must of rubbed off into that pan, 'cause that was some sure nuff good eating. Can I ask you your name?"

"Noon," she said as she busied her eyes at the table and swept crumbs into the dirty plates.

"Noon? Now that's a different name, a mighty different name. Was you born at noon or something like that?"

She laughed quickly and then blushed through her cheeks and said, "Close, real close. Actually I have a birthmark on my forehead that runs down to almost here." She pointed to the bottom of her bang, which almost met her eyebrows. "So my brothers named me Noon; they said it looked like a clock stuck at noon."

"Can I see?" he asked. His smile was gone, and his stare was penetrating.

Noon put the dishes on the edge of the table and lifted her bang back and let it fall again against her forehead.

"Beautiful," he said. "That's got to be the prettiest birthmark I've ever seen, I'm not jiving you either."

Noon's relaxed smile froze. She said a quick thank-you, grabbed the plates, and retreated to the safety of the church kitchen.

She immersed a stack of plates into the kitchen tub filled with glistening suds. She thought about Herbie as she moved the dishcloth in wide circles over the plates. She had watched him all morning. His bounciness, the way he crossed and uncrossed his legs, and snatched at his tie, and shifted around in his seat. He was different from the stiffness of the church men. He had a spontaneity about him, an unpredictability that intrigued her. Since that horrific day under the palmetto when she'd gone for huckleberries, she'd not felt anything that came even close to attraction. She had grown up the center of her brothers' and her father's affection. She helped her mother cook for them. She starched their shirts so that the clean stiffness in the collars could be seen all the way from the back of the church. She cut their hair. She hand-sewed their Sunday pants and the work clothes they wore in the hot Florida field. She was devoted to them. And they adored her. She was content just to help her mother take care of them. As long as she was at the center of their protective circle, doing for them, she never had to think about the unspeakable things those evil people had made her do. So her feelings for Herbie, as she put the sparkling plates into the rack, terrified her.

She decided to stay in the kitchen until Herbie left. Just a passerby, she thought. Probably got a string of women all over the place. Women love those good-looking high-yellow men with the half-straight hair. Probably got a wife back home wherever he's from that he runs around on. Wonder where he's from, wonder what he does. No need in finding out, though.

Noon's mother interrupted her thoughts. She pushed a plate heaped with apple cobbler in Noon's hands. "You see that boy over there, the light one, the visitor?" she said.

"Yes, ma'am," Noon answered, not looking at her mother's face.

"Take that boy this plate of my cobbler, spiced it up 'specially for him. It'll help him settle down some."

"Can someone else do it? I want to get the silverware washed down, and—"

"You the one to do it," her mother said firmly. She looked at her daughter, at her arms pulled too close to her sides, at her eyes that had lost their slant and turned to big circles filled with fear. She was relieved. Worldly though this visitor was, at least he had stirred Noon, made her nervous, made her smile and blush earlier. And she'd seen how he'd studied Noon, saw his eyes take her in all at once as his lean face expanded to have more room for drawing her presence in. Plus he had large ears, meant he'd be generous, giving; Noon wouldn't have to want for much in material things. It was time, Lord, yes, it was time. She'd never have admirers from among the townspeople who'd gotten an inkling about what had happened. Tainted for life she was here after those devils got to her.

She plucked a spoon from the silverware bin and buffed it dry in the pleat of her ruffled Sunday apron. She nestled the spoon along the side of the cinnamon-covered apples spilling from the crust. "Give the boy the cobbler, and you look right in his eyes when you give it to him too. You hear me now. And keep the spoon sitting just like I set it so he'll see you twice, once when you give it to him and again in the reflection of the spoon. Go, go do what I tell you now." She almost pushed Noon out of the kitchen.

Herbie ended up staying for the afternoon service. He knew he had a gig that evening. Knew that he needed to be at rehearsal. But his feet had gotten heavy after the thick sweetness of the apple cobbler. He was drawn back into the sanctuary. The solid wooden pew almost pulled him down. He almost felt drunk. He smiled to himself during the service. He thought about how Noon blushed; that excited him. The women he was used to were beyond blushing. He hoped he wouldn't scare Noon off. Don't know much about church girls, he thought. The sun was going down, and the inside of the church was red from the sunfall pushing through the hand-painted windows. He realized then how late it was. He still didn't leave. He reasoned that he could fall in on the band's first set and be right in sync. "Might even have an usher on my arm," he whispered.

SEVEN

Noon and Herbie celebrated their first anniversary with a hug and a kiss and a piece of thawed wedding cake. They feasted on roast duck and wild rice and broccoli spears. They giggled at Noon's attempts to get down a swallow of champagne. They laughed out loud when she stepped on his feet when he tried once again to teach her to dance. Their bodies stiffened though when he carried her up the steps as if she were a bride. "Please, please, let tonight be the night," they both prayed.

But her healing hadn't come. Despite Reverend Schell's supplication that night on the altar on her behalf, despite the word "healing" folded neatly between the gold-trimmed pages of her take-to-church-Bible, her body went as cold as a block of dry ice.

Herbie cried then. He loved her, he said, with all his heart, but he had physical needs, and he had to go. Noon cried too, and begged for his patience, and then used her hands like a teenage girl with her virginity intact just to relieve his pressure some. She closed her eyes tightly and prayed for the Lord to touch and heal, and imagined she was kneading dough for knock-knock rolls.

It wasn't enough for Herbie. He tried not to think about Noon two days later, as he whistled down in the locker room at the train station. He changed from his redcap's uniform into his good navy pants and starched white dress shirt. It was Friday evening, payday, and since he knew he made a good living for a colored man in a job that was sought after by the young and strong, he usually whistled on Friday nights. Working with the railroad was much more stable than the under-the-table money he'd made playing drums in one club or the other. Even though his father had been a Pullman porter and a card-carrying member of A. Philip Randolph's Brotherhood of Sleeping Car Porters, not just a redcap, Herbie prided himself on having the good sense to know that he would have never made it as a Pullman porter. He didn't have his father's gracious, patient nature. Being a redcap suited him, though. He could move quickly, release his coiled energy in bursts, no long train rides to be filled with polite conversation. He could sing his favorite song out loud while he worked, or grumble if that was his mood. And the pay was actually quite good once he added his tips and considered that he had paid cash for their Lombard Street house with a portion of the war bonds from the First World War his father had bequeathed to him.

So Noon didn't have to hunt down a day job, and she could walk to Fourth Street and pick out the finest fabrics of eyelet lace, or taffeta, or even an occasional swatch of pure silk. They ate the best cuts of meat, the richest creams, and Noon tithed generously to support her church. Even the ruby cuff links that he pushed into his sleeves right now were a gift from Noon that she boasted were paid for with household money she'd managed to save by catching specials.

But still, he tried not to think about Noon in the dullness of the locker room. He slapped a little Old Spice cologne along his neck and smoothed at his mustache and pinched at his nose. He whistled louder. He was on his way to see Ethel.

It had been six weeks since he'd seen Ethel under that tent at Gert's. Six weeks since she'd given him the slip using the back-massaging waitress as her accomplice. He still held on to a tinge of anger just beneath his flesh that irritated him like an insect bite, and continued to irritate him, even after Ethel had given him a message through Big Carl where and when to pay her a visit. But right now his excitement doused the sting as he hung his uniform in his locker.

He could hardly contain himself as he walked through the station under the high dome ceilings and into the thick, sweet scent of chocolate coming from Schrafft's candy store. The aroma reminded him of the cocoa butter bar Ethel would slide along her skin after a bath until it melted into the pores on her arms and legs. He hurried into the store and bought a double-decker box of Whitman's chocolates. "Just give me the one on display," he told the clerk, too impatient even to wait for a fresh box from the back. He picked out twelve long-stemmed multicolored carnations and rushed through the throngs of people at the Thirtieth Street Station: Friday shoppers heading home with bulging bags from department stores, assorted travelers lugging duffel bags and metal trunks, the going-out crowd strutting their sharpest threads, and domestics carrying big brown double-handled bags. He stepped outside into the fading sunlight and found more crowds to work through. Shifts from the post office loaded buses hardly stopping. Cabs stopped, but mainly for little old ladies in white lacy gloves. He decided to walk. Bucking the foot traffic, he headed east, passing those downtown bound and worked up a good clip and a sweat to match.

The late-day May sun was pushing out its final rays. Again he tried not to think about Noon as he walked across the bridge. He sensed the currents of the river rushing just below the surface that wouldn't let the sunfall penetrate. She hadn't even asked that morning why he'd packed his best navy pants for changing into after work. She didn't even fuss when he roused Fannie before he left so he could tickle her under her chin and make her laugh. He was relieved. He didn't want to have to lie and tell her he'd be late because he was stopping off at Royale. He hated lying. But it was this, or join the other men toting suitcases and memories as they boarded trains leaving home.

He walked faster, trying to outwalk thoughts of Noon. Past the Christian Street Y, where girls in billowy dresses and pearls and heels streamed in for the Summer Cotillion. Daughters of upper-crust colored folk, doctors and lawyers and teachers, hoping to meet sons of same. He wondered if there was a porter's child among them; a satin belt, a wrist corsage, the interest on his daddy's bonds might get Fannie in fifteen years from now. Noon's refinement would surely help. He shook his head again to dissolve the image of Noon. Came to Father Divine's, Noon again when he thought about their fifteen-cent special: smothered chicken buried in onions and peppers and cornmeal gravy. The showboat across the street was turning on the lights. Chased Noon from his head as he crossed to see who'd be warming up there tonight. Had caught Dizzy there the month before. Maybe he'd stop back through, depending on how things went with Ethel.

Ethel. His heart stopped. He was on the way to see Ethel. Kater Street, where Ethel lived; he paused to breathe and dab at the sweat that was dripping down the side of his face.

Herbie took the six steps in two skips and held his finger against the bell. He looked up smiling, wanting to be sure that when she saw his reflection in the Nosey Susie, the mirror that hung just outside her second-floor window that allowed her to see who her callers were, she would see the smile. She laughed when she opened the window. She laughed a lot, he thought. Her laugh had a melody and a tone that he guessed came from singing all the time.

"I'll drop the key down," she said. "Let yourself in, and come on up."

He fit the key in, impatiently jiggled it around, cursed, then put it in the other way and the door slid open. Somebody in the first-floor apartment was cooking turnip greens, and the scent was all in the vapors that rested along the dull yellow walls in the foyer. He clicked on a light switch to see his way up the steps. He strummed his fingers along the box of chocolates as he tried to slow his pace. He concentrated on the ceiling where upside-down bouquets of pink flowers raced across the white background, a spiderweb spread out between the brown wooden banister spokes. The brass doorknob came into view as he neared the top of the stairs. He just needed to focus on everything around him to still his heart some.

But then he heard the click of the door lock, saw the brass knob turn, and the rush of red and blue lights as the door opened wide. The laugh again, a smooth trumpet blaring through the red and blue, and then Ethel, as she stepped out from behind the opened door, the red and blue lights in the chandelier a fitting backdrop to her silky lounging robe belted tight at the waist, her short hair brushed back, giving a show to her wispy eyes and her pursed lips. He was jelly. She would have to take over from here until he could recover from the first sight of her.

This time when Ethel laughed it was to herself. Herbie's honesty made her feel like a little girl sometimes. The way everything showed on his face helped her reclaim her innocence for a while. She was a young girl all over again and her face was soft brown and clear of hell-fired red rouge. No men yet that needed saving. No man after man that could have been the same man in whose arms she found redemption while she saved his life. Herbie had always been among the most honest. Like he needed healing as much as he needed his physical release.

"Well, come on in, Mr. Herbie. Long time, so long I guess that if I were in a singing mood, I'd break out into a song." She laughed again and pulled him into the living room and closed the door behind him.

"You know like I know you'll save it for the stage, and come give me a hug." He grabbed her, forgetting all about the carnations and Whitman's chocolates and hit himself in the chin with the box and broke off several of the multicolored blooms.

"Here," she said quickly, taking the carnations from him. "Let me put these in my fanciest jar, those jelly jars have those nice scallops along the edges, let me put these in one right now before you break all the heads off." She kissed him on the cheek lightly.

He watched her back as she walked into the kitchen, the way her hips moved from side to side in the lounging set that looked orange under the red and blue lights. It occurred to him that he spent a lot of time watching her back, watching her walk away from him. The way she'd just flit in and out of town, not available more often than she was, no explanations, just business, "Had some things to take care of" was all she'd say. He guessed that was what she'd say this time, so he promised himself he wouldn't bring it up as she walked back into the living room with the carnations in a tall, slender vase.

"Thought you was putting those in a jar?" he asked, trying to keep his irritation at bay.

"Just playing with you, Herbie. You know I got to keep one nice something around me, so I keep this vase. Besides, if I put the flowers in my jelly jar, won't have nothing to drink my ice water out of." She laughed again.

"Have a sit down." She pointed to a high-backed velvet couch that was shaped like a throne and looked purple under the red and blue lights. She set the vase with the carnations on a low coffee table. "Rented this place furnished so I had to settle for what was already here. Couch is faded, can't see it now. That's why I put the colored bulbs in the chandelier. Coffee table all scratched up. Chandelier globes got cracks in them.

Stuffing starting to peek through the little slits in the kitchen chairs. Used shit. Everything in here is used. It'll do for now, though, until I can go shopping. Except for my bed. I can't be sleeping on nobody else's mattress. Went down to Aaron's soon as I got back and bought me my own bedding. And my music box. Lug that Victrola with me wherever I settle. Thing still pushes out a pretty good sound. You want to hear something special?"

"Sounds good what's on there. 'Body and Soul,' right? I know that's Coleman Hawkins, nobody does a tenor sax like him." He was still standing in the middle of the room, still holding on to the chocolates.

Her eyes looked beyond him and stared off into the red and blue air that hung over them like sunfall. "Yeah, I still love my music soft and slow come evening, you know everything's winding down before the fire of night erupts, nice little wind-down music playing now."

Herbie cleared his throat to bring the dreaminess of her eyes back to him. "Bought you some chocolate."

"I see," she said as if called to attention. She laughed and took the box and led Herbie to the couch.

They sat with knees facing as she tore through the clear cellophane covering the yellow box of Whitman's chocolates with her long, sharp nails done up in the newest shade of nude. She lifted the box cover and then the white waxy sheet covering the candy. Liquefied chocolate colored the sheet. Misshapen clumps of tan, and brown, and near-black chocolate oozed their cherry or white cream centers and looked like lava sliding down a hillside.

"Melted," she said. And then she snickered. "What you do, carry these too close to your waist?"

Herbie didn't laugh. He was too embarrassed. Had walked so hard and fast to get to her he hadn't considered that the display box would contain melted candy.

Ethel cleared her throat when she saw Herbie's face; embarrassment raced across it like a red shadow. "I was just teasing you, Herbie. The chocolates will be fine. I'll stick them right in the icebox right now. Even taste sweeter after they been melted down once and then hardened back to shape."

"Fine," he said, waving his hand in the most nonchalant way he could.

He watched her back again and then her return into the living room.

This time she held a tall bottle of Beefeater gin, a short, thick shot glass, and a jelly jar filled with ice water.

"Still remember your drink, Herbie. It ain't been that long." She set the glasses down and cracked the seal on the gin and poured it into Herbie's glass. "Also bought a quart of Ballantine beer if you want a chaser."

"Just the gin is fine for now. You still on that ice water, I see." He raised his glass in a toast.

"Still got to have it out of a jelly jar too," she said as she clinked her glass against his. "Just don't taste right out of anything else. Had to get that through to your buddy Big Carl's head last night. I told him I ain't signing no long-term contracts to sing at that Club Royale unless he can assure me I get my ice water in a widemouthed jelly jar."

"So I guess that means you here for a while. Is that what you saying?"

"Awhile." She said it matter-of-factly. "So"—a sudden pitch of excitement in her voice now—"tell me 'bout your new baby. Heard all of downtown celebrated for two days over that child."

"Baby's fine." He said it impatiently, wanting to hear about her plans instead. "Named her Fannie, cute little thing. Happy baby too, laugh every time she look at me."

"Awl, that's so sweet," Ethel said as her eyes went soft and she sighed lightly. "Must be nice having a cute little baby 'round."

"Nice, real nice," Herbie said, cutting her short. "So what you say about a contract at Royale?"

"Ain't said nothing about it except that I might settle back here and sing at the club."

The matter-of-fact tone was back in her voice and brought Herbie's under-the-skin irritation to the surface. "Till you just up and leave again, right?"

"My good buddy," she said as she slapped at his knee. "You all right? You know that's important to me, that you be all right."

"Then why you always dropping in and out of my life if that's so important?" He crossed his ankle over his knee, mad at himself for asking.

"Now, Herbie, one thing ain't got nothing to do with the other."

"In my book it does. You say you care about somebody, you at least give them a forewarning when you getting ready to up and leave." He flipped at the cuff of his pant leg and then leaned his arms against the throne-backed couch.

"Don't do that, baby. We go too far back for me to have to feel like I got to explain my every move to you." She leaned forward so she could look right in his face. "You understand the entertainer's lifestyle, seeing as how you lived it for a while too. A person got to make sudden moves sometimes for the career to take off."

"When you left seven or eight months ago to settle some business, ain't have nothing to do with your career." Herbie sat up and put his glass down heavily, unable to stop the anger moving through his voice. "When you gave me the slip at Gert's that night, then disappeared till I saw you at Royale yesterday, ain't have nothing to do with your career. Now you sitting up here, looking so good I can't hardly stand to look at you, and I guess you fixing to go somewhere else, let me guess, for your career, right?"

"Wait a minute, Mr. Herbie." She paused to sip her ice water. "Should I remind you that you got a wife? She's the permanent fixture in your life, not me. I don't have chick nor chile to hold me anywhere, and sure as hell ain't got no man weighing me down. I don't owe you no explanation. Don't owe a damn soul one."

"Okay, here we go with Miss-Don't-need-nothing-from-nobody, don't-owe-nobody-nothing routine."

"It's no routine." This time she put her jar down heavily. "Now we always had that kind of understanding. Just don't come in here now like you expecting some kind of explanation for my behavior. You'll kill it, Herbie, whatever we got, you start putting demands on me and you'll kill it dead."

He pinched at the cuff link on his starched white shirt and then looked straight at Ethel, trying not to lose himself in her half-closed eyes the way it felt as if he'd lose himself whenever he looked at her. "What we got?" His voice was steady as his gaze.

"We got us a good solid friendship. We buddies. Good, good buddies."

"Just buddies?"

"You got a wife, you sure don't need a wife."

"Got half a wife."

"Come again?"

"What I say, got half a wife."

"I know you not saying she's running. I've watched her up and down, you got you a good wife."

"She's good in that way." Herbie's words were thick and measured. "Honest, good cook, house so clean I could eat off the kitchen floor, perfect starch to my shirts."

"A good country-girl wife you got."

"Hold her own in a conversation, loving mother to that baby that was left on our steps."

"Who you telling? Anyone can look at her and see she could write a song on being a good mother."

"Helps out the people on the block, in her church, real giving woman."

"Good church woman, Herbie, I know what you got now. In fact, I don't see the problem." Ethel looked at Herbie intently as he talked, at the pain that covered his face a little at a time as he spoke.

"Good in those ways, but not in other ways that count as much, if not more."

Ethel's mouth fell open, and she had to put her jar on the coffee table before it fell through her hands. "What she do, Herbie, shut down when the lights go low?"

"Like a clam over a freshwater pearl." He tried to keep his voice from shaking. He looked at his cuff links. They were gold-toned with a ruby red center. He stared at the center.

"So what, she don't put out once in a while. Not the worse trait you could have in a wife."

"She don't put out."

"So y'all just get together maybe once a month, makes it sweeter when you do."

"We ain't been together."

"In a long time, right? You saying y'all ain't been together in a long time?" Ethel's voice had a pleading to it.

"I'm saying we ain't been together."

"Don't say that. Please tell me you just saying this to try to bullshit me so I'll be extra nice to you."

"But you know I wouldn't lie to you about something like this." His lips turned down, pulling his whole face with them.

"You wouldn't," she said as she thought about all the times she'd heard the "me and my wife ain't intimate" plea, and now hearing it as the truth from Herbie. She rubbed her hands up and down her arms and felt Herbie's honesty so stark in the room at that moment that it seeped through the silky sleeves of her lounging set and gave her chills.

They were both silent, sitting on the thronelike faded couch. The record had stopped, and there was no other sound in the room save the tinkling of the ice in Ethel's widemouthed jar. Herbie stared into the ruby red of his cuff links. He had never sighed a word of Noon's problem to anyone. And now the breath-strangling embarrassment left him and he was ready to talk.

"What makes a woman do that? Just shut down like that? Something I ain't doing, something I done? I'm on the verge of leaving, love that little baby to death, but I still got needs. Shouldn't have to be hunting down women like I'm single when I'm doing my part, work my ass off, doing what I'm supposed to be doing as the husband. And then she just shuts down on me."

"Don't leave her, Herbie." Ethel's voice had a whispered urgency to it. "Y'all got that little baby now. You can't leave her now that y'all got that baby to raise. Maybe she's just shy, or maybe she just having some female problems. You know marriage is an adjustment; maybe she's still in the adjustment period. I mean really, y'all ain't been married that long."

"Celebrated a year night before last." He said it flatly, relieved that the telling of it to another person had extracted the incredulousness of it all and made it all the other person's.

"A year!" she blurted, and then silence as even the room screamed in disbelief. It *had* been a year, she thought, measuring it by her own departure from and return to Philly. "That must be rough," she whispered when she could talk again. "But don't leave her. Give her a little more time. Maybe somebody did something to her that got her messed up in the head. Colored woman act tough, I know, but she's mostly a delicate thing, a very delicate thing."

"And where that leave a man?"

"Right here on Ethel's faded couch," she said as she stretched open her arms. "C'mere. Come to Ethel, it'll be okay, just come on to Ethel."

PART II

EIGHT

Herbie went to Ethel for a stretch of five years, minus three in the middle when the war took him away, shuttled him across the country in the all-Negro 477th Bomber Squad. He wrote to Noon from Biloxi, Mississippi; Terre Haute, Indiana; Texas; Arizona; but no Europe. Trained for combat, but no combat. Told Noon in his letters don't worry about him getting shot at by the Germans, maybe by the white townspeople in Biloxi, though. Especially when he and his GI buddies went into town and had to walk back because the military vehicles picked up only the white GIs. He could do as much back home in South Philly, he'd write.

In South Philly that stretch of five years passed like molasses going over biscuits. Where it was thin, it moved. It dripped and crawled into a puddle in the center of the plate. Fannie was growing like the thin part—movement for sure. Five years old with her true cornbread color, and black, black hair that was long and crinkly and thick like wool. Her full-lipped mouth pursed under her thin nose and was always spilling out observations with such honest boldness that Noon sometimes threatened to take a hand to her mouth. Except that Noon had been noticing that sometimes Fannie made mention of something that hadn't happened yet that sure enough came to pass. Noon adored her, though. Couldn't imagine loving her more if she had been conceived from mixing pleasures with Herbie.

Their pleasures weren't mixing, though. Thick molasses in that regard. Moved so slowly until it stood still. Once Herbie was done with his southern tour of duty, he returned to Philadelphia and long hours as a redcap since the trains were used to transport servicemen back and forth, and sometimes equipment for the war effort. So with Herbie gone so much it was easy for Noon to wrap herself in her church, in raising Fannie, in her sewing and cooking and cleaning, in everything except Herbie's arms under the covers when the night came. She continued to see Reverend Schell for her healing prayers, three, four times a year. And she'd get that slither of warmth deep inside, but it never grew enough for her to let Herbie in.

Herbie stopped pressuring her for the most part. Depending on his mood when she apologized for not being able to do her wifely duty, he'd hold her, or else he'd suck the air in through his teeth and leave the room. He lived for Noon's macaroni and cheese, though, and Fannie's smile. And especially for Ethel's faded couch if it was late enough. Because recently Ethel saw him only when it was late. During his time in the service Ethel had taken in the daughter of her dead baby sister. For the past few years she'd been trying to fit raising her niece into her club singer's lifestyle. That irritated Herbie. As the child got older, he couldn't visit until Ethel had put her to bed for the night. If she woke up crying, calling for Ethel, he had to leave. Ethel's house rule.

᛭

They could have gone on like that, suspended like no-moving molasses: Noon praying for her miracle, Herbie watching the clock until Ethel would let him in. Except Ethel never did move like molasses. She mostly moved like fire.

᛭

"What am I going to do with you, precious Liz?" Ethel said more to herself than to her five-year-old niece, who was napping, curled up on the couch with her head in Ethel's lap. Since Liz's mother had been killed in a car crash three years before, Ethel had been trying to muster up enough motherhood to do right by the little girl. Right now she stroked the child's red hair and rubbed her fingers gently across her forehead. She had just gotten word that she had a tremendous gig singing her brand of bebop jazz if she could just be in New York City in two weeks. Might have the chance to sing with the likes of Charlie Parker, Thelonious Monk, people sliding up and down the scale the way she liked to do, even going off it when need be. But what about Liz? Liz was her dead sister's only child. Surely she couldn't move Liz to New York, where the scarlet nights blazed much hotter than they ever did in Philadelphia, and the mornings were hungover with the deepest shades of blue. The child needed soft pink things, stability. She needed oatmeal, milk and cookie snacks, chicken and dumplings. She needed Sunday school, crinoline slips, and a big brown doll at Christmas. Not New York City. So Ethel did what she always did when she needed a quick miracle: She went to church.

She stood outside the sturdy brick church. It was July, and the gray bricks jutted and seemed to sweat in the hot morning sun. She watched the congregation file in for Sunday morning worship. She had been here a few months before in the spring when Roosevelt had just died and the women seemed to be in mourning in drab grays and blacks and browns. But this Sunday they were dripping in colors—as if they knew the war would end any day now and the last of the men still doing their duty would return. They wore summer-weight town suits, and side-draped waistline dresses, and button-down shifts with kick-out pleats. They wore hats on top of hats: sailor hats and saucers, turbans, bonnets and berets sweetened with veils for the trying-to-be-pious, or flowers and maidenhair fern. Ethel fingered her own swallowtail hat, drew it down further on her head, as she noticed how easily they laughed, a lightness to their steps, heading in the church as if they expected a foot-stomping good time.

She looked deep into their faces. She knew she'd want to see unweathered skin, a walk filled with purpose, confidence, maybe to the hum of "What a friend we have in Jesus." She listened for snatches of conversations and ruled out anyone who appeared to be too much a complainer, gossiper, or too Holy Ghost–filled. And then she saw Noon, the woman whose husband she whispered creamy words to late at night when her set was done and Liz was fast asleep. Noon was as good as mothers came. Ethel was sure of that. She had watched Noon up close several years ago: walked through her block all different times of day, tried to make trite conversation; even had Pop, the man who owned the store at the corner of Noon's block, over for dinner to learn all she could about Noon. Fed him thick slices of roast beef and butter-brushed candied yams; let him whisper "Jesus, Jesus" in her ear. And in the meantime she stockpiled information about Noon's habits and routines, her temperament, her friends and detractors, and her family down South. She could call up those details at a time such as this when she needed a home for her precious child.

Ethel watched Noon walk into the church. A neat girdled stride. Not as beautiful as she could be. Her hat was brimless and centered, not propped stylishly to the side, not filled with gardens. Her baby blue–colored dress hung loosely. No tightly clasped belt to show off her bow-shaped hips, no high-heel shoes to emphasize her calves, no red-colored foundation to touch up her coloring, which was middle-of-the-road. No excesses. Instead efficient, just enough makeup, a small Bible, not the kind that weighed like construction bricks, simple earrings, hair pulled back in a tight bun behind the small, centered hat. Not even a French roll, not doing that soft hair no justice at all, Ethel thought. The thick-haired child skipping at her side wore a crisply starched pink cotton dress under a lacy white pinafore top with a sash at the waist tied back into a healthy bow. Two soft pink ribbons laced the ends of the child's dense plaits to keep her hair from unraveling. The child's coloring, like corn bread, had a just-scrubbed look about it, a healthy look, the way her long legs looked healthy sprouting from her sturdy leather Mary Jane shoes. Ethel knew the child was Fannie. Herbie often made Ethel laugh until her throat ached with story after story of Fannie's outrageous boldness.

Ethel trailed Fannie and Noon inside the church, which was markedly cooler than the fierce July sun. She took a seat just two rows behind them and slightly to the side. She had left Liz with the woman who lived in the apartment downstairs and she smiled now as she imagined her Liz sitting with the neatly appareled Noon and thick-haired Fannie. Such a polite child her Liz. She would be the perfect balance to Fannie, who was fidgeting, and trying to untie her hair bows, and waving her arms imitating people that the spirit hit. Ethel cupped her mouth to keep from laughing out loud when Fannie actually stood and flung her hands in the air and pretended to faint. Liz was such a serious child. Fannie would loosen her up for sure. But it was risky. Herbie came to call more than most. What if Liz had gotten a glimpse of him? His light skin and dark hair were the things a child would remember. What if she had heard his voice, which boomed when he laughed, which he did a lot, especially when he talked about Fannie? What if she remembered the whiffs of Old Spice that hung around for a day or two after he had left? Ethel settled back in the deep brown pew. Her flowing red dress, the center of a chocolate-covered cherry, melted and oozed over the seat. She needed to think.

Between the dancing tambourines and drums that beat out "Amazing Grace," between the waving paper fans that announced cut-rate funerals and the velvet-lined brass collection plates filled up with copper and silver and brown tithing envelopes, she saw Noon's arms. Good wrapping arms. They were wrapped around Fannie, who was falling off to sleep. That's what Liz needed now more than anything, some consistent arms. Arms like her grandmother's that rocked and held and, when necessary, pushed away. Even pushed away her own child, Ethel's mother, when Ethel's mother's mind turned against her, and she went half mad and could no longer do right by Ethel and her sister. Ethel decided right then and there it could work. Hadn't she been extra careful to keep Liz from knowing her night callers? "No, no, can't come over till I put my baby to bed," she'd tell them. Meant it too. If Liz stirred in the middle of the night or cried out for Ethel, company had to leave. And they could never stay until dawn. Not like Ethel's mother, whom the daybreak greeted time and again sprawled out, half clothed, strange man snoring next to her. Ethel and her sister would have to put cold rags to her face to bring her to, make her decent. They as little girls had to take it upon themselves to chase their mother's company away. Liz always woke to Ethel's snuggles, though, in the bed they shared, wrapped in soft cotton sheets scented with cocoa butter and fine French perfume.

It could work, it could. Except for Herbie's reaction. He'll be blazing mad, she thought. Poor Herbie, he was different, never rough, an honesty to him. She cringed at what he'd do when he found out. His sharp nose would flare. The top of his head where the jet black silky strands were growing thinner would pulse and redden. A ball of anger would form in his throat, and when he could talk, his voice would crackle as he whispered her name, demanding, Why? Why, Ethel, why? But this was for Liz. She had to give Liz the best. Noon was the best.

Ethel liked Noon's block. She liked the sound of the trolley as it swished up the street. Intermittent trees gave the shadows a playful never-know-where-I'm-going-to-land dance to them. Even the people who assembled on their steps after their early Sunday dinners to watch the children play hopscotch, and wait to hear what number was leading, and chatter about who got happy in church, or flimflammed on Broad Street, or whose child was sent down South before she started showing, or who got a new couch, or used piano, or inheritance, or work shoveling shit at the navy yard. Ethel liked them too. Close-knit they were.

She walked through the block, hoping to catch up with Noon. Maybe set it up so Liz and Fannie could become playmates beforehand. She was still smiling at the sight of Noon and Fannie in church earlier, Fannie's bounciness, fidgeting, pulling at her hair, Noon's patience. She said a string of how do's as she walked up the block. The men watched her hips move in circles; some smacked their lips; one or two held back whistles in deference to the wives. The women sneered and whispered: Whose man she coming to hunt down, hussy, hot-behinded red devil? A trail of air filled with outright jealousy and suppressed desire followed Ethel as she walked. Her saucer eyes didn't flinch, nor did her thick ruby lips droop. She still smiled as she walked, her head thrown back, almost facing the sky. She was used to the air that her presence stirred up. She knew how to sift through it, not take it in, not let it cause her pain.

She paused in the middle of her slow, sultry stride to stare up at Noon's house. The shade was on Noon's side of the street. She had the notion to sit on Noon's steps. Her high heels were making her feet ache, and she wanted to feel the smooth roughness of the concrete against her. But then the air changed, right at her back. She turned to see Noon staring at her as if she were trying to see clear to her soul.

"Can I help you?" Noon asked crisply.

Ethel groped for something to say. She didn't want to mention Liz just yet. She noticed the window ledge lined with clay pots painted orange and yellow, all proudly sporting gardenias, and coleus, and begonias, and Swedish ivies. "Gorgeous flowers, what do you do to keep them so healthy?"

"The most I did was paint the pots. God did the rest." Noon tilted her chin upward, signaling the conversation's end and then grabbed Fannie's hands to still her bouncing up and down the steps.

Ethel was not put off. She looked at Fannie and smiled and said, "How you doing, cutie?"

Fannie smiled back. A deep smile. "Fine, thank you, I like your necklace."

Ethel looked down. She was sure her necklace was hidden under the low ruffle of her red blouse. She lifted the heart-shaped locket. The goldness bounced around even on this shady side of the street. She stooped down to show Fannie the heart. "You've got some eyesight on you, sweetie; most people don't notice it. It has little tiny pictures of special people inside."

"Babies' pictures?" Fannie asked, running her finger over the gold heart.

Ethel stroked at Fannie's thick braids. "Yup, and a picture of my baby sister." She spoke softly, right into Fannie's eyes.

Noon sucked the air in hard between her teeth and pulled Fannie toward the steps. "Beg your pardon, but we're on the way in."

"How do you keep your daughter's hair so neat? She's got so much of it, a head of hair," Ethel said, ignoring the curtness.

"A comb, a brush, and some Dixie Peach." Noon started to move up her steps.

"Does she take after your side of the family, such long legs, such striking features for a child so young?"

"Not my natural child. Had her since she was an infant, though, like mine, though. Fannie, her name's Fannie. Me and my husband do just about anything for her." Noon stopped then and turned to look at Ethel, to stare at her again, to have it revealed to her what this woman wanted with her, why she paused in the midst of her preen up the block to stare up at her house, and why was she trying to start trite conversation. And now, why was she so interested in Fannie?

Noon's gaze burned Ethel's eyes, dried them out. She blinked several times hard, held her mascaraed lids down for a time, tightly, and then commented on how bright the sun was on this day. "Should really have on my sunglasses," Ethel said. "Doctor says bright sun can mess up your eyes."

"We in the shade, so what do you want?" Noon asked, her voice steady and strong.

Ethel breathed deep, and cleared her throat, and half stammering said, "I have a little girl too, 'bout the same age as your Fannie. Her name's Liz. Actually she's not my natural either, my baby sister's child. My sister and her husband were burned up in a car fire, you probably heard about it, 'bout three years ago, a whole carload coming from Rock-Away Beach, leaking gas tank, my sister and her husband, and his three brothers. People tried, but no one could get to them in time. They tell me his father tried to grab his arm and just pulled back burnt flesh, tell me that's all he talked about till he died, the feel of his son's flesh pulling off his bones."

"And what that have to do with me?" Noon asked, folding her arms tightly across her chest.

"Well, I thought maybe my Liz and your Fannie could play together sometime. Liz doesn't have a lot of friends, and I'm a singer, and well, I just thought—"

"Fannie doesn't mix in much with other children," Noon said.

Fannie had pulled away from Noon and was dancing in the street. Arms and legs going in a frenetic pace. One of her plaits had unraveled, and thick, crinkled hair stood straight up. She looked like an African dancer bringing on the harvest.

"Looks like she'd mix fine with my niece, Liz. My niece could use some of your daughter's spirit." Ethel's eyes watered in the corners from blinking so hard.

"Fannie, let's go in now, come on, let's go." Noon cut Ethel off. Had to. Anybody else's child, fine. But no way would she invite this woman to be switching her ample behind in and out of her house under the pretense of dropping her niece off. Lacking though she was in womanly ways, she at least knew not to unlock the shed to let the wolf come on in, or the devil. She turned away from Ethel. Didn't want to acknowledge that there was a hint of pleading in Ethel's eyes. A humaneness. A tenderness for Fannie that caught her totally off guard. A hussy. That's all she was. A man-grabbing, two-bit singing, devil-loving hussy. She snatched Fannie by the hand and pulled her firmly up the steps. "Like I said, we're on the way in. Fannie's nap time. Plenty of children all up and down through here for your niece to get friendly with. I can't help you out none."

"My best friend, Julep, lives right around the corner," Fannie said as she turned and smiled and waved good-bye to Ethel. "Maybe you could talk to her mother."

Noon whisked Fannie quickly into the house. Ethel dabbed at the corners of her eyes. Water ran and mixed with the mascara and streaked black lines along the tips of her fingers. She rubbed her fingers together and started back down the block. She knew it must look as if she were crying. It didn't matter. She knew she never cried. Even as she tasted the mascara-streaked tears. She was even more determined that Liz should have Noon—and Fannie.

Fannie didn't want to take a nap. She was five and too old for naps, she thought. She wanted to stare out of the living room window and watch Ethel walk down the block. Ethel had made her insides smile. Not many people did. There were Noon and Herbie; her best friend, Julep; and Miss Jeanie next door. Now there was Ethel. And maybe the little girl she talked to Noon about. She had seen the colors when Ethel called the little girl's name. Liz. The gold from the heart around Ethel's neck had come at Fannie's eyes the way colors always did when she was about to see something. Usually when she complained about the colors hurting her eyes, Noon would get quiet, serious, ask her softly to describe what she was seeing. This time she hadn't complained, though. She'd danced in the street instead. So the moving pictures in her head hadn't gotten clear the way they would with Noon's gentle prodding. They turned to fuzzy mush as she danced. She saw Herbie and Ethel and a little girl with bright red hair, crying, and then the outlines faded, and there was just a blob of gray, and Noon was pulling her in the house away from Ethel and the bright gold heart.

Right now she jerked her shoulder from Noon as Noon tried to nudge her from the window.

"Come on now, Fannie, I said it's time for your nap." Noon snipped the ends of her words sharply.

"I don't want to take a nap," Fannie whined. "I want to go outside and play hopscotch with Julep."

"Julep's probably in her house taking a nap too," Noon said, cutting her eyes toward the window to make sure Ethel was gone. "You gonna want to stay up and sit outside later on, you have to get some rest now."

"But I hate naps." Fannie stomped her feet hard against the floor. "And I hate these old big shoes." She kicked at her brand-new black leather Mary Janes made bigger because they were Stride Rites and supposed to correct the way Fannie stood back on her heels.

"Don't kick the shoes against the floor, you know how many rationing stamps I had to use on those shoes."

"Why?" Fannie pouted and folded her arms across her chest.

"Because of the war, Fannie, I told you, some things in short supply so they have to put a limit on you buying certain things."

"I mean, why do I have to wear them?"

"Keeps your feet from spreading. Now you trying my patience."

"But I like spreading feet, and I like blazing hussies too."

"What did you say out of your mouth?" Noon stooped and grabbed both of Fannie's shoulders and shook her one time.

"I said, I liked spreading feet." Fannie whispered it and turned away from Noon. She concentrated on her white, ruffled anklet socks. She knew she had gone too far.

"Don't try my patience, you know what I'm talking about, the other part that you just said."

"That's what you called that lady." Fannie raised her eyes toward Noon and, seeing the deep line trekking down her forehead, looked away again.

"When? When did I say that, Fannie?"

"Just now when we were coming in the house. You whispered it, but I heard it." She leaned down to tug at her anklet.

"You can't go around repeating everything you hear me say. Some things you hear me say aren't for a little girl's ears and definitely not for a little girl's mouth." Noon stood and took Fannie's hand firmly in her own. "And I don't like to have to think about putting a hand to your mouth, but that's just what I'll have to do if you can't learn what to say out of it."

"I'll learn, I'll learn," Fannie pleaded, thinking that if she couldn't get out of a nap, at least she could get out of a soft heinie.

That's what Noon had said the only other time she'd spanked her: "A hard head makes for a soft heinie."

It was Christmastime, and Sister Maybell and her grandson, Willie, had just come in the door, hadn't even shaken the cold off as they'd unbuttoned their coats, when Fannie said to Willie in a voice as clear as water from the spring in Fairmount Park, "You ain't shit."

She couldn't understand the collective gasps of Noon and Herbie, Sister Maybell, the new Deacon Shone. But she did understand Noon as she whisked her up the stairs, proceeded to lift her red velvet Christmas dress, slap her bottom, and repeat over and over her admonition about a hard head making for a soft heinie. Fannie had tried to explain that's what she'd heard Herbie say. Right at the counter at Pop's while she sipped vanilla cream soda and listened to Herbie and Pop go on about the new cat Big Carl had brought on at Club Royale. Maybell's grandson, they'd said. "Young as he is and think he know everything. Ain't shit," they'd agreed in a whispered huddle. "He ain't shit."

Fannie bit her lip now as she remembered that spanking. "I'll take a nap. I'll learn what to say out of my mouth. Just don't make my heinie soft. Okay, Noon, okay."

Noon loosened her grip on Fannie's hand as they walked toward the stairs. She tried to stay mad. She couldn't. Fannie was a good child. Devilish at times, but good through and through. Could also pick out the goodness in other people. That was why it bothered Noon that Fannie had taken a liking to Ethel. Still only a child, Noon reminded herself, as they walked into Fannie's bedroom and she unbuttoned the back of Fannie's pinafore and undid the bow and helped her step out of the crinoline slip until she was down to her sleeveless cotton undershirt and white cotton panties and the oversized black Mary Janes.

"I'll take my nap in the shoes, okay, I don't really hate them." Fannie stretched across the ribbed bedspread and let her feet dangle.

Noon tried not to laugh as she unclasped the straps and peeled the shoes and socks from Fannie's feet. "Just go to sleep." She tickled Fannie's feet and watched her giggle and left her to her nap.

Fannie didn't nap. She tossed from one end of the bed, letting her feet dangle, to the other, where she leaned her head over and walked her fingers through the pink, fluffy hook rug. She could smell the new leather from her Mary Janes, then the talcum powder that Noon sprinkled between her sheets. She thought about Ethel when she inhaled the talc's sweetness. She pictured the gold heart, imagined the pictures inside, was sure there were pictures of babies. Liz. One of them had to be Liz. She settled down then. She fell asleep thinking about Liz.

NINE

The night before Ethel was to leave for New York, she and Liz sat in the center of the bed they shared most nights. This evening they played 21 blackjack even though Liz was only five. "You'll know all your numbers by the time you start school," Ethel would tell her whenever they sat down to play. "Probably be able to add and subtract too; how else you gonna know whether or not I'm cheating you?"

The bedroom was small, and the bed seemed to Liz to take up most of the room. That was fine by her five-year-old standards. The bed was like a patch of land on an angry sea where monsters circled. As long as she was on the bed, they couldn't grab her by her leg and spin her around and then let go so she'd be flung into space, just spinning and turning and getting dizzy without end. Right now the monsters weren't there. At night they'd circle, though. When Ethel would slip out of the bed, taking her warmth with her, Liz would wake with a start, and there they'd be, like shadows that changed shapes daring her to move. She'd hear tapping on the living room door, and whispers, sometimes laughs, and the low beats on Ethel's record player, and she'd want to get up, to run to Ethel, but she could never see an opening through these monsters that were thick and tight and didn't let any light through. Then she'd hear the couch moving, turning into a bed, and the metal leg scraping the hardwood floor. In the morning, when the sun spilled into the living room, she could see the white scrape marks against the brown floor. She'd sometimes want to pat the marks down with peroxide, the way Ethel did her nicks and cuts. Keeps the germs and infections away, she'd tell her. Liz suspected that the floor was infected; the white scrape marks seemed to deepen each day. She thought about the scrape marks as Ethel folded her cards and the bed shifted as she got up to answer a tap on the front door.

Liz crawled back to where the bed met the wall and leaned against the wall and drew her knees to her chest. The ceiling light was on so the monsters stayed small and flat against the floor. She reached her hand back behind the headpost to her spot on the wall. It was jagged and rough, and it felt good to her fingers as she caressed the spot and then pushed into it and caught the tiny bits of plaster that bounced from it. She put them in her mouth and chewed them down and watched the monsters as they cowered in the light.

Ethel came back into the room and was struck by Liz pressed against the wall with her knees drawn to her, staring blankly at the floor. "What's the matter, sweet pea?" She took her place again on the bed and scooped her cards up and fanned them back into position. "You look like something scared the mess out of you. Tell Aunt Ethel what it is."

Liz swallowed the plaster down. She usually didn't swallow it. She usually just held it in her mouth until it turned to gravy and seeped into the balls along her tongue. But now she had to swallow it, and it made her cough, and Ethel lurched for her and patted her back and asked her if she was okay.

Liz said that she was tired of playing cards and that she just wanted for them to go to sleep until it was light outside again. Ethel agreed, even though she had just told Herbie that he would have to come back in about two hours. She really wanted to be up with Liz tonight. She wanted to play with her awhile longer, and tickle her and make her laugh, and chase away the fright in her eyes. Tomorrow she would leave for New York, so she wanted tonight to go on longer. But she relented, and they got ready for bed. And Liz snuggled up against Ethel, and Ethel rocked her and hummed and squeezed her even tighter than usual as she thought about Liz's mother, her dead baby sister, and told herself again that this was right, what she was doing was the best she could do for their precious Liz.

Ethel eased out of bed when she heard the tapping at the living room door. Herbie always tapped. She liked that. Sometimes her company would pound and bang with a rough impatience and she'd crack the door and tell them to go to hell. If they hadn't been raised well enough to respect people's homes, they sure weren't getting in her house. She cracked the door now and saw Herbie standing there in his starched white shirt and a question mark on his face that pleaded, "Now? Is now okay?"

She smiled and pressed her finger to her lips, telling him to tiptoe on in. He did. He did most things Ethel asked him to do without hesitation or question. He knew he could depend on her for a fulfillment that existed nowhere else. Even if Noon could ever get her passion stirred, he doubted that it would rush and bubble like Ethel's. It wasn't just his body that responded to Ethel. It was all the pieces of him— notions that stirred his intellect, his imagination; yearnings that tugged and expanded to a joy that went to his very core, where he was sure his soul was born.

"What music you want to hear?" She whispered it as she pulled him in and led him to the couch.

"Sounds good what's on there right now," he said as he listened to the soft, smooth loops of Sarah Vaughan singing "Lover Man." He could pick out Charlie Parker on alto and Dizzy on trumpet as the music filled the room. "But you'd sound better." He said it matter-of-factly.

"I'm done singing for the night, baby."

"Don't sing, talk. I just want to hear you talk, long as I can hear your words meeting my ears, I get strength to go back out there and face the rotten world."

Ethel sat along the arm of the couch-bed and stroked his shoulder and smoothed at his hair. "Rotten world, huh? Sounds like you was climbing the rough side of the mountain today?"

"No rougher than usual. Lugging people's shit from the platform to the cabstand."

"Lugging extrahard for that penny tip, huh?"

"Lugging so I don't go into a rage." He pulled her hand from his head and pressed it between both of his. "You know, once the train gets through Maryland, and Delaware, colored folks think they up North, think they got rights now, they free and not confined to the colored car and can sit wherever they damn well please." He stood and walked to the stacks of phonograph records and rifled through them. "I see the thrill in their faces, and I just want to tell them, 'Wait till you ready to go in the movie house and can't sit where you want, or one of those fine stores along Chestnut Street, see how they treat you there; and you might not be breaking your back in a hot field, but you ain't really worked till you froze your ass off pulling guts from pigs all day long.' And then all the soldiers coming home, 'specially the ones who were stationed down South like I was; the German prisoners of war got better treatment than we did. Truman better do something with this situation in this country or there's gonna be riots jumping out all over the place."

"Damn straight," Ethel said, moving from her perch on the arm of the couch to sit in its center.

"Then I help little brown-skinned ladies old as my grandmother, if I had a grandmother living, with all her worldly possessions, and I take her to a seat and tell her that this seat is the best because she won't feel the jerks and bumps in the tracks from this seat. And Mr. Charlie's getting mad, 'cause he been waiting for a train too, since they using most of the trains to get the soldiers home, and he feel like I ain't got no business helping this little old colored lady before I help him. So I go back and lug his shit extrahard or I might tell him to go to hell if he thinks I'm gonna deny my-could-be-grandmother for his penny tip. Like earlier today, I took Fannie with me when I went to get my pay—"

"Fannie!" Ethel sat straight up as if called to attention when he mentioned Fannie's name. "What that little Fannie do this time?"

"Well, we walking through the train station." Herbie put the records down and walked to the center of the room. "Just like I'm walking now. I'm in my street clothes, no redcap nowhere near the top of my head, and this regular Charlie, stops me and says, 'Herbie, get on over here and get my bag, boy.' So I tell him that I'm not on duty at the present moment. So he looks at me like he don't believe I'm telling him no when Fannie runs to his bag and lifts it and says, 'This bag ain't even heavy, mister. You could carry this bag your own self.'"

"No, she didn't." Ethel was listening so intently she almost jumped out of her seat in the center of the couch.

"I swear. Then I pull her away 'cause I know anything's liable to come out of her mouth, and I don't want him to be in earshot when it does. Good thing too, 'cause she stops and tugs my arm and proclaims, 'Herbie, that man's a motherfucker, isn't he?' "

By now Ethel's mouth was wide open, and she had to steady herself she was laughing so hard. "She said what?"

"I'm telling you," Herbie said, all of him totally into the story now with Ethel enjoying it so. "So I stopped and stooped and looked right in her eyes that were serious, and I said, 'Fannie, you must never use words like that, do you understand? Where you hear words like that anyhow?' 'Cause I know Noon don't curse not one bit, and I'm very careful with my language 'round her."

"And what she say, Herbie, huh, what she say?"

"She said, 'Lots of places. On South Street, on Ninth Street, in the back of the fish market where the men cut off the fishes' heads and they don't see me back there.' And I told her, 'It's wrong for a little lady like you to use that kind of language, that's for stevedores and sailors.' "

"So did she agree with you or what?" Ethel was talking with her hands as she choked back laughs so she could ask her question.

"She agreed with me all right." Herbie chuckled. "She said in her sweetest voice, 'Okay, Herbie, next time'—and then she whispered— 'next time we'll just call him a son of a bitch.' "

Ethel doubled over and clutched at her stomach she laughed so hard. "Stop, stop, Herbie, you gonna make me pee. Oh, God, that little girl is too much."

Herbie stopped laughing then; he just stood in the center of the room, and his face got angular, serious. Ethel looked at him, and her laughter just hung in the air unfinished when she looked at him. "What? What's the matter, Herbie?"

"No, I was just thinking about how she kept staring at me all the way home after that. And right when we turned the corner of Lombard Street, she asked me if the man was my boss. I told her, 'No. That was hardly none of my boss.' So she said that he seemed like my boss. I told her that the city is filled with people that think they my boss, but that don't mean I got to buckle for them."

Ethel got up slowly from the arm of the couch. She hugged him and said, "Well, you with Ethel now. You don't have to buckle for me, baby, unless, of course, you got something different in mind for tonight." They both laughed as the music stopped, and she went to the record player and started looking through the records.

"That's what got me through the day," Herbie said as he walked to her back and put his arms around her. "I knew tonight was my night to be with you, don't know what I'd do if I didn't have my nights with you to look forward to."

Ethel stopped short as she rifled through the stacks of records. She had planned not to say anything to Herbie about moving away to New York. She'd thought it would be easier that way, for Herbie, certainly for her. She just wanted to make tonight special so that he could remember her generosity. But now she had a heaviness in her chest that she hadn't planned on. She pressed the black shiny record on the center of the Victrola and watched the needle find the groove. A trumpet bleated a long note, and she felt sad for Herbie.

"Do you talk to your wife the way you talk to me?" She turned to him and put one arm around his back, and he instinctively took the other arm and they fell right into their two-step of a slow drag.

"I talk to her. Not the way I talk to you, but yeah, I talk to her."

"You care for her, right?"

"Course I care for her. Care a lot for her, a whole lot."

"Then why can't you talk to her the way you do me?"

"Can't."

"Why can't you?"

"Just can't. She'd just deny me if I tried."

"I ain't talking about sex, Herbie."

"I ain't either. I'm talking 'bout her denying my feelings. She'd just tell me if I prayed, I wouldn't have so much hate in my heart, how I got to go to church, you know, plus she depends on my paycheck, she'd get nervous if she thought I was likely to do something to disrupt that. But mostly her faith would get in the way."

Ethel stopped moving then, right in the middle of their two-step. She pulled her head back from his shoulder, forcing him to look at her. "There's a lot to be said for believing in something the way Noon does, don't ever underestimate the power of her faith, that's probably what brings her joy."

"Well, that's her joy. She ain't trying so hard to make it my joy, that's for sure. And why you defending her anyhow?"

"I ain't defending nobody." Ethel starting moving again. "I just feel for her."

"Well, I feel for you. And as for my joy, I get it from you." Herbie fell into the lead and moved Ethel around the room. Back and up, he spun her and danced her in a circle and then a square, from the table where he liked his gin to the scrape marks on the floor. He leaned her backward in a dip, way back in the arch that was her trademark. "You give me joy. My joy, my joy." He crooned. "I couldn't go on without my joy."

Ethel pushed her body close to his as he danced her under the blue and yellow lights of the chandelier. "Herbie," she whispered his name. "Dear Herbie." She almost told him she was leaving, New York bound come morning. Instead she spoke creamy words in his ear. She almost sang them. Their steps slowed to one-two. Then their feet were still and they just swayed.

The music pulsing from the record player filled the room with long, sultry notes. Herbie and Ethel matched each other's rhythms well. Herbie wished he could stay right there in the middle of Ethel's living room. The blue and red lights in the chandelier traded off shadows of warm and cool that swayed with them. He was calm there. Even though the guilt would roll around in him, like a pebble caught inside him between his shoulder blades, irritating, life-threatening if it got to his lungs, all that mattered was that he was here now, in Ethel's living room, a phonograph record spinning, he was holding her, settled into her presence; nothing else mattered.

Another light flooded the room. The cozy effect of the chandelier was interrupted. The bedroom door was wide open. Liz stood there staring at the swaying bodies. "Aunt Ethel," she whispered, "I'm scared."

Ethel pushed Herbie away. She ran to Liz and knelt in front of her and grabbed her in a close, urgent hug. "What are you afraid of, baby? Tell Aunt Ethel and I'll beat it up."

"That man," Liz said, pointing beyond Ethel to Herbie.

Herbie was still standing in the center of the room, offended by the rush of light and then Ethel's abrupt shove. All he could see of Liz was her pointing finger and her head of bright red hair.

"Make him go," Liz said, her voice picking up strength.

"Come on back into the bedroom, sweet pea; he's not here to hurt you." She motioned to Herbie that she would be a minute, and then she and Liz took the bright light back in the bedroom, leaving the chandelier all to Herbie.

"Little brat," Herbie said out loud to the sound of the bedroom door closing. She spoils that child rotten. He wondered how Noon would have handled a similar incident. He couldn't guess. Fannie never had nightmares. Nothing seemed to scare her. He chuckled to himself at the thought of Fannie wanting someone to leave. He imagined that Fannie would have walked straight past Noon, right to the person, yanked his hand, and said, "You, get the hell out." He laughed out loud at the thought of a five-year-old throwing someone out. He kept the thought going, amusing himself. It was better than the anger the red-haired child was bringing out in him. He had deep resentments for that child. Always calling for Ethel, needing her in the middle of the night, cutting in on his time, which was already too short. Since he'd gotten out of the service, that child had been the great interrupter. He'd come over ready to put on some music, and grab Ethel in a close, grinding slow drag, and she'd meet him at the door and whisper that he had to come back later, Liz was still up. Sometimes he'd get there, and by the time he had poured his gin, Ethel's head would be on her shoulder, half-closed eyes closed for real, exhausted from where she had spent the day doing motherly-type things instead of getting the day rest that a night singer like Ethel required.

The needle on the record slid over a rough spot and kept coming back to the same few notes. Herbie lifted the needle and let the room go quiet. He sat back on the couch. He could hear Ethel humming a lullaby. He watched the bright light sifting under the door and prayed that Ethel wouldn't ask him to leave.

She didn't. She came back in the living room and stood under the blue and red light of the chandelier. She let the belt to her silky robe fall open. Her face was intense. She didn't say anything as she moved all over him. Usually she moaned, "Poor Herbie, Ethel gonna make him feel better." Usually Herbie sensed that it was all for him. But tonight she was feeling something for herself, something she was trying to shake that wouldn't let go. And then she did moan. Not Herbie's name, though, not even "baby, baby, baby." Just "My." Just long and deep. And then filled with air as she gasped, "My," over and over.

Herbie was falling into the sound mixed with the air sweetened with cocoa butter and fine French perfume. She was all over him with the sound, breathing it all in his ear. "Your what, baby? Tell me, baby, tell me, Ethel, what? Tell me what? Tell me, tell me, tell me, tell me what?" And then he couldn't even talk as he tried to keep up with her moans, which came faster and faster. They covered him. He was immersed. He splashed around like a drowning man. And then the pinpoint that started the climax that spread over him in waves, and the confused fulfillment as she pulled the life from his body.

She touched his hand as she walked him to the door.

"What?" he asked as if she had just called his name.

"Be patient with her."

"What you talking about? Be patient with who?"

"Your wife. She'll give you joy. Just take it slow and easy with her."

"You all right? Why you stuck on the topic of my wife?"

"Just want you to be content, Herbie."

They were at the front door, and Herbie leaned in and kissed Ethel and said, "Just tell me I can see you tomorrow, I'll be content as a tree root pushing deep in the earth."

"Not tomorrow, baby. Not tomorrow."

"Well, when?"

"It's late." She lowered her half-closed eyes and pursed her mouth.

Herbie knew the look. It meant his time was up for this night. Ethel was leaving center stage. She closed the door, and the spotlight faded.

TEN

The next morning came quickly, and Ethel had much to do to prepare for her leave-taking. She was bustling about the small apartment, packing, and sweeping, and folding, and opening and closing drawers and closets.

"Where are we going?" Liz asked, eyes searching her aunt's face.

"I told you, baby." Ethel took the child's hands in her own, "You're going to visit the little girl around the corner; she's been asking Noon if you can come play with her."

"Who's Noon?" Liz persisted.

"That's the lady that's raising her, baby, just like I'm raising you." Ethel stopped short, suddenly remembering what she was about to do. She pulled Liz close and held her head to her chest and rocked from side to side. She kissed the top of Liz's red-like-the-setting-sun hair. She squeezed her tighter. She whispered with a whisper that came from somewhere deep, "You know I love you, precious Liz, you know I love you more than anything living, right?"

She felt Liz's head nodding against her chest. "If anyone ever tries to tell you your aunt Ethel don't love you, you tell them they a liar. You tell them if you don't know anything else, you know your aunt Ethel loves you."

Liz pushed her head back. Strained her neck so she could see her aunt. Searched for something in Ethel's face that would take away the circles going around in her stomach. At least if her aunt would cry, then Liz felt like she could too, even if she didn't know what she was crying about. But right now, with her aunt holding her so close, Liz thought that it must be worse than something to cry about. The circles in her stomach got bigger and spun faster.

"My stomach, I have to make a poop." She wriggled from Ethel's grasp, across the small bedroom into the bathroom.

"Don't strain," Ethel called behind her.

Ethel went back to folding Liz's clothes. She placed each item neatly into a brown paper shopping bag: her red and white gingham short set with the matching red lacy socks, her yellow sunbonnet, her white mesh gloves, her pink jumper with the pinch pleats, her black-and-white polka-dot Sunday dress, the one with the long sash that would make a healthy bow. Ethel stroked her cheek with the sash.

And then she noticed the hole in the wall. She pushed the bed slightly to see beyond the bedpost. It was a curious hole. Just the size of a silver dollar. Sandy chunks of plaster peaked and dived and gave the hole a ridged effect. It almost glistened. Ethel rubbed her hand against the roughness of the hole as if that would give her some indication of how the hole had gotten there. She was relieved that this was her last day in the small apartment, especially if there was a strange rodent making holes in the wall right over Liz's side of the bed.

Liz came back into the bedroom and noticed all at once that it had been emptied, swept clean. The dresser was bare. All of Ethel's fancy gold-tone atomizers packed, her stage dresses, her pointy-toe shoes, the silver-framed picture of her and Liz's mother arm in arm, packed.

"Where's everything at?" she asked, rubbing her eyes hard, and then, looking around the room again: "All your perfumes, your makeups, our clothes, where's all our stuff?"

"It's in the front hallway, baby." Ethel controlled the impulse to turn her face away, not wanting Liz's trust in her to fade, not yet.

"Where's it going?"

"With me and with you, baby."

"Where we going?"

"I told you, you're going to play with the little girl around the corner. You'll have so much fun. You can play dress-up, and play jacks, and soon you'll be able to jump double Dutch."

"You gonna play with us too."

"Aunt Ethel won't be there. I'll be away for a while."

Liz stared up at her aunt. They were too many circles in her stomach now. They were spinning too fast, colliding into one another, exploding one by one, turning mushy, pushing through her stomach, running down her legs, spoiling the ruffle around her sock.

"Oh, my God, you're messing all over yourself, Liz. Are you sick? Get into the bathroom," Ethel screamed.

Liz didn't move. Ethel pushed her into the bathroom, saying over and over, "What's the matter? Are you okay? Tell me what's the matter." Saying it over and over again to drown out the clamoring in her own head that might just convince her to pack Liz up and take her with her. She couldn't. She knew of too many horror stories, little girls messed up forever thrust into their parents' fast-driving entertainer's lifestyle. Handled by the men when they were left alone late at night or even during the day while their mothers slept. Not her Liz. Not in New York City, where Ethel had to go for her career finally to take off. "It'll be okay. You'll love Noon, you'll see. Noon and Fannie. It'll be okay. I promise you, precious baby." Her voice was quiet, desperate, pleading, as she tried to console Liz.

Liz grabbed Ethel around her waist and buried her head deep into Ethel's stomach. She cried hard, muffled sobs. Ethel held her. Even as Liz's bowels broke more and ran all over Ethel's stockinged feet, Ethel held Liz close.

🦢

Noon saw it as soon as she turned Lombard Street. Her eye had been jumping all day, much the same way it had been jumping last Sunday right before she'd seen Ethel staring up at her house. That had confirmed for her what her mother always said; a jumping eye means only one of two things: Either something was going to make her so mad that she was going to curse, not just "hell" or "damn," but words that sounded like cymbals crashing or cats fighting, or her jumping eye surely meant she was going to get a strange visit. So she had guarded her temper all morning. When her scrapple burned, she hadn't blamed Herbie, even though she was taking him up his coffee, and had gotten in a conversation with him on the side of the bed where he liked to have his first cup. And when Fannie let the bird out of its cage because she didn't think things should live in cages, Noon had guarded her temper even though it took her a full three quarters of an hour to get the bird back in. And when Fannie's friend Julep dripped Popsicle juice all over the front steps Noon had just scrubbed down, Noon had guarded her temper, even though she had to wash the steps again to keep the flies from hovering around the front of the door. She had managed to keep her temper in check so well that she'd almost forgotten to prepare for a strange visit. She remembered as soon she turned the corner.

She peered down the block and saw the small figure, a straight-backed, obedient figure sitting on her steps. Red hair looked almost orange as the sun hit it. Fannie had run ahead of Noon. Got to the steps long before Noon did. Already knew that the child's name was Liz, that her aunt told her not to move from the steps until they got home, that Liz should give Noon the rolled-up hankie with twenty one-dollar bills, that her aunt said she'd send more as soon as she got it, that everything she'd need for now was packed in the brown paper shopping bag.

"She'll be like my sister," Fannie panted, out of breath from running from the steps back down the block to hurry up Noon, to tell Noon all that Liz had just blurted out to her. She grabbed Noon's arm; she pulled her, demanding, "Hurry up, Noon, she's been sitting in the sun for a long time, let her in the house and give her something cold, c'mon, she's been crying too, hurry. We have to take care of her. Can't you run, Noon, can't you move fast?"

Noon picked up her pace, almost surprised herself at the way she snapped to Fannie's command. More and more she would take it that Fannie knew what she was talking about. Just last week Fannie had peered at the man cleaning Noon's butterfish, and had tugged at Noon's arm, and announced in a voice that the whole fish shop could hear, "He likes you, Noon, but don't worry, Herbie is bigger than him." And Noon collected her butterfish and hurried out of the shop because she knew Fannie had called that one right. And when she was only four, Fannie had stared hard into the blinded eyes of the broom man as he sang out down South Street, "Broom man, get your fresh-strung sturdy straw broom today." And after she had stared deep in his eyes, she bounded down the street to tell Noon that the colors hurt her eyes and that the broom man was going to die soon. And Noon had gotten quiet, and the broom man died the next day. So when Fannie, out of breath, announced that was her almost-sister sitting on the steps, Noon suspected that she might be calling this one right too, that the child was here to stay.

She set her bag filled with pears, plums, and hot roasted peanuts at the foot of the steps. She looked up at the brown-skinned, red-haired child sitting on the top step, hands clasped in her lap schoolgirl style. Her back was stiff and straight. Her breaths were deep, irregular, the aftermath of long, muffled sobs. She was dressed in a high-waisted white sleeveless cotton dress, a pink ribbon threaded through the bodice, a matching quilted jacket folded neatly in her lap. Ribbed anklet socks peeked over the tops of black-and-white oxfords. She looked to Noon like the little girls that adorned the pages of the catalogs from Snellenberg's Children's Shop. Her eyes were fixed on the white ruffled umbrella lying against the bottom step. The umbrella was wide open, and Noon guessed that it was supposed to protect her from the hot sun, but it had fallen and she was too terrified to move from that spot to retrieve it.

"Lord have mercy!" Noon said, dragging the phrase out as if the mercy were in the saying of it. And then she did the only thing she had in her nature to do. She opened her arms wide. Not thinking of another mouth to feed or how could Ethel burden her thus and so. Not thinking of where would she sleep, or go to school, or how long, or why now, or what if. Not thinking of calling on City Hall, or tracking down her aunt, or leaving her out for the night to catch. Noon simply opened her arms wide, the arms Ethel had recognized as the good wrapping kind; she wrapped them around Liz and let the child in.

Liz felt cool inside the house. The shades drawn in the front to keep out the midday sun, window open in the back to let the cool breeze of the yard tree float in. Noon and Fannie were tending to Liz, fussing over her.
"Give her water."
"She needs ice cream."
"No, quiet."
"Turn on the radio."
"Let her be."
"Give her a pillow."
"No. Let her be, just let her be."
They went back and forth until the cinnamon aroma drifted from the pot of water and cinnamon that Noon always kept simmering on the stove, "For calmness," she used to tell Fannie. "As long as this pot is

boiling, everyone that walks through that door will be calm." The calmness reached Liz. The soft green couch pulled her down, stretched her out, opened her hands, and relaxed her stomach. The prints on the rug in the center of the smooth, shellacked hardwood floor blurred together. The cinnamon aroma hovered over her, then fell gently over her body, cradled her, until she tumbled into a cottony sleep.

ELEVEN

Herbie staggered through the street like a drunk, not a drop of liquor in him, though. No chance. After Big Carl had leaned over the leather-clad bar and whispered that he'd heard that his pretty singer did her finale last night, and when it sank in to Herbie what Big Carl was trying to tell him, Herbie banged the steely coldness of his beer mug against the bar without taking a sip. He dashed out of Club Royale and ran straight to Ethel's apartment. He ran so fast that his heart was on fire when he got there and saw it, a big Apartment for Rent sign sitting right in the window. He pretended he wanted to rent the place, and after the motherly type doing the showing made him sit down and drink some water because he was sweating so, she gave him the key and he did a walk through just to force his eyes to see it. Ethel was gone. No note, no forwarding address, not a red handkerchief to remember her by. Even her scent of French perfume mixed with cocoa butter had already been replaced by pine cleaner. The disinfectant aroma came at him in white clouds from the floors and the walls. He took deep breaths. Maybe then his mind could take it all in, that she was gone.

His vision was doubled, tripled, with a tilt. He could barely keep his balance as he wobbled down the steps of what just last night was his sanctuary. He didn't even know where he was headed. To the bridge to jump over the railing? To try to find her, abandon Noon and Fannie and move close to wherever she had gone just for that one night a week with her? Or just walk. Maybe he'd just walk until his heart burst. It was already skipping beats, then racing.

The yellow-orangeness of the day was fading to navy as he walked. It was twilight in South Philly. The going-out-to-dinner crowd, men in wide-brimmed hats and pin-striped suits escorted ladies in patent spike heels and dark hose with seams that curved up muscle-bound calves. Short, stout women bustled along with brown double-handled shopping bags filled with fresh-killed chicken, unbleached flour, white lard, and stone ground pepper. Choir members rushed to get to Clara's, to get their hair washed and pressed straight as silk. Herbie moved through the rush of day meeting night howling inside. He stepped around a line that had formed at the Saunders Funeral Home. Organ music and sobs sifted into the warm twilight air. The exterior sounds of grief intensified his own. He wanted to cry. He wanted to sit right on the curb and scream as if he were five years old. He wanted to kick and throw his fists and holler out her name. He was back in front of the Apartment for Rent sign. He had walked in circles. How many times had he circled? It was dark out, and he could smell fish frying. He wanted to vomit. He swallowed hard and headed back to Royale to tell Big Carl he had been right. Ethel was gone.

Herbie felt better when he left Royale for the second time. According to Big Carl, she was only in New York. It wasn't California or Europe or Kansas City; a train ride away, that's all it was. He would find her, she'd let him in, only a train ride. He fingered the red licorice in his pocket that he bought for Fannie every weekend. He thought he might even take Fannie with him sometimes. They could go to Coney Island and ride the Whip and the Cup and Saucer. Fannie could play with Ethel's niece. He would figure out a way so that Noon would never find out. What way? Who was he kidding? She was gone. He would catch hell finding her or she would have left him a note in a perfume-scented envelope sealed with the red print marks of her healthy lips. He swallowed hard and walked up the steps to home. He opened the door and started to cry.

🖎

Liz listened to the sounds of the house swirl around in the darkness. She was all cried out. First the crying when Ethel left her on the steps, then the crying when her umbrella fell and she didn't have anything to shade the hot, hot sun, now the crying she had been doing since Fannie fell asleep on the bed right next to the one she lay on. The circles were back in her stomach, knocking together trying to push through. But she couldn't let them. Not on these stiff, clean sheets. What would Noon and Fannie think of her? They might sit her back out on the steps when the sun was overhead and let her bake to death the way she thought she would surely die earlier that day. She eased out of the bed, careful not to wake Fannie. She followed the shine of the brass knob on the closet door. She tiptoed to the knob, then opened the door and scurried deep into the closet's blackness. She leaned against the wall and held her knees tightly to her chest. She pushed her fists deep into her mouth and called for Ethel; deep into her fists she said, "Aunt Ethel, Aunt Ethel," over and over; she rocked and called for Ethel. She rocked herself until the cramping stopped. Then she moved her fingers lightly along the wall. She knew there must be one, every wall had one. Whether it was the wall upstairs at that place where Ethel left her when she went downstairs to sing or the wall right over the bed at Ethel's. Even in this house, where the walls seemed smooth and clean. And then her finger touched it. A crack, not much longer than the tip of her fingernail. She pressed against the crack, then dug into it as hard as she could. Granules of plaster spilled out into her waiting palm. She put the crumb-sized bits into her mouth one at a time. She held them there, then chewed them into gravy. Ethel's voice was swimming in her head. "You know Aunt Ethel loves you, precious Liz." The circles in her stomach were getting big again. She had to go to the bathroom. She eased out of the closet, out of the bedroom. Down the hallway. She didn't know the sounds of this house. The sound of the front door closing. Footsteps on the stairway. A grown man crying. She didn't know the shadows in this house either. How to distinguish them from the monsters that haunted her at Ethel's. She did know that one was in front of her now. A light-skinned one. She was frozen.

"Fannie, that you?" she heard him say. Then the click of the hall light. She wanted to run; instead she stood there looking at him, the circles gushing out. This was the man who danced with Ethel last night and made the infection in the floor spread. She let out a gasp matched only by his.

They just stared at each other for seconds that seemed to fade into forever. Two people raw with feelings of abandonment. Both with eyes red from crying over her, whispering her name, asking, "Why, why you leave, Ethel, why?" Both Herbie and Liz had this in common. But there was no empathy in their eyes as they stared at each other. Only confusion wrapped up in gazes of fear and blame. Sandpaper gazes.

Herbie cleared his throat to speak, to say what? You never saw me before, certainly not at your aunt's? He settled on "Who are you?"

Liz didn't answer; she backed up toward the bedroom. Her stare said it all: I know you, I know you.

Herbie moved in closer. "Come here, little girl, tell me who you are, why are you here?"

The manifestation of Liz's fright trailed down her legs and made a line in the hallway floor as she backed up, fists balled the way Ethel taught her to do if she came across a street dog that foamed at the mouth with rabies. Slowly she backed up, dropping her eyes just slightly until her arm touched the archway to the bedroom door. She turned then and ran into the bedroom, calling for Fannie.

Herbie just stood there, shocked. Mouth opened looking at the waste on the floor when Noon ran out of her bedroom.

"Herbie, that you? What is it? Why you looking like you just saw a ghost?"

"I thought I just saw a red-haired child run through here."

"Well, you probably did. If you could come in at a decent hour, things wouldn't have to shock you under the cover of night." She looked at the floor and said, "Lord have mercy. You must have scared the poor little thing. She been through a trauma today. Loose bowels all day long. What you say to her? Me and Fannie was all day getting her calmed down, now you come in here in the middle of the night and upset her all over again. Could you at least bring the mop and bucket up out of the cellar while I go tend to her?"

Herbie moved like a mannequin. He wasn't processing this at all well. That was her; the red hair was unmistakable. He would have to play dumb, as if he didn't know anything. He didn't know much. All he knew for sure was that was Ethel's niece. Liz. That was that whiny, spoiled-assed Liz. What if she was up there right now telling Noon that she saw him at Ethel's last night? He'd deny it. Say the child was confused. She'd only glimpsed at him for a second; the room was half dark at that.

He let hot water run over the mop. The hot water pushed the scent of pine cleaner from the braided mop in cloudy puffs of smoke. The scent reminded him of Ethel's empty apartment. He twisted the thick braids of the mop head to squeeze the water through. He told himself that he must be mistaken. That must be a new neighbor's child or some kin from down South. Ethel wouldn't do that to him. Leave him, leave her niece on him.

"Shit!" he said out loud. She had done it. Screwed him last night, then screwed him over today. He banged the pole of the mop against the sink. Over and over he whacked the sink with the mop's wooden handle as if this wooden handle were responsible for Ethel leaving him, and now her niece upstairs. The pole made a crisp, clean snapping sound and then broke in two. Herbie jumped up and down. He thought if he didn't, he might go into an unrecoverable madness. To save his sanity, he jumped and flailed his arms and punched at the pine-scented cellar air. He fought the air that didn't fight back except to keep the pine scent exploding through his head. He was exhausted. His breaths came in heaves as he told himself to calm down. He tried to get his breathing under control. He picked up the broken mop and headed upstairs.

"I got a sister, Herbie," Fannie yelled as she ran to Herbie and grabbed him around his knees.

"A sister, what you talking 'bout, little lady?" Herbie busied himself cleaning the mess in the hallway.

"Come see for yourself." Fannie tugged on his arm.

"Wait, wait now, Fannie. Let me get this mess cleaned up before you go stepping in it and tracking it all through the house."

"She only did it 'cause she's scared." Fannie was bouncing up and down as she talked, and almost gasping she was so excited.

"Scared of what?" Herbie asked, keeping his eyes at the floor and his ears poised.

"She's in a strange place."

"How she get here?"

"Her aunt left her on our steps for her to live with us forever."

"Forever is a mighty long time, Fannie."

"But she left a lot of dollars, and a bag of clothes, and a toothbrush. Her name is Liz. Isn't that a nice name, Herbie?" Fannie giggled as she talked and clapped her hands. "Hurry up so you can see her."

"Hurrying, I'm hurrying," Herbie said as he kept wiping over the parts he had already cleaned. "Who is her aunt?"

"Ethel," Fannie said matter-of-factly as if Herbie should have already known that.

Herbie's back stiffened at the mention of her name even coming from this five-year-old. "Ethel?"

"Yeah, the lady who Noon calls a two-bit singer. She's nice. Noon don't say so, but I do. Come on, Herbie, it's all cleaned up, come on so I can show you my new sister, Liz."

Pulled along by Fannie, Herbie peeked into the bedroom. The room was softly lit with a table lamp covered over with a pink-etched lampshade. Noon sat on the bed, rocking back and forth. Liz was on her lap, her head buried in Noon's chest. She turned and stared straight at Herbie and clutched her arms tighter around Noon's back. Ethel's voice was in her head again. "Liz must never tell. If you ever see any of Aunt Ethel's guests, you must never tell, must never, ever tell."

"Awl, she's scared, don't be scared, it's only Herbie, he's my dad, he won't hurt you." Fannie ran to her and patted her back.

Liz squinted at Herbie. She felt more confident with Noon rocking her and holding her tight and Fannie patting her back. Even Ethel's caution about never telling calmed her now. She at least had this connection to her aunt, this secret in this monster of a man staring down at her.

"Isn't she cute, Herbie? Do you like her red hair? Do you like my new sister?"

"So you gonna tell me what's going on?" Herbie asked Noon through the fire in his throat. "Who is she and what's all this sister talk?"

"That singing woman left her here. Left her money, clothes, told her she was coming here to live while she goes away for a while. Ain't that mean? Just dropped the poor chile off, no preparation, no nothing. Dirty, low-down, mean that was."

"She just wanted her to have a sister," Fannie interrupted.

"Chile been calling for her, crying for her all day. But that's okay, me and Fannie worked on her, we got her feeling better, till you came in here probably looking mean and scared her all over again."

"You didn't mean to." Fannie laughed excitedly. "You didn't even know I had a new sister, did you?" And then, pulling him down, she reached into Herbie's pocket and snatched out her licorice. "Here, Liz, Herbie bought licorice. If you don't cry, we can eat it all." Fannie fed Liz bits of red licorice as Noon rocked her from side to side. Herbie stood in the doorway, trying with everything in him not to let his broken heart show on his face.

Noon was ecstatic in the still darkness of their bedroom after she'd gotten Liz settled back down. She felt chosen that a blazing, blues-singing whore the likes of Ethel would select her for raising up her child. Unlike with Fannie, whose arrival was more arbitrary, finding Liz on her steps gave Noon a sense of womanness that she thought might be as good as getting her passions stirred. She hated Ethel with everything in her, hated her look, the way she overpainted her face, the way she walked, parading her womanhood as if her backside were a piece of fine china. She thought it despicable the way she'd just abandoned poor Liz. But here was some womanly thing that Noon could do well. She could raise up what Ethel never could. And now Noon knew that if the likes of Ethel recognized her maternal prowess, surely everyone must know. Now she could stop fretting so much over the problems with her body, wondering if other people could tell that she didn't have a nature to her. She was too buoyed by this feeling of being a whole woman, this event of being singled out to love somebody's child.

She acted mad over it on the outside. Right now she buzzed to Herbie, "Terrible thing she did to that poor chile, just leaving her on the steps like that. I knew that hussy was up to something walking up and down this street last Sunday like something she wanted lived on it. At first I thought it was you. Now I know it was a home for that chile."

"She can't stay, Noon," Herbie said, agitated, but relieved nonetheless to be in this darkened bedroom, under the covers and safe from Liz's frightened eyes. "You can't just take no child in and claim her just 'cause she was left on your steps."

"Can, and will," Noon snapped. "Did it with Fannie."

"Fannie was different. She was a newborn; we didn't even know where she came from."

"Well, what am I supposed to do, turn her over to the state? You know they don't care a thing 'bout poor little colored children; stick her in a foster home is all they'll do where all somebody want is the money. I don't have it in me to do that to that child. Reverend Schell said to look at it as a gift from God. According to Round-the-Corner-Rose, her aunt's more into living the fast life than taking care of the chile. So Reverend Schell said to look at it as God giving the child a good home where she can learn about the love of Jesus."

"Tell Reverend Schell to clothe and feed her then," Herbie grunted. "This is the second time this shit has happened. We keep that girl, we might as well hang a sign in the window, 'Tired of doing for your kid, just leave 'em here, good ole Noon and Herbie'll raise 'em up without a complaint.' Or better yet, we'll take out an ad in the *Tribune*: 'Home for unwanted kids, we want 'em when you don't.' I tell you, Noon, we can't keep that child. Fannie was one thing, granted, but it ain't right to let other people burden us with their responsibilities, no forewarning, no nothing. Just dump them on our steps."

"Wait a minute, Herbie, these little colored children is all our responsibilities, the Scripture says, 'Suffer the little children to come unto me.'"

"Oh, now you Jesus Christ. Now you ready to take on all the children."

"You didn't let me finish."

"Ain't nothing to finish when you start quoting Scriptures. If your church is so giving, take the child there. Must be one or two members want a little girl. Now to me that would be the Christian thing to do."

"But she was left here!"

"Don't mean she got to stay here. Shit, Reverend Schell always got so much to say, let him have a greater hand in being responsible for the child."

"For your information he offered to do a collection every other month to help out with her raising."

"Wonderful, and I'll contribute generously just as long as her raising ain't taking place in my house."

"But I already told him we're keeping her. We blessed already with you having a decent job, plus at least the no-good aunt did send more than enough money to start her out. And she promised to send more money. It might not even have to cost us any extra money. And Fannie loves her already. You should have seen her running to tell me to hurry up so we could help her. Poor little Liz. We turn her over and she gonna have to suffer through investigators asking her questions like she a criminal. She ain't the bold type of child like Fannie. That chile has a weak constitution. I see it in her eyes. It ain't right to put her through that,

Herbie. It ain't Christian, especially not when we got the means to give her a good home."

Noon went on talking in long sentences about their moral obligation to keep the child. Herbie got quiet. The last thing he needed was Ethel's niece living under his roof. The eyes, scared and knowing. He couldn't look at those eyes day in and day out, waiting for her to blurt it out to Noon where she knew him from. But then he also understood how to carry things; a porter, he certainly would. He knew the importance of balance. If he carried something slung over his chest, he'd best sling an equal amount over his back. If his right side leaned too much from the baggage, he knew to shift some to his left. If he stooped low, he kept his back straight and his shoulders high, lest he snap his spine. He loved Ethel. Here in the blackened bedroom that was never hot, he had to admit he loved Ethel. He was infuriated for sure, mired in it, sinking in it like quicksand. He even hated Ethel right now for having the incomprehensible gall to leave Liz with them. But he loved her. She wasn't just a hot body that writhed and arched in spasms that spilled over with the smoothness of silk. She wasn't just some sex-crazed whore who'd give it up to anything with a lump between his legs. He could reconcile that given Noon's condition and all, he could come home and sleep next to Noon like a well-fed baby. Even stick out his chest at Royale and whisper about his good thing on the side. She was Ethel, though. And he loved her. That was his crime. Married man had no business crossing the line like that. The guilt that he carried over that would surely break his back if not properly balanced out: left and right, front and rear, high and low. Agreeing to Liz's staying just because that's what Noon wanted would keep his spine erect. Keep it from buckling, warping, even snapping in two from the extra weight he carried on his heart.

"Indefinitely." He forced the word into the darkness as he pictured Liz running down the hallway. "She can stay till we see if the aunt come back or we figure something out to do with her."

TWELVE

Liz ran from Herbie for a solid year. That summer she sat on the front steps thinking that maybe if she sat so still that she was barely breathing the hot air, maybe Ethel would turn the corner and pick her up just like she'd left her. By surprise. Ethel never did turn the corner. Cross-the-Street-Dottie, Sister Maybell, Next-Door-Jeanie, Reverend Schell, Bow the Barber, the milkman, the iceman, the insurance man, the man selling brooms and venetian blinds, they all turned the corner. Each time Liz saw one of them move up the block and she realized it wasn't her aunt Ethel, her stomach sank until it felt as if it were going to fall right through her shorts onto the grainy concrete steps. Then Herbie would turn the corner walking fast, half bouncing, and Liz would think that he was the one that made Ethel leave, always over there late at night.

All winter Liz watched for her. Through the orange November sun and the steady glow of the Christmas lights, she stood at the window and leaned against the radiator until the heat threatened to burn through her pleated wool skirts or pinwheel corduroy pants. The grayness that overtook January settled in her stomach as she pressed against the radiator, waiting for Ethel. Ethel never moved up those steps, though. Herbie did, like clockwork. His form was like a shadow that Liz was sure must be the shadow that Ethel described in the bedtime stories whenever the big bad wolf appeared.

By spring she could still feel the print of Ethel's lips when she had kissed her good-bye that day, the press of her arms when she squeezed her so hard she almost smothered her in the whiffs of cocoa butter and sweet perfume. She could even hear the sound of Ethel's high heels clicking down Lombard Street.

On Easter Sunday she was sure Ethel would come for her. She heard so many high heels clicking against the concrete, over and over. She could hardly settle down. Even when she and Fannie were all dressed up in straw bonnets, and patent leather shoes with T-straps, and pink and green dresses that billowed over three-tiered crinoline slips as they waited outside until Noon came out to take them to Sunday school. Then the tall, light Willie Mann begged them to be still so he could take some pictures; Liz could hardly be still. The sounds of high heels distracted her. But they weren't Ethel's heels.

By the time the year rounded out into summer again, she stopped looking for Ethel, she almost stopped hoping. But she still ran when Herbie appeared. She ran to avoid his eyes, which always stared at her with a question mark as if he were waiting for her to blurt something out. She ran to try to run away from the feeling that she had for Herbie that she knew was hate, even though the Sunday school teacher said that hate was a sin and sinners got sent straight to the devil. Now it was such a big feeling that it needed more than Herbie; it started to spread to Ethel, started to lump Herbie and Ethel in the same circle in her stomach. It was a scary feeling, and she especially ran from that.

But she loved Noon and Fannie. They were her mother and sister now. Closer than real blood, Noon always said. Real blood rises up against itself and turns bad. We're closer than real blood in that way, don't never have to worry about it turning bad. Liz gobbled it up. She so needed that feeling of warmth and protection that she used to get from Ethel when they snuggled at night and Ethel chased the monsters away. Liz needed a monster chased right now as she ran up Lombard Street, gasping, red plaits flopping.

It was 1946. Time for Fannie and Liz to start school according to state law. Noon had gone to register them two weeks before. She'd presented Dottie, her across-the-street neighbor and clerk at the E. M. Stanton Elementary School, with Fannie's papers. Pointed out to her that Fannie's booster shots were up-to-date, that she had no known allergies, and yes, Noon and Herbie were her legal guardians by the official seal on the gold-edged birth certificate Reverend Schell had put his scribble to six years before.

Dottie tapped her pencil point against the long wooden counter in the school office. She was a diligent worker. Even though she'd fought last night with the latest in a series of no-count men and woke so drunk on loneliness that she'd vomited all the way to the bathroom, she was still at her post in the school office by seven forty-five.

The office was quiet and warm, just Dottie and Noon and the eighteen-by-twenty oil reproduction of Abraham Lincoln. Dottie cleared her throat as Noon held her breath. Looked at Noon in her button-down dress with the vertical stripes, the one that had been featured as the dress of the week in the *Tribune*'s Ladies' Sewing Circle section. Seersucker. Got the nerve to use seersucker, Dottie thought. Twenty-five cents a yard. She knew because she'd priced it the day after she'd seen the picture in the paper. Had run all the way home from Fourth Street to pull her spare change from the sock beneath her mattress. The sock was empty, her man in a drunken stupor on the living room couch. Took Noon to wear the very fabric that would remind her of that, she thought. She'd never liked Noon much. Even though they'd worked on the same auxiliaries for the good of the church, met around the same dining room tables to plan for things like block beautification, Dottie had always taken Noon's keep-to-herself quietness as better-than-thou smugness. Even the aroma of salt pork frying and biscuits baking that streamed from Noon's house each morning as Dottie rushed past it on her way to work was a reminder that her own child had just gulped down dry toast and powdered milk.

Noon felt the sweep of Dottie's eyes from head to toe. She chided herself at that instant for wearing her newest dress. Should have put on the faded blue cotton, she told herself, or the gray with the mismatched belt. She'd watched Dottie the past couple of years go out of her way to speak to Herbie, to laugh at his jokes, to let her hand linger on his arm when she told him, "Herbie, you a mess." She knew when she needed something from Dottie's type what her mother said was true: "Homely gets from homely what pretty never could." But it was too late now. She had waved her relative affluence in Dottie's face like a matador's cape.

Dottie charged. Reminded Noon as she shook the pencil in her thin dark hands that she had been there that day Fannie's birth certificate was made out. "You know I know about this seal you ran down and had them put on Fannie's birth certificate. If you want to call it a birth certificate. You know those supposed relatives that you told those people at City Hall gave you the chile for you to raise are as bogus as a three-cent piece."

Noon pleaded with Dottie in a hushed outpouring of superlatives on the bond that happened between them all that day. How they were witness to the workings of the hand of God, just like Reverend Schell had said. How to make mention of it in other than their close-knit circle of those who knew and understood might bring damnation to them all.

Dottie hated even this about Noon. That she would know the very thing, the only thing, to say that would give her pause. She reminded Noon that there was still the other one. Did she have any papers for that one with the red hair?

"You know I don't," Noon said in a tone that also asked, Why do you hate me so? "You know her aunt just left her for me to raise. She didn't go through any official channels, no papers; you know that already, Dottie. You were right out front the day it happened and I was telling Jeanie and Sis Maybell and Bow, didn't you come running across the street to see what was going on?"

"Well, you can't register her without papers. Doctors' forms and a birth certificate or proof of legal guardianship," Dottie answered in a voice that said, Because you think you so much better than me with your steady husband with a decent job and your neat little flower ledge out front. "In fact, I got to turn her name in. Anybody six and not registered gets the name sent in to Social Services."

"And what they gonna do with her name?"

"Don't know, not for me to know. I'm told to turn in the name, so I turn in the name."

"Can't you just tell me what I got to do instead?" Noon looked straight in Dottie's eyes. Past her lips, painted too red for her complexion, her cheeks powdered with a shade too light, to get to her eyes, where the brows were penciled too hard.

Dottie wouldn't meet her gaze. "Get a lawyer."

"Dottie, I don't know what I ever did to you to make you—"

"Look, I'm letting you register Fannie." She tapped the pencil, leaving angry, jagged lines on the pad.

"But you could put Liz's name right there under where you put Fannie's. You could list me and Herbie as her legal guardians. Nobody will ask. Nobody else really cares. Now you could just pretend like I have proof of legal guardianship. You could do that right now, Dottie, and you know it."

"The law is the law," she said as she dropped the pencil against the counter. "I ain't breaking the law for you or nobody else."

"Whose law?" Noon huffed as she snatched Fannie's papers up and rushed from the office. "Whose law at all?"

It was a hungry, fast-moving law. Moved quicker than Noon could get an appointment with the young black lawyer that Next-Door-Jeanie recommended. The following week, his secretary had promised, as she underestimated just how quickly the system would work. For the system had gained some sophistication in the last six years. Where Fannie was easily allowed to Herbie and Noon with all the rights of legal guardianship on their say-so that relatives had left the child for them to raise, now the war had ended, men needed work—a politician's nephew, a poll watcher's son. The patronage system was starving for the enforcement of this law: the need to hire caseworkers, truant officers, writ servers. At least a half dozen good-paying positions could be justified if people like Dottie just did as they were told and wrote down the names of children like Liz, children who were six and not yet registered for school.

Liz was oblivious of the employment boom her situation caused as she decided to try out her independence this day. Usually never going more than a few yards without making sure Fannie or Noon was in sight, she decided to walk all the way around the corner by herself to see if Julep could come outside and play jacks while Noon was on Fourth Street buying buttons and thread and embroidery hoops. Fannie had agreed; while Liz was walking around the corner, she would find the jacks' ball and meet Liz and Julep out front.

Liz was almost to the corner, feeling very big and proud. The sun was hot and bright, and the air had the smell of damp cotton when it's steam-ironed. She started to skip in her rubber-soled buckskins, didn't notice the freckled white man as he cursed at his brakes and bore down hard to park the used De Soto at the corner of Lombard Street. He had one of those jobs supported by the newly enforced truancy law. Responsible for serving summonses to the families of school-age children not registered to attend. Worked on a commission basis. Started out early today so he could do enough business to get his brakes fixed, maybe take his girl to a drive-in motel. These prospective truants were quick and easy. Still two weeks before school started, so these were mostly first notices. Most times the parents couldn't speak the language anyway, so he didn't have to hear long explanations. First one he'd had in the colored section, though. Hoped they had street addresses visible so he wouldn't have to spend time hunting for the proper house. He checked his city-embossed blue-backed papers before getting out of the car. Scanned them for the line that read, "Birthmarks or other distinguishing physical characteristics." Noted that it listed red hair. Thanked his good luck when he saw the red-haired child skipping right by the car. Checked his papers again for the name, then rushed from the car, yelling, "Liz," with a measure of assurance that he had the right child. "Don't run from me, I need to talk to the people you live with."

The sound of her name from this stranger froze Liz at first, made her forget all about Julep, jacks, even the steamy smell of the air and how good the sun felt against her back in her printed playsuit Noon had made that tied around the neck and left a circle of her back exposed. She turned to see who this was calling her, saw the tall white man and a silver badge that he held at arm's length, gleaming in the sun. The sight of the badge propelled Liz up Lombard Street. "Fannie! Fannie, help me," she screamed.

Fannie had given up on finding the ball that she was sure she had seen under the back steps. She did find a fat piece of chalk. Figured hopscotch was as good as jacks and was out front drawing boxes on the ground when she heard Liz calling out her name. She looked up just in time to see Liz fly by her, out of breath, and into the house.

Liz kept running even after she'd reached the sanctity of the house. She raced upstairs, taking the steps two at a time to her closet, which was dusty and warm.

She waited a minute for her eyes to adjust to the dark. Then she moved the three shoe boxes stacked against the closet wall. The hole was growing. She could see that. Soon the shoe boxes wouldn't hide it. I'll stop when it gets bigger than these shoe boxes, she thought. Fingering the hole, caressing it, she found a chunk of plaster sitting out there. She took her shoe off and lightly knocked at the plaster with her shoe. A small rock of a piece separated from the wall and fell onto the dark closet floor. It glistened, sandy-colored, jagged. She picked it up quickly and put it in her mouth. She chewed into the plaster. She moved the rocky bit from the back of her mouth to the front. She played it around on her tongue. The plaster tasted grainy, hard and starchy and grainy. She went into the top shoe box and lifted out the handkerchief that Ethel had sent with the rolled-up dollar bills. She opened what she could of the handkerchief. The bottom of the handkerchief was melded together from wet plaster gone dry. She spit what was left of the chunk into the handkerchief. It was like gravy, sandy-colored, glistening gravy. She shifted her teeth back and forth, breaking down the rest of what was still hard. Mostly grains left. She wiped her mouth and put the handkerchief back into the shoe box. She leaned hard against the closet wall. She would wait in here until Fannie said it was safe.

Right now Fannie stood with her hands folded across her chest and one foot tapping impatiently, the stance she admired in her Sunday school teacher, Miss Pernsley, when the church was hot and the kids were full of the devil. "I said I can't let you in my house, mister."

He dabbed at his forehead with a stiff plaid handkerchief. "And I said I need to talk to your mother."

"Why you sweating, not that hot out here?"

"Is your mother home, little girl?"

"Maybe she is, maybe she isn't." Fannie stuck her mouth out in an exaggerated pout.

"You know, if I don't talk to your mother, you could be in big trouble. You see this"—he flashed the badge again—"this means that I'm on official business, and you're being an obstruction."

"But you sweating too much," Fannie said defiantly. "You even sweating on your nose. My mother says that people who sweat on their nose are mean. I can't let no mean people in our house."

He scanned the blue-backed papers again. "Look, go call your mother right now, girl, you hear me, now! Or let me through the door so I can call her for myself. If she doesn't get these papers today, Liz could become a ward of the state; that means the police will come and put handcuffs on her and take her away." He knew he was wrong for trying to scare the life out of the child. But he didn't have time for niceties. He had a quota to make, commissions to earn.

Fannie was not frightened by the man per se. But this did seem serious. She thought for a second about what to do. "Okay, okay," she said quickly, eyes moving from his face to focus on his shoes. "You can come in, but my mother's all the way in the back of the cellar; you can go on down." She held the door open for him to walk inside the house.

At first he just stood in the middle of the living room floor. "You don't have any dogs, do you?"

"Nope, no dogs," Fannie said, shaking her head hard.

"Can't you just call her up here?" he asked, starting to walk and then stopping.

"She has a bad leg. Once she goes down there, she stays all day till my father comes home to carry her up."

He looked around the living room: Glass figurines on the end tables sparkled, buffed-up shine to the hardwood floors, magazines arranged in the rack by size order, Bible on the coffee table, neat, very clean. He chided himself for feeling tenuous; these were obviously God-fearing colored people. What could this little girl possibly do to him? He knew he should leave. They were trained not to talk to the children. If an adult wasn't immediately available, they were supposed to come back later. But he had to deal with his brakes, was itching for time alone with his girl. He just wanted to serve these papers.

"Well, what you waiting for? The cellar's right there by the kitchen." Fannie was tapping her foot impatiently again.

"Okay, this will only take a minute," he said as he walked through the house into the kitchen and down the cellar stairs. Fannie followed quickly behind him and slammed the cellar door hard and then pulled the doorknob straight through. She listened to his footsteps start down the steps and then stop and then stomp quickly up to the top again.

"What the hell—" she heard him mutter, and then shout, "Little girl, I'm not playing games here. Open this door right now!"

Fannie just stood there fingering the doorknob. The doorknob was large and glassy and had been broken for the past week. So whenever they went into the cellar, they had to leave the cellar door wide open, or else they had to pull the half a doorknob right through the hole and take it in the cellar with them, then insert it back in from inside the cellar in order to let themselves out.

Fannie covered her ears so she couldn't hear his shouts. She stared at the door as it seemed to bulge in and out from his knocking and pushing. She ran in the living room and tossed the knob behind the couch, then went upstairs to see to Liz.

"I did it, Liz," she said through cupped hands, propelling her voice through the white wooden closet door.

"What? What did you do?" Liz moaned through the closet's darkness.

"I locked him in the cellar."

"You didn't kill him, did you, Fannie?"

"Naw"—Fannie giggled—"he might die down there, though, if we leave him and starve him to death."

"But we could get sent to the devil if we kill him."

"No, we won't either. It's for a good reason, Liz. We can't let him take you and throw you in jail."

"What about Noon?"

"I didn't figure out what about her yet. But at least she's on our side; she don't want to see you get taken away either."

"Herbie does."

"Don't say that, Liz."

"It's true, he's always frowning at me."

"Noon said it's 'cause he was shocked. He likes you, I know him, he does."

Before Fannie could reassure Liz some more, she heard Noon's voice sifting upstairs. First like a song, saying, "I'm back, got the most gorgeous buttons for your fall jumpers." And then, like a crack, demanding to know what was going on in the basement.

"Fannie, Liz!" she yelled. "Didn't I tell y'all 'bout playing with that broken knob. Who's in there? Where's the knob? I can't even let you out without the knob."

Fannie ran back into the kitchen like a flash of light. She grabbed

Noon around the waist and burrowed her head in her stomach. "We can't open the door, Noon, we can't; there's a man down there who came to take Liz away, we have to leave him down there."

"What foolishness you got going, Fannie!" Noon snapped, trying to peel Fannie's hands from around her waist. "What you talking about man in the basement? That ain't no one down there but Liz, now let her out."

Then Noon heard the voice for herself, booming. "Open this goddamn door and let me out!" he demanded. "Now!"

"Who is it? What you doing in my cellar?" Her voice screeched through the kitchen.

"Let me out!" he shouted until it all sounded like a continuous growl, deep and threatening as it mixed in with his shoe kicks and fist pounds against the cellar door.

"Just a minute," Noon said nervously. "Please don't break my door down. I'll have you out in a minute, please." She grabbed Fannie firmly by the shoulders. "What you gone and done?" she whispered, looking straight in Fannie's eyes. "Who you got locked in that cellar?"

"He came to take Liz; we can't let him out. He said he's gonna make Liz a ward to the state. We have to leave him down there and starve him to death. He's evil, he's bad."

"Give me the doorknob, Fannie," Noon said roughly, squeezing Fannie's shoulders for emphasis. "He can't just walk in here and take Liz just like that."

"He has a badge, and I bet he has a gun too," Fannie said, poking her mouth out hard. "He's gonna take her, I know he will."

Noon stooped down to Fannie's eye level and stared straight in her eyes. "How you know, Fannie?" Her voice had lost its menace and was now more genuinely seeking. "Tell me how you know. Did you see him take Liz, or you just think he might?"

Fannie looked away from Noon; she looked out the shed kitchen window. She could just see the tops of the clothespins looking like wooden-headed men. She knew what Noon was asking her. Even though she was only six, she already knew the difference between her seeing eye—that part of her that could see around corners, and sometimes into tomorrow, and once in a while straight to somebody's soul—and her imagination. She knew this time that it was just her imagination.

"I just think he might," she said, "but we still can't let him out. Please, Noon, please, he sweats on his nose."

Noon stood straight up, relieved. "Get that doorknob and bring it right here, right now," she said, menace back in her voice.

Fannie stomped into the living room and crawled behind the couch and kicked the doorknob out where Noon could see it and then stomped on up the stairs.

Noon hurriedly fitted the slim black steel part of the knob into the cylindrical hole. She turned it and opened the door. "I'm sorry, I'm so sorry," she said as she grabbed his arm to guide him out. "Please forgive my daughter, she just got scared, you really scared her, she said you had a badge, what do you want anyhow?" She could feel her anger rising. She didn't want to admit even to herself that the ones running things could do pretty much what they pleased. She and Next-Door-Jeanie disagreed over that sort of thing all the time. Such an admission diminished the power of Jesus, Noon thought. But now this white man had just flashed a badge and scared the life out of her children. She knew Liz was probably upstairs in the closet right now, where she'd most likely stay until Fannie could coax her out. And it would take at least another day for Liz's appetite to come back.

He didn't say a word at first. Didn't even look at Noon. He was swelled up to twice his size. He roughly shoved the blue-backed papers into Noon's hands. "That wild child should be put away. I'm a court officer; I could have this whole goddamn household locked up over what she did. The other one gets taken away if you don't answer this summons." He muttered "fucking nigger" and pushed past her and was out of the door.

"Got some nerve calling somebody a nigger," Noon said to his back as she quickly scanned the papers. "You that, plus a fool, let a little child trick you into the cellar."

🖎

Next-Door-Jeanie laughed to herself as she watched the tall, lean man stumble down Noon's front steps as if he were being chased by monsters. She had observed the whole scene. Had her ear cocked to what Fannie and Liz were doing when she saw Noon run out to the store. She was in fact ready to intervene. Had tiptoed into the front door as Fannie and the writ server walked toward the kitchen. And then stepped back outside when she realized Fannie had locked him in the basement. Even shooed Sister Maybell away when she walked from her corner house to ask what that white man wanted with Liz. She didn't like his looks, and she had just seen Noon turn the corner, so she knew the girls were by themselves. Jeanie assured Sister Maybell that everything was under control. Fannie had handled it. And then Jeanie went back into her house and laughed so hard she was doubled over. Especially when she heard the shouts coming from Noon's basement. "Good for you, Fannie," she said to herself as she watched the writ server race back down the block to where he had come from. "We don't always have to buckle 'cause they say we do."

THIRTEEN

Noon read it and reread it. She was a strong reader. Also good at reading between the lines. Fifteen days, it said. So they would have already met with the lawyer by the time the deadline came through. Probably have to involve that no-count aunt. Probably have to send Herbie to find her. She had pretty much figured out what she needed to know about the official papers that made her hands shake. So when she ran out of the door, yelling up to Fannie and Liz that she'd be right back, don't they dare let a soul in the house, it wasn't for a deeper understanding of the contents of the papers—even though she told herself that it was—it was for her hands that shook.

She settled into the wooden-backed chair with the red-cushioned seat and smiled across the desk at Reverend Schell. His study smelled of cedar and lemon oil and still held the whispered hums of the ladies that bustled through here daily, keeping it clean and comfortable for their pastor. Noon was among them when her week rolled around. It was her privilege. Where she came from, a pastor was elevated above the average man and needed special tending to. Especially one like Reverend Schell, whose wife had gone to glory. Noon served with pride on the Pastor's Aid Committee and the Committee for the Beautification of the Pastor's Study. She even placed her name on the list to have her turn at cleaning and pressing his wide-sleeved robes for preaching in and starching the points on the collars of his shirts after scrubbing them to a blazing white. She baked his rolls to perfection, just the right shade of brownness on top before sliding the butter and letting it drip. This was after all her pastor. When he smiled at her, as he did right now, she blushed inside.

"So what brings one of my prettiest flowers out this afternoon so unexpectedly?"

Noon looked at her hands folded in her lap over the blue-backed papers. She pressed them tighter around the papers. Being called pretty was an embarrassment for her. Even though on this afternoon as she hurried to get to the church to consult with Reverend Schell, she had allowed herself a hint of rouge on her cheeks to spruce up her complexion, which was neither light nor dark, just a middle-of-the-road kind of tan. "Oh, Reverend," she gushed, "I'm no flower, at least I don't feel like one most days. A flower is so delicate, you know, free; most days I feel so, so burdened down."

"If you're talking about your healing, Noon, I do believe that's gonna come. We can't rush the work of the Lord, but we must believe."

"Oh, I do, of course I do," Noon said quickly. "In fact that's really not even what I wanted to talk to you about; honest, Reverend, I'm being real patient about that. I really wanted to talk to you about this." She pushed the papers across the desk. "I came as soon as I got them, terrible devil of a man left them. Scared the girls so bad till Liz ran up and locked herself in the closet and Fannie locked him in the basement. I couldn't hardly settle myself down to wait for Herbie to get home, so I rushed right over here." Her voice shook.

He leaned forward and hunched his expansive shoulders as he scanned the pages. Deep lines came up in his forehead, which was black and smooth and tough like leather. Noon tried to control her breathing as she watched him study the papers. Her heart was racing. She rubbed her hands against her cotton dress. Her hands were wet and cold.

"I notice it says there we have fifteen days to satisfy the complaint, Reverend. We see the lawyer next week, but in the meantime this whole thing has me worried sick, just sick, Reverend."

He nodded as he continued to eyeball the blue-backed papers.

"I just wasn't sure what all we have to do besides waiting to see the lawyer."

He raised his finger as he leaned in closer over the pages. "Did he say anything when he served you with these papers?"

"Said they might be back to haul Liz off to a foster home, not in exactly those words, but the gist of it was clear. She needs me, Reverend. She needs me to love her, me and Fannie; they take her from us ain't no telling, chile might go into herself and never come out."

Reverend Schell went back to concentrating over the inked symbols. That's all they were to him. Rows of black scrawl that interrupted the texture of the fine onion-skinned paper. Glasses placed at the right spot along the bridge of his nose. He prayed for understanding as his eyes moved across the pages. Asked the Lord to open up his mind so that the ink on the paper would become understandable. It didn't now. It never had. In all the years he counseled his congregation, this one with a letter from home, that one with a deed to transfer, another with a slice from the Philadelphia *Tribune*, he was never blessed with the understanding of the etchings, not exactly. But the understanding did come from his great ability to size up a situation and the special gift of memory of a genius that let him recall word for word what he'd heard other people read. It was the former that helped him now. Noon. She told him all he needed to know to pull the essence from the papers. Now he could shape that and then give her guidance.

Reverend Schell looked up all at once. "You don't have a problem, my dear Sister Noon."

"I don't?"

"You don't. You won't lose Liz either."

"Are you sure, Reverend?"

"I'm certain. The lawyer will file his paperwork to get a stay. That way Children's Court can't take action even if it takes you longer than the fifteen days."

"Longer than the fifteen days to do what, Reverend?"

"Well, that's the next part. You got to get the child's aunt to sign over guardianship to you and Herbie. Then it'll be permanent and legal."

Noon hung on to his every word as if they were diamonds falling. Her eyes brimmed over with trust when she looked at him. As if the inked symbols had just been interpreted by the Lord himself. She was so glad that she'd had presence of mind to bring this to him instead of schoolteaching Next-Door-Jeanie. Jeanie would have advised her all right, but only after she'd lectured her about how the system is always gonna work against colored people unless we organize, and how the system keeps poor whites and colored apart, for control, keeps them at each other's throats. Noon didn't need that kind of talk right now. She needed Reverend Schell's silky assurances.

"So, so you mean, it's just that simple, get a lawyer, and then find the aunt."

"Just that simple, Noon."

"The lawyer will be the easy part, except for his fee, but we'll manage. The hard part will be finding the aunt. We don't even know where she is, Reverend. She sends money every month like clockwork, but it never has a return address. Lord knows I don't want no parts of her anyhow. I come up against the likes of that woman, the Holy Spirit might not want to live in my heart no more I might act out so."

"Now, Noon." Reverend Schell chuckled. "To forgive is divine. But to be on the safe side, just get Herbie to handle the aunt." He pulled the glasses from his face and folded the arms in and slipped them in his breast pocket. "Herbie can find her; I trust him that far, to be able to find the aunt. He probably knows those clubs where she'd most likely sing." He controlled the smirk that wanted to race across his face. He talked in his smoothest voice. He didn't want to let on that he knew about Herbie and Ethel. Bow had told him years ago. Bow even wanted him to do something about it. Confront Herbie, make him stop. He'd tried to explain to Bow that he couldn't get involved in all the sordid details of people's lives. Too much. Under those big Sunday hats and wide-lapeled suits with perfectly folded bleached white hankies, some were just plain not interested in changing their ways. Best to let it sit. Until they were ready to change. If he tried to stir things around before they were ready, it'd be like a swirling cesspool. "I just pray for their souls," is what he'd told Bow. "When they ask me, I give them counsel; otherwise I just pray that the Lord don't let Satan lay permanent claim."

"But her daddy's a preacher, just like you," Bow had insisted. "Upstanding, well-respected, well-off colored folks. We from the same county. She married down; you know that bag-toting husband ain't of the social standing she's used to."

Reverend Schell was struck by Bow's anger that time, and every time after that when Bow tried to convince him to intervene. Finally Reverend Schell hinted that if he didn't know better, he'd think Bow had designs on Noon himself.

"Just promised her people I'd look out for her," he'd insisted. Then Ethel left a year ago, and Bow let it drop.

So to keep the smirk from giving him away when he talked about

Herbie finding Ethel, he smiled his slowest, brightest smile.

Noon looked at his face, his white teeth showing as he smiled. She melted again when he smiled, showing the whiteness in his mouth a little at a time. She shifted in the red-cushioned seat and rubbed her hands along her dress again.

He leaned back in the chair and smiled completely now. He talked to Noon soothingly, telling her not to worry about a thing. He suspected that was all Herbie needed to do. Talk to her low and smooth. He suspected Herbie didn't even know how to look at her. Like she was the prettiest gem God set breath to. Reverend Schell had never ever touched Noon in indecent places or in indecent ways. But he guessed that he could stir her passions more with a look than Herbie ever could. Herbie was young, impatient, going straight for the treasure without taking time to admire the chest, dust it off, work the lock until it opened easily. He reasoned that Noon wouldn't even need healing prayers if Herbie were a more patient man.

He put the blue-backed papers on the desk. "Promise me you won't worry, Noon."

"Promise, Reverend." She blushed.

"Let's join hands and have a word of prayer so we can leave here on one accord in the sight of God."

Noon took her hands from her lap and placed them on the center of the desk to meet his. She was embarrassed that they were cold.

Reverend Schell cupped his large dark hands around Noon's. "Such a warm heart has she whose hands are cold." He pressed his hands tighter around hers. "Such small, gentle hands, Noon, but I can tell the Lord has picked these hands for large works. They're already doing large works, giving love to those two girls that you didn't even birth, being a good sound member of this congregation, cooking and sewing for the ones that can't do for themselves. What great works for such small, gentle hands."

He prayed a short prayer asking for a quick resolution, for guidance, and for a home in heaven when this life is done. When he finished praying, he drew Noon's hands to his mouth and blew into them. "They're nice and warm now," he said with the satisfaction of one who'd just gotten a stubborn piece of coal to glow.

Noon squirmed in her seat. She could feel that thin line welling up that always welled up during her healing prayers. The line never grew wider than a slither. Right now it was dangerous. Right now it wasn't supposed to happen. Stretched across the altar under God's sacred watch, it was supposed to happen. But no prayer had just gone forth summoning up her miracle. He had only blown his breath into her hands. She pulled at her hands; she needed them for support. She needed to plant them on the red-cushioned seat next to her hips. She needed to ball her fists and will the line away. The devil, that's all it was. The devil trying to mess with her, trying to block her miracle, trying to keep her mind in a fog over this situation with Liz. Trying to scare her off from her Reverend Schell.

Herbie got home before Noon. He was in the back bedroom with Fannie on his knee and Liz still holed up in the closet. Fannie was talking fast. Pouting. Telling him all that happened with the mean son of a bitch who came to take Liz away. Herbie got madder the more she talked. He was so mad that he didn't even stop the cursewords that peppered her tirade.

"He did what, Fannie?"

"Called Noon a nigger, I heard him when he was leaving saying 'fucking nigger.'"

"You did the right thing locking him in the cellar. He didn't have no right talking his way into this house anyhow. You just a child; by right he should have come back later. I just wish I had been here, I'd have kicked his you know what."

"His ass! Right, Herbie, you'da kicked his natural ass." Fannie jumped off his knee and ran to the closet door and cupped her hands around her mouth and pushed her voice through the thick wood. "You hear that, Liz, Herbie woulda stood up for you, I told you he would."

"Why she always hiding in the closet like that?"

Fannie picked up the agitation in Herbie's voice and jumped back on his knee and rested her woolly hair against his starched white shirt. "She's scared, Herbie; she's just a scared little girl."

"Well, you a little girl too, but you not always running and hiding the least little thing that happens."

"'Cause I know my big, strong daddy will fend for me, I don't have to let nothing scare me."

Herbie hugged Fannie and tried not to laugh out loud at her too-obvious attempts to charm him. At the same time, though, he blushed with the warm flood that he always got with Fannie from the time he lifted her out of the cardboard box. This was true love. For this little girl pushing her woolly hair against his chest, thinking him a hero, as he sat on the pale pink bedspread with the evening sun falling through the pink and green flowered handmade drapes, he'd go to hell and back, and fight fire-breathing dragons, and even kick the shit out of white men with badges. For this one, whom he didn't make in the way a father makes a child but who was made for him as his barometer of goodness—as long as she trusted his worth, he was worthy indeed—he might even let a thought slip through pertaining to Liz that was a nice thought.

"Tell her to come here." He exhaled as he said it, not hardly able to believe it himself. Until Liz stood in front of him, white lines on her face where the tears had dried to ashen streaks. Red hair sparkled with dust from the closet. He tried not to look at the hair. The hair would remind him of Ethel and he'd ache for her. He looked in her eyes instead, brown eyes almost as brown as her skin. He had not looked in her eyes since that night she shocked him in the hallway. Fearful, pleading eyes stared back at him.

Fannie was at Liz's side, nudging her on. "I told you Herbie won't let anything happen to you. Didn't I tell you, Liz, huh? Tell her, Herbie, tell her you'll protect her."

"Why don't you tell me what happened?"

Liz's mouth hung in disbelief. He had never said more than two words to her since she'd been dropped off on their steps. And when he did, it was only at Fannie's reminding him that he hadn't said good morning to Liz or how do you feel? Even then his words were like the bark of an old dog that didn't want to be stroked. But now his tone was soft, and that line that always came up in the middle of his forehead whenever he looked at her was gone.

Liz leaned on Fannie, who pushed Liz to Herbie, gently, until Liz was right at Herbie, her hand on his knee.

"Well, are you going to tell me?" Her fingers with the nails gnawed to the cuticle rested on his knee and almost burned through his pants.

Just a scared little girl, he told himself. Still, the hate that he felt for her started to rise up and stopped as a lump caught in his throat. He tried to swallow, tried not to think of all the times she'd gotten in the way of his enjoying Ethel. And over the past year even got between him and Fannie. Whether it was a walk to Pop's to get a coloring book, or a water ice, or a trip over to Forty-fourth and Parkside to watch the Negro League's Philadelphia Stars play, or a trolley ride to the train station to get red licorice, or even a sit-down on the front steps to count the lightning bugs at dusk, Fannie wouldn't unless Liz could too. He watched the eyes glass over and then spill down, following the ashen tracks straight down her cheeks. She tried to talk. No words, though. Just sobs that made her whole body seem to crumble. He did swallow then. He lifted her small hand from his knee and squeezed it and pulled her to him and sat her on his lap and told her not to cry; he wouldn't let anyone take her from Fannie and Noon.

Fannie pushed her hands to her mouth to muffle her gleeful squeals. Even with her seeing eye she didn't notice that Liz's back was straight as a board, and Herbie's arm was stiff even as it circled Liz's back.

Noon's thoughts beat her home. Her focus was back to Liz and convincing Herbie to help Liz stay. She knew he wouldn't protest finding the aunt. A chance to ogle over the aunt at a club with a shot of gin and a beer chaser, he wouldn't protest at all. It was the money for the legal work that bothered her now. If she had to, she'd dip into the money her mother had wrapped in palm and tucked in the bottom of the cedar chest with all the linen and cotton Noon would need for keeping house. And then there was what the aunt had been sending for Liz's upkeep over the past year. It was growing fast. But she'd kept Herbie from knowing how fast. She was afraid he'd insist Noon use the aunt's money for the expenses of Liz's upkeep instead of the money he worked so hard for. Noon wanted a savings for Liz, though, maybe for a church wedding or college education, something to balance the great wrong done to her so early.

She rushed through the street saying how do's to the men on their way home from jobs at the navy yard, or on Dock Street, or the ones wearing ties who worked in town. She decided she'd need to appeal to Herbie's basic goodness. Like a blind person that relies on smells and sounds and touches to see, she'd have to call on her other womanly ways since she couldn't whisper in his ear late at night and move all over him and make him shout yes, yes, to whatever it was she wanted. She could appeal to his goodness, though, that part of him in every man that makes him yearn for the feeling he got when his mama told him how good he was, how proud he made her feel. Mother's love, mother's love. Raised up with all brothers, Noon understood that kind of power. It'd make a six-foot man humble his shoulders and blush like a schoolgirl, and a leaned-over man of seventy straighten his back and strut. It protected men from the commission of heinous acts that might have otherwise seemed like the natural thing to do. It was their conscience, their guilt, their goodness. For Mama, even when they weren't aware, their best was always done for Mama.

She walked up her well-swept steps and into the house thinking about what a man wouldn't do for mama, until she peeked into the soft pink haze of the back bedroom and saw Herbie leaned against a pillow. Both Liz and Fannie had their heads on his chest, staring into the oversized book that he read from in his softest voice. "For mama," she whispered to herself. "Or for baby girls."

Back in the kitchen she put fire under a pot of greens and mixed flour and water for quick bread, brushed it with cinnamon for calmness, and sliced up the chicken. She set the dining room table, covered it over with her best white lace tablecloth, and pulled out her stark white handmade candles. She called them down to dinner and announced that they weren't going to ruin their meal with talk of the devil of a man who'd been there earlier.

Fannie agreed, but after grace was said, she blurted, "That man don't matter anyhow 'cause Herbie's gonna stick up for Liz, aren't you, Herbie?"

"Give it a rest, Fannie," Herbie cautioned. "Didn't your mother just say we're not talking about that now?"

Fannie made a face that Herbie didn't catch from the corner of his eye. But Liz did, and she started to giggle. Noon looked up, amazed. Liz had never giggled or smiled, for that matter, when Herbie was around. Fannie knew that too. So she kept it up, exaggerated faces she made. Even Noon laughed. And then Herbie caught her, and he laughed too. All four of them doubled over, eyes watering they laughed so hard. Noon prayed, as she laughed, that Liz could stay, that they could be a family.

FOURTEEN

Noon and Jeanie hung clothes on the line in their adjacent backyards. The air was still pink with the new sun, and the subtle breeze of August held a tinge of coolness. Noon chattered on to Jeanie about how expensive that lawyer was that they had to hire to file the paperwork so Liz could remain. But she thanked Jeanie for recommending him. "Smart young colored man, worth every dime. Or should I say every dollar? Even though Herbie would have pitched a you-know-what if he knew just how many dollars."

"Well, I'm sure he'd work out a payment scale if you were really in a bind." Jeanie wrinkled her nose at the sun and pushed her straw hat farther on her head and then smoothed a white linen napkin on the line. "One reason I like him so as a lawyer is that he's sensitive to the fact that a lot of us can't afford legal representation. That doesn't stop him from giving his best service."

"Thank God I did have all the money for him," Noon said as she reached into her apron pocket for a clothespin. "I guess I could have tapped into the special needs loan fund at the church. But I think they like to use that to help people with more basic needs, like coal for heat, food too if someone's really down-and-out. So I just dipped into some of what my mama and daddy sent me up here with. My mama said, 'Noon, no matter what, don't you ever let a man know that you got a little money socked away; he'll sweet-talk you into spending it just so you'll be totally dependent on him.' "

Jeanie laughed. "Wise advice, Noon, listen to your mama."

"Oh, I surely listened. Not that Herbie's not a good provider, he brings in more in tips alone than some people make in salary, but I think there's some wisdom to what Mama said. Definitely in this case. I could pay off the lawyer and didn't have to listen to Herbie's mouth while I was doing it. And now the lawyer's got it all worked out, plus Herbie's even going to New York this coming Friday to see that the aunt gets the papers and tell her when she's to appear in court."

Then Noon went on to berate Ethel for leaving the child the way she had. "No preparation, just traumatized her, just left her sitting in the sun, wonder the bout of loose bowels hadn't killed the poor little thing. But I brought her back around." She pushed a stubborn clothespin through a washcloth to affix it to the line. "I do believe between me and Fannie, we saved the poor little thing's life. Why, even that smart young lawyer said it was cruel the way the no-good aunt abandoned little Liz."

"There were other, better ways of leaving her, I suppose," Jeanie said as she stood the prop to her clothesline straight up, making the line go high so that her clothes were cast in the sun like waving flags.

"Of course there were, and then that turncoat Dottie didn't help matters any."

"Dottie doesn't know any better. She allows herself to be used by the powers that be." Jeanie walked to the short black iron gate that separated her house from Noon's.

Noon dropped a heavy towel she had pulled from her washbasket. The loose dirt of the backyard mixed with the towel's wetness and became muddy streaks. "Shucks," Noon said, snatching the towel up and waving it like a banner. "I been thinking about concreting this backyard, but the girls love playing in the dirt so much, making mud pies, digging up worms—but excuse me for cutting you off, Jeanie, what were you saying?"

Jeanie walked out of her yard and the few steps down the buttercup- and honeysuckle-lined alley into Noon's yard. "I need this big old beautiful shade tree that's in your yard," she said as she sat on the steps. "Your nice brown skin can handle the sun. My old sallow coloring turns to red; then I'm burnt but good."

"Got to be careful in the sun, for sure, especially when it's right overhead. I tell Fannie that with her light complexion, even though she gets as golden as a piece of fried chicken when the sun hits her, but too much of anything is no good. I tell Liz that too, even though she's a little brown, like me, she still got that red hair, means she's sensitive. I know she's sensitive, definitely got a sensitive stomach—"

Jeanie cleared her throat.

"Lord have mercy, listen at me going on and on, Jeanie. Just tell me to hush if I start talking about those girls anymore." Noon flung the muddy towel over the wooden fence that separated her house from the alley and stood her line prop straight up as well.

"I was just saying how Dottie gets used by the system," Jeanie said as she slid her feet from her sandals and leaned her back against the step above her. "They know she needs a job, raising a daughter by herself, give her a couple of hours of work at that school office, then tell her don't ask questions, just do as we say do—"

"That still don't give her the right to act the way she did." Noon pushed her remaining clothespins in her apron pocket and sat on the steps with Jeanie. "Then she got the nerve to speak to me the next day, imagine that. 'Morning, Noon,' she said like nothing happened, like she had just registered Liz like she could have done."

"So shouldn't that tell you something? You can't totally fault her, Noon. You've got to be cognizant of the bigger picture. This system, that white man, ruthless son of a bitch."

Noon winced. She hated to hear Jeanie curse. High school teacher, refined-looking woman with her elegant cheekbones and straight back. "This ain't gonna be another one of your hate-talking sessions, is it, Jeanie?"

"I got strong reason for being the way I am," Jeanie said as she shifted on the step. "The things I been through." She fell silent and stared off into the pink and blue sky.

Noon looked at Jeanie sitting next to her on the steps, at her cream-colored arms in her sleeveless dress, her straight brown hair that hung under her straw hat in billows around her shoulders. "Now, Jeanie, let's be truthful, you look as white as the whitest person I ever did see, you could pass for white if you wanted to, I just want to know what's been done to you that got you in a separate category called 'the wrongest done to'?"

Jeanie dug her feet into the yard's dirt floor. "Breeze off your tree is wonderful."

"That it is," Noon said, looking at Jeanie intently.

"It'll make this August heat in the afternoon easier to take, the memory of the breeze. When you take those sheets off the line and stretch them tight over the bed, they're gonna carry the memory too, keeps the morning breeze with you even late at night, even have traces of that honeysuckle scent in them." Jeanie paused and adjusted her straw hat lower on her forehead. "I've seen and heard things, Noon. Been taken for white, been privy to things because of my complexion." She fell silent, then started to speak, then pulled her words back and was silent again.

Noon forced a cough, almost embarrassed that she should have to call Jeanie back to the yard, back from other times and places that she could tell by the deep wrinkles that folded in Jeanie's brow were not as peaceful as these yards filled with the pink and blue morning air.

She didn't have to. The fishman's loud baritone did as it floated down the alley. "I got porgies, silver trout, butterfish, catfish, bluefish, stripes," he sang.

"But is it fresh?" came the response from two or three doors down.

"My fish, it still wiggles, it still swimming in this bucket, you come see, come see."

Noon laughed, grateful for the distraction. Jeanie cleared her throat but didn't laugh. Noon went into her apron pocket and pulled out a knotted handkerchief. "Over here, fishman," she said, mocking his strong South Carolina accent. "Let me get a whiff of your fish."

"Where you, lady? Oh, there you are. Miss Noon, Miss Mother of my little friend who tells me how much fish I sell." He walked into the yard half singing, half talking. "She look in my bucket one morning and say, 'They all be gone by lunch.' Well, that day I sell out in one hour. Another time she tell me, 'Long day, Mr. Fishman,' and that day I don't think two people buy."

Noon gushed as she untied her handkerchief and pulled two quarters from beneath a small roll of dollar bills. "That's my Fannie, mnh, that's my chile. Give me six butter, the ones still wiggling." She laughed again.

The fishman set his silver bucket on the ground and pulled newspaper from the oversized pocket of his coveralls. "Yeah, I call that girl my friend," he said as he reached into the pail of ice-covered fish with knuckles where fingers should be. His knuckles were quick and deft, and Noon and Jeanie politely looked away as he dropped the fish in newspaper and wrapped it on an angle. "Either she know what's in tomorrow, or she put the whammy on me; either way, I stay on that girl's good side." He laughed louder as Noon dropped the two quarters in the center of his palm. "The other one is quiet, I bet she be smart, but my friend, that girl something all right. What Mr. Noon feel about having a daughter with the present of sight?"

"Oh, Herbie"—Noon waved her hand—"he just humors me, said if she can't tell him what number to play, what good is it?"

"Now that be a fine present for sure, you and Mr. Noon be rich, yeah?" He motioned his knuckles to his pail and looked at Jeanie. "No fish for you today, Miss Book Lady?"

"Not today, sir. Later in the week maybe. Just me in my house and I'm an old lady, don't eat much, no refrigerator—"

"You welcome to use mine, Jeanie. I'm surprised your refrigerator didn't come in yet. Didn't you order it last year?" Noon interrupted her.

Jeanie nodded. "I'd read in the paper around the time I ordered it that the War Protection Board said to look for the war to be over for at least a year before the household goods were back in ample supply. Even though I'm willing to bet those white folks aren't waiting as long as us."

"Maybe that why I can't buy no radio, yeah?" the fishman said as he tuned his voice up to sing again. "I got silver trout, catfish, porgies, stripes." He trilled it as he left the yard.

"Beautiful voice," Jeanie said to his back. "Young man missed his calling. Should be in the theater."

"Or on a church choir," Noon said as she stood and shook out her apron. "I got to put this fish on ice until I can get to it to clean it. So excuse me, Jeanie, you welcome to sit, though, sit as long as you like. I need to run a dust mop through the downstairs, then promised Fannie and Liz I'd take them over to that new city pool. Don't know if I'll let them get in, though, depends on how clean it looks, and the looks of the other people using it. Can get polio swimming in those dirty pools."

"Oh, it's okay, Noon." Jeanie sighed her words quietly. "I don't mean to disrupt your schedule. You run on such an organized schedule."

"Now, Jeanie, you know you're welcome anytime. Anytime, you welcome to come sit over here. If the girls are out here making too much noise, just shoo them on around to the front to play." Noon had her hand on the doorknob. "Got to get those sleepyheads up. Must be almost seven-thirty, girls don't budge before eight if I don't call them, definitely got sleeping habits of city folk."

Noon was inside the door. She let out a long breath. Didn't really have time or desire for a lesson from Jeanie on the woes of being colored in Philadelphia in 1946. "Should come to church and lean on Jesus," Noon muttered as she put her fish in the sink. She had more immediate things to concern herself with. Like frying up the butterfish for Herbie, keeping him in a good mood, laughing, so he wouldn't protest when Friday came and it was time for him to get on that New York–bound train so Liz could stay.

FIFTEEN

Herbie did get on that train when Friday came, but he wasn't laughing as the train whooshed toward New York. Headed to track Ethel down at the club where Big Carl assured him she'd be, so she could sign the papers making Liz his and Noon's adopted child. Feeling as if fireflies were all through his joints, flickering, making him twitch unexpectedly, no order at all, just jumping and jerking.

The train was almost empty on this Friday night. A few men in suits, a fat lady with a big straw basket filled with pieces of brightly dyed fabric. An occasional newspaper rustled above the fast clacking of the train. Herbie leaned back against the headrest. This could have been a good car for napping. The lights were low and buzzed with a faded hum. His muscles wouldn't cooperate, though. He was even blinking more than usual, and yawning, so much that water starting forming in the corner of his eyes. He went into his vest pocket and pulled out his neatly squared handkerchief. Last thing he wanted was for Ethel to think he'd been crying over her. A whole year since she'd busted his heart wide open. He wanted her to think he'd gotten beyond her. He hadn't, didn't know that he ever would be, but he was angry too. So he didn't want to act like a whimpering puppy. He dabbed at his eyes and then looked around the car lest these last-minute Friday night travelers think he was crying too. He fingered his wide-brimmed Dobbs on the seat next to him. The hat was gray and matched his tailor-made suit. The suit gleamed from Noon's repeated hits with the whisk broom. She had fussed over him so. Made sure his tie was perfectly straight and that his handkerchief peeked through the top of his pocket, clipped his mustache, even got down on her hands and knees and shined his black-and-gray wing tips. He hadn't been this decked out since his father died the year he and Noon were married. He had protested the expense of these new clothes. But Noon insisted, said they'd cash in one of the bonds left by Herbie's father. Since he was going to New York on a Friday night, he needed to look the part.

He tried to think about Ethel to the hum of the faded lights. His thoughts melted before he could see them as pictures. Noon spoiled it for him. Dressing him the way she did. Telling him how sharp he looked, as if he were a little boy. He should have stayed casual the way he'd planned, everyday pants, shirt opened at the collar. He felt overdressed, as if he'd been sent out on an errand by his mother just to impress the shopkeeper. Noon's prints were all over him. He pictured her fingers curled, going for his neck to straighten his tie. The tie pressed against his windpipe now and made him want to gag. He loosened it. He took off his jacket and folded it over in his lap. He undid his top shirt button. He kicked at his heels and slid his feet from the the confines of the shining wing tips. He begged the fireflies to leave his joints; his muscles settled down to just an occasional twitch. He wet his lips, which were dry. Now he thought about Ethel.

He'd met Ethel in Albany, Georgia, ten years before. She was no more than seventeen. He, a couple of years older. He'd just left his Mississippi home for the call of the drummer's life. He loved to lose himself in the beat of smoke-filled blues halls, pretty women, straight gin, hard-living colored folks tougher than any he'd ever met. Gamblers and other hustlers, and sometimes people with soft insides just out to catch the beat and clap a little to tide them over until they could get to church. He'd figured Ethel for the soft type. The first time he heard her sing at Colt's, the biggest dance hall in the heart of Albany, the stirring that went on inside him, he was sure she must have been singing about Jesus. Must have gotten her songs mixed up between what she sang on the church choir and what she sang out on Saturday nights. But when he listened to the words, once he could get beyond her look, which was more sensual than any he'd seen, she was singing the blues. He was transformed, lifted out of the muck and mire of everyday life by the face and voice of this girl-woman.

He followed her home one night past the concrete along Albany's main roads, down a dirt trail to a clump of houses that sat in a cloud of smoke that the residents sent up to keep the mosquitoes at bay. He walked faster to get to her before she disappeared in the cloud. Her walk was easy, uninhibited. Her hips went from side to side in a rhythm that would have lulled him to sleep if he were not a young man. Her head was thrown back. Her faced looked up toward the sky. Her hair was short. Nothing interrupted her face from the God that he was sure must have kissed it to arrange it so. The saucer eyes that drooped, the short nose that crowned the healthy mouth, the fleshy lips, ripe for kissing, or for pushing out those notes that had thrilled him so.

She was getting closer to the houses in the cloud. He had to say something before she crossed over into the cloud. He cleared his throat. She turned quickly, not with fear or apprehension, almost as if she expected him to be there, but with a quickness.

"Oh," he said. He felt so stupid then; he still felt stupid when he thought of it, right here on this New York–bound train. He had just followed her through the night, stealthily like a snake, and all he could say was "Oh."

"Oh?" She repeated it with a chuckle. "You better say more than 'Oh'!" She imitated him again. "I suspect you been following me, and my grandmom keeps her shotgun loaded by the porch door, see, right over there. C'mere."

He followed her curled finger motioning toward him. He wasn't sure what his face looked like, but his knees were buckling for certain. He hated right then that his light complexion couldn't be covered over with the night.

"Don't you see it?" She pointed to the houses in the cloud. "The butt of her gun is leaning right against that windowpane, see it?"

He squinted and peered and couldn't see it. He could barely see the house through the cloud of smoke. He nodded, pretending to see it. He was close enough to her to pick up her scent that was like hot chocolate, no, it was cocoa butter, only sweeter, richer. He turned to look at her, and when he did, he saw her saucer eyes all over him. He felt the flood of her eyes burning him her gaze was so hot. She moved to him and kissed him right on his lips. Not a peck, a kiss that gushed. She laughed when she pulled her lips from his.

"I saw you watching me at Colt's. You ain't a cool cat yet. I like that.

Your face can't hide shit." She laughed again and then smiled right at him. It was a warm smile, the smile a church girl might give. "Uh-oh. Got to go," she said as she turned quickly and moved toward the cloud. "I think grandmom's got her gun aimed, don't you see it, you better duck till I get in and tell her you ain't one of those cool cats." Her laughter hung behind her as she faded into the cloud. Her laughter stayed clear.

He went back to Colt's night after night after that. Walked her home. Decided he cared for her. Proposed them joining up, putting their sounds together. Her voice to the beat of his drums. She agreed, recruited a piano man, a horn player, then a road tour through southern back streets, corn liquor barn parties, and she'd laugh. Late at night, when she'd allow him in her bed until four in the morning, when she'd ease out, to walk, she'd tell him, "Clears my head to walk." And she'd laugh. Then he'd met Noon, and he and Ethel did one more tour that ended in Philadelphia, the joy bells, his father's connections with the railroad, the steady salary of a redcap, found his way back to Florida to make Noon his bride. "You! getting married, Herbie?" Ethel had said, and the laugh.

Herbie could hear the laugh now on this train, bouncing around in his head. In a little while he might hear it for real. And see her. Touch her. Tell her that was low, low-down dirty the way she did him. He might even call her a bitch. That would get her for real. He had never called her a bitch before. Even when they were touring in Florida and she got word that her grandmother died, and he wanted her to cry on his shoulders, and he wanted to give her the money so she could skip the rest of the tour and go back home, and she refused him both, told him no man would ever claim her and buy her off. And later that night she went home with the waiter at the club they were doing. He didn't call her a bitch then. He just got up the next day and found a nice little stable church that turned out to be Noon's daddy's church.

He squirmed in his seat as the train blew a loud whistle. They were almost in New York. He sat up and slipped his shoes back on. He could feel the fireflies coming back. He was starting to panic. Just sign the papers, please, bitch. That's what he'd do. No overtures, no niceties, no asking for explanations. He'd beat her at her own game. He'd be the cool one this time, the one that didn't need her this time. The train lurched to a stop.

People were standing all around him. The woman with the basket of brightly dyed fabrics stood in the aisle, blocking his exit. He wondered what she'd do with the fabric. Make a quilt. They were just pieces all different colors. And now they were falling all over the place as the train backed up and then lurched forward again. She plodded quickly down the aisle trying to pick up the pieces. The suited-down businessmen almost walked over her. Herbie started to walk right over her too. Just stamp the prints of his wing tips on the purple and green and orange cuts of cloth. Then he said, "Damn," under his breath, and leaned over and walked up and down the aisle until he had retrieved every last colorful piece. He handed them to her as she stood with her hand to her chest trying to catch her breath from the quick, unplanned moves up and down the car.

She stuffed them in her basket and held one back and extended it to Herbie. "Take this one; it matches your suit." It was a silver gray piece of fabric, silky on one side, nappy wool on the other.

"No, thank you, ma'am," Herbie said as he looked in her face for the first time. She was coal black with clear eyes and dark lips and soft white hair knotted in plaits at either end.

"Take it, young man, didn't your mama teach you not to refuse nothing from a old lady, especially when you just done something good for her? Hard luck to do that, old lady like me too close to heaven to be refusing something from."

Herbie sighed and took the fabric from her plump hands. "Thank you, ma'am. Can I carry your basket to the platform?"

She smiled, and her clear eyes crinkled and soft lines surrounded her eyes like the crisscrosses on a road map. "Basket's light enough to carry, son. Go on and take care of your business on a Friday night in the city."

He didn't argue or insist. He stuffed the fabric square in his pants pocket and stepped out onto the platform through the grandness of Penn Station on a Friday night. And then into the loud lights that made New York City.

The city blared with lights. Traffic lights honked and car lights screeched, and the neon dripping from everywhere shouted so loud he thought he should muffle his ears. He knew where she'd be. He hopped on a bus to Harlem and went straight there. To the spot they talked about playing when they were much younger, when he still made a living stroking a drum pad. They'd always talked about playing here, Club Eden.

The air around the club glittered as if it'd been spiked with silver dust. Herbie inched his tongue out into the air just to taste it, a drop of a dream that he'd never have even in his deepest sleep. Not now. Not after he married Noon and promised her father and her five brothers that he would do right by her. Get a respectable job of a God-fearing man. And now too much time had passed even to consider striking a drum pad before a crowd of whiskey-gulping, loud-talking clubgoers. The swing sound of the thirties was quickly becoming passé; bebop was the new sound with its mixed-up beat. This was the closest he would come, a bit of silver dust on the tip of his tongue on the outside of Eden. He straightened his tie and tilted his brim like the cool cats and walked down the steps guarded by thick black iron railing.

He pushed open the door on bare-backed, small-waisted women and men in suits as sharp as his. Red carpet ran from wall to wall under gold-framed smoked glass mirrors, round tables under low lights, and a square of hardwood floor for jitterbuggers where the spotlight glared and rushed. Large fans whirled and sliced through the laughing air scented with perfumed sweat and cigarette smoke that formed a silver gray cloud that bounced along the ceiling. The band bounced too, as did the hips and shoulders that crowded the square of a dance floor, and Herbie's heart too as he inched through the laughter to a long bar and leaned in and ordered a straight gin with a beer chaser.

The bartender was efficient, almost clinical, and lacked the jolly warmth of Big Carl at Royale. Even the clubgoers here were different from Philly's, lined against the bar, glasses poised like soldiers saluting as they watched the dancers on the hardwood floor. A woman taller than Herbie with hair piled high on top of her head bobbed to the beat, and her whiskey did too as it splashed over the rim of her glass and onto Herbie's suit coat. She pulled a tissue from her cleavage and handed it to Herbie without a look, not an "excuse me, please" or "beg your pardon," just a brisk hand with the tissue and a slow walk away. Herbie shook his head and sopped the liquid with the tissue. The band took a break. The Victrola spun out slow songs. The laughter that was hard went soft as bodies swayed on the hardwood square.

Herbie watched the band walk to the side of the club and down a dark, narrow hallway. Their dressing rooms or closets pretending to be dressing rooms would be through that hallway. Ethel's too. He wanted to get to her to hand her the legal papers concerning Liz before she did her set. But a tall, wide bouncer kept guard and slapped hands with the band members as they turned the corner into the darkness. Herbie reasoned that there must also be a door that led into a side alley. In all his time working clubs, the smallest, dowdiest clubs still had a door that led to an alley or side street for the quick getaways that sometimes accompanied the lifestyle. He drained his beer and stepped through the breeze of the whirring fans back out into the silver dust–spiked air.

He walked around to the side alley. The air was much blacker here. He almost missed a thick wooden door painted black. His heart jumped as he turned the knob. It was sealed tight. He leaned his back against the door, suddenly weak from the prospect of finding her on the other side. He figured that he'd just have to settle for waiting for her to do her set. Then he'd try to see her afterward, hand her the papers, tell her when she had to appear in court. Scowl at her, he reminded himself; call her a bitch and leave her standing with her mouth hanging. He got comfortable with the thought as he leaned up against the door in this black alley that was remarkably quiet considering all that was going on in Eden. It was so quiet that he could hear the click of fan blades whirring the air somewhere inside. He followed the sound deeper into the alley, and right there, just above his head, he saw curtains pushing against an open window. He picked up a beige-colored pebble and threw it into the window and poised himself to duck should anyone come investigate. Nothing. He tossed another one; still nothing. Nobody home, he said to himself, time for Herbie to get in and find Ethel when her public's not around.

He lifted himself onto the low ledge. Peeling wood scraped his palms. He would have dropped right then and dusted his hands and tried again, but the curtain swung out, and with it the unmistakable scent—cocoa butter mixed with fine French perfume. Jackpot. No having to sneak through here, down the dark hallway, dodging and peeping until he found her room. This was her room. Just a leg swing away and a push through the curtains. After a year of plotting to leave Noon, and deciding to stay for Fannie's sake, and dreaming about Ethel, crying over her, cursing her in his head, he was here, one leg in, now the other. He was standing here in her dressing room.

It was a small room. A narrow bed strewn with dresses, mostly red and black, or red and gold, or red and white. The red predominated. A desk lined up with nail polishes, lipsticks, makeup brushes, perfumes. A large oval mirror with looping etchings around propped against the back of the desk turned the desk into a dresser. A calendar taped to the bottom of the mirror, the flip-through kind of calendar. Inked markings all over the month marked "August": hastily written notes, numbers, circles, check marks. Herbie peeled the back of the calendar from the mirror and flipped through it. All the months looked as full as August. He tried to tape the calendar back to the mirror, but it wouldn't stick. He tried to lean it against the mirror, but it kept falling. He picked it up to fan out the pages as a base to lean it on and noticed a sleeve in the cardboard at the back. He ran his thumb through the sleeve and pulled out a photo. A photo of two little girls. At first he thought it was Ethel and her sister when they were children. But he looked closer. It was Fannie and Liz. It was Easter Sunday. He could tell because Fannie was carrying the black patent leather pocketbook that he had picked out for her. It had a big bunny rabbit carved on the front. She had lost it that very Sunday. In the picture she was smiling big, showing her gums. She had her arm around Liz, who wasn't smiling. They had obviously posed for the picture.

"Now where the hell did she get this?" Herbie said out loud. He turned quickly to look around. It almost felt as if someone were in the room with him. Just the fan blades clicking. Somebody would think she really cared about Liz the way she got this picture tucked away. I wonder if she been creeping back into Philly spying. He started to take the picture and then decided he didn't have it in him to be that mean. He stuck it back in the sleeve and tossed the calendar on the dresser-desk. He went into his wallet and pulled out the lawyer's card. And then dipped into his breast pocket for the folded papers for her to sign. He picked up one of her red lipsticks, and mashed down on the envelope, and wrote, "If you really care, sign these, call this lawyer." He was just about to write "bitch." But then the fan blades seemed to get louder, clickety-clickety, then footsteps just outside the door. He stretched his arm. Tried with everything in him to get to the little black hook on the door to slip it into the hole, to lock the door. Almost but not quite. The door opened with force. Too much force for it to be Ethel. Too much force for it to be anyone he'd be glad to see. Damn. The tall, wide bouncer glared at him, then came at him asking him what was he doing there.

"Just taking care of some business I got with Ethel."

"What kind of business?"

"Personal business." Herbie couldn't keep the edge from his voice.

"Yeah, well, how'd you get in here?" His face was wide as his shoulders, and his mouth was big, like his nose, which was flaring at the ends.

"Walked in." Herbie said it as matter-of-factly as he could.

"Oh, walked in? You one of them smart asses. I been standing out in the hallway I sure as hell ain't see you walk in."

"Look, man," Herbie said, scanning the room for something he could wield as a weapon should the need arise, "I said I walked in. Now, if you'll excuse me, I'll walk on out."

"Not yet you're not. 'Cause I don't like no yellow niggers like you just appearing in my lady's dressing room. Now I'm gonna ask you one more time, how did you get in here?"

"All right, I flew in."

"Oh, you got wings, huh, motherfucker?"

"And a brain, asshole."

"I don't think so; only a dumb ass would get smart with me."

"Come on, man." Herbie starting backing up until he was right at the dresser-desk. "I walked in. How the fuck you think I got in?" He flipped at his lapels and flexed his shoulders.

"Well, guess how you going out, you smart-assed son of a bitch?" He slapped his mountain of a fist into his palm and moved toward Herbie.

"After you, motherfucker." Herbie said it loud as he called on every molecule of strength he ever had or hoped to have and balled it in his fist and swung high and landed it square across the wide-open target of the bouncer's jaw.

He watched the bouncer stagger, as if he were getting to ready to fall; he prayed for him to fall. That had been his best shot. His knuckles were sore and bruised. The bouncer was shaking his head back and forth; he wasn't staggering, he wasn't going to fall; he was breathing fire from his nose and his mouth. Herbie balled his fists again, ready to summon what strength was left. He saw the bouncer's fist coming at him. He ducked. The punch went inches over his head and sounded like the crack of a bullet. He forced his sore knuckles into the bouncer's gut, which was hard as Herbie's knuckles.

"You no-good yellow bastard," he said, bending only slightly after Herbie's fist went into his stomach. "I'm gonna fuck you up for real now. Then when I find out what you doing here, in my lady's dressing room, and I don't like the reason, I'm gonna fuck you up again."

Herbie was breathing hard and moving his feet fast and bobbing and weaving trying to stay alive. "Where's your neck, you fathead dunce, you neckless asshole, fuck you, fuck that bitch Ethel too. Tell her I said that too." His words were spilling fast as his feet were moving.

"You calling my lady a bitch?"

"Your lady? She ain't nobody's lady. I know 'cause I been with her. She was mine too—"

Surprisingly he didn't feel anything when the bouncer's fist quaked against his head. It was as if all of his senses had shut down except for his hearing. The clickety-clickety of the fan blades, the roar of the air as the bouncer's fist pushed through it. His skin splitting just above his eye sounded like a watermelon when the first cut opens it wide. He could even hear the cracking sound his head made as it met the floor, and then the tap-tap-tap of his eyelids closing shut.

He just lay there when he came to. One eye looked out into grayness, the other into a fuzzy haze. Too much pressure on his head. As if sandbags used to hold a cresting river at bay were holding his head down, keeping him from moving. His first instinct was to jerk forward, look around, determine where he was. He couldn't. Not until he could move the sandbags from his head.

He was on a bed, he could tell that. He could feel the mattress pushing against his back. He moved his fingers along his sides, up to his head; his hand touched his lip, what was his lip doing so far from his face? Farther along he moved his hand until it came to his eye, the one that stared into grayness. Covering of some kind. Then on up to his head. No blood on his head from what he could tell, no wrappings like the one over his eye, just the sandbags that he couldn't feel but knew must be there. His thinking was blurred like his vision. All he was sure of was that he had gotten his ass kicked. Hadn't been beat like this since he was fourteen, down home. He had the same feeling then coming too, numb confusion, angry humiliation, supplications to Jesus Christ that the fathead wouldn't come back until he could pull himself together and locate a two-by-four, or switchblade, or good solid baseball bat. Something to even the odds a little. He was praying that prayer now.

He heard a door open and braced himself. The footsteps were light, though. The laugh was melodic. The voice vaguely familiar. He was certain only of one thing: It wasn't Ethel's voice.

"You woke, huh, sweetness? Well, you messed around and got your head good and caved in."

Herbie struggled to speak but could only push the word "Where?" through his swollen mouth.

"Where are you? That's what you trying to ask me, handsome? Least you used to be handsome before you got beat up. You in Miss Ethel's dressing room, in her bed. Now ain't that right where you was trying to get to? Ain't that what caused that Grand Canyon right over your eye?"

"No!" He said it so emphatically he almost sat up. He tried to focus through the blur of his uncovered eye to see the woman he was talking to. He only saw streams of light. "It can't be daylight," he groaned.

"Yeah, sweetness, you been stretched out on Miss Ethel's bed all night into today. And she ain't been in it. Now isn't that a cruel turn of fate?"

"Where's she?" he managed to ask.

"Gone, left this morning."

"I left papers." Herbie half moaned, half spoke. "On the desk."

"Papers? She got those. She love that little girl. Both of 'em. Got her own lawyer on it too. Miss Ethel hit the big time. Keeps her people on retainer."

"Who are you?" he asked as he struggled to remember where he'd heard that voice.

"You mean you been listening to me go on and on and you don't even know who I am? I guess that one eye ain't working yet, huh, sugar? Maybe I should flip that persistent body of yours on your stomach and mash my magic fingers up and down your spine, maybe then you remember me. Huh, Papa? Huh, Mr. Sad-Eyed Married Man."

He thought that he must be dreaming or delirious; this couldn't be the woman from Gert's, the woman whose name he never knew, and when he went back to try to find her under that tent, nobody knew her either. And since the smoky haze from the barbecue had kept her face in a kind of cloud that night, all he could describe were her lips. But that voice, the way she said, "Papa." That was the voice for sure. He blinked several times to try to clear the vision in his uncovered eye. He managed to lift his hand to the covered eye.

"Don't touch that, baby," she said quickly. "Nasty gash right over your eye needs to stay covered. Lucky for you I found that strip of material in your pocket. Club ain't want to even offer you a piece of toilet paper the way you broke and entered. Yeah, sweetness, I been all through your pockets, even found the rubbers in your wallet. You was planning on a hot night. I took out a dollar to pay for the whiskey that I had to use to clean that cut. Still a corner left in the shot glass, you want it? Guess you got one hell of a headache."

She sat on the bed and lifted Herbie's head and put it in her lap. His uncovered eye was starting to focus, but now her face was too close to his to see. She was lifting the covering and peering into his other eye. He could see the pores in her brown skin exaggerated like a doctor's skin during an eye exam. Her breath was warm and soothing.

"You'll live, Papa."

She sat back, and he could see bits and pieces of her through the blur. Her hair was tied down with a scarf filled with swirls of color. Bright colors. Yellows and purples and hot pinks. He couldn't look at the colors for long and had to shut his uncovered eye.

"That is, I think you'll live, long as you let Miss Ethel be. Come on, Mr. Married Man, let me help you up. I got to get to my other job, and with Miss Ethel gone, leaving you here alone will be like leaving a mouse in a trap for my hungry cat. Ever tell you 'bout my cat, course not, last time I saw you was itching so to get to Miss Ethel's dressing room, wouldn't hardly settle down for me to massage your back. Well, my cat's name is Liver, cat likes onions, and I love liver and onions, so I named him Liver. Anyhow, good cat, ain't seen a mouse since I had him. I feed him his onions once a day. Fried with catsup and salt. Well, awhile back, he'd just finished eating, I'm sitting with him in my lap pulling at his fur, gently. So first he nestles his head, kinda like the way you trying to nestle your head, but then, out of nowhere, he turns around and bites a chunk out of my arm. Bite was so bad I had to keep it wrapped in cloths soaked in witch hazel for a solid week. Now what made Liver do that? Probably the same thing that made Miss Ethel tell Chip, that's the big guy that took you out last night, imagine that, big as he is got the nerve to have a name like Chip. Anyhow, same thing that made Miss Ethel tell Chip to come in here and kick your butt. Just don't want you pulling on her fur no more."

Herbie sat up with force. He forgot all about the throbbing in his head and stood and stomped his feet and swiped at the air with his fists. "You ain't saying she sent that big, dumb motherfucker in here. You better not be saying that, or I'm a—"

"You gonna what, strong thing? What you gonna do, and who you doing it to? Tell me please 'cause I'm interested now. I want to really hear this."

Herbie's response was a long, deep groan as he and grabbed at his throbbing head. "I got to get outta here. I gotta get back to Philly. My wife'll be worried sick. I don't believe she sent that fathead SOB in here to kick my ass. You sure you ain't lying. You lied to me anyhow, told me I could find you under that tent any Friday or Saturday. Went back and no one even knew who you were. Who the hell are you anyhow?" He was sitting straight up now, trying to focus through the blur. "Well, you gonna tell me?" He patted the bed around him. Then stretched his hands in front of him. "I ain't in the mood for no game playing, okay?" Dead silence. He snatched the covering from his eye. This eye could see clearly. He looked around the room. She was gone. So were all of Ethel's clothes, the notes taped to the mirror, the makeup, perfumes, even the fan. All gone. Just the curtains blowing in and out through the half-opened window. He touched the gash over his eye. He winced when he touched it. He looked at the covering he had just pulled from the gash, and beyond the circle of blood turned purple he recognized it as the gray fabric from the woman on the train. He poured the corner of whiskey onto it and put it back over the gash. It stung so bad he shouted out loud. He heard deep voices moving closer to the room. He felt for his wallet and grabbed his hat and left the same way he had come. Through the window into the alley, this time into the sun, which made his blurred eye water, and now he could see clearly again.

PART III

PART III

SIXTEEN

Ethel had done her part after all. Appeared in court right on time. Sashayed up to the judge decked out in her gray pin-striped walking suit and red feathered hat tilted to the side. Handed him the signed papers and let no emotion out when Liz turned away from her when she blew Liz a kiss, and Noon sucked the air through her teeth in disgust, and Herbie held his face like stone so the soft spot on his heart wouldn't ooze and show through on his face. She let no emotion out until Fannie smiled at her and waved. Then the corners of Ethel's mouth turned up just slightly in the most proper way, and she lowered her head as if Fannie were a queen and she a grateful member of her court. She kept her head lightly bowed as she strutted out of the courtroom, right back out of their lives.

Liz's rationalizations for why Ethel left ripened over the years. At six she was sure the woman was not really her Ethel who batted her eyes at the judge in court that day. Just some evil person pretending to be her aunt, dressed up like Ethel the way Ethel used to dress her up for Halloween. Her real aunt Ethel was tied up in the back of someone's chifforobe, living off of mothballs and rainwater that seeped in through the chifforobe's cracks, planning her escape so she could get to her Liz. By the time Liz was ten and had outgrown anklet socks and wool leggings, Santa Claus's lap, and the wooden pony in front of the five-and-dime, she was sure Ethel had fallen for some fine Arabian prince. Rich and kind, but with an evil mother who put the whammy on Ethel and made her mind go blank when it came to her niece.

But now she was thirteen. Too big for undershirts with sleeves, barrettes with clowns, and wading in the children's pool. Now she had her period and a new tapered haircut. And on this second Sunday, as she stood straight-backed in church, ushering, feeling almost grown in her white gloves and navy pleated skirt, and cotton blouse with a rounded lace collar, she knew for sure why Ethel had left her on Noon's steps that hot afternoon. Thought it to herself as she handed out church programs and signaled to Cross-the-Street-Dottie's-Barb that she could sit three up front behind the trustees' row. She knew as she passed around the brass collection plates, and dispensed wooden-stemmed paper fans to the likely-to-faint, and smelled the cabbage simmering downstairs for the after-service meal. And she was surer than sure when she took her post in the middle of the center aisle, right where the strips of red carpet that ran up the center and midway across met in a T, where only the best of the Young People's Usher Board were allowed to stand, where all the other ushers looked to get their cues on when to face front, or sideways, or turn to the rear. She caught Noon's approving eye when the preacher gave his text and she made her way off the floor. And there was Fannie, patting her on the back, telling her how well she'd done. "I'll never make it to lead usher," Fannie said. "I can't help but fidget when I'm out there." Liz didn't tell Fannie that now she knew why Ethel left, and the knowing weighed so much it just pressed on her heart and bolted her to her post in the center of the red-carpeted T.

Liz talked about Ethel only when she had to. When Fannie's prodding about this or that detail of Ethel's habits or demeanor forced her, and she'd taste the bitterness that covered her tongue like a bad case of strep.

Right now Fannie and Liz weren't talking about Ethel as they headed through the lemon-colored September day on their way home from church. They avoided the cracks in the sidewalk as they talked instead about last week and their first day as eighth graders at Barrett Junior High. Liz told Fannie again about the ninth grader who had squeezed her butt. "Right in the middle of the hallway," her voice screeched. "I had just left sewing, on my way to U.S. history and I feel this hand, I mean right there on my butt, it was the most disgusting thing. I couldn't wait to get home to take a bath."

"I told you you should have knocked the living shit out of him,"

Fannie said. "I'm just waiting for somebody to try that mess with me, I'm gonna be ready for him."

"Well, actually, Fannie"—Liz snickered as she shortened her steps when they got to the corner of Club Royale—"you really don't have much of a butt, but at least you're in proportion since you don't have a chest yet either."

"What you mean I don't have a chest!" Fannie stuck her chest out, and her rear, and then said, "Hey, Liz, who's this?" as she walked around in circles pretending to be built.

Liz immediately recognized it as Cross-the-Street-Dottie and stopped right in the middle of the street to laugh out loud. It was a stoop-down-to-the-ground kind of laugh that came from the pit of her stomach and dissolved, if only temporarily, the bitter remnants of Ethel usually coated there.

Fannie and Liz laughed so hard they held on to each other to keep from falling. Both in their navy and white usher's garb, Fannie, still flat-chested, but tall, standing a full head taller than Liz. Liz was in a B-cup bra, though, and her hips had already curved. Fannie's hair was pulled back in an oversized puff that resembled a cheerleader's pompom; Liz's was tapered softly at the nape of her neck, the cut she'd begged Noon for, for weeks, every day, saying, "Please, Noon, it's not like it's going to grow long like Fannie's. Please, it will be easier to take care of. Please, Noon, I made lead usher." Until Noon ran out of excuses and let her loose to go to Clara's beauty shop for a wash, hard press, and cut and curl.

They started to walk again, still laughing; Liz ran her hand through her hair as she laughed. Loved the smooth feel of the waves in the back that Clara had told her would hold longer if she slept in a stocking cap after brushing it down with VO5. Then Liz looked behind them and nudged Fannie and said, "Speak of the devil's chile," and their friend Julep from around the corner ran to catch up with them, with Cross-the-Street-Dottie's-Barb following quickly at her heels.

"What you acting the fool about?" Julep asked Fannie. "I heard y'all laughing all the way down the block. I said that ain't nobody but Fannie acting the fool."

"Fannie trying to act like she got a shape," Liz said, voice still shaking from laughing.

"Well, tell her." Fannie turned to Julep and asked, "Ain't I built?" Fannie stuck out her chest and butt again, and Julep caught on who they were teasing, and she laughed too.

Barb just stood there feeling like an outsider the way she always did around Fannie, Liz, and Julep. Her mother had told her that sometimes people think they're better, like old high-yellow Fannie with all the hair, don't even know where she comes from anyhow. Of all people, she got the nerve to think she better. And now Barb was sure Liz thought she was better too because she had gotten her hair cut and had made lead usher. And Julep, well, everyone knew Julep thought she was better because her hair was straight and light brown and her father was a dentist. Overcharging people just to pull their rotten teeth, is what Dottie had told Barb about him. Barb didn't know why she was standing here with them anyhow, watching them laugh at their private jokes, and now listening to Julep go on and on about Liz's haircut, telling Liz how good she looked, how it brought out that almond shape to her eyes, and her cheekbones were more pronounced, and that hard press made her red hair look even hotter. Barb felt fatter, uglier, the longer she stood at the edge of their words.

"You better watch it, girl." Julep teased Liz. "Fine Willie Mann gonna think you older than you are."

Liz giggled, and Fannie smirked. "I agree my sis looks good," Fannie said. "Now, don't get me wrong, but she can sure do better than the likes of Willie Mann. He could almost be her father he's so old."

"Willie Mann?" Barb tried to find her way into their circle. "Liz, you be looking at Willie Mann?"

"I just think he's cute, that's all," Liz said seriously. Her voice always got like that when she spoke to Barb.

Dottie's Barb looked Liz up and down the way she'd seen her mother do. "You best be careful that you don't turn out like your aunt," she said.

"Who you think you talking to?" Fannie squinted her eyes and stepped toward Barb.

Barb didn't look at Fannie. She did look at Liz, though. "Everybody knows your aunt's a whore," she said confidently. "So I'm just saying you better be careful, make sure the eyes you got for Willie Mann ain't just the whore in you coming out."

Julep gasped quietly and lowered her eyes in embarrassment for Liz.

Fannie grabbed Barb by the white collar of her usher's blouse. Liz's eyes welled up, and she ran. Straight around the corner to Lombard Street, into the house, almost knocked Herbie down on his way out, straight up to her closet, where the dusty warmth usually calmed her.

"She is a whore," Liz sobbed to herself as she swiped at the cardboard trunk that hid her hole in the wall.

She settled back against the wall. "Whore," she said to herself again. She pulled her hairbrush from the trunk and dug the dented wooden handle into the hole's fringes. She snatched a rock of a piece of plaster that emerged from behind the stark white wallpaper. "Whore." Now she screamed it in her head as she gnashed into the sandy-colored rock that glistened like glass. She chewed it down until it was pasty gravy, and then she just held it in her mouth. "Dirty, stinking whore." That had been the revelation that had descended on her as she'd ushered earlier: The real reason Ethel had left had nothing to do with evil mothers-in-law or chifforobes locked tight. The real reason was simply that she got in the way of Ethel living the life of a man-snatching, selfish, fuck-anybody bitch. She let the image fill her head the way she couldn't allow it at church. She chewed down another piece of plaster, and another, imagined that was all that was left of Ethel, the creamy pulp that she spit from her mouth.

🦢

Liz listened to Fannie stomp into the room and then flop heavily on the bed. She could never tell how much time passed when she sat in the closet and chewed plaster to bits. Sometimes she'd get a hint from Fannie, who'd remark through the closet door that she'd been in there for an hour, or an afternoon, come on out so they could get in on a game of double Dutch, or skate over to the schoolyard and spy on the janitor who lived in the basement to see if he and his girlfriend were doing it, or stuff stockings in their blouses and walk on Thirteenth Street just to make the prostitutes mad. Or if she really wanted her out, she'd tempt Liz with a long walk to Chestnut Street to look in Snellenberg's window.

But this afternoon Fannie didn't say anything. Liz could hear activity downstairs, though, clamoring and high voices screeching, the low, steady pace of Herbie's voice, then the front door closing hard.

"What's happening?" Liz asked almost sheepishly.

"What's happening," Fannie blurted, sarcastically, "is that I kicked Barb's fat ass. Something you should have done. I can't believe you just let her call your aunt a whore like that and just ran."

Liz breathed in deep. "Well, it's not like she said it about you or Noon or somebody really close to me." She projected her voice through the closet wall.

"It was wrong." Fannie's voice was loud and angry "Even Miss Jeanie stood up for Ethel and said that Barb had no business saying that to you."

"Miss Jeanie was out there?" Liz hated to ask. Hated the thought that it had turned into a big scene.

"Yeah, Miss Jeanie, on her way to get a paper, and of course, it hap-pened right on time for all the grown people who'd hung back longer at church. So yeah, it was a show, if that's what you're asking, Noon and Dottie came running too, and then Miss Jeanie and ole Dottie almost started fighting, and Herbie, yeah, Herbie, had to practically drag the ole skinny thing to her house with Barb limping behind her." Fannie stopped to catch her breath. "Then Noon made me come home to see about you. Not that you deserve it, not even willing to stick up for your own family."

"Ethel's not my family." Liz said it defiantly.

"The hell's she's not. Noon may be your mother now, but Ethel is still your natural mother's only sister."

"So why haven't I heard from her?"

"Why haven't you heard from her? How do you know it's not hard for her to—"

And then silence as Fannie pushed open the white wooden closet door, suddenly, something she'd never done while Liz was harbored there. Then her words hung in the dusty closet as she walked into Liz's safe haven. Mouth gaping, Fannie looked at Liz and then at the hole in the wall. "What are you doing in here?" she asked as she looked from Liz to the dented, plaster-covered hairbrush to the wall.

"Girl! Why you just bust in here like that?" Liz pushed at Fannie as she tried to put the cardboard trunk in front of the hole.

Fannie rammed her body against Liz's, sending her to the corner of the closet. She got down on her knees and crawled to the spot and rubbed her hand against the roughness. "Termites?" she asked as if she were sure the answer was no. She picked up a chunk of plaster that had fallen against the floor. She rubbed it between her fingers and smelled it and held it back and squinted as if she were an archaeologist and this plaster bit a significant find. She looked at Liz against the seam of the wall. The rush of the afternoon sun poured in through the open closet door and reached even in the corner to show off the sparkle of the plaster streaks around Liz's mouth. Suddenly she knew why Liz spent so much time here. She pushed the chunk in her mouth and crunched down and grimaced hard.

"What are you doing?" Liz demanded. She watched in horror as Fannie's jaws rose and fell over the meaty chunk.

"You do it," Fannie sputtered as she started to cough and gag and turn red.

"You don't know what you're doing." Liz rushed to Fannie and whacked her back. "Are you choking?" she asked, voice filled with worry. "Are you okay?"

"Get off me," Fannie managed to say as she spit the rocky bits from her mouth. "You eating the wall! Why didn't you tell me that's what you did in here all the time? You could choke to death in here eating these plaster rocks."

"I don't really eat them."

"You put them in your mouth." Fannie held out her hand, accusing Liz with the plaster crumbs she had just spit in her hand.

"Yeah, but not big pieces."

"You chew it."

"Sometimes."

"Well, then you eating it. You eating wall plaster, Liz."

"I don't always eat it. Sometimes I just come in here and sit to be by myself."

"Look how big that hole is." Fannie stood, pointing, tapping her foot impatiently.

"I didn't do that whole thing. Sometimes it just falls off and I just throw it in the trash." And then with pleading eyes she said, "You not telling, are you?"

"How can I not tell? Huh? You could die in here eating this shit." Fannie's face was still red from where she had almost choked.

"Please, Fannie," Liz begged. "I'll stop, I promise."

"What made you start doing this anyhow? I can't hardly believe you eating the wall." Fannie shook her head, trying to shake away the confusion, and then the horror, and confusion again, as she looked at Liz crouched on the floor, her knees pulled in tight to her chest.

"I don't know what made me start; I don't even remember starting; it's just something I always did." Her voice shook as she tried to keep from crying. "Please, Fannie, please don't tell. I'll do whatever you ask for the rest of my life, just don't tell."

"Does that include not letting people like fat-assed Barb call your aunt a whore?"

"I knew you'd take Barb on, did you get her good?" Liz could see Fannie was softening.

"Got her very damned good if I say so myself." Fannie half laughed. And then she looked at the hole in the wall and frowned and said, "I won't tell, but you got to stop, I mean absolutely stop digging in that wall. Noon have a fit if she know you up here messing up the wall. Eating it at that. She'll be ready to kick your butt."

"She only comes in this closet to hang up clothes. She wouldn't move my trunk; that's the only way she'd see it."

"Well, you still better stop, you don't even know what's in that plaster, plus you could choke."

"I'll stop, I'll stop," Liz said, throwing her hands in the air.

"And you won't tolerate no one calling your aunt Ethel a whore?"

Liz looked down at the plaster bits shining against the closet floor. She played with her fingers, short nails jagged and gnawed from digging into the wall. "How you know she's not a whore?" She whispered it, as much to herself as to Fannie.

" 'Cause I know it." Fannie stooped and grabbed Liz's shoulders and shook them. "And you got to know it too, Liz; you got to believe she's not."

"She let a lot a men do it to her, that's all a whore is." Liz still played with her fingers.

Fannie couldn't deny that. Over the years snatches of conversation would catch their ears, between Noon and one woman or the other who'd berate Ethel, say Ethel had been running with so-and-so's husband or brother or uncle, congratulate Noon for taking Liz in and giving her a good Christian upbringing. Or sometimes Fannie and Liz would be walking to Pop's, or to school, or to church, and the whispers would walk with them. "That short brown one with the red hair, that's the one that man-snatching singer saddled Noon with." Fannie would watch Liz's reaction, the way the skin on her face tightened with embarrassment and her eyes settled into a pained blankness. Fannie would rush to console Liz, to paint a composite of Ethel that she hoped Liz could love.

"So what, she did it with a few men." Fannie sat on the closet floor next to Liz. "That don't make her a whore. A whore is like the women who walk up and down Thirteenth Street and carry butcher knives and don't have no feeling. I bet your aunt Ethel has a lot of feeling."

"How you know what she got?"

Fannie drew her knees to her chest. " 'Cause I know. I can tell when a person has feelings and when they don't. If Ethel is a whore at all, she's a good whore. Like a good witch."

Liz wanted to tell Fannie about Herbie, see if she'd still think she was a good whore if she knew Ethel had done it with him. She drew lines in the plaster dust that had settled on the closet floor. She looked at Fannie, at the dreaminess to her eyes as she stared through the dust. She decided against it. Fannie could afford this fairy-tale image of Ethel. She knew better, though.

"Somebody's coming up the steps," Liz cautioned as she hurriedly covered the plaster hole with the cardboard trunk.

Fannie reached up and pulled the door shut and nestled back against the closet wall. Liz leaned her head against Fannie's shoulder. Fannie shifted to give Liz more leaning room. "Tell me about her singing again, Liz."

Liz swallowed the paste that had settled along her tongue and described what she could remember about Ethel in the clubs, and what she couldn't remember she made up. She told Fannie how Ethel would take her with her to Ike's or the Postal Card, how people would go crazy over Ethel's singing, how they'd dance and clap and stomp so much "you'da thought you was in church."

"What did the nightclubs smell like?" Fannie interrupted her.

"I don't remember for sure, but if I had to guess I'd say it's like a cross between Noon's Manischewitz Concord wine, the Camel cigarettes the insurance man smokes, and body sweat mixed with thick perfume."

"Well, how did it feel, you know, what did the air feel like?"

"Felt just like church right after someone gets saved and the people are wild and free."

"Mm, anything that much like church couldn't have been all bad. Probably why Ethel sang in those places. Probably why she still does. Just trying to save people's souls is all."

Then Fannie told her that when she was four or five, she used to think the air was really red and blue inside the clubs. "You know how they use those blue and red bulbs, when I'd walk by one and the door would open, I thought that was just the color of the air. Then one night me and Herbie were coming from the drugstore on South Street, and this man stumbled out of Freddie's Bar and Grill all bloodied up around his head, blood dripping all over his shirt. So I asked Herbie what happened to him. Herbie said, 'Bad air in that place, my man was just in the wrong place at the wrong time.' So I thought for the longest time that when it got late, the red air melted and settled on the heads and shoulders of people who weren't supposed to be there."

"You were one smart child," Liz teased.

"Well, this was before I had you around to make sense of the world for me." Fannie patted Liz's head.

"What was it like before I was around?" Liz asked, the laughter gone from her voice.

Fannie was quiet. Then she said, "It was like things were incomplete, like we were waiting for you so they could be complete, we knew you were coming and we just wished you'd hurry up."

Fannie and Liz were silent sitting on the closet floor in their usher's uniforms facing the trunk that covered the hole in the wall. "That was nice of you to say that, Fannie." Liz sighed through the plaster dust that swirled around them lightly. "Very nice."

SEVENTEEN

Fannie and Liz laughed their way through thirteen and fourteen. They skated to Nat King Cole tunes at crepe-paper-strewn parties at the Y and sniffled over Dorothy Dandridge movies at the Standard Theater on Tenth and South. They slow-dragged with the boys they'd invited over to Julep's house when Julep's mother was shopping in New York and her father was in his adjacent dentist's office filling teeth with the thank-God-it's-so-loud drill. They pierced each other's earlobes with burnt needles and then toothpick sticks and got Saturday afternoon part-time jobs: Fannie worked the soda counter at Pop's; Liz arranged the displays at Betty's Dress Shop on South Street.

Liz was a straight A student at Overbrook High School, where Jeanie was one of the few black teachers, where most of the students were white, and where Liz had begged to go because that's where Julep and her cousin went. The teachers loved Liz because of her exceptional reading skills, her perfect posture, her every-thread-in-place appearance, and her manner, which was quiet and polite. Fannie could have gotten all A's too, except that the teachers said she had a fresh mouth, and the way she'd stare at them bordered on disrespect.

So Fannie and Liz tumbled through thirteen and fourteen like children rolling down a hill where the grass is lush and buffers the lumps and protruding tree roots along the way, hands high in the air, laughing, then catching their breath to laugh some more.

Around fifteen, though, life turned serious; almost every couple of months, it seemed, their laughter was interrupted.

The first time was in October, when Fannie and Liz were on their way home from Julep's cousin's Halloween party at a castle of a house on Osage Avenue in West Philly. Herbie picked them up in his '48 Chrysler, which, even though it was seven years old, still drove like new because he mostly kept it parked. Liz nestled in the backseat, grateful that they didn't have to walk all the way back downtown, and thought about the high-style elegance of Julep's cousin's house with the marble mantel and the grand crystal chandelier. She decided right then she'd live like that someday. That's when Fannie cried out "Oh, my God," and Herbie slammed the car to a stop and was immobilized by the sight of Fannie as she bounced around in the front seat, flailing her hands and screaming, "Noon's daddy. Noon's daddy's gonna die."

Then, in January, Jeanie leaned over the short black fence out back and blew smoke from her mouth as she told Noon she'd heard a rumor about a road, a high-speed road, slated to run right through where they lived. Noon, who rarely cursed, dug her heels in the frozen dirt and said, "The hell they will." She listened to Jeanie then. Where she used to list off chores and excuse herself politely when Jeanie started her talk about the evil nature of the system, now when she went out back to empty the garbage or spread crumbs for the birds, she put on a jacket and gloves so that she and Jeanie could talk for a while. And when she'd go back in the house, she was so agitated over the very thought of being bulldozed from her block that she'd bang pots around and snap at Fannie and Liz and argue with Herbie over the smallest things for hours afterward.

Then one Wednesday in May, Liz sneaked around the corner the same way she had every Wednesday since the weather broke. And this Wednesday, like always, she dabbed rouge on her cheeks, smeared an extra coating of Vaseline on her lips, tucked her bobby socks all the way in her penny loafers, and tied a scarf around the waist of her pleated jumper so the print of her hips would show. She managed to fade into the simmering stream of activity on Catherine Street just so she could watch Fine Willie Mann direct the ritual of getting Club Royale's weekly inventory into the cellar through a hole in the ground. But this Wednesday he noticed her, extended his hand; said, "You're Ethel's red-haired niece, the one Noon and Herbie took in." He invited her down into the cellar then for a cup of tea.

Willie Mann moved the crates around in the cellar at Club Royale so he could offer Liz a seat. He was tall and light with straight hair that he slicked to the back: his eyes were brown with a hint of gray. His forehead jutted and made his brown-gray eyes appear deep-set and intense. "Fine Willie Mann" the women called him. He knew it too. Even dressed like it. Even when he was just pushing boxes around in the cellar, separating imported from domestic, dry from sweet, red from white, he still wore good wools, or pure silks, or soft cottons. Matching leathers; a lizard belt meant lizard shoes meant lizard strap to his watch. He'd started at Royale when he was only thirteen. Happened to be walking by as Big Carl heave-hoed with cases of bottled beer. Willie Mann offered to help. Suggested they lower them down through the opening in the ground using a rope or chain. Would take some time to devise, but it'd be a huge savings of manpower in the long run. Big Carl liked the way Willie Mann's mind worked. Hired him on the spot to unpack inventory after school. Winked and smiled when he occasionally showed up with a giggling long-haired classmate to help.

Sister Maybell protested at first. "That pretty boy there is the only grandson I got in the world," she'd told Big Carl. "Don't hardly want him caught up so early in all the devilment that goes on in that Club Royale."

Big Carl eased her mind. Promised to keep Willie Mann in the cellar for most of his work. Until he finished high school. That's when Willie Mann started in the main room, and the ladies ogled over that fine young thing. And ordered double their usual when he flashed his perfect smile. And it was always easy for him to talk one or the other of them into the cellar on most any night of the week. So he quickly jumped ahead of bartenders twice his age and became Big Carl's right-hand young man.

Liz looked at his watch strap now. She couldn't look at his eyes. The eyes would just fuel her blood, which had drained from her hands and feet and was splashing around in her head making her woozy, making her feel as if she had to faint. She couldn't let herself do that. If she fainted, she wouldn't have every detail of this place to recall each night before she fell asleep: the deep soft couch that held her at its edge; the open-top wooden crates filled with bottles of Seagram's and Ballantine beer; the desk with an oversized adding machine on its top, the muted throw rug that ran from the desk to just under the couch, the three-legged desk chair with wheels that he sat in now, and swiveled toward her, smiling, extending a cup of tea in a dainty china cup.

"Thank you," she said as she took the cup and sat back a little on the couch. She took a sip of tea and then looked at him as he smiled. She could finally look at his smile and not pass out. She wanted to return the smile. The chin-thrust-out Lena Horne kind of expression that she and Julep would practice that Fannie said may be okay for Lena, but on them it was fake, phony, and full of shit. Her mouth was filled with the thick silver wires of her braces anyway, so she settled on a closed-mouth, eyes-lowered smile like the shy church girl that she was.

"So, what occasion led you to be standing on my corner?" he asked as he ran his hand through his hair.

"Oh—" She hesitated, took another sip of tea, and thought about which excuse she'd use. She had at least four excuses should Noon or Herbie or somebody from the block want to know what she was doing there. "I was pricing taps for my penny loafers. Taps save the heels, so I figured I'd get some with the money I make at Betty's Dress shop."

"Work at Betty's, do you?" He sat cross-legged, swinging his foot, elbow propped on the arm of the chair, looking at Liz with her grown-up hairstyle and little girl's face.

"Sure do," she said as she tilted the cup to her lips again. She held the cup by the handle without putting her fingers through the hole and allowed her pinkie to curve back just a bit, away from the rest of her hand, the way she'd seen Julep's mother do, wanting to make sure Willie Mann knew that she had class. "Just working there on Saturdays for right now, but Betty said I'm doing so well she may talk to my mother about adding on Wednesday evenings."

"That well?" he asked, letting his eyebrows go up as he tried to decide.

"Yes. I was actually hired to help her dress her window, but she said I have a real eye for quality, you know fabric, and how well a piece is put together, so she wants me to help her pick out her line for next season." She sat back farther in the couch. The tea was settling her stomach and her head, and she could feel her hands getting warm again; her confidence was coming back. "This is very good tea," she said.

"It's only Salada. So you like clothes, I see. You seem to have a sense a style. I mean, I've noticed you walking by, and you're always much more pulled together than your sister."

Liz felt a flush of warmth along her cheeks at the realization that he'd noticed her. She giggled and sipped her tea again. "Fannie," she said, "she's hopeless. She just throws on the first thing her eye hits. Her attitude is, if it's clean and pressed, who cares if the colors match or the patterns clash?"

"I used to date a lady like that," he said as he swiveled on the chair. "Drove me crazy. We stayed in more than we'd go out because I'd get to her place and see the wild getup she had on, and all I could do was say, 'Let's have Chinese tonight, baby. Take out.'"

Liz forced herself to laugh. She didn't want to think about him in context with another woman. "Well, I just love clothes," she said determinedly, to prove herself worthy. "I love the feel of material when it's good. The way the threads come together in a finished piece is very exciting to me. Noon sews, she sews well, but then I see a dress, or a sweater, or a suit in John Wanamaker's window, and well, Noon's work is just not that good. I would never insult her like that, but I am glad I'm earning a little money and can save and start buying some store-bought outfits, you know; even if I have to start at Betty's, I can work my way to Chestnut Street."

"After you get taps for your loafers." He threw his head back and laughed.

Liz could see gold crowns around three of his teeth when he laughed. She had never told anybody, not even Fannie, about how she felt about her home-sewn clothes. She felt suddenly guilty, as if she had betrayed Noon. She placed her cup and saucer on a sideways-turned crate next to the couch. "Well, yes, and maybe I'll go ahead and let Noon keep making my clothes; she is good, quite, quite good."

"But not as good as you," he said as he stopped laughing and moved the wheeled chair in closer to the couch.

"Beg your pardon?" Liz said, not following him.

"I'm saying, Liz"—he lifted her hand from her lap and held it in his own—"Noon's ability to sew does not surpass your ability to spot superior workmanship in a finished garment. So you'll keep yourself bound to wearing less than the best because of, of what shall we call it, Liz, not wanting to hurt Noon's feelings, or loyalty? Neither can really justify settling. Do you understand what I'm saying?"

She did understand exactly what he was saying. He was saying what had been rolling around in her head that she hadn't been able to put into words. He held her hand tighter. He fingered her watchband. She started feeling weak and clammy again. She squeezed her thighs together. She had never felt such a stirring, not even when she had slow-dragged with the boy at Julep's, and rubbed his butt while they danced, and let him put his tongue in her mouth.

She thought she might pull Willie Mann to her, that's what she'd do. Just pull on the arm that held her hand, right to her on that couch. But all at once he squeezed her hand and placed it softly in her lap.

"Listen," he said as he pushed the wheeled chair back to the desk, "I've got to settle some balance sheets and get the rest of these crates unloaded—"

"Can I help you do something?" Liz asked, rubbing her hands together so the left hand could share equally in what had just thrilled the right. She shifted in the seat and stared straight at him.

She looked a little like Ethel to him as she sat there now. Ethel's eyes were larger, and her mouth, fuller. But she and Ethel had the exact same cheekbones, the deep-set kind that made a woman beautiful. He reminded himself then that Liz was still very much a girl despite her stacking that was also like Ethel's. If his calculations were right, Ethel had left Philadelphia about a year after the war ended, because she had stopped playing at the USO on Broad Street and had come back to Royale full-time. So that would mean that she had left about ten years ago, yeah. So Liz couldn't be more than fifteen. He was almost twice her age. He decided then what he'd instinctively known when he'd invited her into the cellar, this pretty young thing facing him on his couch with a plumpness to her eyes, like that unmistakable plumpness of a cat's tail when it stands straight up and the fur gathers in a circle, or a kidney bean when it swells right before it bursts and sends up shoots, or the bulging to the eyes that a calf gets when her sacs are swollen and ready for that first release: This plump-eyed girl sitting on his couch where he had sweet-talked the best into giving it up was just too damned young.

He stood and straightened his striped shirt and refit it into his navy pleated pants. "I've also got to get ready for a meeting; in fact, it's at Reverend Schell's church, your church, right?"

"Oh, my God!" Liz shouted as she jumped up and grabbed her books from the other side of the couch, grateful for the opportunity to turn away so that her disappointment wouldn't show. "I was supposed to come straight home; I was supposed to be going to that meeting; it's important, about some highway coming through here! Oh, God! I'm in trouble, I probably missed dinner. Oh, uh, thanks—thanks for the tea and everything." She put her hand to her forehead. "What am I gonna say! Noon's gonna be mad!" She ran to the leaned-over ladder that served as stairs out of the basement.

"Liz," he called behind her, almost authoritatively, "you were pricing taps for your loafers, remember?" He hoped she did remember as he watched her big, curvy legs with a hint of bobby socks peeking from the back of her shoes rush up the ladder. He surely didn't want any lip out of her evil-assed so-called father, Herbie.

EIGHTEEN

Noon sat on her back steps and watched her freshly hung clothes flap in the start of the sunrise. She had so much to do today. Another meeting at church tonight over the highway. The first meeting last week hadn't accomplished much. City people hadn't even shown up. Plus she'd been in such a state over Liz getting home so late, she was just calming down about the time Reverend Schell called the meeting adjourned. But at this one tonight they were supposed to be presented with real facts. Humph! Not enough facts in all of God's universe to justify them being uprooted for a road, she thought. Then there was Fannie and Liz's sweet sixteen birthday party at the Christian Street Y, less than two weeks away. All of downtown would be there. Even though Fannie and Liz were a couple of months apart, Noon decided to throw them a combined party to save all the preparation and expense of doing them one at a time. She had cakes to bake, had to finish Liz's dress, Liz so specific when it came to her clothes, had to be a certain fabric, highest quality, even went with Noon to Fourth Street to pick out the thread. Couldn't fault her, though, straight A student; if the worst she did was overspend on material, Noon could live with that. Fannie could be a straight A student too if she'd get her mouth under control. Smart as a whip, just always so quick to fresh-talk the teachers when they did something she didn't like. She hadn't even started Fannie's dress. Then there were the decorations; she'd get Maybell to help with those.

She tried to clear her mind of the road business and all she had to do otherwise, so she could enjoy the sun getting ready to splash in the sky.

Today's sunrise would be glorious; she could tell because the air had been unusually black just an hour ago as she'd pressed wooden-headed clothespins on to her wash. Now the first streaks of red and blue were starting to separate the horizon that hung over downtown and made her say, "Jesus, Jesus how great Thou art." She'd just sit here for a little while longer, just let her thoughts tumble around in the newness of the day.

She reached into the depths of her apron pocket and pulled out a vial of spirit of peppermint and rubbed it against her teeth. Her backyard peeped into the side of the Saunders Funeral Home, which took up a quarter of the block around the corner. Lush rosebushes that the Saunderses raised to cut down on the cost of flowers climbed along the plot next to the building and sent their fragrance to befriend the as-strong scent of the wild honeysuckle that lived up and down the alley. Noon breathed it all in now, the roses, the honeysuckle, the peppermint, and felt dizzy from the air that was new to this day.

The side window to the Saunders Funeral Home was cracked a quarter of the way, and she could see light streaming through the opening interrupted by a to-and-fro of people moving quickly. She wondered who died last night. Wondered if Fannie had been right when she woke last week crying, saying that Miss Pernsley, her Sunday school teacher, was going to die soon. Noon and Liz had calmed her down. The only time Fannie cried, the only chance they ever had to console her, to hug her and smooth at her hair, which was long and woolly and ever so dense, was after a vision. The only time she seemed to need the press of flesh that she so readily gave to them all was after her seeing eye had shocked her with a revelation. But that night last week Fannie's period had started too. As Noon and Liz had hugged Fannie and stroked the back of her neck with cool rags, Noon noticed her sheets, and told her maybe that's why she was so upset. Maybe it wasn't her Sunday school teacher at all, just her emotions running wild.

Noon folded her hands in her lap now as the sun continued its entry into the morning. She prayed for the family of whoever it was causing the lights and the bustle at the Saunders Funeral Home so soon. Probably was Miss Pernsley that the Saunderses tended to now. Fannie hadn't been wrong yet. Sometimes months would go by without Fannie seeing anything, not even whether a storm was brewing or whether a melon had sweet insides. But when she did, when she got still and stared and squinted and then lost control, whatever it was she'd seen came to pass. Like when she'd seen Noon's father's death six months ago and through her hysteria told Herbie and Liz. And Herbie, as gently as he could, told Noon. Noon packed Liz and Fannie up and boarded the first train Florida bound. She'd gotten there just in time to squeeze her father's hand and hear him shout, "Death, where is thy sting? My baby Noon made it here in time."

And when Noon's mother had asked her how, how did she know to come when she did? They were just about to pick up the phone to call her when the next thing they knew she was standing there right at her father's deathbed. How on earth did she know? Noon didn't tell them it was Fannie. Child found in a box the way they'd found Fannie caused enough talk about witches' babies and the like in that part of Florida where they had migrated from islands in the Bahamas with names like Exuma. Islands so small they didn't get a pinpoint on the map. Islands that had served as docking stops for slave ships North America–bound. They picked up Jesus there but never really put their other ways down. They already knew that Fannie had dropped into their lives on their front steps one cool predawn morning like magic; they didn't need to know that she had a seeing eye too. Noon's mother's smooth, oil-rich brow would have wrinkled in fear; what with all that was done to Noon when she was twelve, they would have started talking witches' children for sure.

Noon thought she could hear wailing coming from the Saunders Funeral Home now. Family probably followed the hearse over from wherever they picked up the body. Probably died right at home. Most colored people died at home, she thought, or close to home. Trying to get home.

Like that morning when she was trying to get home back when she still lived in Florida. She had stopped herself from thinking about that morning over the years. But her trip home for her daddy's death had revived it all. Now the memory of that morning would rise at her like a serpent that uncoiled so slowly she wasn't even aware it was there, right there at her feet, and then suddenly at her face sticking out its ugly tongue; the memory caught her like that. She had started seeing that morning again in the oddest things: the nub of the fishman's fingers, the red basting strips for trimming Liz's dress, the dried bits of dough she'd flick from her rolling pin, even sitting here on her back steps watching the Saunderses prepare the dead for the living.

She was only twelve years old that morning. Breasts not fully sprouted, hips not even rounded out, hadn't even started her monthly. Her mother had warned her. "Noon," she'd said, "heard talk about some heathens running through South Florida performing a ritual that sacrifice young girls to whoever it is they pray to."

"Who do they pray to?" Noon had asked her mother as she shuddered at the very thought.

"Don't know, don't want to know. If I did know, wouldn't call out the name. All I know is it ain't Jesus. From what I hear they did to a little girl not far yonder, scraped her insides like they was cleaning a chicken for roasting, devil worshipers is what I call them. Hear tell they don't stay in no one place for long. You just stay close to home till they pass on through these parts."

Noon didn't think she had wandered that far from home. Not even a mile past the church that stood solid as the lead structure into town. She had woke that morning before the sun did with berries on her mind. Huckleberries. Her daddy had remarked the night before that he had a taste for huckleberry dumplings. Noon knew where the blackest and sweetest berries grew. Where the juice flowed with just a pinch. Perfect berries for wrapping in strips of dough and dusting down with butter and cinnamon and cooking until the dumplings plumped. She thought about her dumplings as she half skipped, half ran into the sunrise. Her pan was already greased down waiting on the ledge, her dough patient under the covered bowl. All she needed now were the berries that dripped their juice like crystal melting, so black and shining until the juice looked clear.

She left the white stone pavement of town and stepped out of her huaraches onto the opened dirt road that was the beige color of sand. Her toes pushed deeper into the earth that was a softer sand as she moved into the woods. The air was moist under the thick green canopy of palmetto. It settled along her hair, soft and thin, and seeped down along her forehead. Morning birds called to each other, and possum rustled through the understory as she saw her tree. The one that would yield up the best huckleberry dumplings her father'd ever tasted.

But then there was a stark silence. Not the birds, not the possum, not even the drips of the clear dew from leaf to soil. Just no sound. She had never heard the booming of no-sound before. She stopped, terrified, a silence as loud as this surely meant a supernatural power was close.

And then another sound interrupted the no-sound. The ripping squeals of calves that almost sounded like the cries of a young girl. The caws-caws of chicken. The chanting of people filled with words she didn't know.

She knew to run. As soon as she'd heard the no-sound, she knew to run. Before the chanting even, she'd dropped her basket meant for her sweetest blackest berries. Tried with everything in her to move her feet through the sandy earth that held her feet captive and slowed her even as she tried. Tried to get to her mother and father and brothers who praised a gentle God, not the heinous devil these people chanted to in words she didn't know, except for the word "blood."

Her feet were no match for theirs. Three of the men caught her before she could even get back to the morning, to the beige-colored dirt road that led to the white stone pavements of town where she left her hua-raches waiting.

They carried her writhing, screaming body back in the woods as they chanted and called for blood. Her blood, which was supposed to nourish the babies she dreamed of having. Her blood, which she would one day whisper about to the other women saying that hers came this day or that, the way her mother and the ladies whispered as they stirred over pots for the meal after church. "Mama," she cried. "Mama, Mama, Mama," she screamed in a continuous wail as she kicked and punched and hollered for her mama. Her mother would know what she was up to when she saw the buttered pan and the dough under the bowl already cut in triangular strips. So organized she was. She'd smile and say that Noon done gone for berries this morning. And when she wasn't back, her mother would know to send her father and brothers with their shotguns cocked. "Hurry, Mama," she screamed.

They tied her fighting body down and dressed her in oil, and sprinkled her with powdered herbs the likes of which she'd never smelled. Acrid smells like turpentine, burning hair, decaying flesh. The women slapped her face and told her not to fight it. Easier on her if she didn't fight it. Then the men among them took her. Old and young, each more violently than the one before. The onlookers chanted and fainted and came to calling for blood. They wouldn't stop until they saw the blood. Not the trickles that fell with the first searing pain of a young girl being stretched wide, but the gushing that came later, seemed like hours later, when calf after calf had been placed around her in a circle. The calves bled too. They cried out and moaned for Noon when she no longer could. When she wished all of her would die but only part of her did, the part where her womanly passions were just starting to come to life.

The wailing coming from the Saunders Funeral Home got louder now, the daybreak wider as Noon sat on her back steps and rubbed more spirit of peppermint between her teeth. Then she could hear Mahalia Jackson singing "His Eye Is on the Sparrow." The Saunderses were good in that way. When the family members stood in the funeral parlor and stared in death's eye and wailed and pounded their chests and cursed God, the Saunderses knew to put on Mahalia, knew to let her gospel songs rise and fall and fill them up, knew to let a singing voice do what a speaking voice could not.

Noon thought about what she'd cook to take over to the bereaved family as she listened to Mahalia sing. Potato salad. She'd pull down her largest, fanciest bowl, the one with the thick beveled edges that made a prism when it caught the light. Then she'd take the large fancy bowl of potato salad over to the bereaved. Most of downtown would be there with their food donations. House full of people would be there. Noon and the other neighbors would console the grieving family, even help them clean the house. When they all sat down to eat, Noon would just have her potato salad. No meat today. She'd lost her taste for meat hearing that wailing from the Saunderses' so early.

By the time she left the grieving family it would be time for the meeting at church. She would be exhausted when she finally got home. So tired she'd fall right in the bed like stone. A quick sleep would come. She'd be dead asleep when Herbie pressed himself into bed. Not that it mattered anymore. He had long since stopped reaching for her, stopped pleading with her in a desperate voice to just tell him why, why it was she didn't have a nature to her.

Now Mahalia was singing "Swing Low, Sweet Chariot." The sunrise was complete, and the yellow chased the red and pink streaks behind the blue. Miss Pernsley. Fannie's Sunday school teacher. Noon was sure that's who it was right now on the gurney in the room where the Saunderses dressed the dead. She caught a whiff of formaldehyde through the roses and honeysuckle still making friends in the alley. "Sleep on, Miss Pernsley," she whispered. "Better that all of you should die than just a part."

NINETEEN

The church was going through something. Noon could feel it as she and Fannie and Liz walked through the door. At first she thought it was the shock of the news of Miss Pernsley's death. Then she thought it was just her; she was still feeling shaky from her early-morning remembrance as she'd sat on her back steps. But there was something else too. People were jumpy, smiling too much, trying too hard to be cordial. They were saying, "Praise the Lord," louder than usual with a determination, a hardness. They were like lovers on the verge of separation, when each partner knows it but they deny what's imminent and make love anyhow.

Reverend Schell was in his office, in an upper room just to the side of the main sanctuary and behind the Baptismal Pool. Willie Mann was with him too, and a representative from the city, Tom Moore, a tall, balding white man with a nervous tic that made his left cheek jump up and down as if he couldn't decide whether he wanted to smile or grimace. Reverend Schell sat behind his expansive wooden desk, a gift from his congregation acknowledging his thirty-fifth anniversary of pastoring the church. Willie Mann and Tom Moore sat catercorner one on each side of the desk. They sat where people usually did when they'd come for counseling.

Willie Mann was smiling. He handed Reverend Schell a small brown envelope filled with dollar bills that could have been a tithing envelope except that it bulged.

Reverend Schell waved the envelope away. "Can't accept that, I said. Can't really say that I understand all of this highway business, certainly

I can't accept money to endorse a plan I'm not even sure I understand."

Tom Moore coughed. Without looking up from a diagram spread across his lap that he seemed to study now, he said, "Just accept it as payment for your time, Reverend. That's all, no strings."

"But I don't even know all the details." He motioned to the stapled sheets of paper on his desk and patted his breast pocket. "Left my glasses at home so I can't even begin to read through the background. All I know for sure are the same rumors been floating around here for the past few months. That you want the people to sell their homes so y'all can come through and bulldoze for a highway. This little community is home to these people. Lot of these folks don't even travel north of Market Street or west of the Schuylkill River even. Plus, people start moving, it'll siphon off the membership rolls of the church. I don't think this highway business is gonna go over well, not well at all."

"Reverend, Reverend, Reverend." Willie Mann interrupted, and laughed softly as he allowed the envelope to slip from his hands onto the desk. "We're just talking tonight, sir. That's all."

"You keep saying 'we,' William. Explain your involvement." Reverend Schell leaned way back in his chair and peered at Willie Mann.

"I've been hired on as a consultant to what we"—Willie Mann laughed softly again—"they are calling simply the Highway South Project." He walked to the window with Reverend Schell's eyes still on him. "Lots of involvement, Reverend. Not just the city either, private concerns, even some state and federal. Big, big fish involved, Reverend. You ought to consider jumping on the wagon, sir. Quite a train"—he cleared his throat—"a gravy train, if I may say it and not be insulting." He returned Reverend Schell's stare. "It's the way things are done now, Reverend. It's 1956. That Eisenhower is a different sort, really. Maybe it's his military thinking, but his type don't go right to the people, they work through the leaders. So of course the first thing I said when I was approached about working with this project is that we need to bring Reverend Schell on board. A pivotal leader in this community, I told them."

Willie Mann walked back to his seat and glanced at Tom Moore. He didn't tell Reverend Schell that Royale owed the city for back real estate taxes, that he'd racked up citations for violating the blue laws when he served liquor on Sunday mornings, that he had been caught buying wholesale from a nonlicensed distributor in New Jersey. He didn't tell Reverend Schell that he was working with the project not only to protect the business Big Carl had built up over the years but also to keep his own pretty ass out of jail.

Reverend Schell swiveled his chair around so that his back was to them. He turned then to face Willie Mann. "The church," he asked, "is the church sitting in the path of the road?"

Willie Mann and Tom Moore exchanged glances.

"No," Tom Moore said. "Not at all."

"Not at all," Reverend Schell repeated, as if he had some doubt. He positioned his chair back to center so that he could see them both. He addressed only Willie Mann, though. "So I guess these big fish, as you call them, brought you on so you could pour a little persuasion with the whiskey, and now I'm supposed to pour my brand of persuasion with the prayer." He shook his head and drummed his fingers along the desk. "I don't think they'll move. Most of them won't. Too tied to this area. Won't move."

"But, Reverend"—Willie Mann stood and thrust his hands in his pants pockets and walked to the window and looked out again—"it's not a matter of whether or not they'll move; it's a matter of when. The people may reject Highway South's first offer, may say, 'No, we're not selling our homes.' No problem, we'll back off then, give them six months to think about it. Come back with another offer, some may still reject that. Still no problem. In the meantime some of the people will have moved by, say, the second offer. Their houses will be sitting, and since they'll be targeted for demolition, no one will certainly move in behind them. They'll be, you know, a change in the neighborhood. A year and a half from now, we anticipate they'll still be some holders-on, but think about it, Reverend, it's the people that make it a community, would you want to hang around when all your neighbors are jumping ship? Three years, this whole area should be cleaned out and ready to be razed." He walked back to the desk. "Yes, siree, in about three years, you won't even know this area."

"So why do you need me?" Reverend Schell asked. "You saying it's going to happen regardless."

Willie Mann leaned in almost to Reverend Schell's ear. "They'll need help cutting the cord, sir," he whispered. "They'll be coming to you, asking your advice; they'll be more amenable to move if you lead with the example, you know, that it's okay, better in fact than being crammed down here the way we're all crammed down here like sardines in a can. It's going to happen, like you've said, regardless. Better that it happen sooner. That's what we need you for, to keep them from challenging it, tying it up in a court battle that could go for years."

Reverend Shell held up his finger sharply. "And I'm supposed to go along with that and just watch my church membership fall off to nothing."

"We can set you up in a new church building." Tom Moore spoke. "You just tell us what area; that will be the least of your concerns. We can even match your salary if your membership falls off and your congregation can't meet your salary; that's not a problem."

"It's more than salary," Reverend Schell said, a measure of anger in his voice. "This church does a lot in this community. We put towards sending deserving ones to college, our young people's union gets out each and every Saturday and goes shopping for our sick and shut-in, they even wash down their steps if need be, we make sure our members have coal through the winter, we extend credit with our revolving loan program, so it's not just my salary."

"Understood," Willie Mann said quickly. "And you can still do all that, from here, if you choose to remain in this church building, or from much better surroundings." He rolled his hands as he talked and moved his shoulders in and out, and sat back and up until it looked as if he were conducting an orchestra. "Your—our people deserve better. Now's our chance to have better." His voice had an urgency to it.

Reverend Schell drummed his fingers again the way he always did when he was in deep thought. Both Willie Mann and Tom Moore watched the preacher's eyes stare blankly; they listened to each other breathe for several minutes. When Reverend Schell spoke again, his voice was dry and he had to clear his throat. "Let's just say I'm neither for nor against you right now. I need to pray on it. But I won't speak out against the highway right now. That's a help to you, trust me. If I go in that meeting now and tell the people to pay you no mind, you've got a fight on your hands."

Reverend Schell stood—his shoulders squared, eyes straight ahead, stately stance in his dark suit. He looked down at the bulging envelope on his desk. They all did. The room was completely quiet save the rumble in the sanctuary sifting into the office. The piano started to play; it was old and out of tune.

"Just payment for your time, sir," Willie Mann said again. "You're a leader. Your time is costly. We've had your ear for the past hour."

Reverend Schell cleared his throat and straightened the knot of his tie. "We really shouldn't keep the people waiting." His voice cracked, and he had to swallow hard. He picked the envelope up and dropped it quickly in his inside breast pocket where his reading glasses should have been. "No strings," he said. "And definitely no promises."

"They'll be more where that came from, Reverend, should you decide to come on board and be a full player in this venture." Willie Mann whispered it, almost gasped it, like the voice he used when he breathed into a woman's ear after he'd taken her on that couch in the cellar at Club Royale.

Noon and Fannie and Liz had made their way to the front of the church and found seats along the side aisle. They could see the members filing in. Liz listed them, trying to make Fannie laugh and chase away the strange look to her eyes. "There's Hurry-up Hank from the fish market, and here comes Johnnie Mae Makeup from Bea's Beauty Parlor, and there's Sad Sandra Saunders from the funeral parlor, and Look-Out-Louie, the number man, and Cross-the-Street-Dottie, mnh, Fat Barb getting bigger every day." Liz whispered out the ones she knew and made up names for the ones she didn't, and then she gasped and dug her hand into Fannie's arm.

"What's your problem, girl?" Fannie snapped, pulling her arm from Liz's tight grasp.

"Fannie, Fannie," Liz whispered, out of breath, "it's him, he's looking at me."

"It's who?" Fannie demanded. "Who the heck is worth you squeezing my arm to death?"

"Him, Fannie, it's him, Fine Willie Mann from Club Royale, he was just looking at me, Fannie, honest to God he was, I think he winked his eye." Liz had not yet told Fannie about her cup of tea the week before on the couch in Royale's cellar. She had meant to, but then Fannie had

had the vision of Miss Pernsley's death, and she was so irritable with getting her period, Liz thought it better to wait. Even now Fannie didn't look quite right to Liz. Her lean face looked even smaller, and her yellow skin easily showed shadows under her eyes.

Fannie shook her arm and rolled her eyes at Liz. "Him? Thinks he's too pretty for me. Miss Jeanie said you should never go out with a boy that thinks he's prettier than you. Plus he's not even a boy, gotta be well in his twenties. He's not worth the emotions, Liz."

"Who said anything about emotions?" Liz asked defensively.

"My bruised arm," Fannie blurted out so loudly that Noon told her to hush.

"Quiet now," Noon said, leaning her head so both Fannie and Liz could hear her. "They're getting ready to start, and I don't want to miss a word."

Noon sat very straight and still. Her memory earlier as she'd watched the sun come up still had her unsettled. The rest of the congregation had filed in and tried to settle down too. But there was still too much of a jumpiness in the air, a ferocity. And then Reverend Schell took to the center of the pulpit.

Reverend Schell didn't look immediately at the church body. He looked instead at the gavel he held in his hands, his dark hands almost lost in the darkness of the wood. The deep lines in his fingers almost matched the etchings in the gavel. He turned the gavel over several times, looked at it even more intently as he tried to guess the tree that the wood had been carved from. He shifted the gavel from one hand to the next, trying to guess its weight. The congregation got silent watching him. Even the scrambling toddlers stopped. They all watched him study the gavel. Finally he looked up. All at once he looked up and out at his waiting congregation.

"Let's open with prayer," he said in a voice somewhat raspy, drier than his usual richness of tone. He prayed hard. Eyes clenched tight. Hands opening and closing, arms raising and falling, head going up and down. "Bless us, Lord," he shouted.

"Please, Lord," the congregation responded.

"Take us through the storm, Lord," he sang.

"Yes, take us, please take us," the congregation sang back.

"Just give us Your guiding light, Lord."

"Please give us the light," they repeated.

He prayed for a full ten minutes, the congregation chiming in and helping him pray. He prayed a ferocious prayer.

And then he looked out on the congregation again. Suddenly they looked weathered. Many had worked all day as domestics, and dish-washers, and in factories making fine leather belts or fancy draperies. Some poured sand at the shipyard; some hacked freshly slaughtered, healthy-looking pigs. Some lifted heavy pieces of French Provincial furniture onto dark, musky vans; one or two had won at card games. Most had put in a hard day's work, he could see that. Even if it was spent fretting over how they were going to get milk to feed the babies or keep their son away from the prostitutes, or their daughter from the hustlers, or their wife away from that devil-filled Four Roses whiskey. Even the well-to-do property owners, the teachers, the shopkeepers, the government workers, the ones who had college and professions—they especially worked hard because they worked under the illusion of having made it. In the light of the upper sanctuary it all showed on their faces. Why shouldn't they have more than these tight blocks? he thought. As he scanned the congregation, he wrestled with his conscience. Knew that his judgment might likely be clouded by the bulging brown envelope he'd just slipped into his pocket. He tried now to convince himself that his people did deserve more than these South Philly blocks. Much more than these weathered expressions.

"It's no secret why we're here, Church, am I right?" he began.

"No secret at all," one shouted back.

"Seems the city has plans for this area we call home," he continued.

"They can keep their ole plans and do you know what with their plans," another voice said.

Nervous snickers rippled through the church. "Please, let's be respectful," Reverend Schell said. "Now the city, or should I say a representative from what's now being called the Highway South Project, has sent a representative to talk to us tonight. That's all we're going do tonight is talk. We're going to talk and listen, but nothing is going to be decided tonight. Let's just say we're in the phase where we're collecting information. Can we all agree to that?"

"Mnhuhs," and, "yes, Reverends," and, "sure nuffs just listen," and, "that's reasonable" floated around the church. Heads were nodding and turning to meet other heads in whispered "I guess it ain't no problem long as we're just talking."

"Now we're going to hear from Mr. Thomas Moore." Reverend Schell continued. "He'll probably be around to visit you-all over the next several months. My understanding is that he'll go block by block, tell you what your house is worth, make you an offer. Some of you may be ready to take him and the city up on the offer immediately. Some of you will tell him flat out no. But we'll all be prayful, prayful and respectful throughout this process that my understanding is can take some years. Now if we're in agreement, we'll hear from Mr. Moore." He looked down and motioned to Tom Moore.

Tom Moore was sitting at the front of the church, not up in the pulpit with Reverend Schell, but behind a school desk—type table at the front of the church. He wanted to sit in the pulpit, wanted to be able to look down over the congregation the way Reverend Schell did. But the good reverend had explained to him that only preachers were so exalted. So Tom Moore sat behind the small table looking awkward, looking almost as if he were being punished and had to sit in the front of the class where his classmates could jeer at him when the teacher wasn't looking. The congregation wasn't jeering, though. They were polite. Waiting, expectant.

Tom Moore stood; his cheek was going up and down; his glasses hung around the bottom of his nose. Right now he looked over the top of them. "Moonhead," Liz whispered to Fannie, who didn't respond; she was rubbing her eyes hard with her fist.

Tom Moore didn't look at anybody in particular, at least not for any length of time. He looked over them as he stood. He looked at the tops of their hair. He looked at their foreheads of black and brown and yellow and olive and tan and red. He looked at the creases in their furrowed brows. But he didn't look at their eyes.

"Reverend Schell is correct," he began. "I will be around to visit all of you who live in the affected area. The Highway South Project is prepared to purchase your homes and relocate you to more spacious areas in other parts of the city and maybe even out into the suburbs. I have no doubt you all will be pleased at the amount of money the city is prepared to offer, much more than the current worth of your properties."

"How you calculating worth?" one irate member shouted. "Some of us have kids in school down here we'll have to yank them out of."

"I don't have a car," another called to Tom Moore. "Everything I need I can walk right to. Am I gonna be able to do that somewhere else?"

"And how 'bout to getting to church?" Sister Maybell asked. "We supposed to have to get on a bus or trolley every time we ready to go to church?"

"Listen good," called one of the mothers of the church, "I'm in here every Saturday morning at the break of day washing down these pews with oil soap, so I don't want hear a thing about having to travel no distance to get here."

"Those City Hall white people don't understand our kinship with our blocks, why we even gonna listen to what they got to say?" asked Pop. "I have a business. How am I gonna be compensated, not just financially, but how they gonna replace the streams of 'Morning, Pop,' I get from y'all on your way to your day jobs."

They got louder as one by one they offered up their emotional ties to the neighborhood. A steady background chorus of why here, why now rose and fell and resonated through the building like a gospel song. The comments were circling so loud and fast that Reverend Schell had to bang his gavel and shout, "Order. We serve a God that does things decent and in order. Let's have some order here and now."

"You're asking individual questions that need individual answers," Tom Moore shouted when they had quieted down enough for him to be heard. "Just hear me out." He hated this part of his job the most. He liked the negotiating, the closing deals part of it, but this part, the group part, particularly when he had to deal with colored groups, he hated the most. They were so unreasonable or so easily led, he thought. Polar, either hot or cold, no middle ground with these people, he thought. "Like I said, if you all would just let me continue, I'll be quick and out of your way. We need the area where your houses now sit because this is where the road is slated to run. We really need your cooperation."

"I ain't cooperating at all," Noon whispered to Fannie and Liz. "Not at all."

Fannie squinted as she watched sweat gather along Tom Moore's forehead. Her head was pounding. Everything around her took on a clarity as if she had been seeing things through a dirty screen. She could even see the white marks along Reverend Schell's fingernails as his hands gripped the sides of the podium.

Tom Moore waved a red-tipped pointer in the air. The pointer looked like red lightning to Fannie as it cut through the yellowness of the church air. He unfolded maps and diagrams and indicated with the red-tipped pointer what was targeted to be torn down, leveled, demolished, swept up, so the highway could run through.

"You still haven't answered the main question. Why here? I mean, why now?" demanded Bow. Almost sixty years old, a member of the church for at least half that long. The muscles in his shoulders flexed through his light blue shirt as he put his whole body into his question.

Fannie saw the shirt as a light blue ocean giving up its tide as Bow's arms moved up and down and jabbed into the yellow air. She turned away so she wouldn't be swallowed by the tide.

"This is where it has to be," Tom Moore said. "We've studied this. Our staffs have worked overtime. I won't even bore you with the names of all the type studies we've done."

"Bore us," shouted Jeanie. She scowled at Tom Moore and repeated, "I said, bore us. Talk to us like you talk to your colleagues. We can understand. Explain the studies, what do they show, why does the highway need to be right here? And furthermore, why are there suddenly blocks and blocks of available houses in West Philadelphia? If it's so wonderful there like you claim, why's everybody suddenly moving?"

"Jeanie, if you don't mind, I'd like to hear him out," said Dottie.

"I want to hear him out too, Dottie," Jeanie shot back. "But I want some answers first. Sounds to me like they rode through the streets of West Philly like Paul Revere shouting, 'The colored are coming.' "

"You don't even go to this church, Jeanie." Dottie's voice was getting loud. "I don't know why you come here trying to monopolize things so the man can't even make his point."

"This a community meeting, not a church meeting," Jeanie shouted. "I'm a member of this community, a homeowner in this community, I think I have a right to have my questions answered."

"Mr. Moore," Dottie called, exasperated, "could you please just ignore this distraction and continue with your presentation?"

"What's the matter, Dottie?" Jeanie turned to the back of the church where Dottie sat. "Isn't your job secure yet? You been working for the city how long now? And you still have to be their neighborhood yes-girl."

"Who you think you're talking to? You half-breed, half-assed educated fool." Dottie moved out toward the aisle side of the pew.

"Ooh, Fannie, a fight," Liz whispered, sitting up, rubbing her hands together. "There's getting ready to be a fight."

But Fannie didn't respond. Her head was throbbing too much to respond. The colors had gotten too glaring. The red velvet strip that hung down the center of the wooden podium, the gold trim to the pages of the altar Bible, the orange and blue reflecting from the stained glass windows. The colors were too angry, too noisy. She balled her fists trying to anchor herself, to center herself. She didn't want to be beaten down by the intensity of the colors. Her eyes opened and closed hard and fast, and she started to bounce up and down in the pew.

Liz wanted to nudge Noon, to tell her Fannie must be getting ready to see something. But she didn't want to call attention to her. What if Fine Willie Mann was looking? He wouldn't understand that once in a while this happened to Fannie when she was getting ready to see something. He would think Fannie was crazy, probably think that about the whole damn family.

Liz didn't have to nudge Noon. Just as Dottie called Jeanie an atheist bitch, right out loud, she hollered it straight through the sanctuary, "Come on you atheist bitch," she said, and right when Jeanie planted her feet solidly where she stood as Dottie moved down the aisle with her fists raised to the beat of Reverend Schell's furious gavel, Fannie let loose.

She jumped up and shouted, "It ain't no road, it ain't no road." She was on fire, convulsing. Her arms flailed; her legs kicked; her hair stood on end, electrified. "It ain't no road, no road nowhere," she screamed.

Noon pulled Fannie down. Wrestled with her. Held her arms while Fannie shook. Liz tried to help hold Fannie down while she sloped in her seat and prayed that Willie Mann had left early. Noon pressed her face close to Fannie's. "What you see, Fannie? Tell me what you see."

"I don't see no road," Fannie moaned.

"What you see?" Noon pleaded. "Tell me, please, what you see?" Noon spoke deliberately, softly right into Fannie's ear.

"Houses, I see houses," Fannie whispered.

"Where you see houses? What kind of houses? Tell me, tell Noon what you see."

"Here, all around here," Fannie said, gasping in Noon's cradled arms. "Brick houses, bright, new, red brick."

"Shush, you sure it's here, Fannie?" Liz whispered, holding her head low. "Everybody's looking."

"Here!" Fannie yelled. Her eyes were shut tight; tears ran down her face. Noon dabbed at her cheeks with her handkerchief.

"Take your time, Fannie," Noon said, talking gently, encouragingly. "Do you see a highway?"

"No!" Fannie, said, and then her eyes opened all at once. "No," she said again, and then started to cry. "I don't see no damned highway. It ain't gonna be no road through here, Noon." She sobbed while Noon rubbed her back, and Liz tried to push down her hair that was wild and standing straight up.

"It's okay," Noon whispered. "It'll be okay."

Fannie's outburst got in the middle of the fight between Jeanie and Dottie. Broke it up better than the fifteen or so who had run center stage to try to prevent it. They gasped at a teenager having such an outburst as that.

"The devil in her," one of them said.

"What she say about houses, what was that all about?" another one asked.

"She might be right," another one insisted. "The chile just might know what she talking 'bout."

"Well, it don't give her no right to curse, the chile ain't getting proper home training considering that the one raising her think she so proper," said Dottie. "I would say she like her real parents, 'cept don't no one know who her real parents are. The chile could be a witch, could be the devil's chile for all we know. Act like someone possessed to me if I ever saw it."

"Can we go?" Fannie cried. "I just want to go home."

"Sure, baby, let's get you home," Noon said as she helped Fannie to stand.

She and Fannie and Liz moved out of the pew and down the aisle. The church was completely silent as the three moved up the center aisle to get to the door. They breathed in unison, it seemed: Noon and Fannie and Liz inhaled; the congregation exhaled. Even the colors settled down to a pattern. Liz kept her head looking at the floor, at the occasional feet pushed out into the center aisle. She was too embarrassed to look in the faces. Too terrified to look up and maybe see Willie Mann staring at her, shaking his head in disdain.

He wasn't. He smiled, in fact. Bared his perfect teeth from end to end. He looked at Fannie as she leaned on Noon. He liked her graceful slenderness. And her wild dark hair against her light skin, and the way the intensity of her eyes interrupted what could have been a soft face. He chuckled to himself at Fannie being called a devil's child.

They were right at his pew pulled along by the congregation's unified breaths. Willie Mann cleared his throat and grabbed Liz's hand and squeezed it. He winked and smiled right into her eyes, eyes that turned to saucers filled with shock before they melted into the look of a young woman in love.

TWENTY

Ethel stretched across the soft gold bedspread on the king-sized bed in her Harlem brownstone. It was afternoon in May, and a perfect breeze riffled through the leaves on the tree outside her window and sounded like bacon sizzling in a hot black skillet. She tore open an envelope with her done-up nails slicing through the paper like a penknife. She knew Willie Mann's handwriting. Most good-for-nothings got the nerve to have the best handwriting, she thought. She dumped the contents on her bed, tossed aside his note, and went straight for another envelope, opened it, and recognized it as an invitation. Oh, my God, she thought, it was an invitation to Fannie and Liz's sweet sixteen party. She read Willie Mann's note. "Just thought you'd like to know," it said.

She smiled when she thought about Fannie and Liz turning sixteen. My, my, my. Sixteen.

Her face broke out into a complete smile as suddenly the thought occurred to her to sneak back into Philly, spy on Liz at her party, see what type of young lady she was turning out to be. Even though Willie Mann pretty much kept her up-to-date with his persistent notes and letters, even sent her pictures a couple of times of year, she wanted to see for herself.

She stared at the invitation, at the word "sixteen" in big block letters and listened to the leaves sizzling and the antique wooden clock with the solid gold face ticking away on the stand next to her bed. Usually this time of afternoon she was preoccupied with songs for her set, what she'd wear, the next tour that always came too quickly on the heels of the last one, counting her money—making sure her manager wasn't cheating her. Or else she'd be thinking about what man she'd bring home after her set was done to share her passion that was too wide, so wide that she had to give it away. Night after night. If she wasn't free with her passion, she feared it might settle in her chest like a bad pneumonia and take her breath away.

But right now her mind was clear of all she had to do and she was thinking about Liz being sixteen. Suddenly she was cold stretched across the king-sized bed in only her black lace slip. So she wrapped herself up in the gold bedspread mummy style. She took a deep breath as if she were trying to reach a high note. She rolled herself tighter in the bed-spread and thought about what she could say to a sixteen-year-old about why she'd abandoned her.

She'd start off telling Liz about her mother, Coreen, how well she married, how smart her daddy was, had college even, had a good job as a chemist when they were all burned up in that car fire. She'd whisper to her about how her own mother had suffered from what her grand-mother called a weakness in the brain. Smart enough, but sometimes her judgment came from the weak part of her brain and made her do things without thinking: go out with strange men, bring them home with her all times of the night. That's why her grandmother had to raise Coreen and her.

And then Ethel wasn't even thinking about what she'd say to Liz anymore, rolled up in the soft gold bedspread. She burrowed her head in her arms and tried to blot out the loud ticking of her bedside clock. She didn't want to go back there because she knew she wouldn't be able to turn her thinking off when she got to that part. But she was back there anyhow, eleven years old and back there in Albany.

She and Coreen were standing by the front window waiting for their mother to pick them up from their grandmom's, where they had lived for the past year. It was like Christmas to Ethel, not that her grandmother wasn't a gem, but she reasoned everything living wants to be with its own mother. Her grandmom held them close and whispered, "Your mother's a good woman, just got a problem making decisions now and then. Sometimes when she gets tired, she listens to those voices coming from that weak part of her brain. Now she's been away resting for a full year, and those citified doctors say they can't tell whether or not it's gonna flare up again. So y'all got to be strong for her, and you got to tell me if she start slipping back to her old ways so I can reclaim you and get you raised up right."

They said, "Yes, ma'am," to their grandmother and waited by the window until they saw their mother coming up the road to get them. Pretty woman. Face got completely round when she smiled because her cheeks pushed out so, shapely curves to her hips and legs, soft skin had red tones to it, big innocent-looking eyes, a gentle brown. They ran and met her and jumped up and down all over her. Her hands shook a little when she gave them each soft pink hair ribbons and white anklet socks with the daintiest pink embroidery. Ethel made much over the socks but pretended not to notice her mother's hands; she just wanted her mother to take them home.

That first night back home with her mother was like heaven to Ethel. They slept in the same bed, the three of them. They snuggled against one another, and their bodies were like pieces of a jigsaw puzzle the way they just fit. They sighed in comfort, and Ethel felt as if she were floating as she went to sleep in her mother's arms. Those were the things she liked to remember about her mother. All that was good and honest about her. The lip-licking meals she'd cook from breakfast to supper. And how she'd kept their house clean as the inside of a church on Communion Sunday. And how she'd play old maid, and hide-and-seek, and any other kind of game that kept them in stitches, running and laughing and hugging when the game was done. She even wanted to think about her mother's hugs, how sometimes she'd hug them so hard and Ethel would feel something desperate in her arms. Years later Ethel came to understand it as a pleading. She wanted Ethel to save her with the hug. Hold her back from those voices trying to pull her to the other side of their cozy country house, voices that were stronger than her little girl's arms.

She stopped her thoughts and lifted her head. The clock on the nightstand seemed to be ticking right in her ear, so she rolled to the other side of the king-sized bed. "Loud-ass clock," she muttered as she shifted under the bedspread to get comfortable again so she could think about her mother's goodness.

But all she could think about right now as she listened to the leaves sizzling on the tree right outside of her window was that damned bacon frying. It was burning in the black skillet, and her mother was just shaking the pan back and forth, letting it burn. The smoke was white and rose to the ceiling and then just settled over her mother like a fog landing. She and Coreen stood there watching their mother's back muscles flex in and out as she shook the pan. They held hands like two children afraid to cross a busy road, still in yesterday's school clothes. They had fallen asleep by the front window the night before waiting for her to get home. The first time since they'd been back with her that she wasn't there when they got home from school. Smiling. Holding out her hands for them to guess which one held their after-school treat. Coreen had cried herself to sleep in Ethel's arms, and Ethel had consoled her as best she could considering that her own chest was on fire.

"Went to get bacon," her mother said, her voice wavering from shaking the pan. "That's why I was late, trying to find the best bacon in all of Georgia. Only the best for my girls."

"Bacon's burning, Mama," Ethel said gently. "Whole kitchen might catch fire in a minute."

"Bacon's burning." Her mother imitated her with a vicious-sounding voice, and Ethel felt a lump come up in her throat and Coreen's hand tighten around hers.

"Mama, are you okay?" Ethel was breathing hard, and the smell of the bacon as it burned was nauseating.

"Yes!" her mother shouted as she pulled the pan from the fire and stumbled to the sink and let the bacon fall into the sink. The sizzling echoed through the whole kitchen. "What do you think, I burn a little bacon and I can't raise you? You think you'd be better off with your grandmother, huh, go back to her then. Both of you, pack your bags and go the hell back."

Coreen started to cry and ran to her mother and wrapped her hands around her back. "Please, Mama, we want to stay with you, please let us stay with you. The bacon's okay, it's okay."

Ethel shuddered when she heard Coreen cry. She shuddered right now rolled up in the bedspread. In those six months that they had been back with their mother life had been perfect. She flexed her feet now under the spread and tried to shut her thinking down. But once she got to this point, she never could. The point when her mother turned around and the whole side of her face was raw flesh, as if she'd been dragged through the road all night long. Heavy black circles wrapped around both of her eyes, and her top lip was separated and still oozing blood.

Need to unwrap this damn bedspread right now, Ethel thought. Need to get up and put on some music. It was easier for her not to think about it if she had some music going. She tried to move from under the bedspread, but a chill had found its way through and raced inside of her from her toes to her scalp. Must be catching something, she thought. Probably need to close that window, storm must be kicking up out there or something. She couldn't get up, though. She was shivering too bad to get up. Even as sweat inched along her skin like a child's sticky fingers, she convulsed with chills.

The same way she got chills that morning when Alfred, their neighbor two doors down, tapped on the door and then walked on in. He was holding her mother's gold-toned beaded purse. Nice young man. Stocked the shelves and sometimes worked the cash register at the penny store in the center of town. Trustworthy young man looking clean and honest as he stood in their smoke-filled kitchen in a starched checkered shirt, waving away smoke with one hand and holding Ethel's mother's purse in the other.

"Morning, Miss Charlotte," he said, smiling the proud smile of someone doing a good deed. "You must have dropped this. Found it in my front yard this morning. Just peeped in it long enough to see the ID card in the little flap." Then his face turned to stone when he looked at her. "My God, Miss Charlotte, what happened?" He took a few steps closer in, waving away the smoke as he walked. "Are you okay? Maybe you should have that checked out." He walked closer still to get a better look, holding the beaded purse loosely in his hands.

Ethel always wished she'd cautioned him right then and there to run. She'd noticed the wild look that came up in her mother's eyes as she stared at the purse. She'd watched her mother's body stiffen more with each step he took toward her. And then it was like slow motion as her mother grabbed the paring knife from the silverware bin and let out a yell that made Ethel's blood go to ice and her skin bead up with chills. But by the time Ethel screamed at her mother to stop, it was too late. By the time she pushed Coreen out of the way and tried to get the knife from her mother's hand, her mother had already landed it over and over, yelling, "You, why you'd do this? Why you'd do this to me so my girls would have to see me this way?"

"It wasn't Alfred, Mama, it couldn't have been him. You're making a mistake, Mama. Stop, please, you're killing him, Mama." Ethel wrestled with her mother. Tried to hold her mother's hand high in the air in a distorted Indian wrestle that relied only on the smoky air for support. Ethel's little girl's arms were too short, too weak. As her mother pulled rank on her, showed her who was in charge in a final tug and wrench, Ethel's little girl's arms went along for the ride as the knife plunged right where Alfred's chest rose and fell.

Coreen ran out the back door, screaming for help, and Ethel's mother squatted on the kitchen floor, fading in and out of consciousness. Ethel took Alfred's head in her lap. "Don't die, Alfred, please don't die," she begged as she choked and gagged on her sobs. "She didn't mean it, Alfred, please don't die." She cried and pleaded to the erratic tune of the bacon still sizzling in the skillet in the sink as she tried to push the blood back in Alfred's chest that was spurting like wine from a fountain at a wedding feast.

Ethel was sweating now rolled up in the soft gold bedspread. She thought when she tried to explain to Liz why she'd left her, she'd have to tell her about Alfred. About that feeling she gets when a man moans in her ear right before his release, and his heart is pounding with such a weightiness to it until it seems it might just get so heavy until it just stops, and he's holding on to her for dear life. And she imagines it's Alfred. She's saving his life; she's freeing him up, giving him pleasure, saving his life over and over again, night after night. Liz would never understand, Ethel was certain, but if she were to tell her, she'd have to describe her appetite, her craving for a man's life force. That's where her redemption was. Not in raising little girls but in saving grown men. That's when she felt the purest, the cleanest, when she was exonerating her mother's crime by bringing a man back to life.

The afternoon was noisy under her window. The evening paper hit the door with a thump and sounded like a body being thrown against it. Schoolchildren were returning home. They crunched leaves under their thick-soled school shoes and turned the sizzle to a whip cracking. They clapped their hands hard in a rhyming game. One little girl with a voice sounding just like Liz's sang out louder than the others. "Old Lady Mack," she chanted, "all dressed in black, with silver buttons, all down her back. She asked her mother, for fifteen cents, to see the elephant, jump over the fence. He jumped so high, he reached the sky, and never came back; till the Fourth of July, lie, lie."

The gold-faced clock ticked to the beat of the chant and made Ethel realize how late it was. The little girl's voice, the tone to it, the way she said, "lie," went straight to Ethel's heart, changed it. Decided she'd skip the sweet sixteenth party after all. Maybe next year. Do this one more tour; then she'd think about going back.

TWENTY-ONE

Tom Moore couldn't have known this was the absolutely worst time to be walking up Noon's front steps. It was less than two hours before Fannie and Liz's sweet sixteen party at the Christian Street Y. Better that he'd walked in on their wedding day, or the day one or the other brought her firstborn home, not today, not while a tornado was spinning through that usually immaculate row house. Nerves frayed, like short-circuited wires popping and smacking with unpredictable sparks all over the place.

First Fannie and Noon. Fannie got a run in her nylon just as she attached it to her garter belt. Made her say, "Oh fuck!" Noon heard her. Ran into her room with her fist balled at hearing such language come from her mouth. Then Fannie told Noon she didn't know why she had to wear stockings anyhow. Furthermore, she was still upset with Noon for making her get her hair pressed out.

"I like it crinkly and bushy and pulled back in my pompoms," Fannie said.

"The hair don't have a thing to do with that language I heard coming out of your mouth," Noon retorted.

"No, I just look like one of the Lennon Sisters on *Lawrence Welk*, is all, with this straightened hair all the way down to my shoulders."

"The mouth, Fannie, I'm talking about the mouth."

"Awl, Noon, give her a break," Herbie called from downstairs. "If the worse she do is say a four-letter word every now and then, what the hell." He chuckled at his unintentional cleverness. "Now tell me which of these boxes spread all down here got to go to the Y."

"The bud vases, I told you the bud vases."

"What the hell's a bud vase?"

"The box with the vases wrapped in newspaper. Should be ten. One for each table. The carnations are in the icebox. My hospitality members from church gonna set it all up. Just make sure Maybell gets it. She's there already. And don't forget the cake. Lord Jesus, not after I was up half the night icing that cake, please don't forget the cake."

And then of Fannie, she demanded, "Go see if Liz got a nylon that comes close to matching this one. I'm gonna run my bath. And let me know quick if she doesn't. Have to catch one of those kids playing in the street to send them to the store."

Fannie pushed open the white wooden door to Liz's room. Liz had the larger room thanks to Fannie's generosity. The one with the walk-in closet that Noon said must have hidden slaves because people back then surely didn't believe in closets.

Fannie drew her breath when she looked at Liz. "Oooh, Liz, you're—you're beautiful." Liz's dress was white brocade, strapless, cinched at the waist with a wide pink satin sash, and then fanned out softly to the scalloped hem that hit just above her ankle. Her flaming red hair was freshly tapered, the rounded hairline prominent in the strapless dress. Her face was made up in lipstick and rouge and pink powdery shadow to her almond-shaped eyes.

Liz wrinkled her nose and went to her window and slammed it down. "Somebody on this block cooking cabbage, can't stand that rank smell of cabbage cooking, smell gets all in your clothes."

"What's your problem?" Fannie asked as she went to Liz's stockings drawer and rifled through it.

"Number one, don't be rummaging through my drawer. Number two"—she lowered her voice and sharpened the ends of her words—"there is no way I'm wearing this jacket." She held up the jacket that matched her dress. Waist-length, leg-o'-mutton sleeves, scalloped neckline to go with the dress's hem.

"What's wrong with the jacket?"

"Look at the sleeves," she said, letting the jacket dangle by one sleeve.

"What about the sleeves?" Fannie turned from the dresser to study the jacket.

"They're puffy."

"So."

"So! So, they look homemade. Noon's not good with sleeves. I asked her not to put sleeves to the jacket."

"Just put the damn jacket on, you know how hard Noon worked on that dress. I haven't seen her work as hard on anything as she did on that dress."

"I'm not wearing the jacket," Liz said as she smacked it against the bed as if she were trying to swat a fly. "I won't go before I have to wear something botched up looking like this jacket looks."

"Well, guess what—you should have made your own fucking jacket. You being spoiled and ungrateful."

"Why should I have to settle because my ability to see the flaws is greater than Noon's ability to do sleeves?"

"What? What are you saying? Studying Plato or some damn body." Fannie started going through Liz's drawer again. "Think about Noon's feelings, put the jacket on, and loan me a stocking to match this one so I can finish getting dressed."

"You weren't so concerned about Noon's feelings when you was around here all afternoon yelling at her about your hair."

"Clara did the hair, Liz. Noon's hands didn't get crampy and stiff taking hours on the hair. The hair and the dress are two entirely different things."

"Well, I don't appreciate the way you holler around here whenever you get ready, and as soon as I have the least complaint, I got to be selfish and spoiled. Furthermore, my stockings are too short for you and I don't wear anything that light anyhow. You should have thought about extra stockings when you got paid like I did. I told you I could use my discount at Betty's for your stockings—"

Right then there was a crash of a noise downstairs, followed by Herbie's voice saying, "Oh, shit!"

Then Noon's voice rising and falling to quick thumps bounding down the steps. "Not the vases, Herbie, please tell me not the vases!"

Silence. Then Fannie and Liz looked at each other and in dreadful unison said, "The vases."

🐍

Tom Moore's cheek was jumping up and down as he rang the bell to Noon and Herbie's house. He knew it was late on a Friday evening to still be making calls. But he had a meeting first thing Monday with the board of the Highway South Project, wanted to squeeze in as many calls as possible between now and then. His stomach was full and tight. He hoped Noon didn't offer him anything to eat. They all offered him something when they asked him to take a seat at their dining room tables. Ham hocks and beans, coffee and pie, port wine, ice cream, Jell-O and pound cake, quick bread, peanuts and mints, a slice of fruit, a chunk of cheese, a slab of ham on lettuce. He hated that about them, that they had to be so courteous. Especially when he sat at some of the dining room tables and they pieced together pennies to send to the corner store for an envelope of Kool-Aid just so they could offer him that. He especially hated when the poorer ones laughed. And the half-dressed, barefoot children played outside on the pavement waiting to grow up. For what? he wondered. Grow up for what? God, how he hated this project.

The door opened with such force that he stepped back at first. "A quarter apiece," he heard a woman's voice moaning. "I paid a quarter apiece for those vases. Now what we supposed to do for centerpieces? What we supposed to sit the carnations in? Water glasses!"

And then to him, a male voice: "Can I help you please? Well, don't stand there like you scared, you letting flies in, come in or stay out, one."

"Tom Moore," he said as he quickly pulled a card from his shirt pocket and touched his cheek to still it some. "I represent—"

"The people trying to chase us out is who you represent," Herbie said as he closed the door behind him. "I got an earful from the wife about you the other night when you did your pitch at the church."

"Mr. Moore," Noon said, a greeting and a question at the same time, remembering Reverend Schell's plea to at least be courteous when Tom Moore called. She walked toward the door where Tom Moore stood.

"If this is a bad time—" He extended his card to Noon.

"It is, it's a very bad time," Herbie called over his shoulder as he stomped toward the back of the house with the box of newspaper-tangled broken glass.

"Listen, Mr. Moore, you can come on in," Noon said, exasperated. "I can offer you some lemonade, but it won't take me too long to tell you I'm not interested."

"But once you understand the facts," he said as he looked around the living room, freshly painted, well maintained, very neat, save the clump of flowers and boxes on the floor. "You stand to make a huge profit on this house, you own it, you've got a clear title, even your taxes are up-to-date."

"She said we're not interested right now." Herbie walked back into the living room carrying the box with the cake.

"Lord have mercy, Herbie," Noon breathed, "please be careful with the cake." And then to Tom Moore: "I wasn't looking to move on account of a road. Now I don't even believe there's gonna be a road, so you can well imagine I'm definitely not looking to move for a lie of a road."

"I think we should hear him out," Liz said as she and Fannie made their way down the steps.

From where he stood in the living room, Tom Moore had a clear view of Fannie and Liz on the steps. The one looking like a bride, the other in a housecoat, one foot bare, and a stocking dangling from her hand. He thought about Fannie's outburst when he looked at her. He'd have a hell of a time explaining that to the board. He didn't even understand it himself. Real estate was his specialty. Not this hocus-pocus seeing eye business and all the singing and praying and preaching these people did. "Just get it done," the board had told him. "Do what you have to to prevent the court challenges that could tie it up for years." How could he explain that it might take somewhat longer now that some of these property owners may have been fueled by a teenager who thought she had a vision?

"Grown folks talking, Liz," Herbie said as he rested the cake on the coffee table and picked up the bunch of carnations.

Liz rolled her eyes and pushed past Fannie to come all the way down-stairs. "Julep's cousin lives in West Philly, and she has a huge house, three floors, a porch, a backyard where they barbecue. You can even get to upstairs through the living room or the kitchen."

"Julep's people come from money, Liz," Noon said, looking at Liz in the dress. "God, that dress is fabulous if I say so myself." Her voice went quiet as if she were watching a sunset. "Can't wait to see it in the jacket. Mnh, that hem is perfect. Those scallops took some time, but they were worth every minute."

"When she start wearing makeup?" Herbie asked, looking at Liz now too. "Maybe that's what made her think she could talk like she's grown, 'cause she got on a little lipstick."

"Why is he here?" Fannie asked, motioning to Tom Moore with the hand that held her torn stocking. "I thought we had a party to go to." She said it more to prevent the back and forth between Herbie and Liz that had intensified over the years and threatened to turn ugly than to make Tom Moore actually leave the house.

"Fannie, what did I tell you about your manners?" Noon smoothed at the pink satin sash adorning Liz's white brocaded dress.

"Fannie's got a point." Herbie waved the carnations up and down as he spoke; pink and white petals began to litter the floor. "Riled up as you were over this road thing the other night after you left that meeting at the church, and now you actually gonna give it an audience."

"Noon," Liz whined, "he's getting ready to do with the carnations what he just did with the vases."

"You wanna trade places with these carnations," Herbie said, looking at Liz with a flash of anger.

"Come on, Liz"—Fannie tugged on her arm—"please help me find a matching stocking."

Tom Moore coughed and hit his chest and rubbed his cheek again. "Well, if one of you, an adult, could sign that I've been here and presented the option to you—"

"No-o-o, siree." Herbie dragged it out. "We ain't signing nothing."

"Well, it's just to say that I've been here. I've got bosses to please. Or— or if you just tell me when I can come back, at your convenience, at least if you hear the offer, the dollar amount—"

"What's it gonna hurt to hear the dollar amount?" Liz asked from halfway up the steps.

"Won't be needing to come back at all." Herbie opened the front door. "What else besides the cake needs to go, Noon?"

"That bag sitting in the corner with the crepe paper and balloons. And you could stop past the church and see if they're any vases we could borrow; otherwise no need in even taking the carnations."

"Royale got some vases. Big Carl'll be glad to help out. You can follow me on out the door, Mr. Moore; like I said, we're not changing our minds on this thing."

Tom Moore hurried down the steps behind Herbie. He started to offer to help him carry the large box, the brown paper bag, the flowers. Then he remembered Willie Mann had told him Herbie was a porter; used to having his hands full, he thought. No need in offering to help now. He'd be as bad as they were if he started offering shit.

TWENTY-TWO

Big Carl sent the vases, the church sent linen napkins, and pink and white crepe paper crisscrossed the ceiling and dipped in the center where the dance floor was. The room was expansive and dimly lit and smelled sweet and salty like mints and peanuts and Noon's butter cake. All of the Young People's Usher Board, friends from the block, and around the corner, and classmates showed up with gift-wrapped packages or cards with quarters, no doubt, taped inside.

The young women were off in one corner, throngs and clumps of satin and lace, seamless hose, hot-curled bangs, and patent leather clutch bags. The young men in another, wearing single-breasted suit jackets and baggy pants with cuffs at the hem, strong cologne from South Street Drugs, and waves in their hair from sleeping in stocking caps and Murray's hair pomade the night before.

Right now nobody danced, only the balloons as they bobbed to the beat of the Platters singing "Only You." Fannie swayed to the rhythm and grinned in her pink and white flowered, cocktail-length blouson dress with slightly mismatched stockings; Liz sulked in her jacket with the puffy sleeves. Julep and her cousin were all over Liz, telling her how gorgeous she was, what shade of lipstick was she wearing, and the pearls, those pearls must be antiques. Liz looked at them in their store-bought evening wear from Snellenberg's, peeled the jacket to reveal her strapless dress, said the lipstick was by Helena Rubenstein; fingered the pearls that were Noon's, and said yes, yes, of course they were antiques.

Herbie and Noon, Maybell and Jeanie and Bow sipped coffee next to the table that held foil-draped trays of chicken wings, sliced ham on lettuce, and hors d'oeuvres made with Vienna sausage and Colby cheese. Bow was describing the shape of Jackie Robinson's head, he knew because he'd just cut his hair that very morning, and Herbie, tired of the story already, decided he'd get the party started by dancing with the prettiest sixteen-year-old that ever lived.

Now the Dells were singing "Oh, What a Night" as Herbie sauntered across the room, all eyes on him. He extended his hand to Fannie and bowed slightly, his Cab Calloway bow. Fannie was all teeth as she threw her head back and laughed out loud. She put her hand in his and let him lead her in dance.

"Well, daughter, might I say you're looking smashing tonight," he said as he held Fannie loosely around the waist and spun her across the floor.

"And, Father, you are quite debonair."

"Well, tell your old dad, how does it feel to be sixteen?"

"Well, you tell me, dear old dad, you've been there."

"Look"—he fell out of voice—"don't remind me about being sixteen or I will declare you off limits to any of these think-they-hep-cats getting within two feet of you. Furthermore, you see how we dancing right now, don't nobody have no right getting any closer than I am right now. And if they do, I'm, I'm—"

"Oh, Herbie, you so cute." Fannie kissed him on the cheek.

"I ain't gonna be cute if I see anybody even act like they putting the moves on you—"

Then Herbie felt a tap on his back. He hunched his shoulders to shake it off. Again. Again he shook it off. Then he heard laughter; the whole room laughed. Then Fannie yanked his arm and stopped following his lead.

"Herbie, he's trying to cut in." She laughed too.

"What? Oh, oh, I was wondering what that was on my back, I thought it was one of these balloons that's floating all over the place." He turned to the young man, Pop's nephew from Norristown. "You drink or smoke, boy?"

"Herbie, it's just a dance." Fannie shook his arm again.

Herbie stepped back and extended Fannie's hand to Pop's nephew. "I got my eye on you, boy. Anybody with enough nerve to cut in on me, I'm keeping my eye on."

Fannie winked at Herbie and mouthed the words "Dance with Liz."

But Herbie didn't want to dance with Liz. Liz would suck the air through her teeth, roll her eyes up in her head, complain that he was out of step, ask him why was he still wearing that cheap Old Spice. When he looked in Liz's eyes, he still saw remnants of that anger and fear he'd seen that night when she shocked him in the hallway. With Fannie, though, he'd see his own reflection. Like the way she looked straight at him that predawn morning he'd pulled her from the pink-lined box, the way she looked at him tonight; made him feel he was good and decent and full of honor when she looked at him like that. He was back along the fringes of the room. The Dells were holding their notes at the part of the song "That's why I love you so-o-o-o." Herbie swallowed to get rid of the lump that came up in his throat as he watched Pop's nephew take Fannie in the circle of his arms, holding her closer, much closer, than he ever had.

"Your father's funny," Julep's cousin said to Liz. "It killed him to give up Fannie's hand for someone else to dance with her."

"I hate to see him on her wedding day," Julep said. "When the preacher says, 'Who gives this bride in holy matrimony?' he'll probably look around and say, 'Well, somebody else better say something, 'cause I ain't giving her up.'"

Julep and her cousin laughed identical laughs, and Liz forced a smile. "He's silly," she said. She couldn't keep the ice from her voice when she said it, and Julep and her cousin looked at her, startled. "He's all right, I guess," she added quickly. "He doesn't have a lot of class or anything, but as fathers go, he'll do."

"Speaking of doing," Julep asked as she flicked a bit of crepe paper from the back of Liz's dress, "what's the latest on you and Fine Willie Mann?"

"You mean since my cup of tea in the wine cellar?" Julep and her cousin squealed when Liz said that, and they joined hands and huddled in a circle so Liz could tell them again how he'd squeezed her hand, and stroked her arm, and understood her as nobody ever had.

The dance floor was getting crowded. They were looser now, mixing. Long legs and arms moved to the sounds of Little Richard, Fats Domino, the Flamingos. The young men sneaked a grind when the records went slow, and when the music sped up, the ladies, shy and demure at the party's start, shook their assets and twirled and teased.

The food was served up from bottomless pans, but with so many throats and other body parts to cool, the punch went much too fast. It was late; Pop's was closed, so Herbie made a call to Club Royale and asked Big Carl to send over a case of Frank's orange soda in quart bottles, "Quick," he said. "Need to bring the temperature down on fifty dry-mouthed teens." Big Carl responded. In under ten minutes the soda was there, hand delivered by Big Carl's right-hand young man.

Liz was in the bathroom when Willie Mann arrived. She was touching up her lipstick, which had rubbed off when she'd eaten a chicken wing. She'd wished Noon hadn't served fried chicken. The finger sandwiches Julep's mother always served would have been more appropriate. But she had to eat the chicken. Especially after the disappointment that had washed over Noon's face when she'd told her that she didn't think the jacket added to the dress. Right as Noon attached the pearls around Liz's neck, Liz had blurted it out quickly, then looked away, then caught Noon's reflection in the mirror. Noon's soft skin tightened in a way that went straight to Liz's stomach and made her want to cry. She had to wear the jacket after that and eat the chicken wings and the too-thick slices of ham on lettuce.

When she walked out of the bathroom and into the gray hallway that connected to their party room, she had a clear view to the dance floor. She had to stop where she was to laugh out loud as Fannie jumped around in the middle of the dance floor imitating Dick Clark's *American Bandstand*. They'd tried to get in one afternoon, walked all the way to Forty-sixth and Market, where the show was broadcast, watched the white kids in bobby socks and hoop skirts saunter on into the place like they owned it. And when it came to Fannie, Liz, and Julep, the man at the gate said simply, "Sorry, kids, can't let you in, capacity limits, it's the law."

"Who wants to get in there anyhow?" Fannie had said all the way home. "This is how they dance." And she'd kept it up until it broke Liz's mood and she had to give in and laugh.

Now Julep was on the dance floor with Fannie, and it was twice as funny, and Liz was just about to pass through the grayness of the hallway, back into the party room, she'd run onto the dance floor with them, Fannie would really put on a show when she saw Liz out there. But then she saw him instead. He walked right out of the men's room right into that hallway where she stood.

Black shirt, white jacket, the slicked-back hair, the smile, the smile, the smile. She touched the wall lightly, for support, commanded her knees that they would not buckle, then extended her hand. "Why, Willie Mann, so nice of you to come to our party."

"I wished I'd been invited," he said as he squeezed her hand. "I just dropped off the soda. I'd seen the invitation your father had given Big Carl, but Herbie doesn't care for me much, and then you didn't even mention it the other day."

"I didn't think you'd want to be in a room full of teenagers." She looked at the weavings in the black shirt, the marbleized buttons.

"Liz," he said, "if I'd known you'd be here, looking like you just stepped out of a fairy tale about a beautiful, very beautiful young lady, I would have been here, and stayed here, and enjoyed myself just watching you laugh."

His words were like silk to her in this hallway that was dark and close and out of view. She just wanted the softness of his words to wrap around her, to make her feel rich and precious, the way Fannie must have felt rich and precious when Herbie had bowed and asked her to dance.

"Tell me the fairy tale," she said as her eyes moved up the buttons on his shirt. She counted them as she listened to him breathe.

"Let's see," he whispered as he moved in closer, fingered the back of her pearls. "There's a beautiful lady with red hair who lives with a kindly stepmother, a sister who's half crazy, and an evil, fire-breathing step-father."

Liz smiled and touched the button on his shirt right at his collarbone.

"She has an aunt who sings who really doesn't know what she gave up when she left our red-haired girl. If she only knew, she'd take her, you"—his fingers left the pearls and squeezed her neck—"and rock you in her arms like I wish I could."

"You can." Her voice declared it while her eyes begged.

He pulled his hand from her neck, thrust it in his pants pocket. "Liz, you're so young, too young. I shouldn't be talking to you like this—"

"But I'm sixteen now."

"Sweet sixteen," he said, "so very sweet."

"And never been kissed." She said it seriously, her eyes agreed.

"Never?" He half laughed.

"Not in a meaningful way," she said, thinking that if she were to give in to her urging in this hallway the way she wished she had in the cellar at Club Royale, it had to be now. Now, while Fannie held everybody captive, in stitches, with her floor show; in another minute the song would stop, people would appear in that hallway to use the bathroom or to see where she was. It had to be now.

She reached up and wrapped her arms around his neck. His cologne was light and easy for her to breathe. She could feel the grains of linen in his jacket as she moved her hands along his back. His lips were thin and soft as she pushed her mouth against his.

It was a hungry, openmouthed kiss. The longing in the kiss caught him off guard. Made him wonder what she was starving for. Ethel. Maybe, but more than that even. When he could, he peeled his lips from hers. He kissed her nose, her forehead, her chin. "I've got to get back to the club," he said.

"Take me with you."

"You know you can't go in there, you're too young."

"Those fast girls from Fitzwater Street go in there all the time."

"Liz, enjoy your party with your family and friends; this is where you belong."

The Ink Spots were singing "If I Didn't Care." She watched his tall back in the white jacket move against the close hallway air. She could hardly breathe. Fannie was on the dance floor again with Pop's nephew; he was getting bolder, holding Fannie the way he did when they met over Julep's when Julep's mother was away. Now she could hear the familiar squeals of Julep and her cousin as they ran down the hallway.

"Liz, Liz, there you are," Julep said. "You missed him, Liz, he was just here, Fine Willie Mann was just here!"

"This is the best, the absolutely best party I have been to in my entire life," her cousin chimed. "Come on, Julep, let's go check our hair."

People were streaming into the hallway to get to the bathroom. Then Noon turned in. "There's my baby, I been looking for you. You just missed your sister acting the fool. I'm gonna put that girl on *Ted Mack's Amateur Hour* yet. We gonna sing 'Happy Birthday' and cut the cake directly."

Liz tried to breathe as the gray hallway air caught in her chest. It filled up in her, even down to the circles in her stomach. She couldn't even understand it when she ran to Noon and hugged her and started to cry.

PART IV

PART IV

TWENTY-THREE

Philadelphia winters could be brutal; February was the worst month of all. The sun lied so. Rolled out of bed with a wink and a smile across the sky as if it were going to do something, cut through the blustery air or at least melt the ice that settled overnight. Nothing, though. Just hung there looking pretty until it was time for it to go in and anybody outside prayed that maybe the moon would do what the sun hadn't.

By 1959 Herbie knew about February in Philadelphia. He was severely bundled as he headed home from the north side. He'd stopped off at the Moonglo café after work; he'd taken to Arch Street for his physical release. The moans and body thrusts on Thirteenth Street had gotten predictable. And the women there on that third floor ace-deuce-tre knew him well enough now to want to try to talk. Herbie didn't want conversation. Just wanted to be able to whisper Ethel's name and pay his tab and leave. Didn't want the women there thinking they understood him. The way Dottie tried to act as if she understood him. The day when Fannie busted Dottie's daughter in the nose, Herbie had to drag Dottie home before she and Jeanie started fighting, and then he had to stay to convince Dottie not to call the police and press charges against Fannie. The only way he'd been able to do that was to move with her passion when she'd pinned him against her dining room wall, whispering, "Please, please, Herbie, please. I know what you need." He avoided Dottie after that, lest she'd be led to believe she understood him. Only three women ever had. His mother, and she was dead. Noon, she was dead in a sense. Ethel, might as well be dead. So he took to Arch Street, where he was a stranger and didn't have to worry about understanding.

He turned onto South Street. Even in the twilight he could see how South Street, the whole neighborhood, was starting to show signs of wear and tear. He occupied his mind against the cold by counting who'd moved out in the almost three years since they'd been approached about selling their house: Betty's Dress Shop had packed up and left, Freddie's Bar & Grill, Hank's Clean 'N Press. And the bad part, he thought, is that the properties were just sitting, no one sweeping in front of them, or washing down the sidewalk, or scraping the paint when it peeled so fresh coats could be spread. He trod lightly over the icy remnants of last week's snow; no one was even shoveling in front of these places. He was beginning to believe that maybe Noon was right when she spouted off about a plot to get them out, not for a road but just so they could come in and redevelop and turn it into a high-priced, ritzy area for white folks to live. Plot or no plot, he knew he didn't appreciate the way their real estate taxes were shooting up. Got mad about that every time he walked through here, which was why it hadn't taken much for Jeanie to convince him to join in a class-action challenge to the tax assessment with the thirty other homeowners crowded around his dining room table for one of their long-running meetings. The same lawyer was handling it who'd handled Liz's adoption all those years ago. He was running title searches to see what these abandoned properties were assessed at. Herbie wished he'd hurry up. He had had to put the tax money in an escrow account, and he could sure use it to help pay Fannie's tuition at Lincoln. Fannie had alienated so many teachers with her smart mouth, no one recommended her for a scholarship. At least Liz was on a full academic scholarship, thank God for that and for the church, which had chipped in to help Fannie from their education fund. Otherwise Fannie and Liz would have had to flip a coin to see who got to go.

He adjusted his scarf higher on his face and blew into it so his breath could warm his cheeks. This whole road thing was taking a lot of time and energy to oppose. Noon was running herself ragged over it too. In fact she was actually turning into one of the leaders of this whole crusade. Egged on by Jeanie, of course. They'd sit and talk for hours, and Noon would start using language that sounded foreign, like eminent domain, gentrification. He'd have to stop her, tell her to get an interpreter if she wanted to talk like that. And then she'd always come back to Fannie's vision, "You can understand that, can't you?" she'd snap at him. "Chile saw it, plain as day; she said it's no road. Houses, she saw red-brick well-built houses." He wasn't sure about the vision part of it. Had always attributed Fannie's visions to part lucky guess, part coincidence, part intelligence. Figured when a child had a quick mind like Fannie's, she just processed the logic without letting the steps show. The way old folks down home said it was gonna rain even when the sun was hot and bright. Then, sure enough, it'd turn dark and rain. If he didn't know they were basing it on a combination of their swollen joints, the way the birds were taking cover, the direction of the wind, he'd have thought they were psychic too. Tried to explain it that way to Noon. She wouldn't accept it. As far as she was concerned, Fannie had the gift of sight, and that's all there was to it.

He turned onto Lombard Street, which remained surprisingly intact considering how the blocks all around it were starting to fall. A clear path not troubled by ice or snow ran the entire length of the block. People had even started putting awnings up on Lombard Street. They had just gotten theirs. Bright red. Fannie had talked Noon into getting red.

Ɩ

He walked into the house, into the kitchen, where Fannie sat at the table staring into one of her oversized textbooks. He yanked on her thick puff of a ponytail.

"What's up, daughter mine?" he said as he started peeling off his hat and gloves and scarf.

"Just the books," she said, grimacing.

"You didn't go in to work at Pop's today? Saturday. Thought you worked there every Saturday. To hear him tell it, you practically run the place, said he might leave the place to you in his will." Herbie laughed.

"Studying. Midterms coming up," is all Fannie said.

"Never saw you read this much, ever, not during your whole twelve years of school. Not even last year, when you were a senior." He pulled back a chair and sat and strained as he kicked off one boot and the other and then sighed. "Ooh, feels good in this kitchen. You in the right spot, I tell you that, 'cause outside's no place to be."

Fannie kept reading.

He noticed her eyes were frowning as she read. "You sure you and Pop's nephew didn't have a lover's spat, and he convinced Pop to fire you?"

"I'm sure," she said nonchalantly. "Actually Pop's nephew is working for me today, you know, doing me a favor 'cause I'm just swamped."

"You mean to tell me," he said as he got up and walked his boots and coat into the shed kitchen, "you wait to get in your first year at that Lincoln U to let it start getting hard."

"I guess," she said, trying to sound absentminded about it. She didn't want to admit that she'd fallen behind, way behind. Because then she might have to admit that all those nights she'd spent on campus because she'd gotten so absorbed at the library, she'd told them, and missed the last bus back to Philly, but not to worry, she had plenty of friends in the dorms who would lend her a sleeping bag and floor, it was mainly one friend, Pop's nephew from Norristown, who'd pick her up at the library, sneak her back to his dorm room at Cheyney State Teachers College, where she never slept on the floor.

"I guess Noon's over Jeanie's," he said as he came back into the kitchen.

"You guessed it," she said, never taking her eyes from the page.

"And Liz?"

Fannie pushed the sleeves of her sweatshirt higher on her arms. It was blue and faded and given to her by Pop's nephew. "Probably in her room doing what I'm doing if she got any sense." She hoped Liz had that much sense. Probably in that closet going at the wall like somebody crazy. At least she was in the house, though. For a change she wasn't laying up in that cellar at Club Royale. She'd tried to talk some sense to her just before Herbie got home. Liz had come in from her Saturday job at Wanamaker's, and after Fannie told her that no one should be spending the kind of money on boots that she was sure Liz had spent on the black suede ones she was wearing, and damn, was that another new dress, ribbed knit at that, how many dresses could a person wear in a lifetime, and she wished she would stop using that light-ass powder on her face, as pretty as the color of her complexion is, if she were Liz she'd tell John Wanamaker, fuck you and this job if I got to be high yellow just to work on the selling floor, after she'd gotten beyond all that, she told Liz she had to start making it to class or she would surely lose her scholarship. But Liz just reminded her that at least she'd gotten a scholarship. And then Liz threw Pop's nephew in her face, told her not to come off like Miss Polly Pure Bread to her. So Fannie only ended up defending herself, telling Liz how at least she did take that long bus ride every day to go to classes, and by the time she saw Pop's nephew, she had put in some time with her books. And at least Pop's nephew could put on a jacket and tie and come by on a Saturday evening, shake hands with Herbie, chat with Noon, and then take her out on a date in a respectable way. She'd like to see Willie Mann try that. Especially the way he was working to undo all the challenges Noon and Jeanie and their group had filed against the latest barrage of zoning notices.

She didn't notice that her eyes had drifted from the page and that she was staring off in space. Herbie did.

"Stuff on your mind," he said as he squeezed her shoulder.

"Just trying to understand what I just read."

"Tell me about it," he said as he sat back down quickly. "Might help it sink in if you try to explain it."

She stared at her page again.

A ham was baking in the oven. He could smell the cloves. "You not in trouble?" he asked.

She raised her eyebrows as she underlined words in her book.

"You know, family way kind of trouble?" He asked it quickly, sneaked it in as he took a breath so that it sounded like a whisper.

"Herbie!" She slammed her book shut. "How could you ask me that?" Thinking that if he only knew how careful she was, how careful Pop's nephew was. And now the fact that he'd asked her meant that he assumed they were doing it, and she was embarrassed at the assumption, even if it was true, so the only respectable response was for her to act as if it wasn't. "I'm appalled that you even think that, could form your lips to—"

"Fannie, Fannie," he said defensively, "I mean, Pop's nephew been hanging around here more and more. You know, and I've never actually talked to him about his intentions, I was just waiting to see if anything really developed, so"—sweat started to shine on his brow—"awl, I feel stupid now. I had no right to ask you that. You're eighteen years old, for Christ's sake. I'm relieved, though. Damn." He stood up. "I'm just gonna take my dumb, relieved behind from this table and let you study."

"Herbie." Fannie called him back.

"Yeah," he said from the dining room.

"Liz could probably use some talking to." She hunched her shoulders ready for his barrage of excuses of why he couldn't.

"Lord, Jesus, Fannie, please," he said. "I'd do just about anything for you, you know that, but please don't ask me to talk to Liz. You know me and Liz can't be in the same room ten minutes without going at it. I can't talk to that girl."

She didn't have to turn and stretch to look in the dining room to know he was shaking his head. And now he was mouthing the word "damn." And now scratching his head, considering it.

"What about?" he asked, right on cue.

"Nothing in particular. You know, just tell her you're there for her, if she ever needs it, you know in a fatherly sort of way."

"Like she don't know that. Come on, Fannie, I know there's bad air between Liz and me, but she got to know if she needs me, I'm there." He walked back into the kitchen. "You understand what I'm saying, I know you do."

Fannie did. She shook her head that she did. "I just wish you and Liz talked more, that's all. Like you talk to me."

"Don't try to be a snake charmer, Fannie. Liz and you are different, different temperaments. If I'd tried to ask her what I just asked you, it wouldn't exactly come off like, what's his name on *Father Knows Best*, talking to his daughter, you know a hug and that soapy music they play. I might be trying to pull one of those butcher knives out of my chest right about now."

Fannie laughed, an embarrassed laugh as she thought about Pop's nephew again.

Herbie noticed her embarrassment; she looked away, and a rash of red flooded her forehead. He was so unaccustomed to seeing her like that. He sighed and walked back out of the kitchen. "I'mma change and see if I got the nerve to step back outside to that cold. Hit the club maybe. Tell Noon don't hold dinner for me, rib night at Royale." He paused. "If you think of it, tell Liz I asked about her too."

Right now Liz was in her walk-in closet, where the hole had grown along the seam from the floor to almost the ceiling, where she kept her thick wooden coat-tree, and along the baseboard, the full width of the closet, where she kept her shoe boxes stacked. She promised herself that when the hole got yea big, she'd stop. Until it was yea plus several inches, and she was adding another shoe box. Sometimes the hole seemed to have legs and feet the way it crawled along the wall, and the outline got jagged like a river on a map, and she'd use her butter knife to scrape off chunks in a straighter line because the jagged edges were hard to look at. The chunks were easy to take, though. She laid a piece of its substance inside her mouth; it almost melted like a clump of brown sugar and turned to that glistening gravy that left hardened crumbs along her tongue.

She worked the crumbs between her teeth as she told herself that her life was darn near perfect so she wouldn't cry right now. Had been perfect in the eight months since her high school graduation, she told herself. Summa cum laude. And chosen by her classmates as the best dressed. And won a scholarship to Lincoln U. And got a promotion at her part-time job at Wanamaker's from the stock room to the selling floor, which meant an automatic charge card and 25 percent discount; even though her main job was to keep the racks in order and go for coffee for the assistant buyer, she was one of the first black persons ever assigned to the store's exclusive third floor.

And then, as if life weren't perfect enough, on her graduation night, right while she, Fannie, Julep, and Julep's cousin walked home from Bookbinder's, where Julep's parents had taken them for dinner, Willie Mann walked up behind them, grabbed Liz around the waist, and kissed her on the lips to the gasps of Julep and her cousin and Fannie's scowls. He took her back to the wine cellar, presented her with an exquisite pair of solid gold earrings, and finally, after having put her off for two full years, he gave in that night and took her on the couch. She hadn't even gotten pregnant that night and went the next day to be fitted for a diaphragm.

She shifted her teeth. The more she tried to concentrate on how good her life was right now, the more she wanted to cry. She'd overcharged on her employee card, and the amount she owed far exceeded her paycheck. The assistant buyer liked her, though. Liz could tell because she asked her opinion on colors and fabrics before she went to her sales meetings. So she'd arranged for Liz to work Monday through Friday for a week. It would mean missing a week of classes, but she could work off her debt and then go back to her regular hours. She'd told Liz she'd arrange that for her anytime; she thought all that college business was a waste anyhow; you could have a real future here, she'd told her.

So bad enough she'd missed a week's worth of classes, leaving each morning with her books in her bag so Herbie and Noon wouldn't know, last night, right on that couch in the cellar of the club while she sipped dry sherry and looked at Willie Mann's perfect smile, she'd gone and sold out her dear Noon. Listed for him the subjects of the strategy sessions Noon and Jeanie hosted right downstairs in Noon's dining room. Told him who was challenging the tax assessments, who was wavering, who'd probably sell by spring. She'd stopped herself and covered her mouth and begged him please not to use the information against Noon. She just forgot, for a minute, that they were on opposite sides. He circled her lips with his fingers. Told her that deep down she knew they were on the same side. He respected her loyalty, he said, but she was settling—again. She knew they deserved more than that little Lombard Street row house, didn't she? He kissed her. Didn't she know it? He kissed her again. Didn't she have to admit they were on the same side? He was all over with his kisses. Until she closed her eyes and arched her back and whispered, yes, yes, they were—yes—they were on the same side.

She crunched down hard on another sandy-colored chunk and liquefied it into paste, but the inside of her mouth stayed dry, and a sharp edge scraped the roof of her mouth so she tasted blood too. Plaster, blood, and guilt.

It was then that she heard Noon calling her. "Liz-zy." Noon almost sang her name, which Liz knew meant that she was pleased about something. So Liz reached in the top shoe box, where she always kept her soft white handkerchiefs, and quickly wiped her mouth. She was neat with her habit. Covered her clothes with plastic so the dust wouldn't settle on her nice wools, and soft cottons; dusted down the closet floor, and rubbed her tongue against the cut in her mouth as she went to the top of the stairs.

She saw Noon sitting in the deep green chair, and Fannie sitting along the chair's arm holding on to a thick textbook. She breathed in deeply as she walked down the steps and noticed Noon swinging a tattered brown shopping bag with such a broad grin on her face that it puzzled Liz. Noon had been so tensed up over the road, snapping at her and Fannie for little reason, bundling up and sitting out back by herself for sometimes half the night, more and more agitated over each property sold and then left abandoned. She couldn't imagine what had caused this sudden change in Noon's disposition.

"Well, hurry it," Noon said to Liz as she noticed her slow walk down the stairs. Her voice bubbled with excitement. "Can't hardly wait to say what I got to say. What you doing anyhow, up there so quiet?"

"Studying. Midterms coming up, can't believe how much work I got to do."

Fannie looked up at Liz and immediately knew what she'd been doing. She'd stopped arguing with Liz about it for the most part. An occasional "Would you get out of that fucking plaster hole," if Liz had been hitting it often that Fannie knew about. But Liz timed her episodes when Fannie was least likely to be around, so it was only times like these, when she'd have to stop abruptly, that Fannie could see it in her eyes.

"What's up?" Liz asked, smoothing at her hair as she sat on the deep green couch across from Fannie and Noon. The crumpled brown shopping bag swayed lightly in Noon's hand.

Noon half laughed as she stood and wiped at her yellow apron and waved the shopping bag like a banner. "Just got done talking to Jeanie and found out Round-the-Corner-Rose is moving."

"What!" Fannie and Liz shouted in unison.

"Moving, I said, going back down South."

"And what about her property?" Fannie was standing now too, looking at Noon with a question mark. Rose's property was prime, right in the middle of a short block, actually two houses, gutted, redone, turned into one. Noon should be upset; Rose after all was on their side.

"She got to sell it. Needs the capital. Seems someone in her family died and left a lot of land down South to Rose and her thousand cousins. And the cousins are selling the land a little at a time, parceling it out so it's hardly worth the weeds growing on it. Rose is gonna buy it from all the cousins willing to sell it so it can stay in the family and keep its value.

I tell you, that white man's gonna try and get our property one way or the other."

"So I don't see the good news," Liz interrupted her, not thinking she could stomach her tirade right now, sounding more and more like Next-Door-Jeanie the deeper she got into the project.

"The good news, my darling Liz," Noon gushed as she walked to the couch where Liz sat and cupped her chin in her hand, "is that you are going to buy Rose's house."

"Me!" Now Liz jumped to her feet.

"Liz!" Fannie was just as shocked.

"You!" Noon grabbed Liz and spun her around and almost danced a jig, the brown shopping bag dangling from her arm like an oversized bracelet.

"With what? Thought they wasn't giving mortgages down here," Liz said, almost mad that Noon should suggest such an undoable thing.

"Now you know that they not."

"So Rose is just gonna transfer the title?" Fannie asked, looking at Liz, hunching her shoulders to signal she had no idea what Noon was up to.

"No, already told you she needs the cash."

"But if we can't get a mortgage, that means we'd have to buy the house with cash." Liz was getting more agitated.

"Exactly right."

"Noon!" both Fannie and Liz said at the same time, exasperation filling their voices.

Noon put her hands to her hips and danced across the living room and looked as if she were doing a holy dance except that they knew she never did a holy dance. She waved the tattered brown double-handled shopping bag and bounced it up and down to the rhythm of her feet and almost turned it into a dance partner. She held the bag high and let it fall open so its contents spilled, and suddenly it was raining money. Right in the middle of the living room. Dollar bills, and fives, and tens and twenties. Twirling and floating and softly landing on the coffee table and the couch and the deep armchair. They papered the floor and interrupted the buffed-up shine. Lightly they fell, taking their sweet time, because they knew about time. Some of those bills had been patient in that tattered bag since Liz was five and had been left on the steps. Fifteen years a secret between Ethel and Noon and then Herbie; Noon had told Herbie, but he never knew how much, how often the envelopes came. Even though Noon hated the ground Ethel walked on, she'd figured the least Ethel could do was provide financially for her own flesh-and-blood niece. So Noon had taken her money, slid the crisp bills from the envelopes each month. Laid them to rest in that very shopping bag Ethel had left on the steps the day she abandoned poor Liz. Every dollar Noon had saved; every envelope she'd burned. Never one for cursing, except when she'd set the match to the fine paper envelopes. "Bitch," she'd say. "This is the least you could do, provide for your child. Low-down, dirty bitch."

Liz scooped up the dollars, inspected them, made sure they weren't play money. Heart pounding, stomach turning. Mouth and eyes and even nose gaping, not even able to talk at first, and then shouting, laughing, asking where? Where did it come from?

Fannie walked slowly to one rumpled green bill that had landed in the corner, away from the center where the mounds rested. She picked it up slowly and put it to her lips, as if her eyes were in her lips and through putting it there she could see. She did see as she pursed her lips against the bill. "Ethel," she said softly. "Ethel."

"What Ethel got to do with this?" Liz asked as she threw the money in the air and let it fall down on her as if she were playing in the snow.

"This is Ethel's money, isn't it, Noon?" Fannie caressed the dollar and stared off into space, past the money twirling that Liz scooped and tossed. "Isn't it, Noon?" she asked again, staring at her now, almost looking through her.

"Wait a minute." Liz walked slowly to where Noon stood so that she was looking right in Noon's face. "Ethel, my aunt Ethel, this is Ethel's money?"

"Was, at one time." Noon walked to the deep armchair and fell into it, suddenly tired, deflated, after having waited so long to make this presentation, buoyed by the very prospect, and now in an instant it was done and she was drained.

"Ethel sent all this money?" Liz's voice was strained as she followed Noon and stooped at the foot of the chair. "When? Why?"

"She sent it over time," Noon said as she leaned forward and took both of Liz's hands in her own. "From the day you were left here. She been sending it monthly for your upkeep. Ten, sometimes twenty, lately as much as fifty, sixty, dollars at a time."

"For me?" Liz had to stop, to swallow and catch her breath. "You saying this is mine, must be thousands of dollars here and you saying it's mine? Mine? I'm rich? Mine?"

"I think she was sending it for Noon," Fannie interrupted. "Probably to pay for your food and clothes; you know how you always had to have the most expensive of everything."

"I had a mind to send it back." Noon almost sighed. "But I figured the least she could do was provide for your future. So I kept putting it up for you. Figured the day would come when you'd need it for something big."

Liz's hands shook, and she could feel Noon squeezing them tighter. A homeowner. She was about to be a homeowner. A deed in her name. Eat-in kitchen. Private bath. Open weave drapes, French Provincial chairs, a shiny copper teakettle. A lock, a key, all night long with Willie Mann, all night long. Suddenly when she thought about Willie Mann, she had to go to the bathroom. She was sweating, and she pulled her hands from Noon's and ran up the stairs.

She made it just in time before her bowels broke. "Be still, circles," she whispered to her stomach. "Didn't tell Willie Mann anything he couldn't have found out on his own. He's smart, got good people sense, knows who's for and against him, hardly needs me to tell him that. Be still, circles," she whispered again, the way Ethel would whisper to her when she was small and cried because the circles were spinning too fast in her stomach. "Be still, circles; I didn't tell him anything that would really hurt Noon. I'll make it up to her; I'll help her push her plan; I'll never sell my house to Willie Mann. My house. My house." She said it over and over until her stomach settled enough for her to go downstairs and look Noon in the eye.

She walked right to where Noon sat and grabbed her and held her as tight as she could. "I don't deserve how good you been to me, Noon. Too good, you just been too good."

Noon stroked Liz's bright red hair and nodded and smiled. "You deserve me and more. You been a good chile, a sweetheart you been."

Liz felt the circles again as she sat on the floor and rested her head in

Noon's lap. "But you did the work, you always been there with whatever I needed. I don't deserve you," she said again.

Suddenly Fannie was furious as she caressed the faded, crumpled dollar between her fingers. That Liz could so easily discount Ethel's generosity, just take the money, and buy the house, and let Willie Mann try to swoon her for it. And not have a soft, kind word to say about Ethel. "Don't forget about Ethel." Fannie's voice cut through their embrace and stiffened it. "Wish it was some way you could thank her, Liz. We know how good Noon's been to you, all of downtown knows. Nobody knows about Ethel, though. I told you she always loved you, I told you she always cared."

"But Noon did the work," Liz said weakly.

Fannie wondered how hard Ethel had to work for the dollar she rubbed between her fingers. Did Liz even consider that? Didn't she wonder like Fannie if Ethel had to stand at some oversized microphone until her feet swelled, until her throat ached from pushing out notes night after night? Did she have to give it up to some club owner to extend her act and watch her drink so it wouldn't be spiked, making it easy to cheat her out of her due? Did they whisper "nigger" behind her back when she wanted to travel first class and make her go in through the kitchen when she played the finer clubs? Did they schedule her tours with no time off, forcing her to work whether she had cramps, or the flu, or a stiff neck, pink eye, or just sick to her soul? How hard? Fannie wondered. All that money papering the living room now, how hard Ethel must have worked. Selfish bitch, Fannie thought about Liz. If she can just wave her hand over Ethel's efforts like she's shooing a persistent fly, how easy would it be for her to do the same thing to Noon. When Willie Mann breathed in her ear, what would stop her from selling out?

"I'll bet this is one of the first dollars she sent." Fannie walked to Liz and pushed it in her face, almost rubbed it against her nose.

Liz waved the dollar away. Fannie shoved it harder against her face, this time mashing her nose for real. Liz jumped up from where she'd sat at Noon's feet. She pushed Fannie's hand from her face. "What's your problem? You act like you mad 'cause I got a little bit of money."

"I'm just trying to make a point, Liz. Like I been saying to you all these years, this proves how much Ethel cared about you. She took time every month to make sure you was being provided for." She continued to wave the crumpled, faded dollar bill. "But you so concerned about the money, you haven't even given a second's thought about Ethel. Maybe it was a sacrifice for her. Maybe she even did without so you could have."

"Oh, Fannie, how she supposed to act?" Noon interrupted. "I doubt that woman did without too much except maybe some religion. Now get off your high horse and help clean this money up before Herbie gets in here. Come on now, let's go around the corner right now and talk to Rose. You gonna be living right in the house with Liz, so you benefiting from the money too."

"I'm not looking to benefit." Fannie's voice was angry. "And you know that, Noon."

"Get it up, hurry." Noon talked right over Fannie.

"And you know it too, Liz." Fannie leaned into Liz as she stooped to pick up the dollars.

"Let's go over to Levitz's when we leave Rose's; couch in the window that is so gorgeous, Noon." Liz ignored Fannie. She'd heard her, though. Knew exactly what Fannie was saying. No, she hadn't thought about how hard Ethel had to work. Probably wasn't hard enough, leaving her the way she did, lying to her. Should have sent more. Should have worked twice as hard and doubled what she'd sent.

TWENTY-FOUR

Liz got the couch she wanted and first pick of the bedrooms, the largest one that got the sun in the morning, the one with the smoothest walls. Even though before she and Fannie moved, she had to redo the walls in the closet at her bedroom at Noon's. Fannie cursed the whole time about how she better stop eating that shit 'cause it was gonna kill her sure nuff, but Fannie helped her with the walls just so Noon wouldn't find out, the same way Fannie kept the secret of Liz seeing Willie Mann, to protect Noon. Noon was in such a volatile state these days. Obsessed with winning out over the road. Day into night, meeting with Jeanie, and Bow, and the Saunderses, and Pop, and the other faithfuls who refused to sell out. Hearing the report from the lawyer on the latest appeal he'd filed. Noon was turning into a walking, mumbling wreck.

Herbie was too. He had never seen Noon in such a state. Thought that maybe all those years of never getting her passion stirred had finally taken its toll. Drifted to her brain and confused her. Except that she wasn't really confused, just emotional, high-strung. Stopping people on the corner so they could hear her out. Going door to door to tell them about the hype. "No road," she'd tell them. "My daughter saw it, and it's not gonna be a road."

"Get some rest, Noon," they'd say as they shook their heads sympathetically. "You're working too hard. Now go, go get some rest."

She didn't even listen to Reverend Schell when he said it, and she'd always listened to Reverend Schell. Even at the last session when he prayed over her body, asked the Lord to touch and give her a nature of passion so she could do her wifely duty, Noon had sat straight up. Got off the table in the middle of the prayer. "What's the use?" she'd said. "Nineteen years passed. What's the use?"

"But the Israelites wandered for forty years, Noon. Forty years before their deliverance came."

"No use. It's no use," she'd said, and walked out of the church before she could even get that thin hot line that was her glimmer of hope. "It's just no use. Devil get a hold of you, get inside of you, scar you up like the devil did to me, it's just no use."

Her brothers called from Florida. Each night a different one would call. "Take care of yourself, Noon," they'd say. "Get some rest, Noon, or I'm coming to bring you back home," they'd caution. "Let it go, Noon. Just let it go," they'd counsel. And Noon would promise them she would. Then she'd throw a sweater over her shoulders, and sit on the back steps facing the Saunders Funeral Home, and rub spirit of peppermint between her teeth, humming, "Come by here, my Lord. Come by here."

🐦

Herbie went to work and to the club because he couldn't stand being home anymore. Now with Fannie and Liz gone, the house was just too quiet, too many memories, reminders in the quiet of what he and Noon had never shared. The stretch of time turned on him like a two-faced friend and made him start to blame himself. Maybe he should have gone to church with her; maybe that would have loosened her up. Or forced her. Maybe if he'd forced her just once, and she saw it hadn't killed her, maybe she would have been willing the next time. Or maybe he shouldn't have been so quick to take up with other women, especially the prostitutes after Ethel left; if he'd forced himself to go longer so that he really needed it, maybe he could have been more convincing to her, more creative with his pleas. The maybes and the two-faced stretch of time were too large in the quiet house. They fell over him like a heavy blanket, covered him until he felt he had to fight himself out. So he went to work and then to Royale, until it closed, until he had nowhere else to go except home to be with the quiet.

🐦

Then one night Big Carl leaned over the leather-clad bar and said, "What's doing, Herbie? Now you having your mail sent here?"

"What you talking 'bout?" Herbie asked as he tilted his thumb-sized glass of gin to his lips.

"Letter came for you the other day," Carl said as he leaned in closer across the bar. "Don't know who it's from, but it smells sweet." He handed Herbie a short envelope with a fine textured feel to it.

Even through the dark blue air of the club, Herbie recognized the inked symbols. He used to tease her about her handwriting. Said it was pretty as all getup, but you couldn't understand a word of it. Herbie's heartbeat stepped up; his fingers were sweating now as he tore across the end of the envelope.

Carl moved the candle in the red-tinted jar closer in. "Little candlelight to read by." He laughed.

But Herbie didn't need the candlelight. He had already read the too-few sentences. "I'm coming back to Philly, maybe for good this time, looking to settle down. Hope to see you. Love, Ethel."

"I'll be damned," he said out loud.

"Somebody die?" Carl asked, filling Herbie's shot glass.

"No, but somebody might, somebody damned sure might."

"Just keep it outside of the club." Carl chuckled. "Bloodshed ruins the reputation of a nightspot, especially when it's the domestic variety."

Herbie barely heard Carl. He was too distracted by the jumble of emotions. His rage percolated. That she would just bounce back after all these years as if she'd just left that morning to go shopping. And the way she'd had his ass kicked in New York. But then he also wondered if her laugh was still easy and loud. When her gaze fell on him, would he feel that flood of warmth mixed with tingling anticipation? The desire, still there, still as strong as it had always been, fought with the rage now. Damn, almost thirteen years since he'd seen her that day in court, and just the thought of her still had him turning to jelly.

"Herbie, 'nother one?" Carl asked as he tapped a bottle of Beefeater's gin against the leather-clad bar. "Herbie, you with us, or what?"

"I'm gonna split, man. I got to work some things out. I'll see you tomorrow, Saturday, you know I'll be by tomorrow." Herbie turned to get up and then hesitated and said, "By the way, man, what you hear from Ethel?"

"Hear she doing good, doing real good. Still in the Big Apple. Last I heard, she was kicking ass at Small's Paradise. Hear she packs in the crowds wherever she goes."

"Guess the cats cram into the place just to see her move," Herbie said, his facial expression very far away.

"Awl, c'mon, she gotta voice too. It ain't just her body; they could sit right where you sitting on any barstool in any club, and see just 'bout any shape they wanna see."

"Oh, I know it ain't just the body, it ain't just the voice or just the face," Herbie said, almost having to shout now as the club was starting to fill with the Friday partyers. "It's all of it, the eyes, the lips, the arrangement of her songs, the way she walks, and throws her head back when she gets mad, and looks at you when she talks like you the only living thing on earth. Her shit is perfectly arranged for greatest effect, and she knows it, you know what I mean?"

"Do Noon know what you mean?" Carl asked, laughing.

Herbie exaggerated a grimace and said, "This ain't really about me and Noon; me and Noon, well, we're well, we're me and Noon, you know. But since we raised Ethel's niece, and all, I just like to know how she's doing."

"You should hop on the train and catch her act," Carl said, moving down the bar some to pour for other patrons.

"Yeah, I'd love to catch that act. Love to catch the shit out of that act," Herbie said as he spun off the barstool and headed for the door, fingering the finely textured envelope as he went.

&

He reached for Noon that night. He hadn't reached for her in years. They had settled into a pattern, like doing a ten-thousand-piece jigsaw puzzle. They had started at the edges and gotten all the blue pieces for the sky, except that sometimes a blue piece belonged deep inside of a green area, a tree that was allowing a little light through. But they'd tried to make it fit at the top. Herbie tried to force Noon to move to the beat of his passion; she was capable only of stillness. "Still waters run deep," she'd tell him time and again. And she tried to force him to settle down, to grow out of some of his playfulness, to go to church, to walk slow, to be patient with her until her healing would come. "A rolling stone gathers no moss," was his response. And they'd go back and forth until they accepted that the puzzle piece didn't fit at the top, that it belonged deep within the green of the tree, that it was just a little light coming through after all. That the puzzlemaker threw in such tricks to keep it a challenge. The way he'd thrown in Noon's illness, which had become almost ordinary over the years. The eye after all adjusts itself over time, making what first seemed horrible appear normal. Like having a wife with palsy; soon the shaking becomes as much a part of her as the slant of her mouth.

But tonight Herbie reached for Noon as gently as he could. She didn't move. How could she not move? he thought. She even seemed to stop breathing. He needed Ethel. He almost called out Ethel's name. He almost whispered in Noon's ear that he needed Ethel. He wanted to hurt Noon. In that instant he wanted to hurt Noon for being the one that he'd desired all those years ago in her daddy's church. He nudged her, and then he pushed her, right in the small of her back, he pushed her hard. He could see her back shaking, he could see she was crying. He clenched his teeth and held his hands stiffly to him. If he didn't, he might hurt her. He didn't want to hurt her, not really. He ached all over. Noon was crying hard now, he could tell by her back, it was convulsing so. At least she was moving. At least her back was going in and out. Some nights she didn't even move. Some nights he had to fight the impulse to get his thickest strap just to make her move.

He felt ashamed. He got out of bed and went downstairs and opened the front door. The night air was cool and full of movement. He sat outside on the front steps. Cross-the-Street-Dottie turned her bedroom light on and off three times. She had told him if he ever wanted to visit for a late cup of coffee, just watch for her light. "No, thanks, Dottie," he said to the fast-moving night air. "No, thanks, no, thanks."

The morning after Herbie got Ethel's letter, Noon woke with a soreness right in the small of her back where Herbie had pushed her. She soaked in Epsom salt. I hope that don't cause me to have arthritis right in my back, she thought, as she stretched out in the tub and let the hot water cover her. She listened to the church bells chime their 4:00 A.M. wake-up call. She watched daylight peek through the skylight. She tried to clear her mind enough so she could say her morning prayers. Her mind was too crowded. The road mess. People falling for the lie. Treating her as if she were the one crazy when all she was trying to do was expose it for what it was. Abandoned houses starting to pile up, block by block. People who swore they never would buckle were crumbling like day-old bread. And that turncoat Willie Mann smiling up in her face, Liz's eyes going bright whenever he crossed her view. Liz not looking quite right, either, as if she were getting ready to come down with something; not coming to visit regularly, not even stopping by with Fannie for morning coffee on her way to classes. And Herbie pushing her in the small of her back late at night. "Oh, no, he's not either," she said out loud. Her voice bounced around in the bathroom. The loudness of it shocked the quiet and pulled her from her thoughts. The water was barely lukewarm now; her fingers were prunelike; daylight was completely overhead. Must be at least six, she thought, as she pulled the rubber stopper and let the water rush through the drain. She sat in the empty tub. Now she said her prayers.

$$\text{\Large ✒}$$

Herbie passed up breakfast. He just wanted to get out of the house away from the two-faced stretch of time and the emptiness. He and Noon argued before Herbie could get to the door. How dare he let her fry up all that city dress salt pork, and scramble all those eggs, and he had no intentions of eating. And how dare she expect that he hang around the house on his day off when she was gonna be gone quick, straight over to the church to a meeting or rally or prayer vigil or, at the very least, in a huddle on the back steps with Jeanie.

"I told you I'm not going to a service. Didn't I tell you we were getting petitions signed today?" Noon asked, irritated. "Didn't I say yesterday that when I left this morning, it was gonna be for a petition meeting? Why you can't never remember what I tell you?"

"All I heard you say was that you was going to church, Noon, which is all you ever do, since Fannie and Liz moved, might as well say you moved too, at least I knew they were leaving."

"All right, Herbie, what else is it?"

"What you talking about?" He moved quickly toward the front door.

"This ain't about me and church, I always spent a lot of time in church. Something else is going on, I can feel it. I could feel it when you walked through the door last night. Now you can treat me like you think I'm going crazy, like other people been treating me." She followed Herbie into the living room as she talked. "But you know I ain't going crazy, you know my feelings are usually right on the mark."

"You and your feelings again, huh, Noon? Too bad your feelings don't operate when it's time for you to feel something. Past twenty years your feelings ain't kicked in once when it really mattered. So don't give me no shit about your feelings."

Noon flinched. She breathed in deep the thick, angry air. The air was heavy in her chest, painful. She flicked a tiny spot of dust from the otherwise spotless coffee table. She shifted the orange gladiolus so that they were more balanced in the vase. She turned the table Bible so that it sat on an angle to meet in a point with the *Ebony* magazine. She sucked her teeth and swallowed hard.

Herbie was sorry; he was angry and sorry at the same time. "I got to get the hell outta here," he said as he moved quickly through the front door.

Noon was beginning to trust her instincts—everything that culminated to shape her assessments of the present moment. It would catch her by surprise. Like knowing that something was going on with Herbie. It was a sound that the quiet house made, like a sad trumpet blurting out notes that ended too soon.

The thud of the door as Herbie left jolted Noon. She watched him half run, half jump against the wind up Lombard Street. A trolley sliding up the street crossed her view. The clang of the trolley was distorted by the wind, carried to a higher note, swirled around against the blue and sun-lit Saturday. The clang faded too quickly. That disturbed Noon. She had come to rely on the sound of the trolley, much like the church bells that rang every hour. Stability was in those sounds. The trolley coasted through the wind on down the street. Herbie had already turned the corner.

It had rained the day before. And then the March winds had come through like a vacuum cleaner and sucked up all that wasn't clean. Now the sun was out; it sparkled out. Herbie walked. He walked up to the bridge and stared into the wind-rippled water. He walked back on the other side of the tracks past Ninth Street and the smell of Italian sausage and pepper cheese. And then down to the waterfront, where the air was moist and cool. He stopped off at Bow's for a cut, a long wait for a chair. He was glad for the wait. He could shoot the jive with the other men waiting about the up-and-coming Cassius Clay, the demise of Lady Day, the Warriors' stats, Willie Mays's hits, and South Street, the way it used to bounce in the old days before all the talk of the highway had people closing up shop.

When he left the barber's, dusk was settling in. He got the urge to talk to Fannie; he walked over to Pop's, stuck his head in. "Just missed her," Pop said. "I let her go a little early tonight, reward for her doing all my balance sheets."

Herbie acknowledged Pop with a nod and a wave and then headed around to Fannie and Liz's new house. He had to walk back past his house to get to Fannie and Liz's. He walked on the other side of the street. A trolley was sliding up the street. The wind pushed the clang of the trolley deep into his head. It followed him around the corner.

Fannie and Liz's house was in the middle of a short block. The house on one side had been completely gutted; now it was a shell. The other still had occupants, renters; the owner was selling, though, so they would have to find somewhere else to live.

Herbie walked up the five concrete steps and noticed the familiar glisten. The sand in the concrete sparkled like diamond pins, the results of a good Saturday morning scrub. Noon did all right by those girls, he thought. He knocked on the middle of the door that was beveled into three big squares. No answer. He shook against the wind and knocked again. Then he heard the window on the second floor open. He saw the crop of red hair through the mirror push into the air.

"Hey"—Liz waved—"hold on, I'll drop the key down. Come on in; I'll be down in just a few minutes."

"Shit," he muttered. He was hoping Fannie had beat him here. He had to be in a certain mood to tolerate Liz; today wasn't it. He picked up the jagged key, fitted it into the door, and went on in.

"Wow," he yelled upstairs to Liz as he walked from the small hallway into the living room. "Y'all done more in here since the last time I was by, what, a week? And new curtains, this coffee table new too, isn't it?

Look like the furniture department at that store where you work. What you doing, sneaking shit out in a Mack truck at night?" He laughed and then sat on the deep navy velvet couch that sported brightly printed pillows. No crocheted doilies sat along the arm of the couch the way they did where he lived. The coffee table had at its center an oversized vase and a copy of *Life* magazine. Lacy curtains, open weaves, hung in billows from the tall windows and almost scraped the freshly shellacked, almond-colored hardwood floors.

Liz laughed too. "Be down in a sec," she said.

"Take your time," Herbie said as he nestled back into the lushness of the velvet. "I'll just sit still and enjoy the quiet." He thought he heard whispers, movement from two sets of feet upstairs, and that revived his hope that maybe Fannie was indeed home.

But then Liz was right in his ear. "You! Sit still," she said as she emerged into the room and leaned over from behind him and pecked his cheek.

Herbie sat up, startled. "Don't be sneaking up on me like that. Damn trolley bell almost busted my eardrum, so I'm a little on edge, you know."

"You always on edge, aren't you?" Liz took a seat across from the couch where Herbie sat.

"Please, Liz, don't give me the Noon routine." He glanced at his watch. "What you do, get off early?" he asked. "Just a little past six. I thought your place didn't close till six."

"I switched a day with someone. They worked today for me, I'm gonna work a Monday for them week after next."

"How you gonna work a weekday when you got classes?"

Liz sucked the air in through her teeth. "They do give us a spring break, you know, a week and a half off when we don't have class."

"Yeah, well, what do I know about college life? I'm just a dumb old country boy." He laughed to himself, then asked, "Where's Fannie?"

Liz pulled the sash of her silky robe tighter and folded her hands in her lap. "Not here."

"Not? Thought I heard someone else upstairs."

"Yeah, the ghosts. You know this house is haunted, noisy things too." She laughed hard and slapped her lap.

"You could have just told me it's none of my business," Herbie said as he noticed her silky lounging set for the first time.

"Well, if you heard voices, it must be ghosts 'cause no one's here but me, and I wasn't talking to myself."

"You know where Fannie went?" He ignored the sarcastic edge to Liz's voice. "Pop said he let her go early tonight."

"She probably stopped off at the store, or else she's somewhere giving the winos all her spare nickels."

"Why you say that?" he asked, looking at her fancy silver-tone slippers.

"Oh, you know Fannie," Liz said, smirking. "She's knows 'em all by name, wouldn't drink it if you paid her, but she feels sorry for them, so she'll get on down in the gutter with them, pal around with them, give them her spare change."

"That's Fannie, though," Herbie said, sitting up from his comfortable slouch. "Arrogant as she gets with people, she still got a heart. She snaps, and then she forgets about it; she don't carry no hurt feelings around with her."

"I tell you one thing," Liz said, standing up and walking to the lace-draped window, "all that's getting ready to come to an end. They getting ready to bulldoze all those buildings to get ready for the expressway, so the winos gonna have to find some other curb to wallow on, unless they wanna volunteer to be the cones that separate the traffic."

"Damn, Liz!" Herbie said, hitting his thighs. "You never used to be this cold. You move around the corner and now you wanna kill all the winos. What you do, meet some new cat that's swooning you with his politics?"

"I just want it to hurry up and be over with," Liz said, lightly tracing the looping curtain threads and then slipping her hands under the curtain to open the window. "It's been dragging on forever; now that it's close, I just want it to happen, level the blocks, so we can get on with life."

"Noon disown you if she hear you talking like that. You know how strong Noon feels about this expressway thing."

"I know they making final offers," Liz said. "Just might take them up on it." She turned to look at Herbie, to get his reaction. She stopped short when she saw the top of his light forehead turning red.

"Liz, you can't even be thinking that!" Herbie said, jumping to his feet. "You can't even be thinking about selling this house; you can't turn on Noon like that, not after all she's done for you."

"I didn't say that I was selling it. I didn't say I was absolute about this." She walked around Herbie into the dining room, not daring to look in his face, and then, half mumbling, said, "I just know it was the money Ethel sent every month that we used to pay for this house."

The window fell down with a bang, egged on by the angry March wind. The window caught the lacy curtain just as it was flapping in, trapping it.

Herbie caught up with Liz, grabbed her shoulders from behind, and turned her briskly to face him. "Listen good," he said, "Noon didn't have to save that money. She could have rightly spent it on your food and clothes, taking you to the doctor, and getting your teeth fixed, you know how many little colored girls ever had the chance to wear braces on their teeth. You know where all that came from, from me."

"I'm not saying I don't appreciate everything Noon ever did for me. I'm not saying that at all. But I surely never asked *you* for anything." Liz's head was cocked to the side, her hands on her hips, picking up steam.

"I knew this was gonna happen one day," Herbie said loudly as he balled his fists. "I told Noon to use the money on you, that's what Ethel was sending it for, even when we had to go and pay a lawyer just so the state wouldn't take you, I told Noon then to use that money, I begged her to, argued with her about it, but Noon wanted to do right by you. I see now she should have listened, you a ungrateful—"

Liz shook her shoulders hard. Herbie moved his hands back, held them straight up in the air. "Hands off," he said. "Never let it be said I put my hands to you. But I feel like just shaking some sense into you. You know that would break Noon's heart if you turned on her like that."

"I didn't say I was," Liz said, rolling her eyes hard. "I just said I had the thought. Of course I'd talk about it with Fannie."

"Oh, no! No! No! Don't go bringing Fannie in this." Herbie shook his head, and wagged his finger, and almost jumped up and down. "Fannie would never agree to signing this property over; she got a bit more family allegiance."

"Maybe Fannie was treated more like family than me." Liz's eyes narrowed to just slits.

"Noon never showed no distinction between the two of you."

"Talking about you, though." Liz sneered. "You always favored Fannie over me."

"That ain't nothing but your insecurity talking." Herbie stomped his foot hard.

"Truth talking," Liz retorted. "You never liked me."

"Poor little Liz," Herbie said in his most sarcastic, mocking voice. "Nobody likes me, so I'm gonna break the heart of the woman that raised me and sell the house that she saved the money for."

"Why don't you just go? Just get on out. Fannie's not home; that's who you came to see." Liz was shouting. Her voice was clouded with angry tears.

"Not until you admit that it's a big mistake to sell this house. That would just crumble Noon; it would just kill her." Herbie was at Liz's back as she walked into the kitchen.

"Leave me alone, Herbie." Liz's voice had gotten quieter, threatening.

"Yeah, what you gonna do, huh, you gonna grab a butcher knife and stab the life outta me, huh? Why don't you just do that to Noon? Just kill her quick."

Liz turned to look at Herbie all at once, her eyes as red as her hair. Her face was pointed, her lips, her nose, her forehead, even her chin was jutting out, poised for a fight. She looked right at Herbie. Her voice was so low and chilly when she started to speak that Herbie drew back, caught off guard.

"You know why you never liked me, why you never smiled when I came around like you did with Fannie, why you never laughed if I said something funny, or hugged me first. You know why, Herbie? 'Cause you know I know the truth."

"What you talking 'bout, girl?" Herbie could hardly look in Liz's eyes.

She pushed her finger into his chest; she punctuated her words with hard finger stabs in his chest. "You know I know the truth about you and Ethel."

Herbie stood in the kitchen under the light. He wished he had stayed in the dark dining room. He wanted to turn and walk from under the light, but his feet were frozen. After fourteen years the other goddamn shoe had finally fallen. After wondering if she recognized him, even making up little games called "guess where you seen me before," to see if she knew. After bracing himself each night before he went in, wondering if tonight was going to be the night that Noon met him with balled fists. After Liz pretending all these years that she didn't remember anything, it came down to this game of tit for tat. You can't tell on me or I'll tell on you. Evil little bitch, he thought.

"What you say, girl? You talking crazy," he said when he could talk again.

Liz walked away from Herbie. Suddenly her stomach felt as if it were on fire. She filled her shiny copper teakettle with water from the tap. She turned the water on full blast. She let the water run loud, long after the kettle was full. She watched the dense white sprays bounce off the mouth of the kettle.

Herbie moved toward the living room, maybe on out of the front door. He wasn't sure; he just couldn't stand the sight of Liz's back.

The front door exhaled as it separated from the frame, and Fannie was back home. "Fannie!" Herbie said, dragging the name out, almost sighing it out, relieved to be able to say something to get rid of his pent-up breaths.

"Hey now," she said, smiling broadly, putting her bag down on the living room floor, and then opening her arms wide. She ran to hug him. "What's up, what's the matter? You stiff as an ironing board," she said as she drew back to look in Herbie's face.

"Just got in a conversation with Liz about the highway thing and got riled up, is all," Herbie said as he looked over the top of Fannie's tall, bushy hair.

"Well, have a sit down. I'll make you some tea." Fannie picked up her bag and walked into the kitchen.

"So what's up with you and Herbie?" she whispered to Liz.

"Nothing, just nothing," Liz said, her back to Fannie as she pushed a match under the kettle, and then jumped back when the flame whooshed around the circle of the pilot and out around the kettle's side.

Liz stared at the flame, she wondered if that was what the inside of her stomach looked like at the moment: orange and blue fire fanning out in circles, each breath feeding the flame with new heat, insides burned, blackened as the fire grows.

"Turn it down!" Fannie yelled. "You want to burn us out of here?"

"Oh, shucks," Liz said, snapping to attention as she quickly turned the knob on the stove. "My brand-new kettle almost got scorched. I paid five dollars for that kettle."

"Why you walking around in all your good shit?" Fannie asked as she looked at Liz in her silky lounging ensemble and silver-toned slippers.

"I was just in my room when Herbie knocked, studying. I was studying, and I just threw this on when Herbie knocked on the door." Liz avoided Fannie's eyes.

"Studying, huh?" Fannie said.

"Fannie," Herbie called into the kitchen, "I got to go, I was just making a pit stop. I'm just gonna run past the club and grab a brew. I'll see you tomorrow, you be by in the morning to have coffee with Noon, right?" He fidgeted with the zipper on his windbreaker.

Fannie knew it was no sense trying to talk Herbie into staying. "See ya later, alligator," she said, running into the living room to let him out.

"After while, crocodile," he said, slipping out into the wind.

Fannie walked over to the living room window and retrieved the curtain that had gotten caught in the fallen window. She watched Herbie step fast down the steps.

&

"So what you say you was doing when Herbie knocked?" Fannie asked as she opened the copper flour canister and poured in flour from the sack she had just brought in. Liz poured steaming water into her blue-flowered china cup. She lifted the delicate string on the Tetley tea bag and bounced it around in the cup. She didn't answer Fannie. She wrapped the tea bag around a spoon and squeezed it against the side of the cup. The pressure of the spoon tipped the dainty cup. Tea spread out over the stove top, down into the grooves that separated the pilots. It made a hissing sound as it touched upon the pilot that had just boiled the water.

Quiet on top of quiet was building between Fannie and Liz. And then the sound of the water hissing against the hot stove made Fannie jump.

"Oh, shucks," Liz whispered. She quickly sopped up the spilled tea, put her china cup in the empty sink, and said, "Look, Fannie, I don't feel that well, my stomach is bothering me. I'm going to my room; maybe I'll be down later, depending on how I feel. I'll tell you about the chat me and Herbie had. Maybe later. Okay?"

Fannie was sitting on the kitchen stool; she had finished pouring flour and had moved on to the sugar canister. She knew Liz's "maybe later" meant that she'd be in her room for the rest of the night with the door closed. "Me and Julep and Pop's nephew are taking in a movie a little later, *Imitation of Life*, you wanna come go?"

"Julep's home?" She didn't look at Fannie. She bent down to wipe a spot of water from her slipper.

"Yeah, for the weekend. Said she went to Wanamaker's looking for you this afternoon, then came over here and knocked and didn't get an answer." Now Fannie filled the salt and pepper shakers. "She said she really wanted to see you before she goes back. She met this new guy at Howard and might go home with him for their spring break; she wanted to tell you about him, get your opinion. We'll probably go over to Lawnside for barbecue after the movie."

"Tell Julep I love her. Tell her I've got superbad cramps. If she's going to church in the morning, I'll see her there."

Fannie shrugged. "If you saying you don't feel well, I'll just tell her you don't feel well. I hate to see you miss a good time, though. Plus Julep said she probably won't be back home till Penn Relay Weekend."

Liz was almost to the kitchen door. "I really don't feel well," she snapped. "I'm not just saying that."

"It's only seven o'clock on a Saturday night. You saying you in for the night?" Fannie asked, trying to hold Liz in the kitchen, to talk to her.

"That's what I'm saying, Fannie. Okay?" Liz made her voice chilly and rolled her eyes when she said it. She walked quickly out of the kitchen.

"Well, stay the fuck in then, okay," Fannie said to Liz's back.

🐎

Liz let out a long sigh when she walked into her bedroom. She closed the heavy wooden door lightly. Navy blue paisleys decorated the burgundy background of the bedspread. Liz looked hard at the bedspread and thought that it made the room too dark. "Got to get another one," she said to herself. She curled on her bed and rocked back and forth. She pressed her arm tight into the small of her stomach. Her stomach was spinning, like a scratched record playing the same few notes over and over, stuck in the groove. Liz had gotten used to the notes. She felt that maybe if she could vomit, it would relieve some of the spinning. But she knew she had to lie and rock herself for fifteen minutes, a half hour, for as long as it took for it to pass. Then she'd have to run to the bathroom and let it push on out. And then the relief of flushing the muddy waters down. Tonight was no different. She flushed the toilet, went back into her bedroom, and closed the door tightly behind her. She knew Fannie wouldn't come in. As close as they were, Fannie always respected the doors between them, whether the closet door at Noon's or now the thick oak door that separated Liz from the rest of the house. Liz smoothed at her bedspread. The spread matched the curtains and the dresser scarf and the big pillow that adorned the chaise lounge. She pushed the bed from against the wall. The coaster wheels on the bed frame made a squeaky sound against the hardwood floor. The hole was growing, but she reasoned that she had at least another foot high and two feet wide until the headboard would no longer hide the hole. "Months," she said out loud. "It'll be months. I know I'll have stopped by then."

Tonight the first snatch at the plaster didn't take much work. Usually the first snatch at the first chunk excited her the most. Her heart beat faster as she peeled off the pink and green wallpaper, small prints that didn't clash with the larger bolder ones on her bedspread. The part closest to the wallpaper was chalky white, smooth. But farther in it was grainy, tiny bits even sparkled. That was the best part. Sweat formed along her hairline. Plaster bits pushed up beneath her well-done bright pink nails. She pushed the skinned chunk into her mouth. At first she just held it there. She just let it rest between her tongue and the roof of her mouth. The roughness felt so good inside her mouth. Then she moved it to the side, between her teeth. She crunched down on it, hard. The explosion of tiny grains of plaster going through her mouth, sifting down her throat made her cough. She put her hand to her mouth and spit the biggest portion of the chunk out. It was like a clump of gravy, liquefied at the top, hard at the center. She licked at the soft part; her saliva broke it down more. She put it back in her mouth and just held it there. And then she chewed it again. Sometimes gnashing, sometimes just letting it roll along the length of her tongue, sometimes pushing it to the side of her jaw and holding it there as if it were a sweet cherry candy ball. She finished the first chunk and spit what was left into the center of a soft white hand towel. She snatched at another chunk, and another, breaking each down and then letting go of it. Sometimes she muttered to herself as she peeled back wallpaper or worked a stubborn chunk from against its foundation. Tonight she even let a curseword slip through.

"Damn you, Herbie. I'm not living down here in a hole-of-a-wall part of the city if it's just gonna get more and more run-down. Damn you, Herbie. That was you. That voice, I know that was your voice at Ethel's. I could feel that voice deep in my stomach when you and Ethel were in the other room late at night. I know that was you. How dare you have done such a thing to Noon, then gonna talk about me not having no feeling of family? What about you, Herbie, huh? You were fucking around. What about that, huh? If I want to sell this house, I will. Ain't nowhere near as bad as fucking around."

Liz chewed and spit as she muttered about Herbie. Then she used a butter knife to chip away at stubborn chunks. The crumbs hit the floor with a chinking sound. Liz continued to work, trying to keep the growing hole in proportion, not higher than wider, the headboard still needed to cover it.

When she was done, she went to her closet and pulled out the gray and black feather duster. She dusted the remnants into a neat pile and then scooped them up and into the shiny metal trash can. They made a whooshing sound as they slid down the piece of cardboard she had scooped them onto. They fell into the bottom of the can heavily. She stood in the middle of the room and waved her hands, trying to disperse the dust that just hung there. She dusted at her dresser, shined her mirror, scraped her nails, and brushed her hair. She pushed her bed back against the wall. She lay on her bed and thought about the new bedspread she would buy, one that would brighten up the room. If she worked all of spring break, she could afford the one she'd seen with the bold peach flowers. That was one of Willie Mann's favorite colors. She shifted to her side and pulled at her silken pajamas. Noon had told her to always sleep in cotton, cotton's healthier, she used to say. Liz wondered if Ethel slept in cotton.

Back downstairs Fannie grabbed her bright orange hooded jacket and headed for the door. "Be there, Herbie," she said, " 'cause I gotta talk to you." She moved through the March air. The bitter sting of February was gone. The March air was warmer, madder. Fannie moved fast, the way she always moved fast. She couldn't slow down. She had tried before to walk slow, to think slow, to slow down her feelings, which were always building revelation on top of revelation, like a slide show in fast forward. She tried to make her mind quiet and still. But afterward her thinking would make up for lost time. Sometimes she'd just have to blurt out the thoughts, just say what she was seeing at the moment, just to free up time and space in her head. People would say, "Why can't she be nice and quiet like the red-haired child?" People mistook it for meanness. Fannie never intended meanness; she just needed to empty her head.

Fannie tried to smooth at her wind-blown hair as she pushed through the big door into Club Royale. Herbie was sitting at the bar, sipping his gin. Fannie could tell by the way he was hunched that it was gin and not beer.

She moved through the blue air and was at Herbie's back. She tapped him on his shoulder and, in a disguised playful voice, said, "Hey, bud, need to talk to you." Herbie turned around quickly; the muscles in his face gave way all at once and collapsed into a complete smile.

He had just been thinking about Liz, calling her a brat, she was a brat back then, fourteen years later, eighteen years old going on nineteen, and she was still a brat. He was just thinking that he should have called her on it, right then and there; as soon as Fannie got home, he should have put Liz's little scheme right out in the open. He was just thinking that Liz didn't have anything on him. No way can she remember that far back. Shit, can't her or nobody else say anything about him not doing right by Noon. He was relieved that it was Fannie who interrupted his thinking.

He grabbed Fannie and hugged her tightly. "What's up, daughter mine?" he said cheerily.

"You tell me," Fannie answered.

Herbie looked around and saw that Willie Mann was in earshot, standing behind the bar racking wineglasses. "Let's go where we can talk in peace," he said as he picked up his drink and led Fannie to a small booth.

"So you gonna tell me what's up?" Fannie asked as they settled into the booth's coziness.

"Nothing much, I just felt like talking to you earlier. I miss you girls."

"Why you run out as soon as I walked in then?"

"Me and Liz got into a little dispute. She say anything to you?" Herbie looked hard into Fannie's face for any sign that Liz had told.

"Nothing, she wouldn't say anything; that's what I want to know from you."

"Nothing, really, it was about nonsense. I don't even remember. You know how damn sensitive she is, can't say nothing to her, from the time she was a little thing. Noon never helped matters any, Noon always talking about Liz's nervous stomach, couldn't nobody holler at her, chastise her, I just think it's all left her a little too selfish sometimes for her own good."

"Yeah, and . . ." Fannie said, looking at Herbie intently.

"That's all, that's why I left the way I did. Didn't mean to offend you, but I knew if anybody understood, you would. You been more like a daughter to me than Liz."

Fannie waved her hands, trying to wave away Herbie's words. She always wanted Herbie and Liz to be close. But the balance was off between Fannie and Herbie and Liz.

"It's true, Fannie," Herbie said with emphasis. "You even look like me."

"Noon says you feed anything long enough it'll start to look like you."

They both laughed easy laughs.

"What number you like tonight?" Herbie asked.

"Don't know. Haven't seen any numbers for a long time. You on your own."

"Well, sit right here, Fannie, don't move, I'm just going in the back to put mine in, I don't usually do the night one, but I've had this hunch all day, five minutes, give me five minutes, order yourself a Coke, and just be still for a few minutes."

Fannie sat back and breathed in deep. The back of the booth supported her back well. She liked strong wood that she could lean heavily on. This back was like the back of the church pew. Must be the same wood, she thought. She felt that if she could lean hard enough against it, it might suck some of her worries right through her spine; absorbent wood, she thought. She breathed in the blue air. The air was not like the church air, though. The air at church was bright yellow, sometimes almost blinding. This air was transparent, like a blue film, everything showed. The number writers, the prostitutes, the slick-haired hustlers did their business out in the open. There was no need for a blinding yellow light here. They were honest enough with their trade. Fannie closed her eyes and took in more of the blue air. She could smell the fish frying in the kitchen. She could separate the ground pepper from the paprika, the lard from the cornmeal. Trout, she thought. It had a fresh smell. Not like the close-to-rotten fish that was sometimes sold to the church. Club Royale after all had connections, front people. Even though it was Negro-owned, they had learned who to send to the docks to do the buying. Fannie pressed harder into the wood. She allowed herself to be lost in the blue air filled with fresh fish. She didn't see Willie Mann staring at her as he racked his sparkling wineglasses.

🦢

Willie Mann's nature was filled with contraries, paradoxes, that he should have what he wants and in the having not want it. That his desires so well defined, so sought after, so worked for should suddenly turn on him, switch up, and the thing that he presently wants bears no resemblance to his havings. So it was as he watched Fannie sitting at the small dark booth in the back of Club Royale. That he had just left Liz's a couple of hours ago did not matter. That he had sneaked out when Herbie came in, saved only by the bang of the window falling as Herbie and Liz argued did not matter. That he had gone against his grain of quick-hit and move-on approach and instead taken his time with Liz, put months into whispering in her ear, lightly tracing her cheekbones, kissing her chin, her closed eyelids, skillfully unfolding her and then backing off until she was of legal age, did not matter. Nor did it matter that he liked his women like Liz: high-gloss, done up with bright lipsticks and blushes, coiffured hair, and diamond pins. All that mattered to Willie Mann at this moment was the tremendous throbbing urging him on to Fannie.

Fannie's nose was long and thin, like her fingers and her arms. Her waist nipped way in to make her slender hips look broad. Her legs curved at the calves, not muscles that jutted but a soft curve. Her hair was dark and wild and woolly and made her eyes look darker, almost magical set far back from her thin nose. Her skin was light with a brownish tint, like unfinished pine with a deep maple varnish to it. Her chest was small, no voluptuous breasts to tempt with. Her eyes did the tempting, her eyes and her lips. Her lips drew the fullness that was missing from her chest. It was her lips that Willie Mann focused on as he smoothed at his hair, and straightened his tie, cleared his throat, and moved for Fannie's table.

"Good evening, Liz's sister," he said, smiling down at her.

"What you got against calling people by their given name?" she snapped. She pulled her mind from the slippery shine of the silver trout.

He held his hand up in mock defense. "Please, let's not argue," he said, making his voice go softer, smoother. "Can I sit with you a minute?"

"Sit at your own risk. I'm waiting for Herbie, and you know he can't stand your ass."

"Ouch!" he said, wincing hard. "You could have dressed it up a little bit, maybe said, 'He doesn't particularly care for you, Willie Mann.' "

"What do you want?" Fannie asked, staring hard at him.

"A truce is what I want."

"A truce," Fannie said sarcastically. "Now what do you suppose is bringing on this call for a truce?"

"Actually I'm thinking about Liz. Now I know you know that Liz and I have been seeing each other, we're trying to keep it low-key, especially since your family doesn't exactly approve of my, er, affiliations. I just thought it might make it easier on Liz if at least you and me could be on friendly terms. You know this whole thing wouldn't wear her down as much."

"I thought you liked her worn down, you egging her in directions that's pitting her against her family."

"Fannie, let's not quibble, for Liz's sake. I mean you're a good-looking woman, I see Pop's nephew is hot on your trail, probably at least a couple of other cats nursing an attraction to you. Suppose you happened to like one of them that your whole family hated. And suppose they liked you as much as I like Liz."

"Like?" Fannie asked, as if she hadn't quite heard right.

"That's right. I mean, me and Liz have this understanding, it's not a heavy love thing with us, we're not losing our head over this. I mean, of course I care about her, I care a lot about her, in fact a whole lot. But it's probably the same way with you: You wouldn't want to shut down all your options while you're still young and good-looking, you know what I mean."

Fannie didn't say anything; she just stared straight at Willie Mann.

She knew in fact that it was a heavy love thing for Liz. That Liz had shut down her other options. Turned a deaf ear to the compliments of a whole array of options. Even earned a reputation as "stuck up" at Lincoln. "Thinks her ass weighs a ton," the college men said about Liz.

"Furthermore," he went on, "I got to honestly say that I've never been in love, not the head-over-heels variety in the movies. I bet you haven't either. I bet we're a lot alike in some ways. Have you, Fannie? Have you ever been in love?"

Fannie was tilted off center. She'd expected him to come at her with persuasive whispers about the road, how good a thing it was, a blessing in disguise, a way out for people trapped downtown like crabs in a barrel. She was prepared for that. Not this, though. "Not head over heels," she said flatly. Mad at herself then for even responding, for even giving him an audience.

He hunched his shoulders in and nodded his head slowly, not even blinking he stared at Fannie so. "Well, like I said, I haven't been in love either—"

"'Cept for with yourself, right?" Fannie interrupted, forcing herself to look straight at him as she struggled to get her balance back.

He rubbed his fingers gently over the match back. "Rough," he said.

"Me or the box?" Fannie asked, finding her center again.

"Not you." Willie Mann spoke even softer. "You put on a rough front, but you're not rough. In fact, I do believe you might be soft as silk."

"I'm more like cotton. I ain't slippery and I hold up in the wash."

"Okay, then, cotton." He looked down at the match box, fingering it.

"So what's this about?" Fannie asked. "What you after?"

"You and me being friends, is all I'm after," he said. "For Liz's sake. And for your sake, and mine. I think we could do each other good being friends."

"Never happen," Fannie said. "Not as long as you in cahoots with the cronies that's trying to steal our community, you can't be no friend of mine."

"Okay," he said, raising both his hands as if surrendering. "It's no secret I'm into this highway. I think it's one of the best things that could happen to all the Negroes crammed down here like sardines in a can. You know, they give the people a piece of change for their properties, let them move where they can have more space."

"And you get a little piece of change for every little piece of property that gets turned over, right?" Fannie asked.

Willie Mann sat back against the booth. He still played with the match box. He didn't look at Fannie. He was rarely challenged by women. Most women were like Liz with Willie Mann, too grateful to have this fine, slick-haired man spreading them wide to challenge him. He imagined spreading Fannie wide. Might even take Fannie to his apartment. He'd never taken any woman to his apartment. It either had to be her place or his couch at Royale. It was simpler for him that way. They tended not to get too possessive. "I swear to you, Fannie, I believe in this project. But even if I am getting paid, say a consultant-type thing, why should that stop us from being friends? One is business; the other's not."

"It's an honesty thing."

"But I'm being honest with you. Probably more honest than I should be. I trust you. Don't ask me why, but I do. I want you to trust me too, Fannie. I—I like you, Fannie, I like your spunk, you know, I like the way you challenge me. Maybe we could meet some evening and just talk. You could tell me what problems you're having with this whole highway project. Just you and me, you know, without interruption."

"What I look like to you?" Fannie said with her mouth hanging open. "Do I look like a fucking dope?"

"You gotta do something about your mouth, it's not ladylike, you look too good to be talking the way you do. Who you look like anyhow? I know you were adopted, but your mother must be a serious looker." Willie Mann stared at Fannie, to see if she had any idea, to see if she knew, the way he knew.

"Noon is my mother," Fannie said quickly. "The only mother I know, the only one I need."

He could tell that she didn't know as he followed her eyes through the blue air to just beyond his shoulder. He sat up sharply. Herbie was back, standing over him.

"I believe you in my seat," Herbie said icily.

"Can't nobody be in your seat, you be the man," Willie Mann said as he slid out of the booth, bowed his tall frame, and extended his arm motioning for Herbie to sit. "Miss Lady, please think about what I said."

Fannie didn't acknowledge him. She looked instead at Herbie. His face was as red as Liz's hair when the sun hit it.

"Calm down, Herbie, he was just talking shit, he didn't do anything to me. You all right?"

"I just saw stars when I saw him sitting here talking to you, and you look like you really listening to what he has to say."

"Well, what if I said that he sits and talks to Liz a lot, a whole lot? What if I said that he and Liz are doing more than talking? What would you say to that?"

"I'd say that's a damn shame, that's what I'd say."

"But that's all, huh, it's okay for him to talk to Liz, huh, Herbie, is that how that goes? That ain't equal treatment."

"I been suspecting something was wrong with Liz. She's changing her whole point of view. Okay, he done already got to Liz, already ruined her. It'd kill me if the same thing happened to you."

"Let's be real, Herbie, what can he do to me? It's not like I don't know what he's made of."

"I just don't want him around you."

"Well, he's around Liz."

Herbie shrugged his shoulders. "That ain't gonna last long. He's just around her 'cause she's a homeowner. Once he get what he wants from Liz, he'll be long gone."

"Well, why don't you threaten to kick his ass? You almost did just now when it had to do with me, why don't you stick up for Liz? She's the one that really needs it. I can fend for myself."

"Fannie, I ain't saying I don't care about what happens to Liz. But she would resent the hell outta me, I try something like that. She just never been the daughter to me you have. You can't force it to be peaches and cream with me and Liz. She never liked me, she acts civil enough, but the feelings just ain't there. You know, the family-type feelings that she has for you and Noon, it ain't there for me. I can accept that, Fannie. I just wish you could."

"Why ain't it there, Herbie? She was only a child when she came to stay with us. What she got against you that's that powerful? What you got against her?"

Herbie's jaws sunk in. He held the skin between his teeth. The words were trying to push out, but he couldn't let them, not even to Fannie. He bit down hard on the skin of his jaw. He wanted to shout, Yes! I know why me and Liz can't be like family, 'cause every time I look at her, I remember what I lost when Ethel left. Every time my eyes hit her red hair, it reminds me of my shame, fucking Ethel while Liz was asleep in the next room; while Noon was home thinking that the worst I was doing was watching a little ass shaking at Club Royale. Knowing Liz knows it was me on that couch-bed, knowing how scared she must have been when she saw me walk through the door and she burrowed her head in Noon's bosom, how scared I been all these years that she was going to tell, how I always turned it around, made it seem like Liz was spoiled, selfish.

Herbie tried to swallow the words, but his throat closed, so he pulled the words between his teeth. He chewed at the inside of his jaw until he was sure the words were ground to a bloody pulp. He tasted his blood; it tasted salty.

He heard Fannie calling him. "Herbie, you okay? What is it?" Her voice sounded far away, as if suddenly the space between them had obstacles.

Herbie gulped his gin and swished it around in his mouth. The alcohol burned the rawness and then numbed it. "I'm okay," he whispered. "Just bit the shit outta my jaw. Don't worry 'bout me and Liz; like I said, she's just overly sensitive, spoiled, that's all."

He looked past Fannie through the blue air into the mirrored wall. He could see Willie Mann racking wineglasses, watching Fannie as he worked.

TWENTY-FIVE

Sunday morning in South Philly was like buttermilk. There was a quiet smoothness to it. The trolley clanged through Lombard Street less often. No chink of glass against concrete mixed with the fast steps of the milkman. Children played quiet games like checkers instead of tag or rope. The smell of frying salt pork floated easy to the tune of "Steal Away to Jesus."

Noon hummed in her kitchen as she made quick bread for Fannie and Liz and Herbie to have with their coffee. The Sunday morning kitchen had a quiet smoothness to it too. It was only interrupted by the crunch of coffee beans, as Herbie turned the handle to the grinder, and then the sound of the coffee silt spilling into the tin can. Herbie watched Noon as he ground the beans. Her hands were fast as she beat the lumpy batter with the wooden spoon and then poured the batter into the hot skillet. He tried to grind the coffee quietly. Noon's humming was so smooth and creamy. The grinding of the coffee beans might remind her how beat down she'd felt lately. Yesterday's petition drive wasn't the success she and Jeanie had hoped it would be. That was all she talked about when Herbie got in. Even when he tried to apologize for saying what he said earlier about her having no feelings, she had just waved her hand and went on about how now that the weather broke, people were really starting to waver and considering taking Tom Moore up on his latest offer and how glad she was that they now had Liz's house as one of the ones that wouldn't sell, every piece of property helps.

At least now she wasn't talking about it. Once the humming stopped, though, he was sure that the next words from her mouth would be about

238

the road: the devil-filled, conniving developers and city planners and politicians, all of them in it together, she would say. Didn't Fannie warn us? And then she'd go back to Fannie's vision and how that was proof enough for her. And how reluctant people are to stand up to them. But me and Jeanie, we're not giving in, she'd say. Right now, though, she was still humming. No song in particular, just a rich, round tune, slow-moving like the morning.

She reached into her large apron pocket and pulled out a handkerchief. She blew her nose hard. Herbie braced himself and then relaxed when she went back to her rich, round notes.

She flipped the quick bread. The battered side was cream-colored; the done side was unevenly browned with beige swirls running through it. "Mm," Noon said, "bread's looking good. You better start the coffee so both can be hot at the same time."

"Getting ready to do just that," Herbie said to her back.

He brushed past her to put the percolator on the stove. He sat back down and looked again at Noon's back. He noticed that she was smaller. The beige dress she was wearing used to show the print of her healthy hips. He had teased her once about the dress and how she better not be switching in front of Reverend Schell in that dress or the devil gonna get her sure nuff. But now all he could see was fabric, even with the apron tied tight around her waist.

Goddamn highway, he said to himself. Goddamn thing is eating her up. He thought about his argument with Liz last night, how such a thing as Liz selling that house might send her over the edge for real. He rubbed his tongue around in his jaw. It was still tender from the night before. His jaw started to throb. He went over to her as she was turning the cast-iron skillet to tap the quick bread onto a plate. He grabbed her from behind and squeezed her to him. She jumped. The skillet and plate made a crashing sound as they hit the floor. The brown-swirled quick bread was mangled amidst the broken plate.

"Herbie, look what you made me do," she said as she wrenched herself hard from his grasp.

"We'll have store-bought, it's no big deal," he said softly.

"I had my mouth all set to dunk that in my coffee."

"I said we'll have store-bought, I'll go around the corner right now, just take me a minute."

"Well then, go! The girls will be here directly."

Herbie's response was the front door closing hard.

"And don't be sneaking up on me grabbing me from behind no more," Noon said to the thump of the door. She swept the broken plate and bread into the trash and sat heavily at the kitchen table. Her eyes burned as she fought back tears. "Never did like nobody grabbing me from behind," she mumbled. She was almost back there, when they'd grabbed her from behind when the sand had held her feet captive and she couldn't run. She could almost hear their chanting all over again. She banged her fist hard on the kitchen table. Even now, more than twenty-five years later, her body poised for a fight at the very thought. She didn't even hear Fannie come in.

When she looked up, Fannie was in front of her smiling, all dressed for church in the mint green suit Noon had made for her with the cream-colored buttons and a matching beige tam pulled to the side. "Morning, Noon," she said.

Noon jumped to her feet and wiped at her eyes and pulled Fannie in a tight hug. "How's my baby this morning?" she said, holding on to Fannie until she could swallow the memory once again.

"I'm okay, I smell quick bread, but I don't see it."

"Yeah, that bread was so quick it's gone. Herbie made me drop the skillet. Bread and good plate gone," Noon said, turning from Fannie to point to where the bread had landed. She wiped at her eyes and fixed her face for smiling.

"I'm sure he didn't mean it. He never was the most agile person. He tell you I was with him at Royale last night?"

"Hasn't said a word to me. I wish you wouldn't go in those places, not nice places for good Christian girls like you and Liz."

"I mainly went to talk to Herbie; besides, as many devils in church as there."

"Devil's everywhere, but at least in church you got a good backup."

Fannie kissed Noon on the cheek, "God's got a special place in heaven for you 'cause you are consistent."

"That I am." Noon laughed. "Now where's my Liz?"

"Still in bed when I left, said she'll see us in church, said her stomach was upset, thinks she ate some bad shrimp."

"What's with her, Fannie? She ain't herself. She don't look right to me. Like she ready to just jump outta her skin. If she's not at church, I'm just gonna have to pay Miss Lizzy a visit."

"Maybe it's just the trauma of leaving here. You know that was a big step, Liz been so dependent on you just about all her life, and now here she is this big-time property owner. Takes some getting used to."

"Thanks, but no, thanks, Fannie. Now I know you always stuck up for Liz, protected her, but if something's wrong with her, I need to know." Noon stared at Fannie, peered at her, squinted her eyes. "You hear me, Fannie, now I'm gonna trust you to tell me if Liz is going through something that she maybe can't handle by herself, that maybe the two of you can't even handle."

"Yes, ma'am," Fannie said, and then went into the kitchen to pour a cup of coffee.

Herbie walked back in with a loaf of bread. He had walked slowly, took the long way around, hoping it wouldn't be just Noon and him when he returned. He was relieved to see Fannie in the kitchen pouring a cup of coffee.

"Liz didn't show, huh?" he asked.

"I was just telling Noon, she has an upset stomach, bad shrimp she thinks."

"Tell her I hope she feels better," Herbie said as he made his way into the kitchen to peck Fannie on the cheek.

"Or you could tell her yourself. Noon might come by after church, you could come with us."

"Don't think so," Herbie said curtly. "Went by yesterday and we got to arguing, Fannie, I told you last night, she say anything to you about it yet?"

"What was you over there fussing with Liz about, Herbie?" Noon asked, shooting her eyes at him with angry flashes.

"I wasn't fussing, just went over there to pay the girls a friendly visit. I don't even know what got her all riled up, you know how damned sensitive she is, can't say nothing to her." And then Herbie looked at Fannie, needing confirmation from Fannie's face that Liz had not told.

"Well, like I told you," Fannie said as she heaped sugar into her coffee, "Liz doesn't feel well, so I haven't talked to her much this whole weekend."

Fannie poured cream into her sugar-laden coffee. She liked it sweet.

She liked to have a mass of sugar streaked with coffee at the bottom of her cup. Then she would run her bread through it. Noon used to fix Fannie "children's coffee" when she was much younger. She'd add a spoon from her own cup into Fannie's milk. Then she'd add sugar and let Fannie stir it around and dunk her bread in it. Noon and Herbie used to love to watch Fannie drink it. They loved the way her dark eyes shot way open when she got to the bottom of the cup and tasted the sugar. As they both sat watching her now dunk her bread in the bottom of the cup, they beamed and glowed as if she were their baby all over again. Here was the one thing they shared equally, an intense love for Fannie.

Liz brushed her hair hard. She liked to feel the brush whip at her scalp. It was an old brush, a boar bristle. It was the same brush Ethel had packed in the bag when she'd left Liz on Noon and Herbie's steps. She quickly smoothed on lipstick and wiped the dust from her gold-framed dresser tray. Already it was eleven. In only two hours Fannie would be back from church, and he's late again, she thought. She looked out of her bedroom window onto the street below. Three vacant buildings across the street interrupted the beauty of the golden Sunday morning. "Can't wait till I can get off this block, look how run-down it's getting, people moving, and no one moving in behind them. Like rats jumping ship. Where the heck is he? He's only cutting into his time with me, know he got to leave before Fannie gets back." And then as if he had heard her, Willie Mann's tall figure quickly turned the corner.

Liz breathed in deep. The first sight of him always stepped up her heart rate and went straight to her stomach. She ran down the stairs and had the door opened before he reached the steps.

"I was beginning to think you weren't coming," she said, and then smiled a deep smile lest he think she was angry.

"I just wanted to make sure the coast was clear, especially after last night." He walked into the door and kissed her face that she tilted. "Oooh, my pretty redhead," he said when he pulled his lips from hers and looked at her in her black-on-black negligee, "you don't know the effect you have on me." He pulled her toward the steps.

"No, no," Liz said. "Let's come on in the living room and talk first. We used to just talk. Now we rarely do."

"That's 'cause I can't get enough of you, baby. Now you tell me how I'm supposed to act with you looking like you look. My God!" He spun her around and wet his lips and told himself to settle down. Then he sighed, and looked at his watch, and let Liz pull him into the living room.

"Now I got to ask you this one more time. For how long did Herbie run around with Ethel before I came into the picture?"

Willie Mann settled into the couch. "What did I tell you? Didn't I tell you from the time Ethel settled here until she up and split? Herbie was always hanging around the club like a lapdog with his tongue hanging out of his mouth waiting for her to finish her set. I was a teenager, working stock in the cellar. Soon as she'd leave, he'd leave. After you came to live with Ethel, things got a little cool between them, least as much as I could tell. They were still, you know, getting together, just not as often. Then she left, left you, when I was about eighteen because I had already started working in the main room. I remember you too."

Liz grinned and rubbed her hand across her hair. "And what do you remember about me?"

"That cute crop of red hair," he said as he ran his fingers up and down her arm. "Everybody would comment on it. Just ain't common for brown-skinned women like you to have such natural red hair. The prostitutes used to joke about all the money they could save getting hair color touch-ups if they had your hair."

Liz laughed and then just stared ahead as images came and went like waves: red silk, white shoe boxes, the smell of new leather, perfumed hugs. Thumping from below as she napped in the room where Ethel would leave her over top of Royale. Ethel's bedroom, her warmth late at night, and the bed that got too cold and too wide when she could hear Ethel laughing in the living room to the beat of the low-playing record player.

Willie Mann glanced at his watch. He saw the look on Liz's face, knew she was way back there, ready for hours-long descriptions about the past. But it was getting late. He needed to get back to the club. His fullness was on him, and it was hard to talk a woman into the cellar on

Sundays, especially if Big Carl was playing Mahalia Jackson, and the women were weepy and repentant. He almost hated to, but he began to remind her of how wrong she'd been done, misunderstood by everyone. How Ethel had abandoned her so she could live the free life of a jazz singer. How Noon and Herbie took her in so their favorite, Fannie, could have a playmate, how Noon just gave her the money for the house just to help her win the road war, not for Liz, just for her own victory. How she'd been used by people all her life. Not him, though. He really cared about her. He had even sat across from Fannie last night at a booth at Royale and told her how much he cared. And then Liz cried into his open chest. And after that it was easy to rub her back and work his way around and get her passion stirred.

They were back at the doorway. He kissed her face. "Perfect timing, baby," he said. "Church is probably just letting out. So I told you, I want to set up a meeting for you to sign an agreement of sale, and then I got a beauty of a house in West Philly I want you to see. Don't feel pressured, baby doll, but the sooner you do it, the better price you'll get on your new house. Property values in West Philly are going through the ceiling. The ones waiting won't be able to afford homes much better than the ones they're leaving."

He kissed her again. "Call me at the club later on, baby doll." He half skipped down the steps and was around the corner before Liz could pull her mind back. What was Fannie doing sharing a booth with him anyhow? she wondered. I thought she hated his guts so much.

Church was good. They danced and shouted to a frenzy and hollered in sweet release. The women left with eyes shining, lighter footsteps, broader grins. The men were loose, laughing, hoarse, and hungry.

Noon and Fannie left in a hurry. After the disappointing showing at the petition drive, Noon wasn't ready for fellowship with those she tagged turncoats. Plus she was anxious to get to Liz. Another Sunday and Liz hadn't shown up at church. Noon wanted to know why.

"I'm telling you it was bad shrimp, Noon," Fannie said as she and Noon walked arm in arm through the golden air to get to Fannie and Liz's house.

"You don't believe that yourself, Fannie. You ought to be 'shamed of

244

yourself even perpetrating such a lie. Now I know people pegged me as half crazy over this road, but I ain't that far gone to not know when something's wrong with my children."

"Well, we both know Liz has a weak stomach. The least little thing is likely to give her a bout of diarrhea."

"I fault that two-bit, call herself a singer, no-count aunt for that," Noon said as they turned the corner. "The way she left her, just abandoned her the way she did, that's enough to make anybody's bowels run for a lifetime."

"I don't think you can totally fault Ethel," Fannie said, looking at Noon from the corner of her eye. "She at least made sure Liz was well cared for. Look at the money, that's just an example."

Fannie stopped short; she could feel Noon's arm stiffen against hers. "Okay, Noon, I know you can't stand to hear a kind word said about the woman, but you got to give her her due."

"I'm leaving it to the Lord to give her her due. I hope to never be acquainted with no parts of her. The Good Lord might disown me as his child, I might act out so."

They were right in front of Fannie and Liz's. Fannie was fumbling through her purse, pretending that she couldn't find her key, just in case that no-good Willie Mann was there. Noon stood down on the pavement and looked up at the house. She was smiling as she admired it, its general look of being well cared for. The steps clean, windows shining, fresh paint. And then she smiled even more when she saw Liz push her head out of the second-floor window.

"There's my baby," Noon said, beaming. "Get down here and let us in. Your sister'll have us down here meeting nightfall."

Noon adjusted her hat and smoothed at her dress and ran her fingers along the gleaming brass door knocker shaped in the letter L. Then the door opened, and Liz stood in front of her. She had changed from her black negligee into her 'round-the-house stretch pants and cotton shirt. She squinted as the day's brightness hit her all at once.

"Well, look at you in your fresh dress," Liz said, making Noon blush. "And do we have flowers in our hat?" She touched Noon's brim.

Noon loved to hear Liz make much over her mostly simple outfits. Since Liz was a little girl, she tried to get Noon to adorn her hat with flowers, add a dash of lace to her dresses, a splash of color to her nails.

Sometimes Noon would relent and allow Liz to make her over completely. But when she was done, Noon was too close to beautiful. Noon couldn't handle being beautiful. But she would allow herself an occasional adornment, like the large yellow flower pinned to her hat, just to get an admiring smile from Liz.

Fannie pushed past them both to go change out of her church clothes as Noon squeezed Liz to her and held her until she could feel her slipping away. That's what she had been feeling from Liz lately, a slipping away. She followed Liz into the living room, walked right behind her as Liz went to the window.

"Looks like a perfect day out, sun so bright," Liz said, not looking at Noon.

"The curtains are fabulous," Noon said as she touched them lightly and watched Liz from the corner of her eye staring through the sunlight to the other side of the street.

"Abandoned buildings piling up," Liz said somberly. "Can't hardly stand to look out front."

"Just part of the plan," Noon said confidently. "Jeanie said that's what they do, buy them, then let them sit so we'll think the neighborhood's going way down. Rush us into moving that way. We just got to be patient, is all."

"Patience's wearing thin," Liz mumbled.

"What did you say?" Noon asked, turning to look at Liz directly.

"Nothing. I didn't say anything," Liz said as she moved toward the kitchen. "I got some tea steeping, you want it iced or hot?"

"All I want right now is to know why I been missing you at church, and while you at it, I want to know why you don't walk around the corner and visit me. Stood me and my coffeepot up every morning this week."

"Upset stomach this morning," Liz called back into the living room, rolling her eyes hard up into her head.

Noon straightened her hat and smoothed at her dress and settled into the lushness of Liz's new couch bought with what was left over after they'd paid for the house. "Then when Julep came by the house looking for you, said she had gone to see you at your job and they told her you were off, I said to myself, something must be wrong with Liz. Not like her to just not come by at all on a day when she doesn't have classes or work."

"It's nothing, really," Liz said as she walked back into the living room and took a seat across from Noon.

Noon gave her that the-Lord's-gonna-reveal-it-all-in-a-minute-so-you-might-as-well-fess-up look. "You sure nothing's wrong?" she asked.

"I said nothing's wrong." Liz said it so sharply that it surprised Noon.

"Well, it's not just me noticing a change in you, dear heart." Noon tried to soften her tone. "Even Herbie noticed a difference. And Reverend Schell asks about you all the time, you never come by in the morning with Fannie, you always in your bedroom with the door closed."

"Look"—Liz interrupted Noon—"Reverend Schell ain't got no cause for concern long as I'm sending my tithing envelopes, Herbie wouldn't be concerned about me if you paid him money to be, and as for me always being in my room, I mean how would you know that anyhow unless Fannie's running around the corner telling you every time I sneeze?"

"What's that supposed to mean?" Fannie said, walking back into the living room wearing Pop's nephew's faded blue sweatshirt. "I been defending you. I told Noon you had an upset stomach this weekend."

"Well, when don't you have an upset stomach, Liz?" Noon cut in. "That's where your nerves are settling, right in your stomach. What you so nervous about?"

"Not nervous," Liz said, her voice screeching.

"What was you and Herbie arguing about then?"

"Ask Herbie."

"I'm asking you, and I demand that you answer me with some kind of respect." Noon wagged her finger to the beat of her words.

"Respect me then," Liz shouted, fighting tears.

"Lord have mercy, what devil done jumped into my chile?"

"It ain't no devil," Liz said, walking back to the window. "I'm just sick and tired of everybody hovering over me like I can't think for myself or have a simple upset stomach or make a simple decision."

"What decisions you gotta make?" Noon was standing up now, her Sunday hat with the big yellow flower tilted on her head.

"Like where I want to live." Liz's voice quivered.

"Where you want to live?" Fannie and Noon said in unison.

"I'm tired of this whole road thing."

"We all tired," Noon said, sitting back in the chair heavily. "You think I like wearing myself thin with all the work it's taking to oppose it?"

"Well then, why you doing it then?" Liz's voice had gotten harder, more determined.

" 'Cause it ain't right to displace us the way they trying to do."

"People getting paid for properties," Liz said defiantly. "It ain't like they getting cheated, I hear they getting good money for these little pieces of property down here."

"What's good about money that's displacing people on a lie? It's not good money, it's downright evil money." Noon was banging the arm of the couch as she talked.

"How you know, Noon?" Liz said, turning and walking right toward Noon. "What makes you so sure you right? Did it ever occur to you that you might be wrong?"

"Who you raising your voice at?" Noon said as she shifted to the edge of her seat. Her hat was sitting along her forehead now; the bow almost rested on her eyes.

Fannie had gone into the kitchen. She came back into the living room carrying a tall glass of iced tea. "Maybe you should think about what you saying, Liz, and maybe not say anything else," Fannie said as she set her tea on a cork-backed coaster next to the *Life* magazine on the coffee table.

"I been thinking about it, okay," Liz shouted. "I been thinking a lot about it. You know what's with me, okay, I'm sick and tired of all the opposition, all the drives and rallies, and meetings, and prayer vigils. I'm tired of it, okay. You wrong, okay, I said it, Noon, you wrong. I think this could be the best thing that could happen to us, okay. I said it. Just give it a rest, Noon. It ain't got to be no big plot. It ain't just 'cause we colored. It's just a road that they need to run, and we happen to live where it needs to be."

Noon stood very slowly. Her smooth skin turned to granite. Her round, generous face was suddenly angular, lean. Even her arms so ready for hugging were pulled in close to her sides.

Liz cast her eyes down. It was hurting to look at Noon. Her voice went from shaking to a thin, straight line, from loud with emotion to deep and quiet where there was neither love nor hate, just determination. "I'm selling the house," she whispered.

The sun was pouring in through the billows of open-weave draperies and washing the room in yellow and gold. Noon walked deliberately toward Liz. She raised her arm with such force that her Sunday hat with the big yellow bow fell from her head. She brought her arm down quickly, openhandedly, right across Liz's mouth.

Liz felt her lip open, and she tasted her blood. She stared ahead, not looking at Noon. How could she look at Noon? What worse words could have fallen from her mouth? Better that she had called Jesus a liar than to tell Noon this. She let the throbbing in her lip grow. She didn't cringe to try to stop the pain. She didn't grab at her lip or even stroke it with her tongue. She needed the hurt. A good sound punishment. Now she and Noon were even. Now she could go ahead and see what price she could get for the house. She could move from this hole-in-the-ground part of the city. Go to a church where they didn't dance and shout and rejoice in being poor. Now at least she had this on Noon. A hand to the face, a busted lip.

Fannie pulled her ice from her tea. She ran to Liz and dabbed her lip with the ice. "Liz, tell Noon you didn't mean it. Do you have a fever? That must be it, you coming down with something and talking outta your head. You couldn't possibly be thinking about selling this house. Liz, tell Noon you didn't mean it. Tell her, tell her now." Fannie was shouting and almost jumping up down as she held the ice to Liz's swollen mouth.

Noon walked away from Liz. She went back to the couch and picked up her purse. She pulled out a starched white handkerchief with green embroidery and blew her nose hard. She let her purse dangle from her hands folded loosely in front of her. She stood firmly and stared at Liz, a silent, penetrating stare. "I never thought I'd raise a child that would defy me in the way that you just did." Her voice was dry. She cleared her throat several times.

"This isn't against you," Liz mumbled through her swollen lip. "It is my house, bought with money Ethel sent for me."

"This is not about the money," Noon yelled, bringing her voice from deep within her. Her tight fists rose and fell, punctuating her words. "This is about betrayal, disrespect, you thumbing your nose at everything I worked for."

And then Noon cried. Out of hurt that Liz, whom she found on the steps, and comforted, and prayed over, and raised up, that she would turn on her like this. Out of shame, as she looked at Liz with her top lip separated, she had defaced her; she should have seen the signs, should have confronted Liz before her thinking got to this point. Out of anger at the church and the people who wouldn't band together, at the city and the realtors that created this situation where mothers and daughters were pitted against one another, Noon dropped her shoulders and cried.

Fannie ran to Noon and hugged her and shook her and pleaded with her. "Please, Noon, please don't cry, it'll be okay. Liz is gonna come to her senses. She's being influenced, you know how low-down dirty their tactics are, they're influencing her, Noon, please don't cry." And then ran back to Liz and grabbed her by the shoulders and shouted, "How could you do such a thing, Liz, to Noon of all people? I feel like kicking your ass myself."

Liz looked at Fannie. She stared deep into her coal black eyes, and then she flinched. She couldn't stand to stare in Fannie's eyes sometimes. Sometimes all she could see was the darkness and then her own reflection. Sometimes she felt diminished when she looked in Fannie's eyes. It seemed that the worst that Fannie did was to curse on a Sunday. Liz was sure that Fannie didn't have the hateful thoughts running around in her head that were always spinning in Liz's. She even hated Fannie right now: for being in Noon's life first; for not caring what people thought about her, free of always having to hold it together, contained; for being a raw beauty, even now with her hair standing all over her head; for sharing a booth with Willie Mann last night, letting him look into those eyes that held people like magnets. She especially hated Fannie right now for that. So she flinched, and then she had to leave the room. She had to stomp up the stairs. She had to slam her door as hard as she could. She needed the grinding now more than ever. She needed the roughness between her teeth. She needed the solid rockiness of it to scrape the roof of her mouth. She needed to bang up the dust and lose herself in the wall.

"Leave her 'lone, Fannie," Noon called as Fannie started to follow Liz up the stairs. "I'm going. I'm going."

"Come on, I'll walk you home, Noon. Liz'll come to her senses."

Fannie stroked Noon's cheeks with lightly cupped hands and then linked her arm in Noon's.

They were both quiet as they walked back out into the sunlight. The yellow air reminded Noon about her hat. The one she had put the bright yellow flower to just so she get Liz's admiration. It was still on the floor by the couch. She didn't want to turn back now to retrieve it. Later. Later she'd unpin the flower, no need to rip the flower off, no need to ruin the hat; she'd just unpin it and let the flower lightly fall.

TWENTY-SIX

Liz was going down. Once she'd told Noon she was selling the house, she lost her joy. She'd felt justified as long as her plan to sell was a secret between her and Willie Mann. But now she was doubled over with the sound of Noon's sobs bouncing around in her stomach. And that overbearing sunlight that had rushed in through the curtains that day two weeks ago when she'd told Noon had exposed more than her plan; it put a different slant on Willie Mann. Made her heart tingle with a kind of pain that one feels in the tips of fingers that have been asleep for too long. She began to see him cast in that sunlight, imagining what he must have been saying to Fannie when he shared a booth with her at Royale. Started to awaken to the notion that he might stoop so low as to try to swoon Fannie, her own sister, the way she was beginning to realize he had been trying with other women all along. Over the past two weeks she wouldn't even talk to him. She hardly came out of her room anymore. Wouldn't go to classes, couldn't stomach that hourlong bus ride to Lincoln U. Called in sick at her part-time job at Wanamaker's. She'd started losing weight, hollow look to her eyes, red hair fast losing its proud luster. She couldn't even stand to look at herself in the mirror. She looked instead at the wall. She didn't have to worry about seeing her reflection in the grainy roughness of the chunks she tore from the wall's foundation.

Fannie tried with everything in her to reach out and pull Liz back. She'd shout through the thick wooden door late at night, "Hey, Liz, this is me,

Fannie, your closer-than-sister friend. Why you shutting me out? Let me help you, Liz. Let me in." Liz wouldn't. And then suddenly Fannie's seeing eye forced her to let go of Liz. She had a vision that shocked her into a struggle with herself.

⌇

One night when Fannie couldn't sleep because the darkness got blacker than it ever had, her bed sheet whiter, the tips on the hands of her bedside clock that glowed green in the dark hit her eyes like green streaks of lightning striking right in the center of her eyes. And her head pounded from the intensity of the colors, so she just covered her head with the sheets and shook. She saw herself then with Willie Mann. Right in the wine cellar at Club Royale. On the couch. Her thick hair fanned across the arm of the couch, her knees bent wide. Willie Mann moving to the rhythm coming from the club upstairs. A sound coming from deep in her throat like a sound she'd never made before. It was a half moan, half cry, breathless sound that sounded like "Yes." She'd hear that sound reverberating through her head whenever she tried to look Liz in the eye.

She couldn't tell Noon what she'd seen. Noon was already shouldering more than her share of burdens. So she confided in Next-Door-Jeanie. They were up late one night stuffing envelopes with letters to the editors of all the Negro-owned and liberal-leaning newspapers across the country. Just the two of them sitting in Jeanie's spare room–turned–library. The books lining the walls from the floor to the ceiling gave the room a tight, cozy feel, a soundproof feel. Before she realized it, she was saying, "Miss Jeanie, I need to talk to you. I'm plagued by a vision, and I need to talk to you."

Jeanie stopped folding and pushed the envelopes aside. "Anything, Fannie, you can tell me anything, anytime."

Fannie told her the vision just as she'd seen it, down to the sound coming from her own throat that meant Willie Mann was giving her pleasure. It terrified and embarrassed her so.

Jeanie didn't say anything at first. She watched Fannie as she talked, her shoulders slumped, head almost hung, not at all the bold, confident child she'd watched grow up. A reminder, Jeanie thought, child needs to be reminded of all she is. She reached across the table and pulled a piece of paper from Fannie's hand that she was crumpling and straightening out and crumpling again. "You have to confront him," Jeanie said sharply.

"Confront him?"

"Definitely. That boy got no power over you that a good hard stare won't shrink down to size."

"But it was a vision."

"So?"

"So, every time I've seen things they've come to pass. Even when I've prayed to Almighty God they've come to pass."

"Have they dealt with your own will, though, Fannie?"

"My will?" Fannie asked. Needing the paper back, needing to use her hands to let go of some of her energy.

"I'll bet not," Jeanie said as her hand lightly covered the balled-up paper, keeping it from Fannie's reach. "I'll bet they've always had to do with things like birth and death and storms and luck of fortune. Things you can't control, you might have seen them before they happened, but you couldn't have controlled them."

"I never tried to control them. I'm not God."

Jeanie half laughed. "Who're you telling?"

"Never knew you believed in God, Miss Jeanie." Fannie looked beyond Jeanie to the shelf where at least half a dozen Bibles rested, different versions and sizes and colors. "All those Bibles, never pictured you saying morning prayers with a Bible in your hands."

Jeanie laughed again. "Read it as a scholarly pursuit. Not saying I don't believe in a God per se, I just have a problem with religion. People confuse it so. Turn things over to the will of God that they have responsibility for tending to themselves, then fret day and night over what they need to be leaving to their God."

"You saying just leave it alone?"

"No, child. I'm saying that sound you heard coming from your throat that scares you so is of your own will. You always had control of your own will. From the time I watched you lock that white man in the cellar, even before that, even before you could walk and talk, you were staring people down. Strong will. Will stronger than Willie Mann, trust me, Fannie. You got to confront him. You got the power to make your vision not true."

254

"But what if I can't look in his face?" Fannie's voice had desperation running through it.

"Why shouldn't you be able to? What? You ashamed about something?"

"It's just when I saw it, I wasn't fighting it at all. You know, I was, you know, enjoying it." Fannie looked away. She looked beyond Jeanie again to the wall where the Bibles seemed to shove one another for space on the crowded shelf.

"Maybe the man stirred something in you before you even had the vision. Maybe your vision is as much a wish as it is a prophecy."

"But I really have strong feelings for Pop's nephew; he's the nicest, most caring person. I enjoy being with him, you know, sexually, he makes me feel good, yet what I was feeling in the vision with Willie Mann, I've never felt that, that intensely with Pop's nephew."

Jeanie's voice went softer, and she patted Fannie's hand gently over the scrunched-up paper. "You're human. I know Noon always exalted you some because she thought you could see things, but you're still human. Won't be the first time someone smart as you was stirred by a no-good man."

Jeanie's eyes drifted and got such a faraway look that Fannie had to ask, "You? Miss Jeanie."

"No, not me. My husband was a decent soul. My daughter."

"I didn't know you had a daughter."

"Do. At least I did." Jeanie answered matter-of-factly as she scooped the pile of envelopes back in front of her and picked up more pages to fold.

"Died?"

"In a sense. Man she fell in love with convinced her she was more white than black. Walked out that door twenty-five years ago and hasn't been back."

"How come you stayed, Miss Jeanie? You could have easily passed for white. Lived a life of privilege."

"My soul couldn't. Wouldn't have wanted to if it could. Too strong-willed to be pretending to be something I'm not. Like you, Fannie. You got to confront that man. Put him in his place and tell him to keep his sorry ass right there."

"What about Liz?" Fannie's voice screeched like a little girl trying to keep from crying.

"Liz got to come into her own just like you. You never were her keeper. Not really. You never had that kind of power either."

They went back to stuffing envelopes in the room that was quiet save the books occasionally shifting along the wall. Fannie settled in the chair and ran her knuckles along the seam of a folded letter. She thought about what Jeanie had just said about being stirred by a no-good man. That's what she feared the most, not Willie Mann, but the fact that she desired him so. That's what she needed to confront to make the vision not true. Her desire for the man. Eye to eye. She would.

She watched Jeanie from across the table and was struck by the softness of her features. Lived right next door to her her entire life and never realized what a pretty woman she was. Even in her old age. Beautiful woman.

TWENTY-SEVEN

Ethel was back in town. Herbie didn't know yet, not Fannie or Liz, and especially not Noon. Willie Mann knew. He had seen Ethel on South Street buying a pair of shoes. Followed her and learned she had rented a room on Catherine Street. He hadn't yet figured what to make of it. Didn't know if Fannie or Liz had summoned her, maybe even Herbie. The whole damned family was falling apart so. Noon more and more defiant about the highway, telling anybody who'd listen how they all had to work together to stop the properties being turned over one after the other, whole blocks at a time. Herbie fidgety, practically living at Club Royale, sitting and staring in the same shot of gin for hours at a time. Willie Mann had learned from the young girl that rented the house next to Fannie and Liz's that Liz hardly came out of her room anymore and that they must be getting the house revamped because the ferocious knocking coming from Liz's bedroom would sometimes wake them all up.

So Willie Mann really didn't know what to make of Ethel's return or of Fannie saying she needed to talk to him. Right now he was in the wine cellar at Club Royale, fluffing the pillows down there and dusting at the beer kegs. He was moving the inventory around, making it spacious for Fannie just in case. The couch was enough for most of the women he had ever had down there, but Fannie, if he could have a chance at her raw nature, dip into her virgin honesty, topple her prophet status: the one who sees things, who tells it like it is, who sets it all straight; if he could spread her on the couch and even kick over the beer kegs because the spreading was so ferocious, if he could make her normal, tame, ogle over him, be enchanted by him the way women were supposed to be, then he could rest easy. So he moved things around in the wine cellar just to make sure the space was sufficient.

"Two o'clock," she had told him, "I'm taking my lunch break from Pop's at two." He looked at his watch. It was five minutes till. He dashed upstairs and out of the club. He wanted to wait for her on the street so he could usher her down in the wine cellar through the opening on the side just in case Herbie was at the bar staring in his gin.

It was April, but the air was thick and gray. Willie Mann would have blended in with the air dressed all in gray himself, except for his yellow-toned skin. He looked up and down the block and was struck by his handiwork. Every property minus two on this long block had been turned over. Even the club, but they were still open for business until the demolition trucks would come, which was still months down the road. He felt good about what he had accomplished. Whether or not he thought of it as good or bad to sell and move, to run the road, to even get a kickback, his goal was persuasion. Bending wills. The stronger the will he broke, the greater the rush. And then he saw Fannie moving up the street toward him. Such a contrast with the landscape of abandoned structures with their lives all packed up and moved away. Fannie's will had not yet been broken.

Fannie moved swiftly up the street dressed all in yellow. The gray air needed the yellow as a reminder that spring was already here. Willie Mann twisted his pants at the waist and snatched at his collar. He smiled in spite of himself. Calculated smoothness was his usual effect, smiling on cue, laughing just the right amount of syllables, never with abandonment. But this smile, as he watched Fannie move quickly and gracefully toward him, came up involuntarily, unexpectedly, the way his fullness was coming up on him too.

"The lady is prompt," he said as he extended his hand.

"Where we talking?" Fannie asked, ignoring his hand, not looking in his face either.

"I thought we'd go downstairs to the cellar. You know, Herbie might be at the bar, and I didn't know if you necessarily wanted him to see us together."

"Necessarily there's nothing to see." She pushed back on her heels and allowed the double joints in her legs to pop out.

"Well"—Willie Mann breathed in deep and smoothed his hand over his slicked-back hair—"since it doesn't really matter one way or the other, we can just go on around the side down into the cellar. No need to disturb Herb any more than he already seems to be disturbed these days."

"Like you care," Fannie snapped as she followed his outstretched hand toward the side of the building.

Willie Mann watched Fannie walk in front of him. He could have just grabbed her tiny waist from behind right then and there in broad daylight. He could have just pulled her body to him and moved against her back right there along the side of the building. He could have mashed his chin into the top of her tall, woolly hair as he held her around her waist. But he wanted to be wrapped in the darkness of the cellar. He wanted the sounds coming from the partying upstairs in the bar to penetrate down through the cellar ceiling and wrap around them with the darkness. So he resisted any sudden moves out here in the cloudy April afternoon.

The side entrance was a hole in the ground, literally. Its thick wooden door was almost flush with the pavement. The door would trip the drunks as they struggled to get home late at night. It was a simple square. The children jumped hard on it and played foot-type games on their way home from school. It had a latch that flipped over and secured the wooden cover to the ground. Sometimes the latch would catch the high heels of women rushing to get to communion. It was one way to get down to the bottom of the club: Leave the blue air inside Royale, come outside to the side of the building, undo the latch, lift the three-foot wooden square covering, and walk down the iron stairway, right down the hole into the cellar.

Fannie moved down the stairway first. It was more like a ladder propped against the top of the hole than it was a stairway. She had to go down back first. The darkness hit her all at once as her yellow shoes touched the concrete floor. Willie Mann, experienced at climbing down the hole, followed quickly behind her. He pulled on a silver-linked chain, and there was light. Fannie took the room in all at once: the green couch, the beer kegs, the brown cardboard boxes, the lamp with the etched lampshade, the rug that went from the couch to just under a desk that held an oversized adding machine. She saw the whole thing laid out before her just as it had been in her vision. She felt light-headed. Despite her resolve not to let it affect her, despite her repeating over and over Jeanie's words that her will was stronger than his, despite her getting on her knees that very morning banging on her bed, hollering, "Jesus, Jesus, give me the strength to confront him," when Fannie saw the cellar lit all at once, the way it matched her vision in every detail, she felt the blood draining from her head, settling in her knees, making them buckle.

She tried to rationalize the weakness away. Surely in her vision she had seen it all this way because surely Liz had told her all about the cellar when she stretched across Fannie's bed on graduation night after Willie Mann had plucked Liz from her side as they walked home from Bookbinder's. And Liz told Fannie she had done it, gone all the way with Willie Mann. She had bled and it hurt and felt so good. No, she hadn't seen stars or heard explosions. But she did get dizzy from the pain and then the tingle. And he did moan right in her ear until it sounded like a trumpet. And oh, how soft his hair was as it moved against her body. Surely Liz must have dropped in details about the couch and the lamp and the rug. Surely she must have described the feeling that she felt as if she were falling as she walked backwards down the ladder into the cellar. But the more Fannie tried to rationalize it away, the more the weakness grew, and then she couldn't even look in Willie Mann's face.

That she couldn't look in his face was new for Fannie. She thought she could look in anybody's face. She thought if Satan tapped her on her shoulder late at night, she would be able to stare in his face, stare him down until he withered into serpent status and humbly retreated. But despite all of her boldness, her vision of laying with this man down here in this wine cellar and now being in this wine cellar experiencing the very thing she'd told Jeanie she feared the most—not being able to look in his face—was making her weak.

She walked to the desk and fingered the adding machine. She moved her fingers lightly across the humps of large square keys. "So this is where you do your crooked figuring, huh?" Her voice spilled out into the well-lit cellar.

"The yellow looks good on you," he said as he moved toward her back.

"I got to talk to you about—" Fannie talked more to the keys on the adding machine than to Willie Mann.

"If this is about Liz," he interrupted her as he moved closer in to Fannie's back, "I'm not seeing her; she won't even talk to me. I mean, at this point I want to just tell her to keep the house, don't sell it now if it's gonna bust up her whole family. I just hate to see her lose out when they bulldoze it anyhow."

"This isn't about Liz, it's about me." And then she turned to face him all at once. "I want you to understand that we cannot be friends, that you are not to be coming on to me with your bullshit lines, I don't care how many women you've swooned, don't be trying it with me. I'm not about to go under your no-good, evil spell." Fannie's eyes were more pleading than challenging. Her shoulders were slumped, more resigned than squared and determined. Even her legs, usually pushed back hard so that her calves popped out, were bent softly. He could even see the bend through her bright yellow pants.

"Fannie, I don't know what this talk about spells has to do with anything." He was walking slowly toward her. His eyes were locked in on the fear in hers. She moved back against the desk. She wished the desk were not there so that at least she would have inches more to go before she had nowhere else to go. Where else was there? Hadn't it already been laid out before her? Hadn't she had the vision? She, the clairvoyant one who could look down and expose other people's demons to themselves. Now here she was up against this desk with nowhere to go, with Willie Mann, her sister's lover, almost to her, with the substance of the vision all around her, and the voice in her head saying it may as well be now. Hadn't all the other visions come to pass? Didn't Noon's father die, the way Fannie's vision said that he would? And what about all the strings of lesser scenes that had been laid out before her, whether it was somebody's accident, or unexpected visit, or hitting the number big? Didn't they all come true sooner or later? Maybe Jeanie was wrong. Maybe this was bigger than her will.

It may as well be now, she thought, as Willie Mann was at her face-to-face. He moved his face into hers as he pulled her to him. She could feel his heart pounding hard and fast, almost thumping to the beat of the music coming from the club upstairs. She felt his hardness against her yellow pants as he pulled her in closer and closer and stretched his mouth wide open to cover her thick lips, to put her whole mouth in his all at once. And then the thumping was no longer coming from the club upstairs, but from right down there as someone was moving down the ladder-type steps. Fannie heard the footsteps.

She moved her face from his.

He thought it was so he could kiss at her neck.

She stretched her neck way up.

He thought it was so he could move his head on down, undo her bright yellow buttons with his teeth.

She moved her body in closer to get a better view of the feet making their way down the leaned-over steps.

He thought it was so he could move his manhood against her thigh and shift it so that it could be wedged between her legs.

She breathed short, excited breaths as she saw a bright red shoe hit the floor.

He thought it was from her arousal as he undid her buttons and mashed his throbbing against her in big circles.

She knew the shoe, the foot, always knew that was how the foot would appear, in a bright red shoe. She used to make Liz tell her over and over every detail about her down to the slant of her foot.

She made a gasping sound.

He thought it was because she knew he was getting ready to explode, right there pushed up against her at the desk. He couldn't get to the light, to the couch, couldn't even get to his belt buckle, or hers.

The shoe hit the floor, and a figure all in red walked from the shadow of the leaned-over stairs into the light. The figure was in full view now. Fannie thought her heart would jump right out of her chest. Yes, this was her, more beautiful than even Fannie had imagined, right down here in the cellar at Club Royale. This was Ethel.

"Willie Mann, you down here?" Ethel called. "You still the same lying son of a bitch you always were?"

"Shit!" He spit the word out as he pulled himself from Fannie and turned quickly to see who it was.

"Oops, did I interrupt you, Willie Mann?" Ethel asked, giggling like a schoolgirl. "You still bringing your young ladies down here, huh? Been doing it since the time you were a teenager, but what you, thirty-two, thirty-three, and you still got to do it down here in this cellar?"

Fannie stood mesmerized. This was Ethel, not five feet from her. After all the years of constructing an image of her that bolted her to goddess stature, and defending that image over and over to Noon and even Liz; after being ready to kick somebody's ass for calling Ethel a man-snatching whore or, worse yet, a child neglecter; after fantasizing about trying to hunt Ethel down, to thank her for leaving Liz with them, to tell her that she understood why she'd left Liz the way she did; after years of wanting to jump into Ethel's head because she was fascinated so by women like she herself was, who were brash and free and generous and didn't give a good damn what other people thought, here she was standing right in front of her.

"Miss Ethel, what you doing down here?" Willie Mann asked, nervousness crowding his voice.

"You tell me," Ethel said as she stood with her hands on her hips. "You been following me all over downtown. I can't even try on a simple pair of shoes without looking up and seeing your tall ass peering through the window. I said to myself, let me come down here right now and see what this Willie Mann wants with me. So here I am, and cut the Miss Ethel crap, you ain't seventeen no more, at least not in numbers. Now maybe in your head—" She laughed in a way that was full of notes and colors. "Who's the young lady you done slick-talked down here?"

She walked in closer to the center of the cellar. She was right under the light. Fannie thought that she got more beautiful the longer she looked at her. She had large, round eyes that drooped; her cheekbones were like circles that gave roundness to her face; her nose and her hair were short, her lips round and thick. But it was the coming together of it all that made her beautiful, that and her hourglass of a figure. Fannie suspected that it was her shape more than anything that made men ogle after her. But it was her face, the temptress nature of its arrangement softly set in skin the color of cinnamon, that held them.

"We're down here on business, Miss—I mean, Ethel," Willie Mann stammered.

"Then why the front of your pants soaking wet?" She laughed again.

Fannie laughed too. How absolutely amusing to see Willie Mann stammering, caught, and he cares that he's caught, and he's nervous, and his spell was broken over Fannie at least for now, and she hoped forever.

"See, even the young lady thinks you're funny. What's your name, sweetie? Come from behind this no-screwing man so I can see you."

Fannie moved way to the side of Willie Mann, away from the desk that had held her trapped. She stepped out in full view of Ethel.

Ethel's whole face smiled all at once when she looked at Fannie. "Well, you sure look like sunshine all in yellow down here in this murky cellar. You too bright-looking for these surroundings, and if you ask me, you too pretty for this cheap ass that ain't even got enough style to surround you with a little satin and lace." Ethel contained herself. Fannie still looked to Ethel very much like the little girl that Noon would troop through the streets of South Philly back when Ethel was searching out a good home for Liz. She was only taller. Same dark, woolly hair that would never stay contained in those thick, tight plaits, same corn-bread-colored skin, same thin nose, same dancing to the eyes, just taller. She wanted to run to Fannie and hug her, thank her for being such a good sister to Liz. She'd heard over the years how tight they were. And then she stopped her memory because she didn't want to go any farther than that. Not now.

"Actually I'm not at all one of his young ladies," Fannie said as she moved even farther away from Willie Mann. "Ma'am, uh, can I call you Ethel, because I know you quite, quite well, and well, uh, you don't know me, but you probably, well, you might know about me."

"Sure, sweetie, please call me Ethel. It makes me feel young when young folks call me by my first name." Ethel moved in closer as she talked. "Tell me your name, sweetie. And where might I know you from? I hope from being surrounded by people better than Mr. Willie Mann here, and I sure am glad to hear you not really with him, guess he just got himself all worked up over the thought of being with you. Now tell me your name, sweetie."

"Fannie," she said. "My name is Fannie."

TWENTY-EIGHT

Tom Moore's stomach turned inside out and his hands shook as he read the chapter of the City Code, mimeographed onto the Highway South Project's official letterhead. He had no business even working on a Saturday. Cut back, his doctor had ordered. Take a vacation, longer weekends, relax. But here it was a Saturday and he'd gone to work anyhow, and now his hands shook and the turning in his stomach was slowly rising up to his chest as he read the page. It was an excerpt from the chapter of the City Code citing the requirements for demolishing structures. Tom Moore knew what they were asking him to do. Even as he turned the page over in his hands that shook and read his boss's scribble: "Moore, write up something like this: 'In the interest and ultimate safety of the Negro community still residing in the area targeted for relocation, the Highway South Project, which was about to acquire the church, and in so doing had petitioned an independent appraisal, has detected fractures significant enough to warrant further investigation of the church structure.'"

Before he even got to the scribble in red that demanded, "Moore, level the church," he knew they were asking him to justify its demolition. Making it easy for him too, no need to walk from his desk to do the research, no need to ponder how to force this situation with the church to apply to the City Code.

The dark hair along his white arms almost stood straight up as he pushed his half-eaten liverwurst and cheese sandwich to the side of the desk and reached for the phone. The phone was heavy to lift, and he had to catch his breath as he set it down in front of him and pushed his fingers into the black holes and watched the dial spin back around at dizzying speed. His breath caught right at the top of his chest when he heard his wife's voice on the other end. "You know how you been wanting to go away, California? Isn't that where you been wanting to go?"

"Tom? Is that you?"

"California, right? Get us some tickets. Let's leave tonight."

"What? What are you saying?"

"It's gotten very bad here. Very bad."

"Tom, please tell me what's going on. You're making me nervous."

"The church, I mean. The houses, okay, we've made a lot of progress with the houses, but the church wasn't part of the equation. Even the pastor was still resisting. Now they're telling me to write the church up. You do know what that means? It means they'll just level it. All I have to do is write it up and say that the structure has fractures, or a fucking gas leak, or is sitting in a sinkhole."

He could hear his wife breathing heavily on the other end. He wondered if she was wearing the twenty-fifth anniversary diamond ring he'd just given her. He wondered how amenable she'd be to selling it. "They shouldn't have sent me down there to do business with those colored people down there. Haven't I been telling you that all along?"

"Tom, I want you to come home right now. You need some rest. You got no business even being there on a Saturday. Come home. Tell me you'll come home right now."

"I got to do something first." His voice suddenly took on new energy. "I'll be there soon. First I've got one more thing to do."

He mashed the receiver quickly, then picked it back up and dialed another number. He sat up straighter when he heard his boss's voice crackle, "Hello," through the phone line.

"I can't justify leveling the church." He was surprised to hear the words coming from his mouth. He could taste the remnants of the liverwurst and cheese sandwich sifting along his tongue.

"What? Who the hell is this?"

"We can get all the properties, it may take some time, another year or two, but we can get them all out without tearing down the church. Those Negroes down there have become quite aware of processes anyhow.

They'll challenge it. It'll be too damned tough to write it up so it won't be challenged."

"Moore? Is this you?" the voice on the other end demanded. "We don't want to wait another year or two. As long as they got that church down there to go to, the holders-on won't budge. So write it up and get that fucking church off of that corner."

"We'll offer the reverend a higher price for the church. That way they can vote on it or do whatever they need to do amongst themselves to sell it outright. We can just relocate the church, we won't have to tear it down and, you know, just shock everybody like that."

"Hasn't that goddamn reverend been in your pocket all along?"

"But that was just so he would be noncommittal, you know, so he wouldn't resist outright in front of his congregation. We promised him we wouldn't touch the church. It's been easier that way."

"Moore, you're not getting paid for fucking easy."

No shit, he thought, as he let the phone go limp in his sweaty hand. He wasn't getting paid for the most of it. He rubbed his chest, trying to rub away the heartburn from the liverwurst. He wasn't getting paid for the church services or for sitting at the dining room tables down there where he had to look in their eyes. After he'd looked at the pictures of Jesus on the walls, the baby pictures on the mantels, the figurines in the china closets, the fruit bowls on the buffets, the tops of their heads, the plates they set in front of him, the palms of their hands. After he had nowhere else to look and he had to look in their eyes, and he started to know them by name: Mrs. Saunders, Mrs. Jones, Mr. Hicks, Sister Maybell—he even called her Sister Maybell.

"Why bulldoze the church now?" he yelled into the phone. "What's the fucking rush, why the sudden ostentatious show of power? I can't justify leveling the church." He said it again. "You level it your damn self. You go down there and look in their faces when they pray. Then let's see you tear down the fucking church."

He banged the shiny black phone on the receiver. He pressed the mimeographed chapter of the City Code into a long white envelope and addressed it to Reverend Schell. He stared at it for a while. Then he covered it over with a clean white label. This time he addressed it to Noon. He gathered his personal effects and quickly shoved them into his briefcase. He was thinking about the night-owl flight he and his wife would take to California. He couldn't stay here anymore. He had only two options if he stayed here: Be a villain or a hero. He couldn't stomach either. He'd just leave.

🖎

Herbie ran through the house to get to the door. "All right," he yelled. "What is it, a damn fire?" He was just in the bathroom relaxing with his newspaper before the urgent knocking pulled him up. "Better be important," he mumbled, and then looked through the window and saw Fannie all in yellow.

"Where's Noon?" Fannie asked as she stumbled into the doorway, out of breath. "I got something to tell you." She smoothed at her hair and tried to bring the excitement in her voice to a controlled whisper. "But I don't want to tell Noon just yet. Where is she? Is she here?"

"At the church," Herbie said. "Jeanie came running over here not long ago, all excited, talking so fast I couldn't even understand what she was saying. All I could make out is that Tom Moore was fired earlier today or quit. Then something about the church, and Noon was shouting, 'Lord have mercy,' as she ran out behind Jeanie. Don't seem good, whatever it is."

"Uh-oh," Fannie said, concern covering her face. "I got to get over there and see what's going on. And then I got to get back to work before Pop thinks I quit on him. But first I got to tell you something, Herbie." Fannie was still fighting to catch her breath. And then stopping herself and swallowing hard, she said, "I see your folded newspaper, sorry I interrupted you, but you'll never believe who I just saw. She's actually here; she's actually in Philly. I just talked to her."

"Just tell me who, Fannie, without the dramatics," Herbie said as he tossed his paper on the coffee table and walked to the deep armchair.

"Okay, but I don't know how Noon's gonna handle this; she hates her so. But Noon got to understand she been wrong about her all these years. I mean, Herbie, she's so honest, and warm, she's real warm, but then I always knew she would be. I been trying to tell Liz all these years that she has a powerful love for her, that's why she left her. You should see her face when she talks about Liz; you just feel it inside how deep her feelings run."

Herbie was no longer looking at Fannie. He was staring blankly, seeing the letter in his head. He was scanning the loopy inked figures, trying to see the date. Four weeks. She had said. It had only been three. But then he hadn't taken into account how long it took for the letter to reach him. How long it could have sat at the club before Big Carl handed it to him. Damn, this was happening too fast. He had wanted to prepare Noon first. He had wanted to be the first one to see Ethel, to warn her what she was up against. He had even intended on coming clean with Fannie, just so she would know. Now that Ethel was back Liz might be spurred to tell anyone who'd listen. He at least wanted to tell Fannie. But Ethel's feet had already hit Philly's dirt. She was already strutting up and down the tight blocks, in and out the bebop clubs, probably shopping on South Street, and Ninth Street, sipping coffee at Horn and Hardart, hailing yellow cabs when she didn't feel like walking, paying some young head to carry her bags filled up with lemons for her singing voice, going to Clara's to get her hair washed and pressed, her nails done, her eyebrows tweezed. She was back. He could barely hear Fannie rambling on and on excitedly, sounding very far away.

"Herbie, Herbie, you not even listening," Fannie said, walking right up to his face, almost shouting. "I'm trying to tell you something important, and you not even paying attention."

"I know what you trying to tell me, Fannie, okay," he said as he just let himself collapse stiffly into the deep armchair. "She's back, right? Ethel, she's the hell back here."

"That's right," Fannie said, her voice suddenly calm, serious. She stared at Herbie as he sat in the deep armchair. It was almost as if he wore a leaded belt filled with guilt that pulled him down, made everything on him sag, from his hairline to his eyebrows to the corners of his mouth, his shoulders, even his arms as they hung over the sides of the chair. He put his elbows on his knees and slumped forward with his face buried in his hands. Fannie sat along the arm of the chair. She didn't say anything at first; she just sat there.

Herbie was breathing loud breaths into his hands. He shook his head slowly back and forth. He couldn't find the right combination of words. Did the combination of words even exist? How could he explain it to Fannie? Coming home to Noon, night after night, hoping that maybe tonight she wouldn't be like a corpse, still and cold. Making him feel like putting a strap to her just to hear her cry out, just to make her move, to stir her nature, just to get some life-affirming sign, some passion, even if it was just to wrestle him away, to fight him off, just some motion. And not just for his release, not just for his pleasures. He could go to any club on any night and find a body just for his pleasures. He just needed to know that Noon was alive. How could he explain it to Fannie, that he wasn't some sex-crazed thing that ran to Ethel whenever she would have him just to push it to her over and over? That it wasn't just that Ethel moved like fire, and danced, and squeezed and arched. It was more that she was alive, bubbling over with life, unrestrained. He was free when he was with Ethel. No lugging and shouldering, no shit to carry. No cotton to bale, no frightened younger brothers, or sobbing fathers, no whipping up a response from mothers already dead.

"Something I need to tell you, Fannie," Herbie said, startling the air that had become so still around them. "It's shit from the past, Fannie, but since the past and today done gone and met and shook hands with each other, I got to tell you about it."

Fannie ran her hand along Herbie's shoulder. "I'm listening, Herbie," she said softly as she moved her hand from his back and smoothed at the lacy doilies that rested along the top of the chair.

Herbie rocked slightly to and fro and tapped his feet gently. He moved his hand from his face somewhat. "It ain't been peaches and cream with me and Noon," he said, and then stopped and cleared his throat. "I mean I love her, as God is my witness, I always loved her, but she had some problems, and sometimes it sent me to places where I had no business being. You following me, Fannie?"

"I'm with you, Herbie," she said, stroking his back again.

"I spent a lot of time with Ethel, Fannie, when she was here in Philly. Every chance I got. Sometimes I thought that if she would have given me the word, I'd have left. That's what makes me feel worst of all. I would have left Noon and you girls. It's just that Ethel was always so free like. I didn't feel no pressures when I was with her. You know, Fannie, it's hard on a man, it's damn hard on a colored man. Ethel just made it feel a little easier."

Fannie listened to Herbie's words spill out and fill the room. She knew she just needed to let Herbie talk. It was best not to interrupt him and remind him that it was damned hard on Noon too, nor would she counter him with how life was filled with pressures and that's not a ticket to go running around. Because actually Fannie did understand. Sometimes she could see through the action clear to the motivation. Sometimes she could sniff the vinegar behind the syrup in somebody's sweet exterior and mannered niceties. And other times, like now, in the face of a person's indictable wrongdoings, Fannie could see straight through it all, all the way to his true nature.

"I always knew it was something about you and Ethel and Liz," Fannie said as she moved her hand from Herbie's back and smoothed at the doilies that rested along the back of the chair. "I guess I always figured it for what it was too. I just never let it see the light of day. Until just now, watching you, reading your face."

She patted his back. "Herbie, you a good person. You care. And I know Noon would never, ever understand it in a million years, but I do."

"I don't deserve a daughter good as you."

"I ain't so good. I just never saw things in right and wrong in the conventional sort of way. Sometimes what seems right to everybody else seems downright evil to me."

"I ain't been a great help to Liz growing up in this house either," Herbie said as he sat straight up. "In fact I tried to make her life miserable every chance I got. I'm sure that's part why it was so easy for her to turn on Noon the way she did. I never really made her feel like she was the daughter to me you were."

Fannie stood and walked to the window. She couldn't remember the last time she had seen Liz. Three days ago, maybe. She had passed her in the hallway as she rushed to get her bus so she could make it to her first class. She had asked Liz if she was going to school. Liz had looked down, muttered something about having an upset stomach, and quickly retreated to her bedroom. And then the knocking on the wall started again. Fannie knew that part of it wasn't Herbie's fault.

"Liz is going through something that I don't even understand, Herbie. And most of it don't have nothing to do with you. And the parts that do, well, I'm sure God'll forgive you. In fact," she said as she walked back to Herbie and stooped in front of him and took his hands in her own, "I'll bet if God were to condemn you to hell right now for running around on Noon, I'll bet it would be to the luxury part of hell. In fact, when it got too hot, I'll bet he'd even let you have a fan, and not one of the paper ones that they give you in church; I'll bet he'd give you an honest-to-goodness electric fan. And everybody would say, 'See that Herbie wasn't such a bad guy, heard he even got a fan in hell.' "

Herbie's shoulders were shaking up and down as he laughed. Fannie stood and kissed him on the cheek. "I got to go, Herbie. I got to find Noon and see what's happening at the church." And then she paused and looked at Herbie, and her face was as soft as it gets. "You sure you okay?"

"I'm sure," he said, able to smile now.

"Later, alligator," she said, and was out of the door.

"Crocodile, after while," Herbie whispered to the closed door.

&

They were running out of time. Noon knew it. She sat at the end of the long table in the bottom of the church with her forehead resting in her cupped hands. Twenty-five or so had gathered there, hurriedly, to mull over this latest piece of information. They were being asked to vacate the building out of concern for their welfare. " 'Serious structural fractures,' " Bow read the letter aloud to them all. " 'With Tom Moore's untimely departure, I as head of the Highway South Project will step in as interim liaison.' "

Reverend Schell sat at the head of the table as Bow read to the captive twenty-five. His church clerk hadn't been available when the courier had arrived at his office a short time ago while he and Bow talked about the Phillies training camp and the Eartha Kitt play at the New Locust Theater. "Forgot my glasses," he'd told Bow, "can't see a darn thing without them, what the heck does this say?"

After only the first paragraph Reverend Schell had stopped Bow. Said they'd better call Noon and Jeanie and as many of the faithfuls as they could round up. "Doing something like this on a Saturday serious indeed," he'd said.

So now Bow read the balance of the letter, the part Reverend Schell wasn't prepared for. The part that said, "I'd like to continue meeting with you, Reverend Schell. I sincerely hope we can also have the cordial relationship that you and Mr. Moore enjoyed as we continue negotiations for the acquisition of the church and the remaining properties in the affected area." Bow's speech slowed as he read the last sentence. The letter shook in his hands. He turned and looked at Reverend Schell. All twenty-five looked at him. Their faces were contorted somewhere between confusion and horror. Their exclamations too. Some gasped and clutched at their bosoms; others scratched their heads; still others just shuddered as if to say, "Oh, God, no!"

Reverend Schell squared his shoulders in his best black suit, which made him look as if he were set to preach the eulogy at a Friday night funeral. He should have waited for his clerk to read the thing to him alone. He should have figured those meetings would come back to haunt him. He shouldn't have sat on the fence for so long. Should have just told Tom Moore and those Highway South people no, right out. Should have slammed the door in Willie Mann's face. Why'd he even give them an audience? For what? For those brown envelopes they slipped him. Even though his congregation was willing to meet his financial needs, sell chicken dinners all night long to meet his needs. He'd given audience to the devil for what? So he could be exposed here and now like this.

Well, had he met with them? Bow demanded to know.

"Divide and conquer," Reverend Schell boomed. "Don't you know by now those are their tactics? Now that Tom Moore's gone, their tactics are gonna get even meaner. We can't let them split up the few of us left united on this thing."

"Did you sit down with them or not?" Bow stood and pointed his finger across the table at Reverend Schell. "Were you negotiating with them, like this letter says?"

"Once or twice I met with them; as your pastor I had to see what they were offering." Reverend Schell stood now too. "But I made it absolutely clear that I would never endorse their Highway South plan."

"Well, why'd you keep meeting with them?" Sister Maybell asked. "My own pride-and-joy grandson, Willie Mann, been working with them, I'm 'shamed to say, and I wouldn't even consent to meet with them other than the time that man what quit, or got fired, whatever happened to him, when he came down here to explain things as he saw it and made me an offer. Now that was one thing, but to keep on meeting with them, working against us like that. Bet you even smoked cigars with the good-for-nothings."

"Probably bought you that new suit you got on," Pat Saunders from the funeral home yelled. "You probably came that cheap."

Reverend Schell straightened his tie and tightened his jaw and stared straight ahead. He couldn't really say whether he'd come cheaply or not to the Highway South people. He never counted the contents of those brown envelopes they'd given him as payment for his time. He'd just spill the contents into his El Producto cigar box where he kept his spending money. He'd take out a five here, a single there, sometimes enough for a silk tie, an embroidered handkerchief. His lifestyle was modest.

"No, Sister Pat," he shouted. "They didn't buy me this suit. Nor did they buy me out. If that were the case, would I have had Brother Bow stand up and read this to you all? Tell me, why would I have let him do that if I had anything, anything at all to hide? It's because I wanted to expose them to you. Their tactics. We can't let them pull the rest of us apart."

Noon slowly lifted her head from her hands. Suddenly she remembered the day when her hands shook over the papers that summoned them to a hearing about Liz's legal guardianship. The way Reverend Schell turned the papers upside down and seemed to study them before turning them right side up again. It hit her now like a wooden spoon against an empty ten-quart stewing pot: Reverend Schell couldn't read. That's why he let Bow say those incriminating sentences out loud; he'd had no idea what those sentences were. She watched him standing at the head of the table looking almost stately with his shoulders squared. How brilliant he must be to have pulled it off all these years. Pretending to read the Scripture, the songs in the hymnal, the bulletin of announcements for the week. How it must have eaten him up to have lived that lie. How crumbled he would be if she exposed him now right here in the lower sanctuary. So easy. Just stand and ask him to read the letter himself, tell him to spell "cat," or hand him some scribble and watch him pretend to decipher it. It would be too easy to crumble him right here and now. Easiest thing in the world to do. Give a Negro man a little authority, little power, then crumble him like a day-old cookie. It was ugly. How easy it was. Noon couldn't be that ugly. No, sir, it would be too easy, too ugly to crumple the man now.

"We spinning our wheels in knee-deep mud if we gonna sit here and try to make Reverend Schell admit to something that obviously was not wrongdoing." Her voice wavered as she spoke.

"How we know it's not wrongdoing?" Pat Saunders asked.

"Because if it was, he would've been more vocal in favor of the highway, wouldn't he had? Did he encourage anyone here to take Tom Moore up on his offer? Who? Name me one person who he advised to sell and move."

"He hasn't exactly been so vocal in his opposition to it either," Bow said. "I'm trying to think of even one sermon that he preached encouraging us to hold our ground. In all the three years we been battling this thing, surely he could've done one sermon on it. And the fact still remains, he was meeting with them."

"We got to allow our leaders a bit of leeway. We got to get more sophisticated with our politics. By right we should have sent him to meet with them, should have let him be our emissary, shouldn't have forced him to sneak."

"Reverend Schell's rightness or wrongness is not the important thing here." Jeanie stood and spoke in her clear, strong voice. "That letter Bow just read constitutes an eviction notice. We need to put our energy into challenging that. In fact, we need to have a challenge ready to be filed first thing Monday morning. So we need to get our own independent inspectors in here to see what all this fractures business is about."

One by one they went the length of the long table on both sides until they agreed that it wasn't their Reverend Schell that needed to do the proving, at least not right now. Even finally Bow relented and sat and shook his head back and forth.

Reverend Schell looked at Noon and smiled. In that instant he loved her, truly loved her. Should have been my wife, he thought. Surely wouldn't have needed healing prayers if she'd been my wife.

Noon rubbed her hands over her forehead as they discussed the filing of the challenge. They'd get the church building historically certified. They'd demand a waiting period, a public comment period. Her birthmark, the line stuck at twelve that ran from her crown to just above her nose, seemed to deepen as they talked. It seemed she could almost feel it growing. As if it were being stretched as the skin on her forehead, and her entire face, got tighter and tighter. They were losing. Their voices seemed to be getting farther and farther away. Noon fought back tears. She couldn't let them see her cry. She had been their unlikely champion. Keep-to-herself Noon. Egged on by Jeanie's politics, she had become their leader. Surprisingly articulate once she got going, smarter than she ever thought she was, even quick-witted at times; she had begun to feel capable over the past three years as she fought off the running of the road. She began to feel as she used to when she was ten or eleven and she would help her mother take care of her father and brothers. She knew she was good at cooking, at getting just the right stiffness in their stark white Sunday shirts. She knew she could whip up a dress quicker than her cake could rise. She could wring a chicken's neck in the morning and have it plucked, cleaned, stuffed, and roasted by dinner at two. She was good. And then in the midst of her goodness those devils tainted her. They took her goodness from her, scraped it out of her. The same way she felt as if her church were being snatched from her now. Her church: more than a building, much more than the brick and mortar and orange and blue stained glass windows, it was her precious haven, her salvation, her rock.

Suddenly Noon wanted to go home. Not just home around the corner and three blocks to Lombard Street. But home to Florida. She wanted to look in her mother's velvety face, fold herself up in her arms. She wanted her brothers to dote over her, tease her. She wanted to stand in the bedroom where her father had died and feel his spirit wash over her. Suddenly more than anything she just wanted to go home. Just for a while. A few days, a week. She needed to turn her attention away from the lie of the road. She needed to hear her mother remind her, "Noon, when a thing plagues you so and you done all you can, the outcome is no longer up to you. Sometimes the best thing you can do is take your hands off, just let it go, let it go."

Then they all heard heavy-booted footsteps rush down the stairs, and the door to the lower sanctuary flew open. A half dozen uniformed sheriffs stood there, handcuffs shining from their side pockets, nightsticks poised. "We're here to escort you folks out," one of them shouted.

"Escort us out, why?" Bow shouted back.

"Orders from L and I. Inspectors detected fractures in the structure. For your own good, we're to escort you out from here and make sure it stays vacant until they can get it checked out or repaired."

"Suppose we say we're not leaving?" Sister Maybell sat with her arms folded over her ample bosom.

"Sisters, Brothers." Reverend Schell's smooth baritone voice crackled through the confusion. "Let's go peacefully. We'll be back here, we'll have our papers filed first thing Monday morning. This is illegal and they know it. We'll bring the *Tribune* back with us Monday, and the *Bulletin* too. We'll call TV stations; we'll show everybody the treachery going on here. We'll win, we'll win."

"Come on back to the funeral parlor," Pat Saunders offered. "We can even have church there tomorrow if need be. I guarantee you no one's gonna run us from there."

Noon felt a sinking deep in her chest. She walked slowly, heavily to the door. Reverend Schell touched her elbow. "Noon, er, Sister Noon," he stammered.

She looked at him. The blush that usually widened her face when she looked at him wasn't there now. Nor the gentle bend that usually came up in her knees when she looked at him. Her pulse was steady, not that harder, faster pulse that usually rushed when she looked at him. She looked right at him. Just a man. That's all he'd ever been. No better than Herbie even. No magic potions, no sleight of hand to pull a rabbit forth. No special healing powers to make her passions gush. Just a man. A needy, vulnerable man.

"Reverend?" she asked as she looked at him, through him.

"Noon, your, er, your healing time, I mean the place for your healing prayers, well, I just, since we're leaving here now, I just wanted to set up—"

"Heal yourself, Reverend," she whispered as she pulled her elbow from his folded palm, "You bow at the altar and heal your own self first."

Then she saw Fannie all in yellow running toward her, pushing back the barricades that now surrounded the church. "Let it go, Fannie," Noon shouted, afraid that one of the blackjack-toting sheriffs might crack Fannie's skull. "Just let it go."

🦢

"I want the first train to Florida," Noon told Herbie when she got in after being routed from the church by the sheriffs. "Need to go home, need to go home. Need to do like my mama would say do. Need to take my hands off and just let it go."

Herbie was relieved. Would have carried her to Florida on his back if she'd asked. Anywhere to put some time and space between her and her crusade to save them all from the highway. "Seven in the morning, Silver Meteor," he said excitedly. "It leaves at seven in the morning, and it's always on time. I'll see you on the train myself. I'll even go with you if you'd like. Got plenty of vacation time coming to me. Twenty years on the job, I know they'll give me a week off with short notice."

"That would be nice, you go with me. Please go with me." She leaned her head on his shoulders. He kissed the top of her hair that was soft; he'd almost forgotten how soft her hair was.

Fannie went straight to Noon and Herbie's after work. She was as relieved as Herbie that Noon was going home, just for a week to rest her mind. Fannie talked to Herbie with her facial expression over the top of Noon's head, letting him know she hadn't told Noon about Ethel. They'd just wait, they agreed. At least until after her trip.

Fannie settled into the evening with Noon and Herbie the way she hadn't done in a long time. They had dinner together, hoagies from Pop's. They always used to have hoagies on Saturday night. They sat out on the steps until late, until the chill in the April night air made them shiver. Then Fannie ran upstairs and pulled her soft, nappy blanket from the bed, and the three snuggled under it on the steps warm from the cool April night the way used to when Fannie was a child. Before Liz even. They played gin rummy and ate Popsicles and watched TV some. *Perry Mason*, Noon's favorite show was *Perry Mason*. Then Fannie helped Noon pack for her trip home. Cotton nightgowns with lacy bows, open-toed shoes, straw Sunday hats, no aprons. Fannie insisted, "This a relaxation trip, no cooking and cleaning this trip. And I'm gonna call each of your brothers and tell them don't look for you to be doing no cooking, not a yeast roll, not a sweet potato pie, not even a simple pan of quick bread."

Noon smiled as Fannie listed her demands of all she could not do. Home. She was going home.

Fannie held Noon for a long time when she got up to leave. She kissed Herbie on the cheek and reminded him that this trip was his vacation too. She hugged Noon again and walked on out and down the street that was filled with quiet activity, people sitting out, or stepping out, or heading in on this Saturday night. She turned to look back down Lombard Street when she was about to round the corner. Noon and Herbie stood on the top step, watching her, waving to her; they seemed older, sadder. A lump came up in Fannie's throat, suddenly, unexpectedly. She turned the corner quickly so they wouldn't see her cry.

TWENTY-NINE

pring break came, and Fannie lied to Ethel. Told her that Liz was spending the week with their friend Julep at Howard in Washington, D.C. She'd be back on the weekend, she told her. She had to tell her something. She had yelled through the door last night when she could get a word in through the banging on the wall to tell Liz that Ethel was back. "Fuck her" was the reply from Liz, who rarely ever cursed. So Fannie intended to talk some sense into Liz, help her get herself together, make her presentable for Ethel; she just needed some time.

Liz was resistant to any help. Spinning around in that room the way her stomach was spinning, imagining her life unravel. Scholarship probably gone, she thought; job all gone; Noon hated her now, she was sure; Willie Mann probably fucking Fannie by now. So she pounded at the wall until her shoulders ached and she was weak from cramps. Then she'd go to the bathroom until the spinning in her stomach stopped. Then she'd brush her hair, shine her mirror, wave away the dust, and do her nails. She'd go to bed after that. And when she got up, she'd start all over again. See her life tumbling down all around her, then the relief of the wall. She was like an infant with night and days confused in that room. Except there was no one to rock her to ease her into sleep. So she'd rock herself too. For hours at a time she'd rock and even hum, the way Noon used to hum, or was that Ethel, or was that her own mother's humming? Until she couldn't stand the sound of her voice anymore, and she tried to catch her voice spilling out, so she could stop it, she'd clap her hands in front of her lips to smother the humming, until she couldn't stand the sight of her hands. And then, mercy, mercy, she'd fall asleep. Day in, day out, that was her routine, spinning in that room.

$$\text{\Large ❦}$$

In the meantime, since it really was spring break and since Noon and Herbie were gone for the week, Fannie spent all of her time with Ethel. They were inseparable. They'd start with breakfast at Horn and Hardart, then shop on Chestnut Street until lunch. Then chicken salad sandwiches at Lit Brothers, and take in a movie, a play, or just sit in Rittenhouse Square. They'd go to Bea's Barbecue for dinner one night, Fran's Fish Fry the next. Then from club to club for what seemed like all night long. From the Postal Card to the Upper Lounge to Bill's Be Bop Spot. Sometimes Ethel was called on to sing, and she just couldn't deny the crowds. So she'd rapture them, have them begging for more, then leave them with their mouths hanging, the men drooling, the women weepy, stirred by the passion in her songs.

The men often came to the tables they'd adorn. Fannie tall and poised, thick, crinkling hair that Ethel had styled crowning her head like a halo colored by midnight. Ethel with the red luscious lips, and the droopy eyes, and the laugh that came quickly and easily and sounded like a song. "Can I have this dance?" a man would ask, bending slightly toward Fannie if he were young, and to Ethel if he were older, bolder. They'd size the men up and work their signals. Ethel would wink if he looked okay for Fannie; Fannie would clear her throat if she thought Ethel should give him the nod. Then they'd whisper and compare notes at the dance's end and giggle like girlfriends at a high school prom.

They talked over Cokes and orange juice and the rhythmic pounding of party shoes on the dance floor. Fannie was amazed at how easy Ethel listened. She told her about Pop's nephew, how she thought she might be in love, how glad she was Ethel had come in that cellar when she did, like the Lord had sent her, she said.

Sometimes after the clubs closed, they'd sit in the playground and talk until near dawn. And then Ethel would have to go, "have to catch some sleep before my walk," she'd tell her. "I always walk around four or five. Clears my head to walk."

One night Ethel pushed Fannie on the swing with the rusted chain that squeaked and grunted that Ethel said sounded like a man she used to know when he was taking his physical release. And it was then that Fannie asked her why, why did all of downtown say she was a whore?

Ethel stopped the swing so that the playground went quiet except for the hum of the streetlight that was bright yellow and gave the playground a midday feel. She wanted Fannie to understand. She stepped out of her shoes, unhooked her stockings from her garter, and sat along the edge of the sandbox and dug her feet into the sandy-colored granules. "Been with more men in my life than I can count."

"Why?" Fannie asked, following her to the sandbox and sticking her feet in as well. "Your appetite that large? What could you possibly get out of being with so many men? Or is it just because they want you and you're just doing them a favor?"

"Little of both actually." Ethel kicked the sand in the air with her feet. "I love the feel of a man's breath in my face, his weight pressing against me, his heaviness, his release. I love to free a man up. Married, single, engaged, hooked up, pinned, or just lightly chained, they all so bound. They put on an act like they're so carefree. You been dancing with them all week, you must see it too, act like they don't have a care in the world. Full of laughs and good times, and every one of them got their hands tied behind their backs. I just like to untie their hands, for an hour or so. No conditions." She scooped a fistful of sand and spilled it in a stream that glistened in the glow of the yellow streetlight. "I don't remind them of their failings since I'm not their woman. Babies to feed, rent to pay. Even the ones with plenty of money, status, doctors, and teachers, and businessmen, all of 'em got their failings, all of them bound. But they don't have to prove their manhood with me."

"Well, what about their women?" Fannie asked, barely breathing she was listening so hard.

"I try not to think about them. You know, that I might be hurting them by being with their men. I don't hold nothing against their women, that's for sure." Ethel pulled her feet from the sand and sat cross-legged like a preschooler along the sandbox's ledge. "I know how hard it is for the women. I know about the unspeakable things some of them got to do to keep their day jobs. I feel for the women too. I'm just in a better position to help the men, to free them, just for a minute."

She got quiet and watched the glistening sand still shifting, filling in the spot where her feet had been. She didn't tell Fannie about Alfred, didn't try to explain that when she freed the men and gave them pleasure, she was freeing Alfred, exonerating her mother's crime. She didn't explain that was her release, her climax, raising the one from the dead that she couldn't stop her mother from killing.

She did tell her, though, that she knew her lifestyle wasn't right for raising Liz. Told her she and Coreen had been raised by their grandmother because her mother had a weakness to her brain that affected her judgment. "I'm not apologizing for my lifestyle," she said. "Noon's got the lifestyle, though. Refined Christian woman. Good, honest husband in Herbie too. Don't know if the Lord listens much to my prayers, but I do thank him for Noon. Like I thank him for my grandmom. For all those colored ladies that just step in when one of their own goes astray."

And Fannie wanted to tell her that maybe she thanked God for them, but Noon hated her most of all, not just because of what she did with the men, but because of how she'd left Liz. She wanted to warn her that should she see Noon, it'd be best to cross the street, turn the corner, lower her head, because Noon had fifteen years' worth of hate brewing, and proper as she was, it might get indecent should all that hate be uncaged. She didn't say anything, though. They still had three more days and nights before Noon's Florida train would be Philly bound. Tomorrow, or even the next night or the night after that. She could always tell her then.

🐦

And that's when they heard it. A powerful bang that sounded as if a bomb had hit. The sound sent them running, first for cover, then to see what it was. Two blocks and around the corner before they came to the source of the bang. Fannie jumped and hollered. "No, they didn't!" she screamed. She tried to run to them, to stop them, to get in front of the wrecking ball that was swinging like a gold-balled timer on a piano top. Except it wasn't keeping time, it was destroying it, as it knocked, ticktock, bang, bang, and the church tumbled down like build-up blocks that had been piled too high. And Ethel held Fannie back and had to slap her face to make her cry, so she could hold her and lead her from harm's way.

And then all of downtown seemed to hear it all at once as they jumped out of bed, or spilled from the clubs, or rushed from the pinochle games, or got up from their knees where they said their prayers, or rolled from their lovers, or closed their books, or pushed from their tables of middle-of-the-night snacks. They came running asking, What is it? A bomb sent from Khrushchev, a riot, a shipyard blast. And then to the source. They hollered and raised their fists and cursed and cried. No! Not the church. Lord, no! They stormed the yellow truck that controlled the wrecking ball. But it had already done its work under the cover of night so their rage wouldn't get in its way.

The church was gone. There was a sagging, heavy emptiness in its place. Now Fannie had this to have to tell Noon too.

Noon and Herbie came back a day early. Noon had been so buoyed by the trip, so pampered by her mother, doted over by her brothers, propped by their wives, entertained by their children. And at night, when she and Herbie retired to the guest room on the coolest side of the house, Herbie rubbed her back and told her that he loved her, that he always had. That the ocean sprays in the Florida air reminded him, and sitting again in the back of that church, eating macaroni and cheese served by the big-busted church matrons, he had always loved Noon from that first time. He was just sorry, so sorry that her problem had kept her from knowing how much. So she was ready to go back in six days instead of seven. She had allowed the distance from Philadelphia to Florida to come between her and the road business. Allowed the soothing motion of the twelve-hour train ride to dull her thoughts about their eviction from the church, and the abandoned houses piling up, and Liz, the hardest thought of all to dull, Liz's betrayal. So she was ready to go back Friday night instead of Saturday. Because she felt too good. And if she felt too good, she'd surely let her guard down about what had happened not a mile from her mother's house. And a mile was too close, she needed more than a mile, needed the space between Florida and Philadelphia before she could think about that.

So Noon and Herbie came back a day early. Two days instead of three after the church was struck down. And now Fannie tried to fall asleep to the sounds of Liz knocking against the wall, thinking how she'd tell Noon when she met the train. "The church is gone," she'd say, fast and soft the way she'd tell someone her child was dead. She'd give Noon her mail, which she'd been picking up faithfully, even the long white envelope with a fresh label pressed over scribble. But it was already too late. Noon and Herbie were already pulling the covers back on the bed in their Lombard Street row house. Herbie had stopped Noon because of the hour from running over to Jeanie's to get an update on things. Instead of Fannie having a full day to prepare for Noon's return, she had none. They had come back in the middle of the night, a day early, and now it was too late.

THIRTY

Again Fannie couldn't sleep. Liz's banging on the wall. Fannie hated the banging most of all. The banging meant that Liz was off to a new spot. If Liz was just tapping or scratching, that meant that she was just loosening up and then tearing off chunks of plaster. But when the banging came, a new part of the wall was about to tumble its contents. Sometimes still flecked with the pink and green flowered wallpaper, the plaster would dance out coerced by the rhythm of the banging.

Ever since Liz had defied Noon, told Noon she was selling out to the city in its bodacious urban displacement plan, Liz was up until two, three in the morning. She'd spent her entire spring break banging on the wall, tearing chunks out, gnashing and gnawing, and then spitting into paper towels or washcloths or dishrags, or whatever the receptacle would be for that episode. Fannie wondered why it was always a cloth, why Liz didn't just use a spittoon like the people that chewed tobacco. She figured it was so she could clean her mouth often. Plaster dried against the skin probably hurts coming off, she thought. She wondered how it felt going down.

"Liz, please stop it," she yelled. She didn't want to have to get up. She had downed two glasses of Liz's expensive wine, hoping to flood out the sound of the banging; it had only left her woozy. The excitement of spending her own spring break with Ethel, then the wrecking crane of three days ago, now planning on meeting Noon at the train tomorrow, Fannie was tired. She didn't want to have go into Liz's room. Hadn't been in there in over a month. But this was beyond too much.

She pushed her covers down and threw them over to the other side of the bed with such force that her sheet pulled from between the mattress. She jumped out of the bed, stomped against the floor, almost tripped on the muted throw rug. She bounded down the hallway and was insulted again by Liz's door. The heavy wooden nutmeg-colored door was the first thing meeting Fannie these days whenever she approached Liz's room. She'd come home ready for the get-down-with-it-girl-talk she and Liz had grown up with, and instead there would be that opaque door: sealed. She knocked. No response. Just the banging on the other side of the door.

"The hell with this shit," she said as she landed her body against the door. The door relented. The unexpected force of her tall, slender body propelled her into the center of the room.

"Oh, my God!" she shrieked.

The wall was gone, an entire side of the room from the baseboard almost to the ceiling. Slats of wood sporting oval-shaped knots exposed it all. No pink and green wallpaper, not even the jagged roughness of banged-on wall. Nothing. Just horizontal slats of exposed wood. Down to the structure. Clean. Just the wood and the light from the bathroom on the other side of the wall.

Liz was on a chair reaching and banging, trying to find newness, fresh chunks. Plaster dust had settled on her hair. Had doused her proud red flame. Made it look matted, unkempt. Plaster-streaked mucus lined the grooves around her mouth, even hung below her chin like sandy-colored icicles.

She looked down at Fannie. Didn't care that Fannie's mouth was hung open, horrified, frozen. "Get the fuck outta here," she said icily. Fannie drew back in disbelief. Liz rarely cursed. Around people she was proper, poised, a finishedness about her. But here and now, amidst the paisley drapes and matching bedspread, and ornate dresser and chest of drawers, and the backdrop of a wall with its substance torn away, Liz was grotesque, frightening, even to Fannie.

Fannie swallowed hard. "Liz, look at what you're doing," she said softly. "You're eating the wall, Liz, do you see it?"

Liz never looked at the whole wall. Whenever she went into her room, she'd turn her back on it, treat it like a lover who'd done her wrong, busy herself at her dresser, rearrange her gold-bulbed atomizers, line her nail paints from the bloodreds down to the icy clears. But late at night, when the little girls were no longer jumping double Dutch on the pavement below, and the rush of the trolley was done, and even the clicking heels of midnight strollers were still, Liz would glance at the wall. And then, like the wrongful lover offering a dozen long-stemmed roses and a double-decker box of Whitman's chocolates, the wall offered up its newness. The newness excited Liz. Tonight the newness was up high. She had to use a hammer to loosen up the fresh, tantalizing chunks.

"Leave me the fuck alone." Liz sneered, pounding the wall with her furious hammer. "You think you always so right, it's just a hole in the wall."

"It's not just a hole," Fannie said, voice shaking as she tried to keep an even tone. "You're not in the closet at Noon's, you're not a little girl anymore, Liz, you're a nineteen-year-old woman, and you're eating the wall, do you see it?"

"Bitch." Liz spit the word out as she spit plaster specks into the dusty air.

Fannie winced at being cursed at so by Liz. "You're sick," she said, voice rising. "You need help. I'm calling Noon."

"The hell with Noon too, and Herbie, and that no-good, two-timing Willie Mann. To hell with all of you." Liz turned from Fannie to focus instead on the wall.

"The wall is gone, the whole wall, Liz, do you understand, the whole wall." Fannie was shouting now.

Liz banged harder. The louder Fannie yelled, the harder Liz banged. She banged to the rhythm of Fannie's voice rising and falling. She cursed at the wall, almost as if the faces were there mocking her from between the slats of wood. "The hell with all of you," she said. "Noon self-righteous fool, all that damn fighting for nothing. Just let them build the damn road, don't have a thing to do with us being colored . . . and Herbie, still carrying that tattered picture of Ethel around in your wallet. What you do, look at it at night before you lay down with Noon. . . . I've had it with that Willie Mann, lying, high-yellow, two-timing son of a bitch. . . . Whore, Ethel, didn't have to leave me, told me I was just going over there to play, then left me just to go lay up in peace. . . . I hate you, Fannie, fearless Fannie, always-got-to-be-right Fannie, I hate you, Fannie, I hate you."

"Stop it," Fannie yelled. She covered her ears to try to block out the sound of the banging and Liz's ranting. She jumped up and down in the center of the room, screaming, "Stop, please. Please stop." She screamed until the words blurred together into a hysterical stream of noisy air.

Liz couldn't stand the rhythm of Fannie's voice anymore. The way her voice all ran together pushed her off-balance. She wobbled on the chair. She turned toward Fannie. Fannie, who was her closer-than-sister friend, Fannie, whom Liz trusted and adored, since the day Ethel dropped Liz off on Noon's steps and Liz was traumatized until she saw Fannie running up the street to get to her, to claim her as her sister. With all the might left in her, Liz took aim. She whipped the hammer toward the center of the room.

The air in the room was stronger than Fannie. The air was too noisy, too disturbed from all the banging. The air was too heavy-laden with plaster dust. The air was in the center of the room now just above Fannie's head. Fannie couldn't handle it. The anger, the horror joined forces at that instant to wrench away what was left of her strength. She couldn't stop the air as it came crashing down on her head.

At first Liz didn't realize what she had done. And then she saw the blood seeping through the coal black, crinkled wisps of Fannie's hair. Fannie was folded over in the center of Liz's bedroom floor, still. Liz jumped off the chair. Jumped up and down, mouth wide open, but no sound coming out at first. And then the yell, like a terrified newborn, first the outstretched mouth, and then came the yell. "Fan, Fan, oh, my God, oh, Fannie, oh, Jesus, please, sweet Jesus, help, please, I'm sorry, please, have mercy, Lord, please."

She jumped straight up and down, and across the room, big grasshopper jumps. "Please don't die, please, Jesus, don't let her die." She pulled the sheet from her bed and wrapped it around Fannie's head. She cradled her head and worked through her hair to find the wound, to put pressure on it; she held the sheet hard against the wound. She rocked her and sobbed and held the hole shut tight. She cleaned the wound, then cradled Fannie's head and rocked her more. She sat with her head bowed, sobbing. She didn't dare look up. Sitting in the middle of the floor as she was, if she looked up, she'd see the whole wall gone.

THIRTY-ONE

Noon sat up with a jolt that she felt to her head. As if the wooden post of her bed had just collapsed on her. She felt woozy. She reminded herself that they hadn't gotten in until one in the morning. Now it was four, her usual wake-up time. She looked over at Herbie; he was still sleep, snoring, oblivious of the powerful knock Noon felt in her head, all the way down in her chest. She sat on the side of the bed and pushed her feet into her soft pink slippers. Might as well get up, she thought. More than twenty years in Philadelphia and her country body clock had never readjusted itself to the later sleeping habits of city people. This was Noon's time, though. She loved to nestle herself in the stillness of the predawn, right at her kitchen table. But this morning, though, she felt an uneasiness settling in her chest as she smoothed at the tablecloth and opened her Bible to read some. She'd mostly felt a joyful calm her six days in Florida. So when she knelt against her kitchen chair and said her prayers this morning, she prayed longer than usual. "Liz holds hers in her stomach, I hold mine in my chest," she said to herself as she stood, and went to the window and rolled up the manila-colored window shade. It was pitch-black outside. She could tell it was going to be a glorious sunrise by the blackness in the sky. She wondered if today might be the day that Liz came to her senses, came to see her, to tell how wrong she'd been, to tell her she would never, ever sell that house. Three weeks to the day since she had seen Liz, she was even thinking that much longer and she might even make the first move herself, even if it was just to remind Liz how wrong she was. She went to the icebox to see what she could pull out for breakfast. She had missed cooking the past week; her mother hadn't allowed her to so much as split a mango, so she looked forward to a big breakfast by her own hands. She rummaged through the icebox. There were eggs, a block of scrapple she had frozen, plenty of lard and butter; she'd make a pan of rolls. She pushed past the jar of cream to get to the butter, so she could let it soften. The jar tilted. She just stood there and watched its thickness spill out and then make a lush puddle right on her shiny kitchen floor.

Noon just stood there, startled. But not over the cream, no, no. It was past four. It was even past four-thirty, but Noon hadn't heard the church bells yet. The only sounds were from her breathing, which was coming faster now. She listened, trying to remember if maybe she had heard them and they were lost in her head, trapped with all her morning thoughts. She was certain. She hadn't heard the church bells this morning. Every morning for the past twenty years they chimed through the black predawn air. Noon always considered that her first gift of the day. She ran into the living room and grabbed her jacket. She didn't stop to change from her slippers into shoes, nor did she care that her pink and green flannel nightgown hung way below her jacket. She didn't even take the time to untie her head scarf, knotted in the front with tips of twisted pieces of brown paper bag, her curlers, peeking through.

She walked through the darkness of Lombard Street. The mist was settling on her forehead and mixing with her sweat as she almost ran now, around the corner, past Bow's, past Fannie and Liz's, past Club Royale, past the schoolyard, and the jailhouse, and Pop's nickel-and-dime variety store, and then past abandoned house on top of abandoned house that surrounded the church in what now occurred to Noon was a very systematic two-block radius. The air was turning dusty as she walked. The dust was thick with the smell of burnt wood and was mixing with the mist, its thickness seeming to suspend the mist in midair. Her eyes started to tear. Her breath came in heaves. And then she turned the last corner. The same way she had been turning this corner since coming to Philadelphia. She knew when she turned this corner, no matter what burdens she had to bear, her help was always here, just around this corner, her church, her solid rock.

She drew back horrified. "No! No! Please, God, No!" she shouted. The church was gone. Black air filled with misty dust hung in its place. She ran onto the dirt. She stretched her arms in front of her like a blind woman feeling her way. She thought surely if she couldn't see the church, she could feel it. Surely her eyes must be wrong. If she just kept her arms stretched out in front of her, she would have to come upon the brick; she would have to be stopped short by the solid rockness of the church building. But nothing. Noon felt nothing but dusty air. On the other side of the now wide open, empty lot, she saw bricks piled on top of bricks. Not tenderly picked up, not stroked because this one had the founders' names etched deep into it, or that one was paid for by the tithes of Sister Bertha, or this one was dedicated to the birth and death of the Jacksons' infant daughter; instead they were just pushed away, just scattered, just kicked at, not touched, not understood, just bulldozed onto the vacant lot across the way. Noon covered the top of her head with her hands, trying to intercept the heaviness of the misty predawn air.

The dirt was soft and warm. She could feel its warmth through the thin, rippled soles of her slippers. She knelt in the dirt and rubbed her hands against it, as if to soothe it, comfort it. And then she dug her hands deep into it. She grabbed into it, trying to dig a hole, as if maybe if she dug fast enough and hard enough, she would come upon a grave that held her little church. When had they done this, when had they buried her church alive? If she could only get the dirt out of the way, she could reach it before it suffocated; she could breathe her breath into it and bring the church back to life.

She scooped up dirt by the handfuls. She threw it into the air. It fell on her heavily. It settled on her head, her face, her shoulders. Even blew into her eyes, blinding her. She cried out over and over, "No, no, please, Lord, no." She sat back on her heels and reached her arms to the sky and cried out, and then she just cried.

🦢

Ethel woke all at once. It usually took her time to wake. She usually woke in pieces. First her hands, then she'd twist her hips around, her legs, slowly, slowly, her lips would come back to life, then her eyes, and finally her head, her thinking would move from groggy and muddled until she could get outside to walk so her thinking could get clear. But this morning all of her woke in an instant. As if she'd been hit by a sandbag to her head. She reached for her watch. Almost four. She loved this time of morning. She never slept straight through the night. Since she was twelve, she had been singing somewhere or the other until one or two. And afterward she was so revved she couldn't fall asleep till just before dawn. But as she got older, there was always some man needing holding, some man she needed to hold to help her to settle down. Except that right about four, before the world came back to life, Ethel would wrap herself in a coat if it was cold, or just the stillness if it was warm, and go for a walk outside.

She pulled on her red pants, and black top, and red jacket and pushed her feet into her red high heels, and was out of the door, walking through the mist.

She thought about Fannie as she walked. They had become quite the girlfriends, buying new outfits, stepping out, flirting with the fellows, giggling as they smeared their fried chicken wings with hot sauce, talking about the shape of that man's head, the crook in that one's back, the ears on one, the hat on the other, the tie, where in the hell did that one get that tie? She told Fannie that she was dying to meet her young man, had to tell him that he was richly blessed to have someone like Fannie. They were truly like girlfriends even when she styled Fannie's hair. Except for the one time when she piled it high on her head in an upsweep, and then she'd parted it straight down the middle, tried her hand at a little girl's style the way she used to style Liz's hair. She couldn't get a straight part, though, and the braid wouldn't even hold.

She breathed in deeply the black air that was getting dustier as she walked. Three days since they knocked down that church and the air down here still full of dirt, she thought. TV cameras and newspaper reporters all over the place. NAACP had even demonstrated, demanded an accounting. And still dust all over the place.

She was just about to turn around and head back to her empty room when a strangeness fell over her. Up the street, on the spot where the church used to be. She heard moans coming from that space. "What the hell is that?" she whispered as she walked toward the moans, slowly at first. Probably some drunk got locked out of the house, she thought. And then she saw her. A figure covered with dirt, pounding and hollering and summoning up the name of Jesus. Moaning. Ethel drew back at first. She stepped out of her red high heels in case she'd need to turn and make a swift getaway. But the moans wrapped around her like a lasso, and tightened, and pulled her urgently toward Noon. She ran across the street into the empty space, to help this woman, bent over as if she were broken in two.

"Oh, my God, what's the matter? Are you okay? Let me help you, let me help you." Ethel knelt down in the dirt with Noon.

"The bells," Noon wailed, pounding her fists in the dirt, "what they did, look at what they did, they killed my bells, no more, no more, I won't hear my bells no more." She scratched at the dirt and sobbed, and her body shook from ferocious chills.

Ethel took off her bright red jacket and blanketed Noon's shoulders. "Hush, hush," she said as she held Noon to her and rocked her like a newborn. "It'll be okay, you just hush, just hush now. Calm down, that's it, calm down. Breathe deep and easy and just calm yourself down. Hush, just hush now."

Noon didn't want to hush. She wanted to tell her, make it clear what they had done. Without warning, without due cause or due process, they just gave the order, sent the trucks, surrounded the church, so sturdy, so vulnerable, they just flicked the switch, moved a lever, just like that, just moved a lever back then up; that's all it took to send the wrecking ball crashing, crashing. Noon could feel the crashing in her chest, in her head, as she tried to make this woman understand that it was the empty space that was overwhelming. The air. The void. She wanted to make this woman feel it the way she felt it. But she couldn't talk. Her breaths were coming in short, jagged lines. Her body was shivering. She moved deeper under Ethel's bright red jacket. The rocking was settling her down some. And Ethel's voice was like butter, smooth and rich and uninterrupted.

"How you just finding out?" Ethel asked as she waved away at the dust that was making her eyes start to tear. "Thought all of downtown knew by now. Been like one big funeral down here for the past three days, when they wasn't getting ready to riot, that is. People was so mad at one point, throwing bricks at the city officials, I thought they were gonna have to call in the National Guard. Where you been that you ain't heard?"

"Just back." Noon sobbed. "I was away all week, just got back, just got back, oh, Lord, why'd I have to come back to this?"

"This church must have been a hell of a special place to you. To all those people raising such hell over it. The way you was pounding on this dirt, I would've thought it was your man or your chile. Must've been a damn special place."

Noon was nodding her head that was throbbing now. Her eyes were on fire from the dirt and the dust so that she couldn't even see. She wanted to tell her that she couldn't see, that she was blinded by the dirt in her eyes. All she could do was put her hands to her head and whisper, "My head, it's crashing."

"What you say?" Ethel asked, putting her ear close so she could understand her.

"My head," Noon whispered again.

"Maybe your head rag is too tight, you still cold, let's move this jacket so I can get your head rag off." She undid Noon's scarf. "Are these curlers too tight? Let's get these out too, pulling at your scalp probably; that'll give you a headache quicker than anything when ain't nothing else even wrong." She unrolled the twisted pieces of brown paper bag and let them fall in the dirt. "You got nice hair," she said as she took the curlers out. "Nice and soft. I gotta keep a hot comb to mine at least once a week, more if I been working up a sweat." Her fingers worked through Noon's hair as she fluffed at the curls, and combed through them with her hands, and then purely out of habit, started to give Noon's hair a style, flipped behind her ear on one side, lifted in a slight bouffant on the other, then pulled some to the front for a bang.

Ethel's fingers felt good going through Noon's hair. The way they were lightly touching her scalp had the calming affect of tapping rain. She was usually very particular about whose hands she allowed in her hair. Her mother used to tell her that people could put something on her sure nuff if they got a couple strands of her hair. Burn it. She used to tell Noon, if you clip it, burn it, and don't you go leaving no loose strands in your comb. But Noon allowed this stranger in her hair. At least she thought she was a stranger. The voice was familiar, though. She knew she had heard the voice before. She wished she could open her eyes to see who this was. "You from here?" Noon asked, able to talk just a little now.

"Awhile ago, I lived here for a few years awhile ago," Ethel said as she sat up on her knees. "You better now. You think you can make it home?"

Noon almost wanted to stay there. Right there in the dirt with Ethel's fingers tapping her scalp. She wondered what row of a pew she'd be on, if she were in this place in the church. She thought it would be up front. Facing the pulpit. "I'm about ready to go, I just can't see, dirt's all in my eyes. Can't hardly open them."

"Whereabouts you live?" Ethel asked as she pushed herself to standing.

"Lombard Street."

"Well, that ain't far, just keep your eyes closed, keep 'em closed tight now, till you get home and flush them with water. Hurt like hell you try to open them now in all this dust and shit out here."

Ethel helped Noon to stand and dusted them both off. The sky was no longer pitch-black but gray. The gray was streaming down all around the two women, and Ethel looked at Noon through the gray, her eyes clenched tight, her face tilted the way a blind person does. With the dirt no longer covering Noon's face, without the head rag and the brown paper twisted in her hair, Ethel knew the face. She reached in and pushed back the bang along Noon's forehead. The line was there. This was her, Noon. The woman whose husband she whispered creamy words to at night when he cried over Noon that she didn't have a nature to her at all. The woman on whose steps she'd left her child. Ethel reached for Noon's arm. Afraid that if she didn't that Noon would somehow know; even with her eyes shut tight, she might know and push her away.

"Just give me your arm," Ethel said quickly, "and we'll head on to Lombard Street. I just got to stop on the other side and step into my shoes. I kicked them off when I heard you crying like that; those high heels would have slowed me up if you'd been some crazy or something."

"I'm sorry," Noon said, holding fast to Ethel's arm.

"What you got to be sorry about except that they busted up your place of worship?"

"Your clothes must be full of dirt, you probably was on your way somewhere, I'm just sorry I disrupted whatever you was fixing to do."

"I was just fixing to walk," Ethel said as they reached the other side of the street and she stepped into her bright red shoes.

"You got taller," Noon said. "Those shoes must be awfully high; you know you could get bunions like that."

"Already got 'em, corns and calluses too. Generally got bad feet."

"Well, why you walking in them?"

"Habit, you know how it is, some habits you just hold on to even if they hurt, and it helps if they making you look good."

"Here," Noon said, stopping sharply and extending her foot. "Take my slippers, come on now, I won't accept no, just take them."

"And what you gonna do?"

"I'm a country girl. I can go barefoot."

"You'll catch another chill out here like you did back there in the dirt. Here, I'll take your slippers, you take my shoes."

Noon leaned on Ethel as she stepped into her high heels. She swayed back and forth for a few seconds as she tried to get her balance. "How do you do this?" she asked as she stood straight and held tight to Ethel's arm.

Ethel pushed her feet into Noon's slippers. "These feel good," she said, almost sighing.

"Yeah, but not really for outside. I just ran outta the house so fast I couldn't hardly think to put on some real shoes." And then she let out a moan, as the reality of it crashed down on her again, and she started sniffing and tried to muffle her sobs.

"Hurts, I know it hurts," Ethel said. "Guess you feel about as bad as you ever felt." Ethel talked in her most soothing voice.

"You right. I haven't felt this bad about anything, since I was a young girl and got trapped in the woods by the devil." Noon's voice shook.

"Mnh, what that devil do, made you do it?"

"Like I was animal," Noon said, raising and lowering her free hand for emphasis.

"That's not the worst thing," Ethel said, half laughing. "I've done it with the devil a few times myself."

"I mean the real devil," Noon stammered.

"What you talking, I know about the real devil too now. This one joker even wore a red suit. Came by to pick me up, dressed in red from hat to shoes. I said, 'Wait a minute, baby, I know you got to have you a pitchfork in your car trunk, so you might as well pull it out now so it ain't no pretense.'"

Ethel laughed as she clutched to Noon's arm, and Noon almost wanted to laugh too.

"I'm sorry," Ethel said, composing herself, "you was telling me about your devil."

Noon had never told the details of it. Not even after they'd found her tied down in the center of the dead calves, and her mother told her she must never talk about it with anyone else. But if she felt she must, she could talk to her, only her. Noon never could. Except that here and now she had to. With her heart so broken over her fallen church, so gaping, every pain she'd ever felt rushed to the surface like water seeking its own level, or the way blood rushes to an open gash and spills on out. It spilled on out. Stumbling through the street, blinded by the dirt of the fallen church, holding fast to the arm of this stranger of a woman with a buttery voice who walks alone at night in high-heel shoes, Noon had to let it spill on out.

"Caught me in the woods one morning. I was out picking huckleberries for my daddy's doughby."

"What be?" Ethel asked, stark seriousness crowding her voice.

"Doughby, you wrap the dough around berries, then brush it down with butter and cinnamon, then cook it till the dumplings plump."

"Sounds good," Ethel said. Almost wanting to stop Noon. To tell her she didn't have to talk about it, not really.

"Would've been good too," Noon went on. "Those woods grew the sweetest blackest huckleberries in all of Florida."

"And then the devil got you?" Ethel asked.

"It was a lot of 'em all at once. Chanting, killing calves."

"I hate the devil," Ethel said emphatically.

"I was only twelve, a good girl, you know what I mean," Noon said, her voice still shaking.

"Know just what you mean," Ethel said. "Even I was still unspoiled at twelve."

"Now spoiled for life," Noon said, crying again as she colored it all in for Ethel. Each detail, down to the acrid scent of turpentine as they smeared oil over her body, and the sound the calves made as they died.

"Motherfuckers," Ethel said, stomping her feet so hard that she could feel the concrete through the thin soles of Noon's slippers. "Low-down dirty devil-worshiping sons of bitches."

"I thought once they stretched me open, that would be the worst part." Noon stopped and stood and turned to face Ethel. Her eyes were shut tight, and she tilted her face the way a blind person does. "I thought I would just go numb. But I just kept fighting. Even after they were into

298

their evil against me, I kept fighting. My whole body, my whole spirit just kept fighting. You ever seen a chicken after its head been cut off and it still runs around the barnyard? It's already dead, but it keeps on running 'cause it thinks it's still living. I kept on fighting them; even after I lost, I kept on fighting them."

The gray that was streaming down on the two women had turned to blue, then orange, and now yellow. The yellow was bathing Noon's face as she had her head tilted, eyes shut, facing Ethel. Ethel had known it must have been severe whatever it was that had kept Herbie a regular on her couch-bed on Kater Street. "You still fighting them, ain't you?" Ethel asked as she took Noon's arm so they could walk again.

"What you talking about?" Noon asked, stumbling in the high heels as they turned the corner of Lombard Street.

"The devil worshipers that got you, you still fighting them. I bet it ain't never been right between you and your man. You still running around the barnyard without your head. At least if you just go on and lay down and die, you could get a little taste of some afterlife, but shit, ain't you tired, you was twelve, ain't you tired?"

Noon was crying again, and she put her free hand to her mouth, and then to her eyes, which were burning more then ever as the tears stirred up the dirt again. "I'm so tired," she said, sniffing, and coughing, and sobbing. "I'm so tired of fighting everything. The people in the church, the people outta the church, the system, my husband, my daughter, my memories. I'm so tired of fighting my memories. And now my church is gone." She was wailing, head going up and down, feet stomping. "I'm just plain tired of fighting."

"Then stop, just stop!" Ethel shouted. "You been to church all your life, what they tell you to do with the devil?"

"We say, 'Satan, get thee behind me.'" Noon mumbled it like a little girl.

"Well, that ain't enough in your case. You need to tell him, 'Satan, while you behind me, kiss my butt.' Then you need to tilt your backside like you mean it and kick your leg, kick it like you kicking the shit out of the devil, like you would kick an old sewer rat that was trying to take a bite at your heels. Send him flying. He ain't never had no more power over you than what you gave him. Now I know you can do that. I don't care how refined you are. I know you can tell the devil to kiss your ass."

They were right in front of Noon's house. Ethel knew the house. She knew the steps. She knew that middle step where she had left her child. "What you say your house number was?" Ethel asked, not ready to give herself away, not yet.

"Red awnings, only red awnings on the block," Noon said, sniffing hard. "I usually don't like the color red, but my daughter Fannie talked me into them."

"Your daughter got good judgment; we here, we at your house. Step up right here, then right there, one more," Ethel said as she guided Noon up the steps. "Somebody here to let you in?"

"My husband, he's here. I guess he don't know what happened, the sun done come up and I ain't in the kitchen stirring his breakfast in the pots."

"Good luck with your eyes," Ethel said. "I didn't mean to yell at you, you been through a lot for one morning, but I just hate to see people stuck. Even if you moving backwards, it's better than being stuck."

Noon just nodded her head and stumbled in through her front door. And Ethel thought that she and Noon could have been friends if the past really didn't matter.

She liked Noon, and she never had any real girlfriends to speak of. Plenty of men always ready to call themselves a friend of hers, but never the girls. She was the one that the nice girls were not allowed to play with because their mothers called her fresh. "Hot in the behind," they said about her. Even after the town had forgiven her mother's madness that morning and even allowed their little girls to play with Coreen, Ethel got a reputation as the fast one, the worldly one. She was never invited to the afternoon parties where the girls sipped punch from cups with handles and sucked on dainty pink and green party mints. She reasoned that she would have been a misfit anyhow. Her hair never grew long, so she couldn't wear the pigtails with long satiny ribbons; her grandmother's arthritic fingers could no way stitch the puffed-up party dresses with long sashes for tying bows, so she played with her sister, and the boys; she always played with the boys. And then after her sister was burned up in the car fire, and her grandmother that raised them died, there was never a woman she was close enough to call a friend. Except this morning, walking through the dusty mist as the sunrise showed off, propping up Noon, guiding her steps, telling her not to cry, falling right into her anger with her, sinking into the hurt with her: This was the closest Ethel came to feeling like a woman was her friend.

And then Ethel looked down, down at the steps. She knew she should leave before Herbie opened the door, but she couldn't move just yet. The middle step held her. The step where she'd left her precious child.

THIRTY-TWO

If only it had been a boy. Ethel knew boys; she knew men. But she was scared to death of raising a baby girl to womanhood. As much as she loved that infant, what if the mothers kept their girls away from her the way she had been taboo to the nicer girls? Her baby needed lavenders, and pinks, and lime greens. All Ethel could give her was red.

She immediately thought of Herbie since he was the father of the child, and such a good guy at that. But she had to watch his bride up close for herself. It was, after all, the mothers who made the difference between what Ethel wanted for her baby and what she'd turn out to be.

So she spied on Noon. Noon had a round face, and large ears; generous, her grandmother used to say, large ears mean a person's full of generosity. She had stability, routine: Her steps were always freshly scrubbed; she hung clothes on the line on Mondays and bought butterfish for frying on Fridays. She didn't go to card games, or speakeasies, and Reverend Schell was her friend. But still, it was a wrenching kind of hard to leave her child.

She was up late the night before, knitting. She hadn't knitted since her grandmother taught her when she was seven or eight. But when she unfurled the ball of soft pink yarn, it came back to her all at once. Knit two, purl two, count your stitches, Ethel. It came back to her, and she did it all in one night. She had to hurry, before the sun came up. She had to finish the soft pink blanket to cover her baby girl. She didn't have time to close the stitches, but she knew Noon would pick up where she left off. Noon knew about pink things, like soft unfinished blankets.

She lined the box with cotton diapers and wrapped the baby in the loosely knit blanket. She let the fringes hang over the top; she thought the box looked pretty that way. And still, it was the wrenching kind of hard to leave her. For sure, it hurt to leave Liz, but it was a tender, pulsing hurt, a gentle pain. It was all mixed in with memories of her sister. But with this one, her very own baby, the one she birthed by herself because she had no girlfriends to call on, right there in the wine cellar at Club Royale, just her and Willie Mann with the wine that eased the pain, leaving this baby hurt with a rawness, a whipping pain all through her body. She ran through the street. Four o'clock. She had to beat the sunrise. And she put the box right there on that middle step at Noon and Herbie's house. She pressed the baby's dark, dark hair to her breast. And she said, "I'm gonna lay you in this box, and I'm gonna leave you 'cause that's how much I love you. And as soon as I put you down, I want you to cry your ass off, so they'll come and take care of you. They good people in this house. That Noon gonna make you a good mother, and that Herbie, that's your dad, he's a good guy; he's already your dad." And the baby stared up at Ethel with eyes that were as dark as the pitch-black predawn morning set deep in skin the color of corn bread. Her eyes danced, and Ethel knew she understood.

THIRTY-THREE

Herbie was a wreck. First the bewilderment of the spilled jar of cream, puddle all on the kitchen floor, and Noon nowhere to be found. He had just finished dressing and was on his way out to look for her, to make sure she hadn't snapped completely. Even though she'd seemed more relaxed in Florida than he'd seen her in some time, her mental state over the past months had been so fragile.

"Lord, just let her be all right." Herbie said it out loud as he closed the closet door. "Ain't like her to go walking the streets before the sun even comes up." And then he said, "Thank God," when he heard Noon's voice out front. Until he got to the window, and his insides turned to jelly. It wasn't just the sight of Noon, with her eyes clamped shut, struggling to get up the steps. Nor was it Ethel, curvy and soft-looking with a bright red jacket thrown casually over her shoulder. It wasn't even that they both looked as if they had been rolling in the dirt. It was Noon's hair. It was done up a way he had never seen it before, not even when she would let Liz take a comb to it.

She knows, he said. She must know. Liz must have told her about Ethel and me. Now they've been fighting. Except that he couldn't figure the hair done up, the red high heels, the nightgown, why'd she still have on the nightgown. He snatched the door open and pulled Noon inside.

"I'm sorry, Noon, I'm so sorry," he said as he fell to his knees and burrowed his head in her stomach. "As God is my witness, I'm sorry. I love you, Noon, I do."

"Isn't it the worse thing, just the worst thing!" She slipped out of the red heels, bent one knee, then the other, and knelt on the floor with Herbie. "Of all the things they could've done, who'd thought they would bulldoze my little church?"

"What! What did you say?" Herbie asked as he held Noon's shoulders. "Look at me, Noon, what did you say?"

"I can't look at you. I can't see. Dirt's all in my eyes; you got to clean them out for me, I can't even open my eyes. It's gonna hurt, some woman had to walk me home; she found me scratching in the dirt; I just went crazy when I saw what they did. I didn't even get her name, Herbie, I can't even thank her. My eyes, Herbie, my eyes are on fire."

"Wait, don't move, baby doll. Herbie'll take care of those eyes." He jumped up and ran upstairs to the bathroom and got cotton rags and washcloths and boric acid and filled a dish with water.

"Okay," he said softly, settling back down on the floor with Noon, "let's clean those eyes." He worked with what seemed to Noon like amazing skill as he brushed the dirt from her lids, and then took her head in his lap and squeezed the water gently over her closed eyes, and then slowly raised her lids, to Noon's grimaces, and squirms, and whispered complaints of how it burned and stung.

"Poor Noon," he said when he was done. "You been through so much, Noon, and I ain't been no real help to you, I been so impatient with you, I ain't never really been much of nothing for you to lean on. And now they bulldozed your church. Damn."

He stretched back across the floor and leaned his back against the couch and looked at the top of Noon's head that was still resting in his lap. The hair, the way it was lightly fingered and puffed up just on one side was affecting him. He didn't understand it and was surprised when he felt himself throbbing.

Noon opened her eyes slowly, they were tearing, but the stinging was gone, she could see the gray of Herbie's pants; she put her hand there, right there where she saw his manhood rising. She had put her hand there, many times before; that was the best she'd been able to do was put her hand there. But she had never allowed herself the sensation of feeling it rise. And then it happened. Caught Noon by total surprise the way it happened, right there, without being on the altar, without Reverend Schell's supplications for the Lord to touch and heal, right there on her living room floor. The line came up. That same line that welled up during her healing prayers. It welled up now. Then it broke. It swelled; then it burst. Engorged, then released. Twenty years' worth of captive womanly passion gushed from the broken line. It percolated like oil when it's first struck from deep in the earth. It covered her insides, set them on fire. "Thank you, Jesus," she yelled as she moved all over Herbie, kissing him in places where she never had, then blanketed him; even though she'd never done it, she knew just what to do. "Praise the Lord, praise Him. Praise Him!" she shouted.

Herbie was completely still. He didn't even breathe. He was so unaccustomed to the feel of her body all over him. It was warm and soft against him, just as he'd imagined it'd be. It felt to Herbie as if a cloud had just fallen from a lazy summer sky and just covered him right there on the floor. She was so soft all over him, until he found the center of the cloud that pulled him in, all the way in, and held him there.

"Damn," he whispered into Noon's ear when he could breathe again. "You serve a good God, Noon, a damn good God. Minh. Minh. Minh."

THIRTY-FOUR

Ethel headed straight around the corner to Fannie and Liz's. Noon's slippers felt good on her feet. She could walk faster, with a bounce; even her bunions stopped hurting. Slippers were so sensible. That Noon is such a sensible woman, she thought. All of Ethel's slippers had a high heel, a wedge, a lift that kept her from walking flush to the ground. Buying me a pair of flat slippers, she almost hummed to herself. Not red, pink. She paused when she got to the door. She curled her toes around in the slippers and thought that maybe she should come back later. It was still very early on a Saturday morning. Maybe Liz wasn't even back from spending the week with her friend at Howard. The girls might even be keeping company. Liz may have stored up resentments over the years. But I'm already here, she thought, could use a cup of coffee after the morning I've had. I can tell Fannie what happened with Noon, how I comforted her, helped her home after she had been blinded by the dirt. But she would make Fannie promise that she would never tell Noon it was her. She trusted Fannie. She was uneasy about Liz, though.

She knocked hard on the door. No answer. Okay, she thought, this is South Philly. She looked under a large clay flower pot that adorned the window ledge. Sure enough, the key. She knocked again, then unlocked the door and went on in.

"Yoo-hoo," she called. "Fannie, Liz, it's Ethel, anybody home?" She walked into the living room and immediately thought, Liz. Everything was so perfectly coordinated. The navy and green and fuchsia. The lacy open weaves that almost touched the almond-colored floors, fresh blooms in the vase, latest books on the shelf, even down to the way the magazines were slanted on the coffee table to meet at the points. The room was just like the pictures of Liz, polished, finished, each hair in its place, a sterility, though, a sadness about it. She walked to the couch, tossed one of the navy and fuchsia pillows on its side. Then she called out again, "Is anybody home?"

Ethel headed for the stairway. "Wake up, sleepyheads," she called as she pressed her slippered feet against the hardwood steps. "Liz, it's your aunt Ethel, baby, wake up, wake up, remember that wake-up song your aunt Ethel used to sing to you. Do you remember me, Liz?" She was talking faster and louder, feeling nervous as she reached the top of the stairs. The creaking now came from the banister as she leaned on it to step up the last step, onto the hallway floor. Excited, she told herself, supposed to be excited, haven't seen my Liz in fifteen years. And then she laughed at herself when she realized she was scared too. Chile just might possibly hate me, she thought, yeah, Ethel, you scared, that would hurt and you know it and you scared, but you in here now. You right here in Liz and Fannie's house.

Ethel was almost to Liz's room. The door was open wide. She could see the draperies pulled back, showing white sheers over open venetian blinds. The sun rushed through the window, impatiently, and was divided by the blinds into organized rows of dust-filled beams. Ethel knew this had to be Liz's room. The navy and fuchsia and green of the draperies matched the living room so.

She paused at the wide open door and coughed. Dust everywhere, she thought. Outside, inside, I can't escape the dust today. She reached in and knocked. "Liz, baby, it's Aunt Ethel, are you in here?" The quiet was unsettling, the quiet and the dusty sunbeams. She flexed her foot in the slippers and breathed deep and walked into Liz's room.

She didn't immediately look down at the floor, at the center of the room where Liz sat, head hung, cradling Fannie's wounded head in her lap, where they'd been from four in the morning until now, about seven. She wasn't even aware of them at first. She was too taken by the wall. The entire side of the room gone. It didn't have the look of a carpenter's work, systematic. It was just banged out, a desperation to it.

She rubbed her hands up and down her arms. Her horrified eyes traced the jagged outline where the emptiness met virgin wall, right near the top. Chalky white plaster showed under the pink and green wallpaper from the top down along the seam of the wall in a crooked line that peaked and dived. Ethel's eyes followed the line down around the floor where crumbs of plaster glistened, past the bed with its sheet pulled away, past the hammer. And then she saw Fannie and Liz, sitting where they had been sitting for the past three hours.

She tried to scream, but no sound would come through. Ethel, with her trained singer's voice, used to pushing the air through any obstruction to make sound, to make it go high or low, to scat, or shout, or hum, or moan. She couldn't push the sound through. It was caught right in her throat, strangling her. And then it was Liz's own hands, strangling her. Shaking her head, trying to shake Ethel's head from her neck, and hollering, "Bitch, it's all you fault. Bitch. Why you leave me, you dirty whore, bitch?"

Ethel grabbed at Liz's hands. Tried to separate her hands just so she could get a little air through. She wasn't all that scared of dying, but not by Liz's hands. Crazed look in Liz's eye just like the look in her mother's eye that morning Alfred returned her beaded purse. Her red hair matted, dried plaster caked around her mouth. She knew Liz had already suffered. She couldn't die in peace with Fannie in the middle of the floor. Blood around her, head wrapped with a bed sheet. She had to separate Liz's hands. Everyone deserved to die in peace.

"Why you come back here? Why didn't you just stay away? Just die, just die, bitch, die," Liz screamed, out of breath, tired. She was so tired. She could feel her strength leaving her body. She could feel it pulling from her head, draining. On down through her arms, until her hands couldn't even clasp Ethel's neck anymore. Her strength was leaving her body. Seeping. Right on through her stomach, the way everything went through her stomach. At least when it was pulling through her stomach, the circles stopped for a little while. Pushing. They were pushing on through her stomach. Running down her legs. All her strength sliding down her legs. She was too weak to feel repulsed. The sliding down her legs was warm and soft like liquid velvet. Even it moved slowly, tired.

Ethel pulled Liz's limp hands from around her neck and gasped for air. She coughed and spit and ran to Fannie. "We got to get her help," she said hoarsely. She put her hand to Fannie's head and called her urgently. "Fannie, Fannie, can you hear me? Fannie, it's Ethel." She listened to her breathe and undid the sheet Liz had wrapped meticulously around her wounded head. "Did you do this? What the hell happened here? What the hell happened to you?" she asked as she propped Fannie's head in her arms. "We got to get her to the hospital. Who got a car? Don't just stand there like you outta your fucking mind, you can curse me out and try to kick my ass later, right now we got to get her help."

Liz sobbed, "Fannie, Fannie, I'm so sorry, I didn't mean to hurt you, Oh, God, please forgive me for hurting Fannie, she cared more about me than anyone."

Ethel winced at Liz's words. But she focused instead on Fannie's wound. She knew wounds. She had seen stab wounds from butcher knives and ice picks. She had seen straight wounds from razors, and jagged, crooked wounds from broken chunks of glass. As wounds went, this was not that bad: no pus, no swelling, clean, at least it was clean. "Fannie, Fannie," she called again, slapping her face gently. "How long ago this happen? What you do, hit her in the head with the hammer, what was y'all doing fighting, what was you fighting about? Dial for the red car, we got to get her checked out. Don't just stand there, what are you doing just standing there, what are you doing? You shitting on yourself, Lord have mercy, Liz, you still shitting on yourself!"

THIRTY-FIVE

Willie Mann stood on the vacant lot where the church used to be. Three days after it had been demolished and he still couldn't believe it. That's not the way it was supposed to happen. He had asked them. Tom Moore and the rest. They had told him the plan was to keep the church standing. Surely some streets would be widened to accommodate garages. Pavements would be extended for more walkway space. But the church wouldn't be touched. Historical purposes, they'd told him. What had made them do this? After all, his very grandmother went to this church. Damn, the church?

The dirt swirled around at his feet as he rubbed his hand over his slicked-back hair. What power they had. Immense. That they could take something solid as the church and turn it into the thick air that he now inhaled. He picked up a handful of dirt and let it sift through his fingers. Not over me, he thought as he slapped at his hands to rid them of the dirt. Never did have power over me. No person on this earth got that kind of power over me. Except that he thought now about the one who did. Ethel.

As soon as he'd heard the church had fallen, and first rushed to the spot and saw the thick dew that hung in the air and looked like teardrops, he'd thought about Ethel. Wondered if her presence back here had made the earth open up and swallow the church. Chided himself. Too cerebral to let his thinking descend so. Except that she'd always had a supernormal effect on him. He hadn't even been able to get his fullness back since she'd shocked him in the cellar at Royale when he was exploding against

Fannie. Two, three women he'd talked into the cellar since then, but he couldn't summon his throbbing.

Even that week, twenty years ago, when he'd actually taken care of Ethel. When she'd sneaked back into Philly under the cover of night round with Fannie in her womb. And appeared in the cellar and told him she needed to live down there until the child was born. Told him not to tell a soul, and then she'd unfurled a ball of soft pink yarn and commenced to knitting. And she lived in the cellar at Royale for a week. He fed her soup and gave her chipped ice when her mouth was dry. And then, three days after she appeared there, it was time. He turned the music loud to mask Ethel's screams. Then he saw the crop of black hair pushing out. He held his hands there and guided the baby out. And she cried and jerked in his arms. Thirteen. He was only thirteen. And his hands and voice were shaking when he said, "It's a girl. Miss Ethel, it's a girl." And for four days after that, while Ethel healed, whenever the baby cried, he'd turn the music up so the cries wouldn't sift through the walls to the club or the outside world. He'd kept her secret then. Still keeping it. Couldn't explain it to himself, except to say it was a power she had over him, like those white folks never did.

A crowd was beginning to form near the lot. A crowd formed on this lot every morning since they'd leveled the church. Someone would pray, someone sing; then Jeanie would give a status report on the lawsuit they had filed and the investigation the NAACP had demanded. And they'd shake their heads all over again as if they were seeing it for the first time and cry or curse and shout for revenge.

This morning, since it was Saturday morning and they could tarry here awhile, their collective reactions were more emotional, more passion-filled. They even scowled at Willie Mann.

"What's that old no-good Judas doing out here?" Bow called more to Willie Mann than to the gathered onlookers.

"The gates of hell need to open right now and snatch that no-count boy to burn for eternity," Pat Saunders shouted.

Sounds of agreement rose and sifted around with the dirt that was blowing toward Willie Mann. He knew what he could do now. What he could always do exceptionally well. Swoon a crowd. Usually for money, special privileges, but today for his own hide.

"I want you all to know that I was assured, absolutely assured that

the church was to be left standing. And I am appalled at this atrocity."
He coughed and smoothed at his hair and scanned the crowd, locking
eyes with one person, then the next, until he was sure he had them,
salesman extraordinaire, oratorical genius. He loved doing few things
better than this: winning over an audience.

"Well, you been in bed with them the whole time, ain't you now?"
Bow called from the other side of the street. "Now you ready to turn on
them; you ain't true to nothing. Don't come here now with your empty
explanations; if it wasn't for you and your tactics, things wouldn't have
gotten this far outta hand."

"I'm deeply hurt, Bow," Willie Mann said as he made steeples out of
his hands and pushed them to his face as if in prayer. "My very grandmother attended services here each and every Sunday morning."

"Well, why'd you try to force her to sell her house then?" Bow shouted
as he waved his hand in disgust.

"Eminent domain, Mr. Bow, sir. She would have to move regardless.
I only had her financial interests at heart." He paused and went through
the crowd again, looking for the grandmothers, short ladies with hair
soft and white like cotton, large, sagging chests, and wide ankles, some
still in their ruffled over-the-neck aprons with the deep pockets that held
everything from safety pins to money for the milkman, from cotton gauze
to garlic poultice. He made his eyes go soft when he looked at them and
said, "But now it's not her financial interests I'm so concerned about. It's
her spiritual edification. She would have gotten a pretty penny for her
property; she would have had more space than she could ever use had
she relocated; I believe she was wisely guided even though she chose not
to follow my guidance. But this, this crumbled church, where will she
go now on Sunday mornings?" His voice cracked for effect. "Where will
be the coming-together point for all the saints when that place you were
used to is gone? Where? Where is my grandmother to go now for uplift-
ment of her spirit?"

"It's late to be asking those questions," Bow shouted through the
crowd. "You should have thought about all that when you was right in
there with them scheming."

"Let the boy talk, Bow," one of the grandmothers shouted.

"He ain't got nothing that's any use to us," Bow said angrily. "All he
care about is covering his own smooth backside."

"Actually," Willie Mann said, folding his hands lightly in front of him, "all I can offer you today is information. Information that has come to me through sources which my integrity will not allow me to reveal."

"Go on and spill the beans, boy," another wide-ankled lady shouted to Willie Mann. "Don't worry none about who tole it, you just tell it."

He breathed in deep. "We have been lied to. Tricked, duped in the most awful way. We have been persecuted, thrown into the lions' den."

And Willie Mann reasoned that he was standing right where the pulpit should be. He was right there where the Word emanated every Sunday morning. He was standing in the sun, dirt swirling from his stomping now. "All they wanted was your space. Not for a road, not a highway, not even a widened two-lane street, mothers and fathers, sisters and brothers. They wanted your space. Why? Why do they always rise up against us, money, and power, and fear?"

Sweat was coming together on Willie Mann's brow as the morning sun beat down against the lot. "This space, this very space where you all have carved out honest, simple lives, this space that you've chosen to share with your families, your friends, your church mates, this space that has held your hopes and dreams over the years and created the backdrop for some to even come true, people, this space is worth money to them. That's why they wanted you to move, not for the road, not for some contrived idea of an expressway. Do you know what I've just learned? I'll share this with you. The most that will be built down here is a ramp. That's all. One little old ramp."

The crowd gasped in unison and drowned Willie Mann out so that he had to shout to be heard.

"Did a ramp necessitate you all being dislocated? No. Did it mean you all needed to spend hour after hour arguing over whether to go this way or that? Did it mean family member needed to be pitted against family member? No. I say to you on this morning on the once-fertile dirt that held your church, no. In the name of one that I'm not accustomed to call, no! Think of all that you've experienced in this space. Why, I can even think of things that have happened during my tenure at Club Royale, after all I've been employed there since I was twelve years old, started out bringing the inventory into the cellar. I grew up in the place. I know to some of you that may not seem like the ideal place for a lad to grow, but I did. It was like a second home to me.

"I ask you," he continued to the crowd on the lot, "how can we just walk away from this space that's been a part of our lives? Should we have to? I say to you, should we have to?" He shouted louder, as the scene flashed again, the couch, Ethel with the baby on her breast. Boxed inventory all around. And he had done it. He had helped Miss Ethel birth her baby. He had kept the real meaning forgotten for the past twenty years. New life, he'd helped new life slide into the world. Never bragged about it, never whispered a sigh of it, kept tucked in his heart by Ethel's power that covered him like a sheath. "Should we have to forget?" he shouted again to the crowd. "No, I submit to you today on this lot, no." Willie Mann's arms flew up and down to the rhythm of his singsongy speech. His feet moved in the dirt, stomping, and then dancing. He sang. As he spoke, he sang. His eyes were shining. He was on fire.

He didn't feel the first piece of brick that hit him square between his shoulder blades. Nor the second that caught him mid-thigh. It was the one against his forehead that confused him. Made him stop mid-sentence to grunt in pain. Pulled him from his oratorical hysteria to see them converging on him, stampeding, the very ones he thought he was swooning by his accounting of the current situation. "Wait!" he shouted. He backed up, stumbling on patches of bruised earth. "Let me finish, let me explain their treachery."

"No, you let us finish," called one of the wide-ankled women. "Let us finish what your grandmama didn't."

"Always did spare the rod with that one, Maybell did. Always favored him, gave him too much, see what happens when you give a child too much."

"Turn on you quicker than day into night."

He felt another chunk of brick against his chin, in his chest. He ducked. Pieces of the fallen church were flying like missiles. Now he had lost this too, his finest gift. His ability to persuade. He turned to run. Ethel. He was losing everything since she'd returned. She owed him. She owed him for that week in the cellar at Royale. For his twenty years of silence. He'd tell her too; if he got out of this one, he'd tell her just how he felt. He ran hard to outrun the bricks that were keeping pace. Straight to Royale, his home underground.

THIRTY-SIX

Sunday morning Noon woke to an unkempt house. Saturday had come and gone, and she hadn't done her windows, her kitchen floors, changed the bed linen, dusted down the walls, or the venetian blinds. First time ever Sunday morning had caught her with her housework undone. "It's gonna stay undone until the Sabbath is over," she said out loud, and then laughed, and turned on her side and watched Herbie snore. The thought of her crumbled church caught her laugh in her throat, made her moan and gag. "Not now," she said out loud as she swallowed hard. "Kiss my butt, devil, you ain't killing my joy right now."

She mashed her lips against Herbie's in a long, juicy kiss, and he put his arms around her and snored again, and she just lay there. She watched the daybreak push in through the half-opened blinds, hardly able to contain herself. Her body still tingled from their maiden voyage.

They had done it all day Saturday. All over the house. In each room, in the orange and yellow kitchen right on the floor, their feet banged against the oven door and sounded like an explosion getting ready to happen. In the dining room, under the table, cozy and safe between the low turtle-like scalloped legs of the dining room table etched and shaped by Noon's own brother's hands. In the living room, in the deep armchair where Herbie liked to read his paper. And then in the bedroom, where they took their time. They napped on and off because Herbie reminded Noon he was not twenty anymore. And Noon with surprising finesse would bring him back to life, and he felt twenty then. They laughed in between, about the silliest of things, Herbie's foot caught in the tangle of the sheets, Noon's newly styled bang flopping in her eyes. Until they were depleted. They laughed, and napped, and made love all day Saturday, all night long.

If her muscles weren't so tired, so stiff from positions she'd never given thought to, Noon would have jumped out of bed right then and sang and danced and shouted Hallelujah. She almost wanted to go down and open the front door and announce so all of Lombard Street could hear, "I've got a feeling, everything's gonna be all right." She wanted to put her hands on her hips and rock them on down Lombard Street, ungirdled; she wanted to tell the world she'd been set free.

She slipped from under Herbie's arms and crawled out of bed and reminded herself that she did have a little housework that had to be done. The mess in the kitchen, the butter she had taken out the day before to soften had melted and run over the floor. And the puddle of cream. Then the clothes, his pants and shirt, her nightgown, who knew where they had landed? She glowed at the thought of getting the house in order just so they could tear it up again.

Her face was bright as the sunshine after she'd taken her bath and gotten dressed and walked down into the living room. She might as well start straightening up in here, she thought as she leaned over to pick up the hastily kicked-off red high heels that had gotten her home yesterday morning. She glanced out into the sunshine, then dropped the shoes, stunned, and gasped in horror at the figure on her steps.

She hardly knew who it was at first. The sight of the humped-over figure interrupted the tingle that was still racing through her body. Leaned over, the figure was, head hung as if it were ready to snap from her neck and just fall through the concrete. An unkempt version of Liz, the likes of which she'd never seen, sat on her top steps. She tried to form her mouth to call for Herbie, she could hear him moving around upstairs. But already he was in the tub, singing louder than Noon had ever heard him sing before. And then she snatched open the door. "Liz," she said. "Can this be you? Can it? Lord have mercy, can this be you?"

Liz was still in the silky shit-stained pajamas. Plaster dust still sparkled in her matted red hair. When Ethel had run from the house to rush Fannie to the hospital the day before, she'd told Liz to clean herself up and go tell Noon and Herbie. But Liz hadn't cleaned herself up. She didn't have the strength. Took her the entire day and night into this morning to get up the strength to walk around the corner. Once she'd gotten there she just sat on the steps. She had wanted to knock on the door. She had just wanted to fall into Noon's arms. But how could she tell her that she had hurt Fannie? She pulled her knees close to her chest and wrapped her arms tight around her knees. She needed the pressure of her knees in her stomach. Anything to stop the circles.

"Lord have mercy," Noon said again as she pulled Liz inside the house. "Liz, is this you?" she asked again as Liz stood before her with her head hung. "My baby, my baby, what happened to my baby?" Liz tried to talk, but all that came out at first were unintelligible high-pitched sobs. Noon just heard her saying "Fannie" over and over. "What about Fannie, Liz? Tell me, tell Noon. Look at you, I can't believe this is you. Come on, baby, talk to me. I can't help you if you don't talk to me."

Liz couldn't look at Noon. Her eyes were too fixed on the couch. She just wanted to curl up on that deep green couch. The same couch that she used to hate, outdated, adorned with those silly lacy doilies. She just wanted to be on that couch now more than anywhere. She just wanted to sink into it, pull her knees up and rock.

"Liz, you gotta tell me what happened to you," Noon pleaded. Her voice was shaking as she tried to fight back tears over the sight of Liz: frail and sickly-looking, eyes set deep inside of dark circles, unkempt, smelling. Just unbelievable that Liz, who was always obsessed with her appearances, would come to looking like this.

"I—I hurt Fannie," Liz managed to say through her sobs. "I'm so sorry, Noon, I'm so sorry."

"Hurt Fannie? When, where, how bad, is it bad, Liz tell me, now!" Noon went to Liz and grabbed her firmly at her shoulders and shook her one time hard. "Tell me, Liz, right now."

"What happened to Fannie?" Herbie yelled from upstairs. "Noon, who's down there? What's going on?" He ran down the steps still dripping wet from his bath, a towel around him. "What is it? What they say about Fannie being hurt?" His heart was racing; his knees were weak at the thought of something happening to Fannie.

He froze when he looked at Liz. "Liz? That can't be you. What happened to you?"

"Fannie's hurt, she's at the hospital. I did it, I hurt her. Ethel took her to the hospital."

"Ethel!" Herbie and Noon said in unison. "What did you do to her?"

Herbie demanded as he walked toward Liz with one hand wrapped in a tight fist and the other clutching his towel to his waist. "What did you do to Fannie, huh, tell me, did you hurt her bad?" Liz backed up, staring into Herbie's eyes as he inched toward her. His eyes were full of fear. Liz could see that he was more afraid than angry. When he was almost to her, at the point where he'd have to either stop or strike her, Noon jumped in front of him. She pushed hard against his chest. She yelled at him to go throw on some clothes so they could go see about Fannie.

Herbie dashed back upstairs to get dressed while Noon continued to question Liz. "Is it bad, Liz?" she asked softly, no longer able to hold back the tears.

"I threw a hammer at her, Noon." Liz gasped, hardly able to believe it now herself. "She was—she was unconscious, but she was starting to come to when Ethel was taking her to the hospital."

"Your aunt Ethel, is that the Ethel you talking about?"

Liz just nodded and then covered her face with hands.

Herbie was back downstairs in a flash fully dressed. Noon didn't even have a chance to process this information about Ethel. How could she? One child in the hospital maybe near death. The other one standing before her looking like death. She couldn't even let the Ethel part sink in right now.

"Noon, come on, let's go, let's go," Herbie said frantically as he stood with the door wide open, letting the sun rush in. "A hammer? Goddamn, why she hit her with a hammer? Come on, Noon, if you coming, come on now."

Noon didn't have a chance to smooth at her hair, or grab her purse, or even run upstairs to get her shoes. She pushed her feet back into the red high heels and stumbled out of the door behind Herbie.

Liz stood in the middle of the living room—alone. She felt the aloneness in her stomach, where she felt everything. Her stomach was spinning, and now the living room was spinning too. The colors in the muted green and yellow rug in the center of the floor were washing together as the room turned faster and faster and the lamp tilted, and the pictures on the wall flashed in front of her, and the magazine rack, the telephone stand, the deep armchair, the coffee table were all trading places, playing ring-around-the-roses with Liz in the middle of the circle. Except for the couch. She could trust the couch not to move. She stumbled to the couch and fell on it. Then she mashed her body deep into it. So soft this couch was, like cotton. This couch had the print of her body in its substance. She just wanted the couch to swallow her up.

She pulled her knees up to her chest and rocked against the couch. And then she did what all people did when they fell so low they couldn't even see up to bottom, when they had even stopped calling the name of Jesus. She called for her mother. Didn't matter that her mother was dead, had been dead, that she barely remembered the feel of her arms, the sound of her laugh, the way her breath smelled like peppermint when she sighed. She called for her anyhow. "Mommy, I need you, Mommy," she cried. The calling was hurting her stomach more, so she just moaned. "Mommy," she moaned. Too tired even to say it out loud, she just moaned it in her head. She rocked and moaned and felt the room spinning around her, while the aloneness spun inside her. She slid in and out of the circles. Dizzy. Continuous.

She didn't hear the door open. She didn't see Noon kick off the red high heels. She didn't hear her muttering about how no way was she gonna be able to keep up with Herbie in those shoes, but she did feel Noon's hands against her back. Rubbing it in big rhythmic circles.

"Why you here? What about Fannie?" Liz whispered.

"Herbie'll see to Fannie. I came back to see to you," Noon said as she patted Liz's back gently. "I'm gonna run you a warm bath, and after we get you cleaned up, we'll have some tea, just me and you, Liz."

"I'm sick, Noon," Liz moaned. "I'm so sick. I need help. I need someone to help me."

"Ain't I always?" Noon asked as she pulled Liz to her and flicked bits of plaster from her matted red hair. "Haven't I done for you whenever you needed doing for?"

"Why?" Liz asked, almost choking on the word.

" 'Cause the Good Lord means for me to. That's why he fixed it so you would be left on my steps. He gave you to me, you a gift, Liz, you my chile. That's why, 'cause the good Lord meant for you to be my chile." Noon rocked Liz and rubbed her back, and she didn't mind that Liz smelled bad or that her bowels had run all over the deep green couch. She held her tightly and cried quietly because with her church busted up, she didn't know where she would go now when it was time to put Liz's name on the altar for healing.

THIRTY-SEVEN

Herbie stood in the middle of the emergency room, where everything seemed to be colored brown. The hard wooden floors, the benches along the wall, the heavy-looking desk between two thick pillars. Even the walls had a brownness to them. He was just about to run across the hard wooden floors to the desk, to demand information on his daughter's condition. No, he was prepared to tell them, he didn't know the nature of her emergency, just that she had been hit with a hammer, damn, he thought, as it started to sink in. Why in the hell would Liz hit her with a hammer, why not a shoe, a brush, a broom handle, why a hammer? But then he heard Ethel call his name. Same creamy voice, like peach-flavored ice cream, he thought, but with a strength to it, peach-flavored ice cream in vodka. He mashed his teeth hard and turned to the sound of the voice.

"Herbie, it's me, Ethel." She smiled as she spoke.

"Now how could I not know it's you?" he said as he pulled her in a relieved hug, and then asked quickly, "Fannie, you brought her down here, right? Where is she? How is she? Can I go to her? Take me to her, please, Ethel."

Ethel could see the fear in his eyes, hear it in his voice; she even felt it in his impatient hug. "She's still with the doctor. We've been here since this time yesterday. I told Liz to tell you and your wife what happened." She put her hand on his arm and led him to a long wooden bench. "She was coming to pretty good by the time we got here, calling for you and your wife, saying for somebody to take care of Liz. I think she'll be okay; I think now they're just doing that observation thing they do."

"So what, you saying it ain't serious?" Herbie asked as he motioned for Ethel to sit. "Please tell me you saying it ain't serious. I couldn't hardly handle it if something happened to her. All the way down here I kept thinking that she might already be dead. I was trying to notice everything, the granules in the pavement, the veins in the tree leaves, 'cause I knew if she was dead, I wouldn't see none of that no more. I'd just turn into a zombie, you know what I mean, Ethel."

"I know just what you mean," Ethel said as she nestled into the hardness of the wooden bench as best she could, and crossed her leg, and leaned her elbow on her thigh. "I know just what you mean."

Herbie wondered how Ethel could know just what he meant. She hadn't raised any children to speak of, other than the couple of years she tried to fit raising Liz in with her singing career. But she said it with such knowing, he thought. Right now she appeared miles away, her big rounded eyes in a whole different time and place. Her crossed leg swinging lightly to the rhythm of whatever was going on in her head. He sat back and put his arm along the back of the bench. And then he let his hand lightly touch her shoulder. She turned and looked at him. He thought it looked as if she had been crying. He dismissed that. He never knew Ethel to cry. Even when she got word that her sister had been burned up in the car fire, Ethel didn't cry. But there was a weakness to her eyes that he had never recognized before. Maybe it had always been there, he reasoned, but since it was her strong tenderness he needed back then more than anything, he had never let himself see her weakness.

"Thank you for getting Fannie down here," Herbie said slowly. "What—what happened, how did you come to be the one to get her here and everything?"

"Well, I went by to see Liz yesterday morning. I hadn't seen her since I been here, and God, I can't hardly describe it." She pushed her fist to her mouth, as if daring a sob to come forth. She felt Herbie's hand squeeze her forearm; it was the way a friend would.

Herbie asked, "Were they fighting? They're so close I can't even imagine it. Fannie's subject to blow up now and again, cuss a little, but wasn't neither of them violent with each other."

Ethel rubbed her hand across her neck and thought about Liz's hands trying to choke her life out. "Can't speak about it now, Herbie." She cleared her throat. "It was just bad, very bad." She sat back against the hard bench buffered by Herbie's arm.

They were both silent and still for a time. Herbie had softened for a moment at the realization that this was Ethel he was sitting here with, his arm draped casually around her shoulder. But then his whole body gushed with years' worth of feelings he wanted to get out. How hurt he was when she left him; how enraged when she'd dropped Liz off; how desperate when he didn't have her to hold late at night when Noon was still and cold. And then back to angry when she went year after year and no contact other than the money that she sent faithfully for Liz. As he sat in the brown dinginess of this emergency room, quiet activity all around him, words inside of him bursting to get out, it happened. The way it always did with Ethel. He couldn't tell himself that it wasn't there, because it was. Didn't matter that he and Noon had done it for a day and night, done it so much until he thought his heart would stop cold; it was there. He squeezed her arm. He rubbed his hand slowly around her shoulder.

Ethel knew hand strokes. She knew which were friendly gestures, which were acts of compassion, cordial, which were from someone who would take control or inflict bodily harm. It was the way she had protected herself over the years. Through the contact of flesh. Flesh couldn't lie. Just a touch, a handshake, the press of a thumb, the palm of a hand that she'd allow to touch her bare back, and she would know if someone meant her harm. So naturally she knew Herbie's touch; it was there, the way it had always been. The ambivalence even now as his hand circled her shoulder. The desire, tinged with sadness. But an honesty, though. There was always a wholesomeness to being with Herbie. He wasn't just with her just for his basest pleasures. It was like he needed healing. The way he'd cry sometimes afterward and tell her that his wife wasn't right, no natural desires to her at all. And he'd apologize for being there, in a confessional sort of way. And she thought that if she were the settling-down type, Herbie would have been the type she would have settled down with. But she wasn't the settling-down type, and she had felt Noon's flesh earlier as she held her arm to walk her home. And she knew Herbie and Noon were well suited for each other, and to allow otherwise would have been improper, even for Ethel, whose brand of proper ran hard against the grain.

She shifted in her seat. Herbie squeezed her shoulder tighter. She turned sharply so that he was forced to sit up. She took his hand and felt the desire running all through his palm. She turned to face him, to look in his eyes, so there would be no mistaking her point. She saw it welling up in his eyes, his desire, dead center. She saw the muscles in his jaw shift like an earthquake getting ready to happen.

"Just friends, Herbie," she said softly and firmly. "We just friends from here on out."

At first Herbie was insulted that she moved away from him so sharply, forcing him to drop his arm. He expected that she should have leaned into his arm, let him console her for once. He was all prepared to mash his chin into the top of her hair, tell her not to worry, whisper in her ear, blow into it. But her sharp movement at that moment insulted him. "Well, we always been friends. That's never stopped us from being, you know, from being especially good friends." He laughed a sly laugh. And then the words of the high-bosomed waitress that he had met at that Lawnside club years ago tromped through his head. "Miss Ethel got pretty much the same thing your wife got. Miss Ethel just advertises hers a little better." And Herbie realized he had done it. Turned into the type of married man he swore he never would. He'd always told himself that if Noon had had a normal nature, he would have never sought out Ethel; certainly he wouldn't have spent time at those houses on South Street and later Arch Street. But he had just experienced Noon's nature, feasted on it until he thought he'd burst, and here he was ready to talk some jive for a little time with Ethel.

And then the containment. As Ethel's thumb stroked his palm, she felt the containment. She could feel the desire receding from the surface of his skin. She liked that. Maybe now he'll think it's worth it to put a lid on it, pack it on up, and save it for Noon.

"Of course we just friends," Herbie said emphatically, embarrassed too. "It's just that it's been a long time, Ethel, you know, I still got some powerful memories, powerful memories, but yeah, we just friends nothing more, nothing more." Herbie was sitting up on the edge of the hard bench; he was facing Ethel. She was leaning back against the bench, and he looked at her from her head, to her rounded eyes, her healthy lips, and chest. "Just friends," he whispered, "just friends." Damn.

Before Ethel could say anything, the thick brown doors just to the side of the large brown desk swung open and Fannie walked through, escorted by a white-jacketed doctor.

She stood for a few seconds to focus her eyes under the large bright lamp fixture that hung just a foot or so above her head. She blinked hard and squinted and looked across the room at Herbie and Ethel. "Herbie," she said weakly, and before the word was out of her mouth, Herbie and Ethel ran to her, almost knocked each other over to get to her first. Fannie's head was bandaged.

"Are you her parents?" the doctor asked.

"Yes," Ethel said quickly.

Herbie looked at Ethel when she said that. He put his arm around Ethel's shoulder, deciding he'd help her play the part.

"She'll be fine," the doctor said, rushing his words. "It was a bad hit to the head, but the wound is clean. You'll want her to keep it dry for the next day or two, aspirin for pain, and you'll want to get her back here if she develops a fever, blurred vision, dizziness, fainting, or vomiting. But again, let her take it easy for the next couple of days and she'll be fine. Follow up in about a week with your private physician or clinic." He patted Fannie's shoulder and was back on the other side of the brown wooden doors.

Herbie and Ethel blanketed Fannie with hugs. She felt for the bandaging, gently, though, because her head still ached some.

"Can you walk?" Herbie asked, holding her by her waist. "How do you feel, I'll hail a cab, are you okay? Oh, God, I'm so glad you're— you're standing here like this."

"Like what?" Fannie asked, half laughing. "I'm a mess. Bandages wrapped around my head like I'm a mummy, and I haven't brushed my teeth since this time yesterday."

"But you alive, baby," Ethel said, kissing her cheek, "you alive."

"How'd they treat you back there, the doctors?" Herbie asked as he pulled Fannie to him and hugged her again.

"Okay, you know, asked me to count from ten to one over and over, asked who was President. I told them Truman."

They all three laughed.

"I don't know how Eisenhower would feel about that," Herbie said.

Then he stopped laughing and looked at Fannie. "You need watching over, you coming home with me, you ain't going back to that house. And that's settled." He said it firmly.

"I was gonna say you could share my room with me, Fannie," Ethel interrupted. "I'm not working, so I'm there all day and night. I been enjoying your company so since I been here."

"Actually," Fannie said as she balanced her weight between Herbie and Ethel, "I was thinking of going back to my house. Somebody must see about Liz, she needs help, bad, she needs help real bad." Fannie's voice rose in degrees, and her arms moved up and down frantically so that she almost lost her balance.

"Whoa," Herbie said as he grabbed her to steady her, "just calm down there a minute. Wasn't it Liz that did this to you in the first place? Now you got to get your own strength back before you go on this here crusade about saving Liz."

"She's concerned about her," Ethel said quietly. "I am too."

"Well, you in a better position to help her than Fannie," Herbie said, anger rising in his voice. "Maybe this time you could get it right."

"Herbie," Fannie said, yanking his arm, "don't talk to Ethel like that. That's not fair, and you know it."

"It's okay, sweetie," Ethel said, squeezing Fannie's hand. "Herbie's right. You do need time to heal."

"Damn right she does," Herbie said, his anger going full steam now. "You need to be spending time with your own niece. Why don't you go offer to share your room with her?"

"I'm not gonna listen to you be rude to Ethel," Fannie said as she pulled her arm completely from Herbie's. "She's like a visitor, she didn't do nothing to you, why you acting like this?"

"Fannie, it's okay, baby, really," Ethel said, rubbing Fannie's back. "Me and Herbie go way back. I understand where he's coming from."

Herbie was just about to let another insult fly when he was stopped by Ethel's mouth. It wasn't the thickness of her lips that struck him now; it was the way her lips curled when she said certain words. Fannie's lips curled exactly the same way. But then he reasoned that that's where the similarity ended. Ethel's face was round, Fannie's was thin; Ethel's skin was brown, Fannie's was light; Ethel's nose was short, Fannie's long; Ethel's chest was ample, Fannie's slight. But then Ethel did have double joints in her legs that popped out when she leaned back on her heels; Fannie did too. Why was he just noticing this detail about Ethel now? Because Ethel usually wore high-heel shoes, but in the flat slippers it showed: She and Fannie had exactly the same stance. He watched them talking. Fannie apologizing for Herbie's behavior, Ethel assuring her it was okay. And the lips, both of them curling their lips as they talked, standing back on the heels, the muscles in their calves popping. Herbie tried to picture Fannie brown, with a flatter nose, shorter hair, wider hips, and he looked from one to the other and the lips were curling and the legs jutting and they blurred together, the lips, the legs, Fannie, Ethel. "Goddamn," Herbie said out loud. "I'll be goddamned."

Both Ethel and Fannie turned to Herbie. "What?" they said almost in unison.

"Just had a thought," Herbie said as he linked his arm in Fannie's, "a goddamn crazy thought. Let's get you home to Noon, come on, we'll take it slow and easy. We'll hail a cab. Just gonna take little baby steps until we see a cab."

"Here, put the jacket back on," Ethel said as she flung the jacket around Fannie's shoulders. "Let me get your arm."

Fannie walked from the brownness of the emergency room into the glaring sunlight supported on either side by Herbie and Ethel.

THIRTY-EIGHT

Noon was out of her mind with worry over Fannie, but she took it as a good sign that she hadn't heard from Herbie. Surely he would have called if she were near death or worse. So she occupied herself by taking care of Liz. And then she did what usually worked to still the nervous pressure in her chest: She baked rolls and she hummed.

Liz waved her hand lightly, coaxing the steam from her tea straight up her nostrils. The peppermint was sharp and strong as it bounced inside her nose. She took a long sip and swallowed it a little at a time. She could feel it going straight to her empty stomach. The warm felt good going down. It was soothing. Almost as soothing as the warm water in the tub had been when Noon squeezed the washcloth over and over at the nape of Liz's neck, forcing the warm water to ooze down her spine. Right now Noon was humming in the kitchen as she pulled rolls from the oven. Liz mashed her whole body deeper in the chair. How much she had missed this. Sitting at Noon's table while Noon baked, or mixed, or fried, always humming something low and soft that calmed Liz's stomach. The tree out back swaying so that the shadowed designs on the table changed as the sun fell here, then bounced there. The intermittent hum of the icebox, the trolley sliding along out front, sending an echoed swishing sound through the back window. Liz remembered how uncomplicated life used to be as she and Fannie sat at this table listening to Noon hum, chattering quietly to themselves, sometimes Noon joining in with some revelation or other about somebody who went to the church, or someone she had seen on South Street, usually something that would have them in stitches, until Noon could stop herself from laughing long enough to caution them that God don't like ugly and that if they ever, ever repeated what she had just said, the devil would claim their souls sure nuff. And they would laugh again, sometimes until they cried. And Liz would be so content at the table, until she hated it when the craving started. Hated herself that she couldn't stop it. Her stomach would get hard as a rock, and then the rock would turn over and over. The only way to stop it was to run to the closet and close the door. And she would watch Fannie watching her, right before she asked if she could be excused; that she had to go to the bathroom was always the excuse. And she would see Fannie's eyes darken just a bit, almost pleading with her not to leave the table. But she had to stop the turning in her stomach. She could feel the turning starting all over again as she listened to Noon hum. She wondered what the inside of the closet was like now. She and Fannie had papered it before they moved. Filled in the slats of wood with dry wall. She wished Fannie were across the table from her, making a joke about something, and the more she thought about missing Fannie, the more she needed to feel the hardness between her teeth.

She tried to think about something else. She mashed her body into the chair as hard as she could. She wanted to run up to the closet, just a corner she had left uncovered, just a corner just in case. She wanted to get to that corner of the closet. She held her hands under the seat of the chair. She fought her hands. "Noon," she cried, "help me, please help me, I don't want to do it, I don't want to do it."

Noon let the oven door slam and ran to Liz, who was bouncing up and down in the seat now, like somebody having convulsions. "Stop it, Liz," she said sharply. "Stop it. Do what? Do what?"

"The wall," Liz said, her voice shaking, as she grabbed for Noon's arms.

"Wall? What you talking about? Are you hallucinating?" Noon shouted at Liz as she clutched at her shoulders to try to still her.

Liz jumped out of the chair and pushed past Noon. She ran through the house, upstairs, to the bathroom. She just made it as her bowels loosed again.

She felt Noon looking down at her as she sat grunting and clutching her stomach. At least now she felt clean, in the starched white shirtdress, her hair still wrapped in the towel from when Noon had washed it earlier. She didn't feel pitiful the way she had when Noon had pulled her in off the steps. But still, she found it hard to take Noon's gaze.

"You gonna tell me what's going on, or what?" Noon asked in a heavy voice as she leaned against the bathroom door with her arms folded tightly over her chest. All day, since she'd seen Liz's frail body leaned over on the steps, she had been trying to put her finger on the problem. At first she thought it was needles; somebody had fast-talked her into taking drugs and now she was hooked. But she had inspected her body carefully for needle marks as she bathed her earlier. She even wondered if maybe she had gotten syphilis and it had worked its way to her brain and just made her let herself go. But she couldn't understand the chunks of sand she'd pulled out of Liz's hair as she washed it. And now this business about the wall. She watched Liz straining on the toilet now. How much she looked like the little girl that they'd found on the steps. What was her secret? Noon always felt that Liz knew something that she kept from the rest of them. Something having to do with Herbie. She would stiffen so when Herbie came in the room, her easiness would leave, and she'd become mannered; it lasted for months after she came to live there. So Noon was always careful, protective about Liz, watching, always watching, to make sure Herbie wasn't bothering her. Not that she really believed Herbie would ever stoop so low, but something about him frightened Liz.

"I'm waiting," Noon said as she shifted her arms.

"Okay," Liz gasped, "just let me finish, oh, my stomach, it hurts so bad."

"That's 'cause you holding secrets there that ain't got no business there." Noon said as she walked into the bathroom and yanked on the chain to open the skylight.

Liz felt the sun pouring into the bathroom. It moved on a breeze that brushed over her thighs as she sat stooped on the toilet. She lifted her head and looked at Noon. She looked past Noon at the blue wallpaper lined with silver fish swimming in the breeze of the open skylight. "It's plaster," she whispered. "I eat plaster. You ever heard of such a thing?" She spoke in monotones, her arms hung loosely at her sides. She stared blankly at the silver fish swimming toward the ceiling.

"Plaster, what are you talking about?" Noon asked, so perplexed she was near hysteria. "Lord, child, plaster? Plaster? Explain it! Plaster?"

Liz confessed, and took Noon to the closet and showed her the corner of the hole left and described what her bedroom was like now, as best as she could describe it, and told her how she lost control when Fannie saw how bad it had gotten, and she threw the hammer and hit Fannie right in the head, and when she could, she looked at Noon as she talked, but mostly she couldn't: the horrified expression frozen on Noon's face.

When Noon could talk, she told Liz that she had heard about that in other people, that her body was craving something that it wasn't getting, that first thing Monday morning they were going to the doctor to get her checked out, that the way she looked that plaster eating might have caused damage already to her stomach the way everything runs right through her. She tried to act as if it weren't that abnormal, as she choked back exclamations of, "What? Wall plaster? Lord have mercy, wall plaster!"

"We gonna get you well," Noon told her when she could get over the horror of it and talk. "Me and Jesus, me and Jesus." And in her heart she prayed that the Lord would just keep her child living until they could get her help. She would have never guessed wall plaster until she heard it, and then it fit so: the staying in the closet when she was small, even as she got older, always having some explanation about looking for something or other that fell behind boxes stacked on the closet floor. And the look of sickness in Liz's eyes, even though Liz was all cleaned up and starched on the outside, Noon hadn't been able to scrub away the sickness from Liz's eyes.

Liz felt stronger just knowing that Noon knew. As if Noon had pulled some of the burden from Liz and wrapped it around her own shoulders. Noon had taken such good care of her today. Cleaned her up, fed her, got her to open up. Her hair was all done up, washed and pressed, and now Noon was even hot-curling it. Liz felt improved upon. Even the circles in her stomach were spinning slower, not giving off as much heat. Now she was ready to go see about Fannie.

"Let's go see about Fannie," Liz said as Noon looped the last piece of her red hair around the hot curlers.

Noon was relieved to hear Liz suggest they walk down to the hospital. She hadn't had a problem focusing just on Liz until just now, as she did the last curl in her red-like-the-setting-sun hair. She had wanted to suggest it herself, but she didn't want Liz to feel abandoned. Child been feeling abandoned all her life, Noon had been telling herself all day, can't let it seem like Fannie's more important to me than she is. Herbie did that enough for the both of them. But the suggestion had come from Liz's own lips, and she could surely use some fresh air.

"You sure you feeling up to the walk?" Noon asked as she combed through Liz's curls.

"Better than I felt in a long, long time, Noon. I should have come to you weeks ago."

"Sometimes it got to get as bad as it's gonna get before it gets better. You got here when you was supposed to. If you had come sooner, we'd probably just got to arguing over the house or something or other." Noon took the towel from around Liz's shoulders as she talked. "Look in the mirror and see if you like your hair," she said as she flecked bits of red hair that had fallen along the back of the starched white shirtdress Liz was wearing.

"I never did sign the house over, Noon," Liz said as she stood and smoothed at her dress, "I never did. Forgive me even for saying that I would. I know how that hurt you, but I never did sign it over." Liz was standing facing Noon. Her eyes had a pleading to them that softened any retaliation that was rising in Noon.

"Don't hardly matter none now with the church all busted up," Noon said as she turned from Liz and shook the towel out.

"Church all busted up?" Liz asked, perplexed. "What you talking about, Noon?" She walked around to look in Noon's face again.

Noon was shaking the towel hard, over and over again. She hadn't thought much at all about the church once she'd started concentrating on Liz. Liz had done her as much good today as she had done for Liz. But now that Liz was darn near whole again, at least outwardly, Noon could feel it creeping back in her chest, that void that was so deep it was heavy. She could feel it growing in her chest, like a pockmark, fanning out from the center, infecting surrounding tissue, steady and hard.

"It's gone, busted up, knocked to the ground," Noon said, punctuating her words with hard shakes of the towel. "It's leveled, bulldozed, nothing left but dirt, just dirt."

"What do you mean, Noon?" Liz asked, her turn now to be horrified, clutching at Noon's shoulders, begging for an explanation. "You mean the members all scattered, that's what you mean by busted up, right? You don't mean the building busted up, right, you talking in uh, uh, metaphors, right, the dirt, Noon, right, you mean they're some dirty people in the church, tell me that's what you saying."

"I mean dirty people in the church got in cahoots with other dirty people outta the church, now the church all busted. They knocked it down." Noon pushed past Liz and walked into the shed kitchen and stretched the towel over the railing. She smoothed at the towel harder and harder until she balled her fists and pounded against the railing. "Busted up, just busted up," she said as her fists went up and down against the railing.

Liz looked at Noon's back, at her arms raising and falling, the pale blue and white gingham checks on her dress arching and caving with her back. Noon had been holding on to this all day; while she brought Liz back to life, she had been holding this on her back. Liz needed to know that, as much as she needed the caretaking Noon had doused her with her all day; Liz needed to know that she was that important to Noon that Noon could put on hold all her other burdens, just to carry Liz for a while. She ran to Noon's back and wrapped her arms around her waist and pushed her head into her back. "Let's go for a walk, Noon," she whispered. "Let's walk to the hospital and see about Fannie."

❧

Fannie leaned on both Ethel and Herbie as the three walked from the hospital. Hospital shifts were changing, and the cabs stopped first for the blond-haired nurses and patient visitors who were white. Fannie insisted that they walk. The back-and-forth jerking of a cab ride might make her vomit, she feared. "Slowly," she begged. "Please let's just walk slowly; I really need to walk."

They headed west, where the sun was dropping in the back of the sky like a tangerine falling from a fruit cart, leaving its juice suspended as it falls. Her head throbbed some; she was a little wobbly, but other than that she reasoned that she was darn near back to normal. Except for her seeing eye. She had actually been surprised to see Herbie and Ethel on the faded brown bench together. Herbie sitting stiffly, Ethel leaned back, confident. Ordinarily she should have known that. As the doctors had examined her and turned her head this way and that, and shone light after light in her eyes, and had her walk a straight line and hop on one foot, and count from 999 to 989 backward, she should have sensed that Ethel was already out there, and she should have known the moment that Herbie walked through the door. She wouldn't necessarily have seen it, the way she saw things pretty exacting when a vision came down on her, but a thought should have bounced in her head almost like a voice and should have cut through whatever else she was seeing, or hearing, or thinking at that instant, and she should have said to herself, "Oh, Herbie just walked in." But that had not happened as she sat along the examining table, the stiff cotton roll-along sheet scratching the back of her thighs, the scent of rubbing alcohol going straight to her head and coming out through her eyes, making them tear.

Even now, as she hobbled down the street nestled between Herbie and Ethel, she tried to picture what was going on with Liz right now. But nothing. All she could see was Liz the way she had been in the middle of the night: on that chair against the backdrop of the banged-out, eaten-out wall, frail, hollow eyes, spit-filled plaster dripping from her mouth, pointing the hammer. All she could hear was Liz cursing and making the dusty air ripple with "I hate you, Fannie." And then she saw the hammer. She felt the crashing down on her head again. She let out a moan.

"What is it?" Herbie said, stopping abruptly. "You sure you okay? I knew we should have stood there and waited for a cab. I should have demanded that we get in before that last couple; don't they know this is 1959, shit, we tip too, don't they know that?"

"You okay, baby," Ethel said softly, touching Fannie's bandaged head.

Fannie didn't have the energy to explain to them that she couldn't see Liz, not even a feeling, a sensation over whether or not Liz was okay. Just the past, that's all she could see was the past. "Just throbs every now and then, I'll be okay," she said as she motioned for them to start walking again.

"If you're sure," Herbie said, himself thinking about Liz. The way she looked when he ran downstairs, dirty, smelly, sickly. He had hardly recognized her. He was almost relieved when Noon couldn't keep up with him in the red high heels and said that never mind, she'd just go back home and see to Liz.

"Sun's gonna make a glorious sunset," Ethel said, breaking into Herbie's and Fannie's thoughts about Liz.

"How can you tell?" Fannie asked, looking straight ahead as they walked.

"Misty this morning," Ethel answered. "Bright and sunny all day, mist still hanging back in the sky, it'll be like a magnifying glass and stretch the sunset clear across the back of the sky."

"How you know so much?" Fannie asked.

"Been around the block a few times, baby," Ethel said, half laughing.

"That you have," Herbie said, chuckling, "that you have."

And then Fannie gasped as she saw the two figures looking as if they had stepped out of the fading sun. Noon's blue and white gingham dress cinched at the waist and flowing from her hips down to her mid-calf. Her hair done up in a bouffant, and her feet slightly elevated in her church pumps. And next to her was Liz.

"What is it, baby?" Ethel said.

"I'm fine," Fannie answered quickly. "That looks like a familiar pair heading our way."

Ethel looked toward the sunset and suddenly felt out of place as she watched Noon and Liz approach. Liz cleaned up, almost had a bounce to her step. Noon crisp, efficient, looking very capable. There was a side street just a few feet ahead, and actually that side street was the quickest route to Ethel's house. She didn't want to appear to be running away, but she did still have Noon's slippers on, and she didn't want to put Fannie through a confrontation. And after all, this was Fannie's real family. Noon and Herbie and Liz. They should be the ones for her to lean on now that she was weak. They should be the ones to see her home.

"Herbie, let Fannie lean all her weight on you. I'm gonna turn off here and head on back to my room," Ethel said as she unlinked her arm from Fannie's. She felt Fannie's arm tug harder, not really wanting Ethel to let go. She kissed Fannie's cheek, and the same wrenching feeling washed over now that had washed over her that predawn morning when she'd first left Fannie with Herbie and Noon. She smoothed at Fannie's bandage and waved at Herbie.

"Don't go," Herbie said to Ethel, a pleading to his voice. He wanted to talk to her, set up a time when he could see her alone; he had to know why Fannie's lips curled exactly like hers, why their leg muscles jutted in identical ways, why Fannie's eyes had danced just like his mother's eyes that morning he'd found her in the box. He already knew but needed to hear it from Ethel.

"Got to go," Ethel said as Noon and Liz moved closer toward them. "Fannie don't need no extra excitement that my presence might stir up, Herbie. I got to go. I'll check on you tomorrow, baby," she said, squeezing Fannie's hand. "Tell my Liz I still love her."

"You not leaving town, are you?" Fannie asked, still holding tight to Ethel's hand.

"No, baby," Ethel said, looking up the street again, watching Noon and Liz get closer.

"Honest?" Fannie asked, feeling suddenly like a helpless child.

"I'm always honest, baby," Ethel said, pulling her hand from Fannie's. "Even when I lie, I'm honest."

She backed away from Herbie and Fannie; she blew a kiss and lowered her eyes, the way Herbie had seen her do countless times when she ended her set. This was the way she mesmerized the crowd before she exited from center stage and the spotlight faded to black. She turned and walked on down the side street. Herbie watched her hips move in circles. If Fannie hadn't needed him to lean on in that instant, he would have gone after Ethel, to know for certain what he already believed to be true. He took Fannie's arm as Noon and Liz both hurried now to get to them.

Noon and Liz ran straight to Fannie and smothered her with hugs. Liz cried while Noon shouted, "Thank you, Jesus, thank you, Lord."

Liz grabbed Fannie in a desperate hug. "Please forgive me, Fannie, I'm sorry, I'm sorry. God knows, I'm so sorry."

Fannie stiffened. She wanted to push Liz from her. Knock her in the street for throwing that hammer. She wobbled again at the thought. Then she held Liz. She could feel her ribs, no flesh, just her ribs through the starched shirtdress.

"Whoa, don't knock her down, she still a little weak," Herbie cautioned as he peeled Liz from Fannie.

"Awl, Herbie's just mad 'cause nobody ran to him and hugged him. Somebody hug him, please." Fannie snickered as she nudged Liz, but Liz didn't budge; she looked down at the ground instead. Noon didn't budge either, but she did look straight at Herbie, as if she were trying to get clear through to his soul.

"Wasn't that—wasn't that Ethel?" she stammered.

"Was," Herbie said as he started to walk. "Why we standing here crowding up the sidewalk? Let's get on home. I'm hungry too, you fix any dinner, Noon?"

"What's she like, Herbie?" Noon asked, still staring straight at him. "Nice," Herbie said as he locked on her gaze and breathed in deep. "She's real nice."

"Nice as me?" Noon asked, hardly blinking she was staring at Herbie so.

"Not as soft," Herbie said as he moved in close to Noon and circled her in his arms. "She 'bout as nice as you, just not as soft. Not my soft big-legged usher, Noon, no. Mnh, not hardly."

Fannie let out a breath all at once. Liz too. Fannie pulled Liz by the arm and whispered, "Well, one good thing, if Noon decided to kick ass out here, at least we in running distance of the hospital. We could have gotten Herbie some medical help anyhow." Liz doubled over, laughing harder than she had laughed in months. Fannie kept it going. "I was waiting for Noon to pull a machete from under her dress and start calling Herbie all kinds of lying mfs." Tears were coming out of Liz's eyes she was laughing so.

"Well, we going home or what?" Herbie asked as he and Noon walked slowly, hands swinging together like teenagers on a first date.

"I guess," Noon said hesitantly, "even though this would be about the time of my evening service, can't go there now."

They were all four quiet as if they'd just remembered a dead relative. "Well, can we walk by there?" Liz asked. "I don't think I'll fully believe it until I see the empty space."

"Yeah, let's walk that way," Noon said as she pulled Herbie's hand, "just see for yourself what they did."

The four walked toward the block where the church used to be. Herbie and Noon holding hands, Fannie and Liz at their heels. "You sure you ready to go through this this evening, Noon?" Herbie asked as they got closer.

"We're with you, Noon," Liz said as she reached forward and squeezed Noon's shoulders. "We're right here at your back."

But before they turned the corner, they heard music. All four at once heard it at the same instant, it seemed. They looked from one to the other, all knowing that the clarity of this music was strange. The way it pushed into the air, not muffled by bricks or mortar or stained glass windows. Tambourines, and were those drums or large wooden spoons against kitchen pots? They weren't sure. Except that there was surely a crowd, the air was crowded even from around the corner, a shouting crowd; the shouts were clear too, straight out and up and mixing with the orange and red of the evening sky.

Noon and Herbie turned the corner first. Then they stopped, both stopped. They stopped so short that Fannie and Liz ran into their backs. There was a crowd for sure. Assembled on the dirt where the church had been. Chairs lined up in neat rows, kitchen chairs, and armchairs from living rooms, and lopsided broken-down sit-in-cellar-only chairs, nice fold-up chairs from the Saunders Funeral Home, a barstool or two from Club Royale, a barber's chair from Bow's, two flowered tapestry wing chairs from Julep's mother's parlor. Clothesline props made a square around the chairs, a tufted, braided rope was strung around, and draped from end to end tent style, with canvas throws and elegant bedspreads, fancy sheets, comfortable, practical patchwork quilts. A long table stood sturdily down front. A vase holding flowers, an oversized Bible, a bedroom lamp. A nightstand seemed to grow out of the middle of the table; a piece of red velvet hung and swayed softly down the center.

The people were swaying too. They were swaying and singing. Bow the Barber, the Saunderses, Cross-the-Street-Dottie, Sister Maybell, Pop and his nephews, the fishman, the lawyer who was leading their charge, Julep and her new young man from Howard U, all of Lombard Street, and around the corner, even people who'd moved, even Jeanie, who never went to church, and Big Carl from Club Royale. The deacons and the trustees sat up front, and a not-yet-forgiven, deeply wounded Reverend Schell.

Noon and Fannie walked easily onto the dirt. "Everybody, everybody," Bow called out, "it's Noon, let's hear it for Noon." And the crowd roared with claps and shouts for Noon.

"She tried to warn us," Bow shouted. "From the very beginning she told us it was a lie."

Pop's nephew grabbed Fannie, linked her arm in his; they ushered Noon to the front, next to the long table and the nightstand of a pulpit. Noon sat in Bow's bright red barber's chair that looked like a throne, and tears streamed down her face.

Herbie and Liz watched from the other side of the street. "You going 'cross, Herbie?" Liz asked.

"Never was one for church." Herbie answered. "Ain't saying I don't believe in God, just found him in places other than church, is all."

"Like the club?" Liz asked, looking at Herbie through the air that was now pale blue and pink and orange.

"Yeah, like the club, I guess," he said as he looked across the street, and then, turning back to Liz, he said, "Long time ago, like at Ethel's."

"Long time ago, Herbie, so long ago I can barely remember. Come on, Herbie, let's go over there. They're seats right there next to Willie Mann's grandmom. Let's go on across."

"I tell you one thing," Herbie said angrily as he and Liz made their way across the street, "that no-count Willie Mann better leave my daughter alone."

"He can't do nothing to Fannie, don't even worry about that."

"Ain't talking about Fannie," Herbie said as they stepped onto the dirt, and he took Liz's hand awkwardly in his own and guided her to a seat. "This time I ain't talking 'bout Fannie."

Ethel stood on the other side of the street. Her bag was already packed. She looked at the shoulders. She was tired, she was, tired of trying to save the lives of grown-ass men. She looked for broad shoulders, not for massaging but for leaning on. She never thought she'd come to this point, wanting to lean on strength that came from somewhere other than herself. She walked over and stood next to a man who was also standing back, not entirely a part of the festive congregation. And his shoulders

339

were wide. She smiled to herself and put her bag on the dirt. And focused her attention up front and leaned in just a little closer to the wide-shouldered man, thinking his shoulders could surely give her something to remember Philly by.

Noon stood in front of the gathering. There were at least two hundred people. They were calling for her to speak. She looked out over the people. And pressed her feet in the dirt. Her shoe touched a piece of paper. A twisted piece of brown paper bag. One of her curlers that her morning friend had gently unwound from her hair. She picked it up and twirled it between her fingers. She cleared her throat. "We never know where our help's coming from. Most times it comes from the strangest places, from people we don't even know, or wouldn't associate with if we did. But one thing I've learned from all this is not only that our help is coming but that it's already here. Right here, like our victory is right here. This is where we start to win, all of us working together, united! With these bed wraps protecting our heads and the bare rich dirt pushing up firmly against our soles."

The crowd was on their feet. They were applauding, shouting, and jumping. These were downtown folks. They knew fertile dirt. Knew that they could work this soil, and the system too, and watch a new church sprout up. Richer, more glorious than before. They were stronger now. They would not be moved. No way, no way.